"If thou gaze long into an abyss, the abyss will also gaze into thee."

—Nietzsche

"Abyss: The primeval chaos. The bottomless pit; hell. An unfathomable or immeasurable depth or void."

—*The American Heritage Dictionary*

You're holding in your hands one of the first in a new line of books of dark fiction, called Abyss. Abyss is horror unlike anything you've ever read before. It's not about haunted houses or evil children or ancient Indian burial grounds. We've all read those books, and we all know their plots by heart.

Abyss is for the seeker of truth, no matter how disturbing or twisted it may be. It's about people, and the darkness we all carry within us. Abyss is the new horror from the dark frontier. And in that place, where we come face-to-face with terror, what we find is ourselves. The darkness illuminates us, revealing our flaws, our secret fears, our desires and ambitions longing to break free. And we never see ourselves or our world in the same way again.

POST MORTEM

NEW TALES OF GHOSTLY HORROR

EDITED BY

PAUL F. OLSON
AND
DAVID B. SILVA

A Dell Book

Published by
Dell Publishing
a division of
Bantam Doubleday Dell Publishing Group, Inc.
666 Fifth Avenue
New York, New York 10103

ISBN: 0-440-20792-4

Reprinted by arrangement with St. Martin's Press, New York, New York

Printed in the United States of America

Published simultaneously in Canada

January 1992

10 9 8 7 6 5 4 3 2 1

OPM

Contents

Introduction

The Phantom Book

GLEN ELLYN, ILLINOIS—ASSOCIATED PRESS

Two weeks ago no one had ever heard of *Post Mortem*.

Today, however, it sits comfortably in the number fifteen slot on *The New York Times* best-seller list and has become the most sought-after book in the history of publishing.

Why?

Because the book apparently doesn't exist.

It's either the greatest hoax since Clifford Irving attempted to sneak his Howard Hughes autobiography past McGraw-Hill in 1971, or a chilling quasi-fictional tale as important to the publishing industry as *The Exorcist* was in 1971 or *The Amityville Horror* was in 1977—a book that transcends its own printed page. Either way, *Post Mortem* has created so much of a stir in publishing circles that its publisher, St. Martin's Press, has been asked by *Publishers Weekly* to produce a copy of the book to verify its existence. So far, St. Martin's has refused comment, though earlier this week they did release the following innocuous statement to the press:

> *Post Mortem* is an anthology of all-new ghost stories written by some of today's most popular writers, as well as some up-and-coming authors who are certain to make an impact on the field in the future. We encourage you to seek out a copy and discover for yourself how far-ranging the contemporary ghost story can be. These stories are not only quietly chilling, they are powerfully disturbing.

Actually locating a copy, however, has proved to be more difficult than one would imagine, even in light of recent documents clearly indicating shipment of hundreds of thousands of copies of *Post Mortem* to a number of this country's most influential retail chains. Although several unnamed sources within St. Martin's have confirmed such shipments, the book has continued to be impossible to find.

Until now.

Now comes a startling new development.

The first verified copy of *Post Mortem* was discovered yesterday at the Glen Ellyn Public Library by assistant librarian Emma Dover. In her statement to the press she claimed to have discovered a copy of the book in the nonfiction section of the library while shelving the newest volume of a Time-Life series called *Mysteries of the Unknown.* Apparently, the book had been misfiled.

"The cover was . . . glowing," she reported. "Not terribly bright, though. Soft. Like one of those soft-white light bulbs. I never would have noticed it otherwise."

Almost immediately Miss Dover realized she had uncovered something special. A quick glance at the copyright page confirmed that St. Martin's had indeed published the book—first edition 1989. The list of contents included new stories by the likes of Ramsey Campbell, Thomas Tessier, Charles L. Grant, Melissa Mia Hall, Kathryn Ptacek, Gary Brandner, Steve Rasnic Tem and Melanie Tem, Robert R. McCammon, and at least nine others. In the back was a discussion of the ghost story genre by Dean R. Koontz, and a unique credits quiz, challenging readers to match the contributors to the volume with their previous publication credits.

"I showed the book to Mr. Larabee [the research librarian]," Miss Dover said. "He held it in his hands. He read the jacket copy."

The reason Miss Dover is so emphatic when she tells her story is simple: She no longer has possession of the book. "He [Larabee] was holding it, turning it over and over in his hands because I guess he couldn't quite believe I'd actually found a copy. Then it started crumbling, little bits and pieces of paper sifting through his fingers and floating like snowflakes toward the floor. In just a few seconds it was gone. All of it."

Larabee confirmed the story of his coworker, adding that he, too, had had an opportunity to check the contents. "I still remember a couple of the titles. 'The Ring of Truth' by Thomas F. Monteleone. 'Timeskip' by Charles de Lint. 'The Servitor' by Janet Fox. The titles . . . I remember thinking that they seemed to speak for themselves, as if they were serving as reflections of something bigger than the stories they mar-queed."

According to several eyewitness accounts, the pile of confetti created by the disintegration of the book turned a sickly gray color within a matter of a few minutes, then disappeared completely.

Local officials have been unable to uncover any direct physical evidence of the existence of the alleged copy, though carpet fibers from the library are still undergoing laboratory tests. Until the results of those tests are known, it appears that once again the mystery surrounding *Post Mortem* will continue to be an open-ended controversy.

Does the book really exist?

Or is it instead a hoax that has hoodwinked the entire literary world?

The editors of the alleged anthology held a short press conference the day before yesterday at the offices of St. Martin's Press, where they issued a statement of their own which, they insisted, fully explains the phenomenon of *Post Mortem:*

Ghosts are perhaps one of the only things in this very predictable world of ours that are guaranteed to be *un*predictable.

That's what makes—and has made throughout the history of horror literature—the ghost story ever-unique and ever-popular.

Vampires are fine as far as they go, but when you come right down to it, there's not much novelty left in stories of vampiric terror. We know, as longtime readers and moviegoers, pretty much how the vampire is going to act. How the victim is going to react. How, within a few degrees one way or the other, rather like a machinist's tolerances, the story is going to end. Notwithstanding some fine iconoclastic vampire tales (*Interview with the Vampire* and *The Vampire Tapestry* spring immediately to mind), the chief joy in reading a new vampire book comes from the author's voice, the little tricks of storytelling style and technique, not from the vampire itself.

Ditto werewolves. Ditto mutated monsters. Ditto zombies and rampaging flora and fauna and maniacs with knives in dark alleys.

But the ghost . . . ah, the ghost. A ghost is always different. A ghost can pop up anywhere, at any time. Like Allen Funt, it's there when you least expect it. In the traditional old house. At a party. In the city. On the farm. In your own mind. And its behavior . . . well, it's hard to find anything more capricious than a ghost. Sometimes it is there to scare you. Sometimes, like a memory that clings and refuses to go away, it is there to remind you of something. Sometimes it wants revenge. Occasionally it is there only to teach. And sometimes—biggest surprise of all!—a ghost appears for no real reason. Its existence *is* its justification, and justification enough. A ghost is usually quiet, almost blessedly so, an understated presence in a neon-and-video world. But just when you're growing accustomed to the whisper instead of the scream, the touch instead of the stranglehold, you might find yourself shocked by a spirit a little louder, a bit more raucous, than the rest.

Maybe that's why the most apt synonym for ghost is "shade." Like a shade—a shadow—a ghost comes and goes, and changes, refusing to conform to your expectations, behaving in almost every way *but* the way you're counting on it to behave.

In the *Post Mortem* stories you're going to encounter some of today's finest writers turning their talents to the ghost story. Seventeen tales. Seventeen hauntings. You'll find examples of almost everything mentioned above: shades benign and malevolent, lessons and terrors, gentle whispers and piercing cries, haunted houses and . . . well, much more. Read the stories and enjoy them. But when that little dark patch in the corner startles you by moving, when that voice speaks from the midst of solitude, or your peace of mind is shattered by a cold touch on a warm day, don't say we didn't warn you.

That's what you came for, isn't it?

They ended their statement by refusing to answer questions. So, for the time being, the mystery continues.

Each Night, Each Year

Kathryn Ptacek

 My father is dead.
He died two years ago.
But every night he visits.

He comes to me, each night of each year.

I am in my childhood bedroom, tired and asleep after a long day at my place of work and an all-too-long evening alone. At first I don't hear anything. But gradually I become aware of a sound.

It is in the hallway—a faint scuffling, a wisping of a breathlike sound.

And despite knowing what it is, despite what I have witnessed each evening for the past two years, I still get up and go stand in the doorway of the bedroom that has been mine in this house since I was two years old. Each night, each year.

While the house is dark and there is only a faint night-light in the bathroom across from me, I can see. I can see what is in the hallway.

It is my father, and he is crawling.

He is on his hands and his knees, creeping across

the stained shag carpet, and his lower jaw, covered with grizzle, is quivering as if he were speaking, but I do not hear any words. Occasionally his nails, grown longer than most men wear them, snag on the loops of the carpet.

He is crawling as he has done before and before and before.

As he did the first time I found him. He had been sleeping on the couch in the living room, having gone there from his bedroom where he said he couldn't get to sleep. And he claimed he couldn't stand up from the low-slung sofa when he wanted to return to his bedroom for the rest of the night. So he crawled. He did not call to me, even though I was in the next room. I would have come to help him stand; I did not sleep heavily in those days when I was tending him.

I would have come to help.

But he didn't call.

And so I found him.

I bit my lip and knelt down and slowly, carefully helped him to his feet. Hanging on to me, he shuffled into his room. I eased him down on to the hospital bed that he hated so much. I took off his bedroom slippers, worn down at the heel, and put them under his bed.

I asked him if he wanted water; he said no; and I remembered all the evenings when I was a child that he had brought me one last glass of water.

In the dryness of the night air, a sweetly rotting smell suddenly pervades the room. It is the smell of his cancer, which invaded his bowels and had eaten its way through his body to his liver, and which somehow in three years had not managed to kill him.

Somehow he hangs.

I ask him if he wants anything. Of course he says no. He does not want to bother me, he says. I tell him it's no bother, Dad, because I'm up already. He says no, go back to sleep, honey. I'm fine, just fine. We do not look at each other.

I go back to my room and lie down on the narrow bed. My feet hang over the end just slightly. With my hands clasped behind my neck, I stare up at the ceiling in the darkness.

And after a while, as I knew it would, a light goes on in his bathroom. The light spreads outward, through his room and down the hallway so that small objects in the bedroom suddenly stand out sharply in the semidarkness, and I listen. I hear the sound of running water. He is up again, washing out his colostomy bag as he does so often during the day. He has never let me help him with that procedure, never let me see what he does even though I have told him I wanted to help. I have only seen that horrible opening with its metallic rim in his stomach just once. That terrible obscene, unnatural opening.

My father is proud.

I wait until the light is gone, and I hear him shuffle back to bed. He groans, and I close my eyes. I hate to hear that from him.

I wait in the darkness, waiting for him to call me, and finally I hear him snore and know that at last he falls asleep.

I wait for sleep to claim me, but it doesn't. I am awake when dawn comes with the coolness of a breeze and the sound of stirring birds.

And when I can put it off no longer, I rise and wash my face and my hair and take a bath. This is the bathroom where he had the hemorrhage that indicated for the first time that something was wrong, very wrong. When I came home from the hospital afterward, I found dried blood across the seat of the toilet, down onto its base, splashed into the tub and beyond, and flecked onto the wall behind the commode. I scoured these stained surfaces, wiping away every trace of the blood. But I still see it, even though it's no longer there.

I apply my makeup and dress in good slacks and a tailored blouse with long sleeves that I will roll up later in the day, and while my hair is still drying, I glance into his room.

Of course, I got rid of the hospital bed after he died. Three days after his death I went through all his things and gave most of them away—his few coats and pants and shirts and the three pairs of new pajamas I had bought him at Penney's but which he'd never worn—to a Catholic mission for homeless men located downtown. Two men in patched flannel shirts and baggy pants and oversize shoes came to get the boxes of clothes I had packed. They did not speak to me; I watched them as they hefted the boxes into the back of a silver pickup. The pieces of furniture—a bookcase and badly painted chest of drawers and an old music cabinet he had salvaged from the city dump when I was a child—I gave to neighbors.

My father's room is bare of furniture, but not of memories.

I remember when I was seven or eight, and he would lie down in the afternoons for a nap when he was home from work or on the weekends after he'd mowed the front and back lawns. I would come in and lie on the other half of the double bed, and we would talk for a few minutes, and then I would get drowsy and fall asleep. And when I awoke, he was gone.

Under the window overlooking the backyard, he had placed an old kitchen table. It was yellow-topped, with rounded chrome legs, and very ugly. He stored his art supplies there, kept his drawing board with the watercolor paper taped to it. He had a German beer stein filled with camel-hair brushes in various lengths and fullnesses, and in plastic boxes he had brought home from work he had rubber erasers, and broken pieces of charcoal in several shades, and left-over paper clips and brittle rubber bands and a couple of pretty rocks he had picked up one day when we were picnicking in the Manzano Mountains.

In his closet was an old ice cream bucket, the kind made of heavy tan cardboard. He always used it as a hamper, even though the laundry hamper was just outside his door. But he would put his underwear and socks—always black or dark blue—into it. Mostly he dropped them on the side of the bucket or on the floor around it, and I remember my mother complaining that she couldn't understand how he could miss it so often and then not bother to pick up the fallen sock. She thought it was very unfair of him. I used to smile, thinking it was such a small matter.

At the other window, facing the neighbors' backyard, is a honeysuckle bush, long overgrown. In the summer, when my father cranked his window open wide, you could smell the fragrant flowers and watch the bees darting among the delicate yellow and white blooms. One day while he stood there, a BB tore through the upper pane of glass, missing his head by only a few inches. Our neighbors' son was testing his new air rifle. My father marched over to their house and took the BB gun away because he said the boy — just a year older than I—was not responsible enough to use it. He put the gun into the trunk of our car, and when I asked him for it, he refused. I never saw it after that. The boy saved his money from his allowance and paid for the new window. We never talked of the incident after that.

I leave the bedroom and glance once at the other silent, empty bedroom next to it. It is my mother's. Or rather, it was. She died six years ago. A stroke came upon her late one night—I had seen her only a few hours before—and then she was gone, a vein in her head bursting without any warning. It was only a few months later that my father was diagnosed as having cancer. It cannot be a coincidence, I think.

I eat my breakfast of toast and unsweetened tea in the dingy kitchen, at the table where he used to eat his breakfast, and I remember making him oatmeal. He never wanted anything else, just oatmeal. Oatmeal was filled with fiber, and he had read that that was good for you, was supposed to prevent cancer. Only it was too late; he had bowel cancer by then. But still he ate the oatmeal every day.

I cooked it for him, and set the bowl in front of him, and watched him as he picked up the spoon, watched as the spoon made its quavering way to his mouth. I would look away, afraid I would cry.

I used to cry a lot around him, and he cried with me. Tears can be cleansing upon occasion, but these were not. They only made us feel worse. But somehow we couldn't help it.

I grab my purse and my jacket and car keys and head out the front door.

I test the door. It is locked, as I knew it would be. I

test it again. A habit taken from my mother, I guess, who always checked things two and three times.

I drive to work, a long commute, even on the freeway. I am employed at the University of Albuquerque across the river from the city. It's a good job, not too difficult but with some challenge, with mostly pleasant people, and I am well paid.

And while I work, I do not remember.

"You don't look so good today," Diana says right before we get ready for lunch. She sits at the next desk in this large office, and we talk often during the day while working. She is probably my closest friend, my only friend. "Aren't you sleeping?" she asks.

I shrug. "Not really." I tell her that I've been having problems at night.

She puts down her pen and looks at me sharply. "What sort of problems?"

I fidget with the handful of paper clips on my desktop, unbending and bending them into grotesque shapes. "Problems," I say.

"Insomnia?"

"Sort of," I mutter. I cannot meet her eyes. I take a deep breath, then look up abruptly. "I have a ghost in my house," I say lightly, thinking she will smile. "It's my father."

She exhales sharply, as if she had been holding her breath. Her expression has not changed. At least she has not laughed at me.

I wait for her to speak, but she doesn't say a word. Had she heard me? I ask her.

"I heard. A ghost? Of your dad, you say?"

I nod.

"A ghost."

"Yes. Every night since his funeral I see him crawling up the floor of the hallway, just the way he did that one time right before he died. It's awful."

Even in the daytime the image remains too bright, too persistent in my mind, and I close my eyes briefly, as if that would clear the picture.

"It's been over two years since your dad's death," Diana says, as if I did not know how long it's been. "I don't think it's a ghost, Becky. Not really."

"Why not? Why isn't it a ghost?"

"I think you're just dreaming. I mean, how do you know you're not? Why do you think you're awake?"

"Well, I see it so clearly—"

"Which means it can't be a dream? Of course not! Come on, it's just memories. For some reason—and I'm not sure why—you still feel guilty about your dad's death and what happened just before it. So your mind, which still hasn't let go of all that, is conjuring up these weird images. They're *dreams*, Becky. That's all. It's part of the natural grieving process. Yours has taken two years; some people take a much shorter time, while others never get through. It's an individual thing. You can't rush it, you can't stop it. But you can work it out—mostly through talking. You haven't done that, you know. Not really."

"I know," I say. I feel guilty again.

"Come on. It's not the end of the world. You're having some bad dreams, but that's all. Your memories become your dreams, and that's why you think you have a 'ghost.'" She laughs. "You don't believe that, now do you?"

I smile. "You're right, Diana. You're completely right, of course." And for the rest of that day I feel remarkably better.

But then at five I must head home once again, head back to that silent house.

It is nighttime again, and for once I am in bed by ten. It is early July and too warm, with no breeze to cool me off, and I have only a light sheet across my body. I hope I can sleep through the night without awakening, but I know I won't be able to. I haven't been able to since I tended my father those last months. Not in two years have I slept completely through the night. I awaken each night, time after time, waiting to hear those sounds, waiting to hear him call my name.

And sometimes he would do that, so faint that at first I didn't hear him. When it happened more and more, I awoke at the slightest sound.

But I would get up and go into his room. What did he want? I would ask, and sometimes my voice would be sharper than I wanted.

He wanted to know what time it was. I would look at his clock with its luminous dial on the bookshelf behind his head, and I would tell him. One-seventeen; three-thirty-three; four-oh-five; five-fifteen. Whatever time it was then.

Sometimes he wanted a drink of water, and I would hold his head up with one hand as I guided his icy hand to the flexible straw in the glass and to his lips. Sometimes it ran out of his mouth, and I would wipe his face softly, as if he were a baby.

Sometimes he wanted nothing, but I think he wanted just to see me, just to make sure that I was really there in the other room, that he hadn't died yet.

Sometimes I would get up and go into his room, even though he hadn't called me, and I would watch him as he slept. Would watch his thin chest rise and fall so rapidly. Surely he couldn't be asleep, not a natural sleep. But he was.

Sometimes, as I watched, his breath would catch and hold for an impossibly long time, and I would wonder if this was it, if this was the moment of death, but then he would exhale, and I knew it wasn't time.

Each night, each day I wondered how much longer it could be.

I prayed for his death. I didn't want him to live any longer, not when it was like that. Not when he wasn't the father I had known all my life, the tall and athletic man who was never sick, who never felt pain.

He had accidents. Sometimes he couldn't make it to the bathroom in time.

Once he peed on himself in the kitchen as he stood at the sink, and I yelled at him when I saw the yellow puddling at his feet. I dabbed at his thin legs and the floor with paper towels, and I was crying for him, and for myself, but mostly I think it was because he was reduced to this, such a feeble old man, so unable to tend to himself.

It is nighttime, and I cry, my pillow uncomfortable, my cheeks damp, and I ache inside.

I am watching the television, looking at it with the sound turned off, trying to read the lips of the actors and actresses, trying to guess what's going on. I think what I make up is much more interesting than what is really going on, and sometimes I laugh aloud, the sound odd in an otherwise silent house.

I am staying up late. I am trying to prove to myself that this is only a dream as Diana claims it is, not a ghost.

I yawn and stretch and realize that I'm getting tired, and here it's only after nine. But I can't go to bed. Not yet.

I decide to step outside; perhaps the cool evening air will wake me up. I go out to the backyard and look up into the sky. The air over Albuquerque has grown thicker with smog these past years, but you can still see the stars, can still watch them.

My father used to sit out here on the patio for hours every summer evening. He'd sit on a webbed chair with a can of beer in his hand and stare up at the sky. Looking for flying saucers, he would say with a knowing grin, and I would giggle.

The memory feels good, and there is no ache inside. Simply a warmth.

Memories, I tell myself, can be good, as well as bad. I grin.

As I watch, I see something shimmer in the sky . . . a shooting star, or perhaps only the lights of a distant airplane. I prefer the former.

The temperature is dropping. Even though it's summer, the nights can be cool, and I shiver. I go back inside and decide it's time for bed.

I take a quick bath and see no blood in my mind's eye, and I brush my teeth and pull on my short nightgown and go back to my bedroom. As I brush my hair, I hear a sound outside my room.

I frown, lay the brush across my knees. Wait and wait and wait.

And once more I see my father.

I am not sleeping. I am awake. Too much awake.

Diana was wrong.

* * *

My father is a ghost, and he comes to me each night, each year. I do not think he means to, but I don't think he has any choice.

I bring him here.

It is my guilt that calls him.

Even though I did all I could, I didn't do enough. There had to be something more that I could have done for him. Something. I don't know what. But there had to be something else.

I look back, and I'm not happy with what I see. I yelled too much. I crabbed at him. I didn't mean to, but I did. Sometimes it was just too much for me, day after day like this, and I would raise my voice. He would always look at me with his yellow-brown eyes, look at me and say nothing, and I would feel terrible, and I would apologize at once. But no words could take back the tone I had used. To my father.

I forget the times when he asked me to tie his shoe-laces, and he would sit on the organ bench because it was high and thus easy for him to sit on, and I would kneel in front of him and gently tie the laces, tie them for the seventh or eighth or ninth time that day. I forget the times when I helped him into the bathroom and he would send me away, too proud to let me see. I forget the times when I read to him from the news-paper or talked about what I had done at work that day. I forget.

I remember only the yelling, the anger, the resentment that my life was dying with him.

During the day for a few hours I had aides come in to take care of him. They were expensive, but there was no choice if I was to continue working and bring-ing in money to support the two of us. Luckily, Hospice provided an aide for a few hours a week, and that was good; that was some respite.

But every evening when I came straight home from the office he was already in bed, his thin chenille bedspread pulled up to his chin, two winter-thick blankets spread across the bed. Even if it was July and August and in the 80s or 90s, he was freezing. Always cold, because the disease sucked the warmth from his blood. In the day he wore a Haines T-shirt under a heavy flannel shirt, thick woolen trousers and a bathrobe over that. And he turned the heat up when he thought I wasn't looking.

I turned the thermostat down when I thought he wasn't looking.

On the weekends my father and I were on our own. No aides came then. It was just the two of us, or an occasional neighbor or friend who dropped by to chat and to see how things were or to bring some food for us. I nearly always ended up eating it because he wanted nothing but oatmeal because nothing else tasted good to him any longer. Things were the same, the neighbor would see after a few minutes; my father was still dying inch by inch, breath by breath.

Often on those long weekends we would sit in the den, the small room off the kitchen, and he would be in his green plaid chair that he had salvaged from my grandmother's house, his hands clasped along its padded arms, and I would sit on a wooden kitchen chair that I had brought into the room. Every morning when he rose, he built a fire in the Franklin stove that he had installed some years ago. He had built the fire wall of brick behind it, the floor of brick under it, and the half-wall of brick between that room and the kitchen. My father had never been trained as a mason.

We would sit in that hot room, thick with smoke from the Franklin because he didn't want the windows opened, and there would be silence.

Sometimes the television was on, but the volume was down low because he was going deaf, and it didn't matter to him any longer what was being shown on the old black-and-white. Yet he would look at the flickering images so that he wouldn't have to look at me.

Sometimes he would say he wanted to tell me some things, and I would ask what things. Just things, he would say, almost slyly. I would wait for a few minutes, and when he didn't continue, I would ask him again, though sharply this time, what he meant.

He would turn his head, and he would look at me with those yellow-brown eyes, the eyes of a wolf, and he would say, "Things."

Things he disapproved of in me, things he thought I should have done with my life, things we had disagreed about so many times in the past. Just things.

He never told me. I asked him now and then, but he just said, "later."

I kept telling him there would be no later, that he was dying, and he would say no, he wasn't. He wasn't dying at all.

I would start to cry then. I would put my head down and grab the Kleenex I kept in my pocket, and the hot tears would come, and my shoulders would shake even though I didn't make a sound.

He would want to stand up then, but couldn't, and so I would go to him and take his bony hands and help him to his feet and watch as he shuffled from the room.

I would watch that sad form, and my eyes would fill with tears again. This was the man who had built the wall of bricks without instruction.

I have a ghost, and I want to exorcise it. But I do not know how.

The ghost of my father lives with me, inside my mind and out.

Each night my father comes to visit me, to remind me what I did not do, to remind me of all that he did not say to me.

I did what was best. At the time. I thought. I did what I could do. I regret the yelling, the harsh tones, the bitterness, but I can't take them back. You can't change what has happened in the past, can you? What is done is done, no matter the regrets.

And yet . . . why not?

Why can't I take them back, now after two years? Two years that I've given to mourning, to a life inhabited only by myself and the ghost of my father. Why not?

If I do, will his ghost go away? Will he leave me alone, my father, so that I can sleep through the darkness, be rested for at least one night?

I am scared. I want to take back all those ugly things that I did to him when he was dying, and yet if he goes, what will I have? He is my only nightly visitor.

He is dead, I tell myself.

He is a ghost, and I am rapidly becoming one myself.

I swallow, lick my lips.

I take them back, I say aloud in the darkness. I take them back, all those angry tears and furious words, and the childish impatience when he took too long to feed himself or to pick up a pencil or to finish his sentence. I take them back.

I take them.

Back.

It is nighttime. I am in my bedroom.

I grow aware of a scuffling, a breathlike sound. As I lie in the dark, I hear the sound grow louder.

And knowing, I still get up.

It is dark as I stand in the doorway of the room, but I can see clearly. I can see what is in the hallway.

It is me, and I am crawling up the length of the hallway.

Mark of the Loser

Gary Brandner

Krager pulled the rented Ford off to the side of the narrow road and jogged the shift lever to park. Up ahead and to his right, silhouetted against the clouded night sky, was a house that did not belong here. Three dark stories of porches, gables, turrets, pilasters, parapets, dormers —it was a relic of the last century and should have stood somewhere in gloomy Massachusetts, not in southern California where the sun shines forever and people live in happy homes.

What was worse, the house looked empty. Dead. No lights shone in the windows. A pocket of silence surrounded the place. The chimneys thrust into the night, cold and smokeless.

Krager thumbed on the map light and dug into his pocket for the envelope delivered to his hotel room that afternoon. It was his name all right, neatly lettered on the outside. He had double-checked that earlier, thinking it might be a mistake. He drew out the creamy notepaper and read again the message:

PLEASE COME TO A PARTY TONIGHT, 8 P.M., AT NO. 1
WILLOWS ROAD. DRESS: CASUAL.

The note was signed with an ornately scrolled *W.*

Krager looked up again at the dark, silent house.
This was Willows Road, all right, he had climbed out
of the car and walked over to read the sign when he
turned off the highway outside of Wildewood. And
this was the only house he had seen in four miles of
driving. The road appeared to come to an end at the
thick forest just beyond the house. This had to be
No. 1.

Okay, it was a joke. Somebody's idea of a prank.
Well, why not? Nothing good had happened to him in
the month he'd spent in this crummy little town. A
mean practical joke would fit right in.

At first coming to Wildewood had seemed like a
fine opportunity to get his life back on track. After the
divorce he had wondered for a while if it was worth
going on. He'd lost his wife, his kids, his home—there
seemed little more he could lose. Then the company
sent him to Wildewood to get the new branch office
operating properly. After a month he had the office
running just fine, but his life was as screwed up as
ever. Now he was scheduled to return to the city on
Monday. This party was to be his farewell to the
town.

His failure to make friends here was not for lack of
trying. Since his arrival Krager had been as charming
and open as he could manage—forcing his face into a
smile he did not feel, talking when he felt like hiding
in his room. He had talked to everybody—room
clerks, bellhops, waiters, news vendors. He had invited strangers to have a drink, agreed with their poli-

tics, asked what they thought about the Dodgers. He had gone to the local date festival, visited three different churches, rooted for the high school track team. He had even offered himself as a ready substitute in the local bowling league.

No good. His conversational forays were cut off with one-word replies or ignored altogether. The people he approached would look at their watches and suddenly remember an appointment. Or they would simply turn away. Krager was so lonely he ached. And he knew why. He wore the mark, and anyone could spot it a block away. Obvious as a facial scar or a missing limb. The mark of the loser.

That was why the party invitation came as such a surprise. Krager was ready to chuck it into the trash can, but a look around his hotel room at the cold, impersonal furniture, the sad wallpaper, and the television set that brought in only two channels, and those badly, changed his mind. He had only this weekend left in Wildewood, and if there was even a small chance to break the desolation of his mood he would seize it.

Now it all looked like just one more cruel joke played on him by . . . hell, by life.

He jammed the car into gear and jerked back out onto the road. A large sloping lawn fronted the house, so at least he could turn around there and head back to town. He would buy a bottle of bourbon, go up to his room, turn on the crummy TV set, and drink himself to sleep. Again.

Krager stomped on the accelerator and the car surged forward. The old house was lost for a moment behind a thick growth of fir trees. When it came into view again, he almost drove off the road before he could bring the car to a stop.

Lights blazed in all the many windows. Pale smoke curled up from the chimneys. And he could clearly hear voices, laughter, music. Unmistakable sounds of a party.

Krager shook his head, rubbed his eyes, and looked again. It was the same house, the same turn-of-the-century Gothic gingerbread architecture. The only house in sight. But where a moment ago it had been cold, dark, and forbidding, now it promised warmth and company. A trick of the night mists and shadows? An illusion of his melancholy mind? Who cared? There were people here. Music. A respite, however brief, from the soul-deadening loneliness of the past year.

A long driveway of crushed rock curved from the road up to a turnaround in front of the house. The party sounds grew louder as he approached. Behind the uncurtained windows people moved back and forth briskly, many of them carrying drinks.

Krager slowed and looked around to see where the other cars were parked. There were no other cars. How had all these people gotten here? There must be a parking area around back, he decided. He could ask someone inside.

He left the Ford at the foot of the wooden steps leading up to a broad front porch, and climbed toward the party. The doorbell was an old-fashioned iron key type, set in the center of the door. He gave it a twist and heard the grinding ring on the other side of the panel.

The door opened. Light and music spilled out. The music was Glenn Miller's "String of Pearls." Krager smiled. At least he would not have to listen to any of that cacophonous crap that passed for music these days.

A stocky blond man wearing a cardigan sweater over an open-collar sports shirt stuck out his right hand. His left held a highball glass.

"You must be Len Krager." The man's smile was broad and real.

"Y-yes, I am. But I don't think—"

"Come in, come in," the man said. "The bar's over there on your right. There's food in the dining room, right through the archway. We've been waiting for you."

"You have?"

The man in the sweater laughed. "Well, we didn't exactly hold up the party, but we've all been anxious to meet you. Come on." He stood aside and made a sweeping gesture into the room where a constantly moving crowd of people drank and talked and laughed in the best party tradition. Little groups combined, broke apart, and recombined like amoeba under a microscope. Most were Krager's age or slightly older. A few were younger. Those whose eye he caught nodded and smiled. Krager actually felt welcome here—a sensation he had missed for many months.

He turned back to the man who had admitted him. "Uh, my car . . ."

"Don't worry about it. It's fine right where it is. We haven't had one stolen all night."

The man laughed heartily. Krager felt the tense muscles of his own face loosen in an answering smile.

"Are you the host?"

"Me? Nah, no way. I'm just another guest. Call me Harry. Call me anything but late for dinner."

The man laughed again at the tired old sally, and Krager joined in. He looked around at the animated guests.

"I was afraid I might be early, but it looks like the party's been going on for a while."

Harry clapped a hand on his shoulder. "Seems like forever, ha ha. Come on and join the gang."

"I really should say hello to the host, whoever he is. Or she."

"Plenty of time for that, Len. Plenty of time. Come on."

He steered Krager toward the long bar where a smiling bartender poured generously from bottles bearing good brand names—Chivas Regal, Jack Daniel's, Tanqueray, Stolichnaya. People wandered in from the other room carrying plates of food. They smiled and saluted him like an old friend.

While the bartender served him, Harry introduced Krager to half a dozen of the guests. Their names flew in and out of his head. Krager had never been good with names. Strangely, they all seemed to know him and to have been expecting him.

Krager accepted the Jack Daniel's on ice and turned to his guide. "So, Harry, what do you do?"

The other man's eyes clouded ever so slightly, though his smile stayed in place.

"Do?"

"You know, what business are you in?"

"Oh, I do a little of this, a little of that." He recognized someone off across the room. "Excuse me for a minute, will you, Len?"

"Sure."

As he watched Harry walk off, a shadow seemed to cross one of the windows that opened on the porch, as though someone had passed by out there. Krager had a fleeting impression of a pale oval that might have been a face that turned toward him for an instant; then it was gone.

"Got a match?"

The purring voice close to his ear made Krager start. He turned to see a lovely woman with soft chestnut hair and cheekbones actresses would kill for. She was holding up an unlit cigarette and smiling at him, though her blue-green eyes held strange melancholy shadows.

Krager found his voice and patted his pockets foolishly. "Uh, no, I'm sorry. I quit cigarettes a couple of years ago. My wife insisted. I'm not married anymore." The words came out in a rush, sounding inane even as he spoke them. He felt himself blushing.

"I should quit too, I suppose," the woman said.

"You'll live longer," Krager said. "So they say."

"Yes, so they say." The woman's voice was a mellow contralto. The kind of voice that could say, "Good morning," and make it sound like poetry.

"I'm Len Krager. I'm staying in town at the—"

"Yes, I know. Call me Carol." She touched the back of his hand with cool fingers.

"Can I ask you something, Carol?"

"Of course."

"How do you know about me? Everybody here seems to know me, and I can't figure it out. I've been in Wildewood a month, and I've seen a lot of people, but—well, I don't recognize any of you."

"People look different at a party," Carol said.

"I guess that's true. Kind of out of uniform. Like

seeing your mailman on his day off. Or your bartender on the wrong side of the bar." Krager realized he was talking too fast, but he did not want to lose the woman's attention. He looked around quickly. "Let me see if I can get you a light."

Carol dropped the cigarette into an ashtray. "That's all right. I didn't really want one."

"Do you live around here?" Krager could have bitten his tongue for the corny singles-bar approach. God, he was out of practice at talking to people.

"Have you had anything to eat?" she asked, ignoring his question.

"I'm not all that hungry," he said. "I had something at the hotel. Didn't want to get here too early."

"Oh, you *can't* come here too early. And you should try the food. It's marvelous."

"Maybe I will have a bite," Krager said. "Will you join me?"

"I've already had mine," Carol said, starting to move away. "You help yourself. It's good."

Krager took a step after her, but stopped as the shadow again appeared at the window across the room. This time it stopped and looked directly at him, and he saw it was the figure of a woman dressed in something black and out-of-date. Then she turned and was gone again.

"Were you on your way to the food?"

A tall, thin man with a wineglass in his hand stood at Krager's shoulder.

"I guess I was."

"Fine. We'll go together. I hate to eat alone, don't you, Len?"

"I—I suppose so." Krager looked into the pale, serious eyes of the tall man. "Do I know you?"

The man laughed. Everybody here laughed a lot.

"Who can say, really, who knows whom? Or does nobody really know anybody? Call me John."

What the hell does that mean? Krager wondered. The tall man took his arm lightly and steered him into a large, bright dining room. An old but expensive hi-fi outfit played Benny Goodman's theme, "Let's Dance." On a long table were platters of beef, ham, turkey, three different cheeses, potato and pasta salads, shrimp, bowls of olives, deviled eggs.

"Nice spread, isn't it?" John said.

"Yes. Tell me, John, who *is* the host here, anyway? All I've met is other guests."

"Enjoy yourself, Len. I've got to see a man about a dog."

Before Krager could call him back, John had threaded his way through the crowd around the table and out of reach. Krager turned back to the food and was startled to see a face at the window directly across from him. It was the woman in black. Her sharp chiseled features were clear now, her eyes bright. Her mouth twitched in a half smile.

A hand dropped on Krager's shoulder. He jumped and turned to see Harry, his original guide, holding out a fresh drink.

"I saw you leave this at the bar so I topped it off for you. That okay?"

When he looked back, the woman was gone. He took the drink from the other man.

"Uh, yeah, thanks. Tell me something, Harry, who was that woman out there just now?"

"Woman?"

"Outside the window. Kind of hard looking. Dressed in black. Bright, piercing eyes. I saw her a couple of times from the living room and just now right out there."

Harry threw back his head and laughed. "By God, I think you've seen Old Mary."

"Old who?"

"Old Mary Grauer. Her father built this house. Mary lived here after he died. Crazy as a coot." Harry sobered abruptly. "I mean really crazy. Killed people. Nobody really knows how many. Bums, hoboes, runaways—said she felt sorry for them. Lured 'em out here and . . . *ker-chop.*"

"*Ker-chop?*"

"An ax. Old Mary used an ax. They finally clapped her in the booby hatch. Kept her there till she died."

"But . . ." Krager gestured helplessly at the window.

"Oh, that must have been Old Mary's ghost. People say she still stalks around the house and grounds on certain moonless nights."

Krager stared at him. Harry's expression was bland and unreadable.

"You don't *believe* that, do you?"

"Hey, in the end what does it matter who believes what? Or why? Hundred years from now, what difference will it make, right?" He plucked a stuffed black olive from the table and sauntered away. "Talk to you later, Len."

Krager started after him, but was blocked by a group of partygoers enjoying a joke. Harry strolled through a doorway opposite the living room. Krager set down his glass and the plate of untouched food and followed.

The room was a library, the walls lined with leather-bound books. There were a heavy old oak desk, an ancient grandfather clock, well-used leather furniture. Double French doors led out onto a flagstone patio. Harry was not in the room. Carol was. She seemed to be reading the titles on a shelf of books and did not turn when Krager entered.

"Hi," he said.

"Hello, Len."

"Didn't Harry just come in here?"

"I wasn't watching."

He walked over and stood behind her until she turned to face him.

"Carol, what's with these people?"

"What do you mean? Have you had trouble with someone?"

"Nothing like that. Everybody's been friendly as all get-out. Too friendly. And they talk in riddles. I can't get straight answers from anybody. I haven't met the host, I don't know anybody's last name or what they do for a living or where they live. Not even you."

"Do those things matter?"

"Well, yes. At least it matters to me in your case. Carol, I'm supposed to leave town in a couple of days, but I don't have to. I'd like to see you again."

"You'll see me."

The big clock bonged the hour, and Carol started for the door.

"Well how about a phone number? Or your last name?"

"You'll see me," Carol said again, and slipped out of the room.

As Krager frowned after her, he heard a sharp rapping at the French doors. He looked over there to see the woman in black—the so-called ghost. She looked very substantial as she stood out on the patio looking back at him. She raised one arm in a beckoning motion. When he did not respond at once, she beckoned again, more emphatically.

Krager looked once toward the door back to the dining room, but Carol was not in sight. Anyway, he had questions that needed answers. He crossed to the French doors, opened them, and stepped out.

It was biting cold outside, and Krager shivered. The woman, dressed in black taffeta and wearing no wrap, did not seem to notice. She looked older when he got close to her. Her face was etched with fine lines like crazed old china. Her eyes were oiled black olives in a delicate white crust.

"I'm Len Krager," he said. "But I suppose you know that. Everybody else does."

"I know." Her voice was brittle and whispery like old parchment. "I am your hostess."

Unconsciously Krager touched the pocket with his invitation. "Ah, then you're the lady *W.*"

. "I'm afraid you misread my script," the old woman said. "The initial is an *M.* For my first name."

He stared at her. "Mary? Mary Grauer?"

Behind him the lights dimmed, the sounds of talk and laughter died, the music faded to silence.

"What's going on?" Krager said.

The old woman pointed at the French doors. Krager turned and peered into the dim interior. The guests stood there in ranks facing him. Harry, John, Carol, all the others. Quiet now. No laughter, no talk, no smiles. They watched him.

Behind him the old woman said, "They have something to show you."

Slowly, slowly, in unison like a phantom drill team, the party guests turned. When they were facing away from him, the lights inside flared momentarily—just long enough for Krager to see the deep, wet wound in the back of each of the heads.

It was the last thing Krager saw before the ax blade sank into his brain.

Timeskip

Charles de Lint

Every time it rains a ghost comes walking.

He goes up by the stately old houses that line Stanton Street, down Henratty Lane to where it leads into the narrow streets and crowded back alleys of Crowsea, and then back up Stanton again in an unvarying routine.

He wears a worn tweed suit—mostly browns and grays with a faint rosy touch of heather. A shapeless cap presses down his brown curls. His features give no true indication of his age, while his eyes are both innocent and wise. His face gleams in the rain, slick and wet as that of a living person. When he reaches the streetlamp in front of the old Hamill estate, he wipes his eyes with a brown hand. Then he fades away.

Samantha Rey knew it was true because she'd seen him.

More than once.

She saw him every time it rained.

* * *

"So have you asked her out yet?" Jilly wanted to know.

We were sitting on a park bench, feeding pigeons the leftover crusts from our lunches. Jilly had worked with me at the post office that Christmas they hired outside staff instead of letting the regular employees work the overtime, and we'd been friends ever since. These days she worked three nights a week as a waitress, while I made what I could busking on the Market with my father's old Czech fiddle.

Jilly was slender, with a thick tangle of brown hair and pale blue eyes, electric as sapphires. She had a penchant for loose clothing and fingerless gloves when she wasn't waitressing. There were times, when I met her on the streets in the evening, that I mistook her for a bag lady: skulking in an alleyway, gaze alternating between the sketchbook held in one hand and the faces of the people on the streets as they walked by. She had more sketches of me playing my fiddle than had any right to exist.

"She's never going to know how you feel until you talk to her about it," Jilly went on when I didn't answer.

"I know."

I'll make no bones about it: I was putting the make on Sam Rey and had been ever since she'd started to work at Gypsy Records half a year ago. I never much went in for the blond California beach girl type, but Sam had a look all her own. She had some indefinable quality that went beyond her basic cheerleader appearance. Right. I can hear you already. Rationalizations of the North American libido. But it was true. I didn't just want Sam in my bed; I wanted to know we were going to have a future together. I wanted to grow old with her. I wanted to build up a lifetime of shared memories.

About the most Sam knew about all this was that I hung around and talked to her a lot at the record store.

"Look," Jilly said. "Just because she's pretty doesn't mean she's having a perfect life or anything. Most guys look at someone like her and they won't even approach her because they're sure she's got men coming out of her ears. Well, it doesn't always work that way. For instance"—she touched her breastbone with a narrow hand and smiled—"consider yours truly."

I looked at her long fingers. Paint had dried under her nails.

"You've started a new canvas," I said.

"And you're changing the subject," she replied. "Come on, Geordie. What's the big deal? The most she can say is no."

"Well, yeah. But—"

"She intimidates you, doesn't she?"

I shook my head. "I talk to her all the time."

"Right. And that's why I've got to listen to your constant mooning over her." She gave me a sudden considering look, then grinned. "I'll tell you what, Geordie, me lad. Here's the bottom line: I'll give you twenty-four hours to ask her out. If you haven't gotten it together by then, I'll talk to her myself."

"Don't even joke about it."

"Twenty-four hours," Jilly said firmly. She looked at the chocolate chip cookie in my hand. "Are you eating that?" she added in that certain tone of voice of hers that plainly said: "All previous topics of conversation have been dealt with and completed. We are now changing topics."

So we did. But all the while we talked, I thought about going into the record store and asking Sam out, because if I didn't, Jilly would do it for me. Whatever else she might be, Jilly wasn't shy. Having her go in to plead my case would be as bad as having my mother do it for me. I'd never be able to show my face in there again.

Gypsy Records is on Williamson Street, one of the city's main arteries. The street begins as Highway 14 outside the city, lined with a sprawl of fast food outlets, malls, and warehouses. The commercial properties give way to ever-increasing handfuls of residential blocks until it reaches the downtown core, where shops and low-rise apartments mingle in gossiping crowds.

The store gets its name from John Butler, a short, round-bellied man without a smidgin of Romany blood, who began his business out of the back of a hand-drawn cart that gypsied its way through the city's streets for years, always keeping just one step ahead of the municipal licensing board's agents. While it carries the usual best-sellers, the lifeblood of its sales are more obscure titles—imports and albums published by independent record labels. Albums, singles and compact discs of punk, traditional folk, jazz, heavy metal, and alternative music line its shelves. Barring Sam, most of those who work there would look at home in the fashion pages of the most current British alternative fashion magazines.

Sam was wearing a blue cotton dress today, embroidered with silver threads. Her blond hair was cut in a short shag on the top, hanging down past her shoulders at the back and sides. She was dealing with a defect when I came in. I don't know if the record in question worked or not, but the man returning it was definitely defective.

"It sounds like there's a radio broadcast right in the middle of the song," he was saying as he tapped the cover of the Pink Floyd album on the counter between them.

"It's supposed to be there," Sam explained. "It's *part* of the song." The tone of her voice told me that this conversation was going into its twelfth round or so.

"Well, I don't like it," the man told her. "When I buy an album of music, I expect to get just music on it."

"You still can't return it."

I worked in a record shop one Christmas—two years before the post office job. The best defect I got was from someone returning an in-concert album by Marcel Marceau. Each side had thirty minutes of silence, with applause at the end—I kid you not.

I browsed through the Celtic records while I waited for Sam to finish with her customer. I couldn't afford any of them, but I liked to see what was new. Blasting out of the store's speakers was the new Beastie Boys album. It sounded like a cross between heavy metal and bad rap and was about as appealing as being hit by a car. You couldn't deny its energy, though.

By the time Sam was free, I'd located five records I would have bought in more flush times. Leaving them in the bin, I drifted over to the front cash register just as the Beastie Boys' last cut ended. Sam replaced them with a tape of New Age piano music.

"What's the new Oyster Band like?" I asked.

Sam smiled. "It's terrific. My favorite cut's 'The Old

Dance.' It's sort of an allegory based on Adam and Eve and the serpent that's got a great hook in the chorus. Telfer's fiddling just sort of skips ahead, pulling the rest of the song along."

That's what I like about alternative record stores like Gypsy's—the people working in them actually know something about what they're selling.

"Have you got an open copy?" I asked.

She nodded and turned to the bin of opened records behind her to find it. With her back to me, I couldn't get lost in those deep blue eyes of hers. I seized my opportunity and plunged ahead.

"Areyouworkingtonight, wouldyouliketogooutwithmesomewhere?"

I'd meant to be cool about it, but the words all blurred together as they left my throat. I could feel the flush start up the back of my neck as she turned and looked back at me with those baby blues.

"Say what?" she asked.

Before my throat closed up on me completely, I tried again, keeping it short. "Do you want to go out with me tonight?"

Standing there with the Oyster Band album in her hand, she'd never looked better. Especially when she said, "I thought you'd never ask."

I put in a couple of hours of busking that afternoon, down in Crowsea's Market, the fiddle humming under my chin to the jingling rhythm of the coins that passersby threw into the case lying open in front of me. I came away with twenty-six dollars and change —not the best of days, but enough to buy a halfway decent dinner and a few beers.

I picked up Sam after she finished work, and we ate

at The Monkey Woman's Nest, a Mexican restaurant on Williamson just a couple of blocks down from Gypsy's. I still don't know how the place got its name. Ernestina Verdad, the Mexican woman who owns the place, looks like a showgirl, and not one of her waitresses is even vaguely simian in appearance.

It started to rain as we were finishing our second beer, turning Williamson Street slick with neon reflections. Sam got a funny look on her face as she watched the rain through the window. Then she turned to me.

"Do you believe in ghosts?" she asked.

The serious look in her eyes stopped the half-assed joke that two beers were brewing in the carbonated swirl of my mind. I never could hold my alcohol. I wasn't drunk, but I had a buzz on.

"I don't think so," I said carefully. "At least I've never seriously stopped to think about it."

"Come on," she said, getting up from the table. "I want to show you something."

I let her lead me out into the rain, though I didn't let her pay anything toward the meal. Tonight was my treat. Next time I'd be happy to let her do the honors.

"Every time it rains," she said, "a ghost comes walking down my street. . . ."

She told me the story as we walked down into Crowsea. The rain was light and I was enjoying it, swinging my fiddle case in my right hand, Sam hanging on to my left as though she'd always walked there. I felt like I was on top of the world, listening to her talk, feeling the pressure of her arm, the bump of her hip against mine.

She had an apartment on the third floor of an old

brick and frame building on Stanton Street. It had a front porch that ran the length of the house, dormer windows—two in the front and back, one on each side—and a mansard roof. We stood on the porch, out of the rain, which was coming down harder now. An orange-and-white tom was sleeping on the cushion of a white wicker chair by the door. He twitched a torn ear as we shared his shelter, but didn't bother to open his eyes. I could smell the mint that was growing up alongside the porch steps, sharp in the wet air.

Sam pointed down the street to where the yellow glare of a streetlamp glistened on the rain-slicked cobblestone walk leading to the Hamill estate. The Hamill house itself was separated from the street by a low wall and a dark expanse of lawn, bordered by the spreading boughs of huge oak trees.

"Watch the street," she said. "Just under the street-light."

I looked, but I didn't see anything. The wind gusted suddenly, driving the rain in hard sheets along Stanton Street, and for a moment we lost all visibility. When it cleared, he was standing there, Sam's ghost, just as she'd told me. As he started down the street, Sam gave my arm a tug. I stowed my fiddle case under the tom's wicker chair, and we followed the ghost down Henratty Lane.

By the time he returned to the streetlight in front of the Hamill estate, I was ready to argue that Sam was mistaken. There was nothing the least bit ghostly about the man we were following. When he returned up Henratty Lane, we had to duck into a doorway to let him pass. He never looked at us, but I could see the rain hitting him. I could hear the sound of his shoes on the pavement. He had to have come out of the walk that led up to the estate's house, at the same time as that sudden gust of wind-driven rain. It had been a simple coincidence, nothing more. But when he returned to the streetlight, he lifted a hand to wipe his face, and then he was gone. He just winked out of existence. There was no wind. No gust of rain. No place he could have gone. A ghost.

"Jesus," I said softly as I walked over to the pool of light cast by the streetlamp. There was nothing to see. But there had been a man there. I was sure of that much.

"We're soaked," Sam said. "Come on up to my place and I'll make us some coffee."

The coffee was great and the company was better. Sam had a small clothes dryer in her kitchen. I sat in the living room in an oversize housecoat while my clothes tumbled and turned, the machine creating a vibration in the floorboards that I'm sure Sam's downstairs neighbors must have just loved. Sam had changed into a dark blue sweat suit—she looked best in blue, I decided—and dried her hair while she was making the coffee. I prowled around her living room while she did, admiring her books, her huge record collection, her sound system, and the mantel crammed with knickknacks above a working fireplace.

All her furniture was the kind made for comfort—it crouched like sleeping animals about the room. Fat sofa in front of the fireplace, an old pair of matching easy chairs by the window. The bookcases, record cabinet, side tables, and trim were all natural wood, polished to a shine with furniture oil.

We talked about a lot of things, sitting on the sofa,

drinking our coffee, but mostly we talked about the ghost.

"Have you ever approached him?" I asked at one point.

Sam shook her head. "No. I just watch him walk. I've never even talked about him to anybody else." That made me feel good. "You know, I can't help but feel that he's waiting for something, or someone. Isn't that the way it usually works in ghost stories?"

"This isn't a ghost story," I said.

"But we didn't imagine it, did we? Not both of us at the same time?"

"I don't know."

But I knew someone who probably did. Jilly. She was into every sort of strange happening, taking all kinds of odd things seriously. I could remember her telling me that one of her professors in Boston was a wizard who had a brown-skinned goblin for a valet, but the thing I remembered most was her talking about that scene in Disney's *101 Dalmations*, where the dogs are all howling to send a message across town, one dog sending it out, another picking it up and passing it along, all the way across town and out into the country. "That's how they do it," Jilly had said. "Just like that."

And if you walked with her at night and a dog started to howl—if no other dog picked it up, then she'd pass it on. She could mimic any dog's bark or howl so perfectly it was uncanny. It could also be embarrassing, because she didn't care who was around or what kinds of looks she got. It was the message that was important.

When I told Sam about Jilly, she smiled, but there wasn't any mockery in her smile. Emboldened, I related the ultimatum that Jilly had given me that afternoon.

Sam laughed aloud. "Jilly sounds like my kind of person," she said. "I'd like to meet her."

When it started to get late, I collected my clothes and changed in the bathroom. I didn't want to start anything, not yet, not this soon, and I knew that Sam felt the same way, though neither of us had spoken of it. She kissed me at the door, a long, warm kiss that had me buzzing again.

"Come see me tomorrow?" she asked. "At the store?"

"Just try to keep me away," I replied.

I gave the old tom on the porch a pat and whistled all the way home to my own place on the other side of Crowsea.

Jilly's studio was its usual organized mess. It was an open loftlike affair that occupied half of the second floor of a four-story brown brick building on Yoors Street, where Foxville's low rentals mingle with Crowsea's shops and older houses. One half of the studio was taken up with a Murphy bed that was never folded back into the wall, a pair of battered sofas, a small kitchenette, storage cabinets, and a tiny boxlike bathroom obviously designed with dwarfs in mind.

Her easel stood in the other half of the studio, by the window where it could catch the morning sun. All around it were stacks of sketchbooks, newspapers, unused canvases, and art books. Finished canvases leaned face front, five to ten deep, against the back wall. Tubes of paint covered the tops of old wooden orange crates—the new ones lying in neat piles like logs by a fireplace, the used ones in a haphazard scatter, closer to hand. Brushes sat waiting to be used in Mason jars. Others were in liquid waiting to be cleaned. Still more, their bristles stiff with dried paint, lay here and there on the floor like discarded pick-up sticks.

The room smelled of oil paint and turpentine. In the corner farthest from the window was a life-size fabric mache sculpture of an artist at work that bore an uncanny likeness to Jilly herself, complete with Walkman, one paintbrush in hand, another sticking out of its mouth. When I got there that morning, Jilly was at her new canvas, face scrunched up as she concentrated. There was already paint in her hair. On the windowsill behind her a small ghetto blaster was playing a Bach fugue, the piano notes spilling across the room like a light rain. Jilly looked up as I came in, a frown changing liquidly into a smile as she took in the foolish look on my face.

"I should have thought of this weeks ago," she said. "You look like the cat who finally caught the mouse. Did you have a good time?"

"The best."

Leaving my fiddle by the door, I moved around behind her so that I could see what she was working on. Sketched out on the white canvas was a Crowsea street scene. I recognized the corner—McKennitt and Lee. I'd played there from time to time, mostly in the spring. Lately a rockabilly band called the Broken Hearts had taken over the spot.

"Well?" Jilly prompted.

"Well what?"

"Aren't you going to give me all the lovely sordid details?"

I nodded at the painting. She'd already started to work in the background with oils.

"Are you putting in the Hearts?" I asked.

Jilly jabbed at me with her paintbrush, leaving a smudge the color of a Crowsea red brick tenement on my jean jacket.

"I'll thump you if you don't spill it all, Geordie, me lad. Just watch if I don't."

She was liable to do just that, so I sat down on the ledge behind her and talked while she painted. We shared a pot of cowboy coffee, which was what Jilly called the foul brew she made from used coffee grounds. I took two spoons of sugar to my usual one, just to cut back on the bitter taste it left in my throat. Still, beggars couldn't be choosers. That morning I didn't even have used coffee grounds at my own place.

"I like ghost stories," she said when I had finished telling her about my evening. She'd finished roughing out the buildings by now and bent closer to the canvas to start working on some of the finer details before she lost the last of the morning light.

"Was it real?" I asked.

"That depends. Bramley said—"

"I know, I know," I said, breaking in.

Bramley, if you can believe it, was the name of her wizard professor in Boston. Bramley Dapple. According to Jilly, one of his favorite topics of conversation was consensual reality, the idea that things exist *because* we agree that they exist.

"But think about it," Jilly went on. "Sam sees a ghost—maybe because she expects to see one—and you see the same ghost because you care about her, so you're willing to agree that there's one there where she says it will be."

"Say it's not that, then what could it be?"

"Any number of things. A timeslip—a bit of the past slipping into the present. It could be a restless spirit with unfinished business. From what you say Sam's told you, though, I'd guess that it's a case of a time-skip."

She turned to grin at me, which let me know that the word was one of her own coining. I gave her a dutifully admiring look, then asked, "A what?"

"A timeskip. It's like a broken record, you know? It just keeps playing the same bit over and over again, only unlike the record it needs something specific to cue it in."

"Like rain."

"Exactly." She gave me a sudden sharp look. "This isn't for one of your brother's stories, is it?"

My brother Christy collects odd tales just as Jilly does, only he writes them down. I've heard some grand arguments between the two of them, comparing the superior qualities of the oral versus written traditions.

"I haven't seen Christy in weeks," I said.

"All right, then."

"So how do you go about handling this sort of thing?" I asked. "Sam thinks he's waiting for something."

Jilly nodded. "For someone to lift the tone arm of time." At the pained look on my face, she added, "Well, have you got a better analogy?"

I admitted that I didn't. "But how do you do that? Do you just go over and talk to him, or grab him, or what?"

"Any and all might work. But you have to be careful about that kind of thing."

"How so?"

"Well," Jilly said, turning from the canvas to give me a serious look, "sometimes a ghost like that can drag you back to whenever it is that he's from and you'll be trapped in his time. Or you might end up taking his place in the timeskip."

"Lovely."

"Isn't it?" She went back to the painting. "What color's that sign Duffy has over his shop on McKennitt?" she asked.

I closed my eyes, trying to picture it, but all I could see was the face of last night's ghost, wet with rain.

It didn't rain again for a couple of weeks. They were good weeks. Sam and I spent the evenings and weekends together. We went out a few times, twice with Jilly, once with a couple of Sam's friends. Jilly and Sam got along just as well as I'd thought they would—and why shouldn't they? They were both special people. I should know.

The morning it did rain it was Sam's day off from Gypsy's. The previous night was the first I'd stayed over all night. The first we made love. Waking up in the morning with her warm beside me was everything I'd thought it would be. She was sleepy-eyed and smiling, more than willing to nestle deep under the comforter while I saw about getting some coffee together.

When the rain started, we took our mugs into the living room and watched the street in front of the Hamill estate. A woman came by, walking one of those fat white bull terriers that look more pig than dog. The terrier didn't seem to mind the rain, but the woman at the other end of the leash was less than pleased. She alternated between frowning at the clouds and tugging him along. About five minutes after the pair had rounded the corner, our ghost showed up, just winking into existence out of nowhere. Or out of a slip in time. One of Jilly's timeskips.

We watched him go through his routine. When he reached the streetlight and vanished again, Sam leaned her head against my shoulder. We were cozied up together in one of the big comfy chairs, feet on the windowsill.

"We should do something for him," she said.

"Remember what Jilly said," I reminded her.

Sam nodded. "But I don't think he's out to hurt anybody. It's not as if he were calling out to us or anything. He's just there, going through the same moves, time after time. The next time it rains—"

"What're we going to do?"

Sam shrugged. "Talk to him maybe?"

I didn't see how that could cause any harm. Truth to tell, I was feeling sorry for the poor bugger myself.

"Why not?" I said.

About then Sam's hands got busy, and I quickly lost interest in the ghost. I started to get up, but Sam held me down in the chair.

"Where you going?" she asked.

"Well, I thought the bed would be—"

"We've never done it in a chair before."

"There's a lot of places we haven't done it yet," I said.

Those deep blue eyes of hers, about five inches from my own, just about swallowed me.

"We've got all the time in the world," she said.

It's funny how you remember things like that later.

The next time it rained, Jilly was with us. The three of us were walking home from Your Second Home, a sleazy bar on the other side of Foxville, where the band of a friend of Sam's was playing. None of us looked quite right for the bar when we walked in. Sam was still the perennial California beach girl, all blond and curves in a pair of tight jeans and a white T-shirt, with a faded jean jacket on top. Jilly and I looked like the scruffs we were.

The bar was a place for serious drinking during the day, serving mostly unemployed blue-collar workers spending their welfare checks on a few hours of forgetfulness. By the time the band started around nine, though, the clientele underwent a drastic transformation. Scattered here and there through the crowd was the odd individual who still dressed for volume—all the colors turned up loud—but mostly we were outnumbered thirty to one by spike-haired punks in their black leathers and blue jeans. It was like being on the inside of a bruise.

The band was called the Wang Boys and ended up being pretty good—especially on their original numbers—if a bit loud. My ears were ringing when we finally left the place sometime after midnight. We were having a good time on the walk home. Jilly was in rare form, half-dancing on the street around us, singing the band's closing number, making up the words, turning the piece into a punk gospel number. She kept bouncing around in front of us, skipping backward as she tried to get us to sing along.

The rain started as a thin drizzle as we were making our way through Crowsea's narrow streets. Sam's fingers tightened on my arm and Jilly stopped fooling around as we stepped into Henratty Lane, the rain coming down in earnest now. The ghost was just turning in the far end of the lane.

"Geordie," Sam said, her fingers tightening more.

I nodded. We brushed by Jilly and stepped up our pace, aiming to connect with the ghost before he made his turn and started back toward Stanton Street.

"This is not a good idea," Jilly warned us, hurrying to catch up. But by then it was too late.

We were right in front of the ghost. I could tell he didn't see Sam or me, and I wanted to get out of his way before he walked right through us—I didn't relish the thought of having a ghost or a timeskip or whatever he was going through me. But Sam wouldn't move. She put out her hand, and as her fingers brushed the wet tweed of his jacket, everything changed.

The sense of vertigo was strong. Henratty Lane blurred. I had the feeling of time flipping by like the pages of a calendar in an old movie, except each page was a year, not a day. The sounds of the city around us—sounds we weren't normally aware of—were noticeable by their sudden absence. The ghost jumped at Sam's touch. There was a bewildered look in his eyes and he backed away. That sensation of vertigo and blurring returned until Sam caught him by the arm and everything settled down again. Quiet, except for the rain and a far-off voice that seemed to be calling my name.

"Don't be frightened," Sam said, keeping her grip on the ghost's arm. "We want to help you."

"You should not be here," he replied. His voice was stiff and a little formal. "You were only a dream—nothing more. Dreams are to be savored and remembered, not walking the streets."

Underlying their voices I could still hear the faint sound of my own name being called. I tried to ignore it, concentrating on the ghost and our surroundings. The lane was clearer than I remembered it—no trash littered against the walls, no graffiti scrawled across the bricks. It seemed darker, too. It was almost possible to believe that we'd been pulled back into the past by the touch of the ghost.

I started to get nervous then, remembering what Jilly had told us. Into the past. What if we *were* in the past and we couldn't get out again? What if we got trapped in the same timeskip as the ghost and were doomed to follow his routine each time it rained?

Sam and the ghost were still talking, but I could hardly hear what they were saying. I was thinking of Jilly. We'd brushed by her to reach the ghost, but she'd been right behind us. Yet when I looked back, there was no one there. I remembered that sound of my name, calling faintly across some great distance. I listened now, but heard only a vague, unrecognizable sound. It took me long moments to realize that it was a dog barking.

I turned to Sam, tried to concentrate on what she was saying to the ghost. She was starting to pull away from him, but now it was his hand that held her arm. As I reached forward to pull her loose, the barking suddenly grew in volume—not one dog's voice, but those of hundreds, echoing across the years that separated us from our own time. Each year caught and sent on its own dog's voice, the sound building into a caphonic brouhaha of yelps and barks and howls.

The ghost gave Sam's arm a sharp tug and I lost my grip on her, stumbling as the vertigo hit me again. I fell through the sound of all those barking dogs, through the blurring years, until I dropped to my knees on the wet cobblestones, my hands reaching for Sam. But Sam wasn't there.

"Geordie?"

It was Jilly, kneeling by my side, hand on my shoulder. She took my chin and turned my face to hers, but I pulled free.

"Sam!" I cried.

A gust of wind drove rain into my face, blinding me, but not before I saw that the lane was truly empty except for Jilly and me. Jilly, who'd mimicked the barking dogs to draw us back through time. But only I'd returned. Sam and the ghost were both gone.

"Oh, Geordie," Jilly murmured as she held me close. "I'm so sorry."

I don't know if the ghost was ever seen again, but I saw Sam one more time after that night. I was with Jilly in Moore's Antiques in Lower Crowsea, flipping through a stack of old sepia-toned photographs, when a group shot of a family on their front porch stopped me cold. There, among the somber faces, was Sam. She looked different. Her hair was drawn back in a tight bun and she wore a plain, unbecoming dark dress, but it was Sam all right. I turned the photograph over and read the photographer's date on the back: 1912.

Something of what I was feeling must have shown

on my face, for Jilly came over from a basket of old earrings that she was looking through.

"What's the matter, Geordie, me lad?" she asked.

Then she saw the photograph in my hand. She had no trouble recognizing Sam either. I didn't have any money that day, but Jilly bought the picture and gave it to me. I keep it in my fiddle case.

I grow older each year, building up a lifetime of memories, only I've no Sam to share them with. But every time it rains, I go down to Stanton Street and stand under the streetlight in front of the old Hamill estate. One day I know she'll be waiting there for me.

Resettling

Steve Rasnic Tem
and Melanie Tem

When Hannah found herself kneeling on the bed screaming hateful things at Perry and punching at his stomach through the tangled bedclothes, it didn't occur to her at first that the house had anything to do with it. Perry, who was her life, whom she'd waited for all her life and lived in fear of losing. Later they made frantic love with all the lights out; it was very late at night, and it was then that Hannah first felt without question the absorbing presence of the house.

She had lived in the neighborhood for nearly ten years, before and since Perry and Ashley. She'd looked at the house for all those ten years and wanted it for most of that time. At first, she remembered, it had seemed overwhelming. It sat on a hill in the middle of a crowded residential block. Not a very high hill, not much higher than the lots of its neighbors, but it seemed to tower over them. Dark red brick with black trim, ivy encrusting all the south wall, high, narrow windows that seemed to reflect any kind of light. Just around the corner Hannah had been amazed to discover a twin, a house clearly built at the same period and from the same design, probably by the same builder, but, for reasons she could never quite determine, a friendlier house, lighter, more open, with white trim and a wide, sunny porch and half a dozen tall bright trees. A far less interesting house. Hannah found herself drawn to the house on the hill.

Routes to the bus stop, to the grocery store, to the cleaner's could, if she went just a little out of her way, take her right past it, and those soon became her regular pathways. She saw the house then in all kinds of weather, at all times of the day and night. In snow it hulked like a Minotaur guarding its treasure. In morning sunshine it seemed cool and impenetrable, and it cast a tall triangular shadow all the way across the street. At night black clouds scudded breathtakingly behind its peaks.

"I hate you!" she heard herself shouting at Perry, the man she loved more than anyone else in the world. "You're not the man I married! I am not going to live like this!"

Perry was crying. She'd seen him cry before; in fact, his emotional openness was one of the things that endeared him to her. But now, for an awful moment, she was repulsed, as if he had turned into a monster. "So leave!" he shouted, and pushed his fist against her chest so that she sprawled back across the bed. "We'd all be better off without you!"

And then they'd stared at each other in horror while the house surrounded them like a palpable spell, and they'd fallen into each other's arms.

* * *

Hannah was determined she would keep her daughter from knowing that anything was wrong, as if she could protect her from being poisoned, too. Ashley was so precious, so fragile, and she always knew when things weren't right, often before Hannah did. Hannah's worry that she couldn't adequately take care of Ashley was long-standing and persistent. And it was getting worse. She heard herself speaking more sharply to Ashley than she would have thought possible, and resolutely turning away from the small, distressed face. It seemed to Hannah that she damaged the child in small ways a dozen times a day, and that she couldn't help it.

As her arguments with Perry became more frequent, Hannah became obsessed by memories of her life before Ashley was born. She and Perry had been alone in their first, much smaller house. Those had been their best years, with nothing but time for each other. But she had wanted children; she'd had no idea what that might be like; she just knew she wanted them. They had tried to have a child for almost ten years, mostly at her insistence; Perry adored his daughter but could, she knew, have been quite content living all his life with just her.

Childlessness for her was, truly, barrenness, and, after a time, conceiving became the most important thing in her life. They'd made love regularly for so long that she'd almost forgotten that sex could be anything but dutiful and charted. They'd undergone every imaginable fertility test, and the doctors could find nothing wrong with either of them. She'd taken a variety of fertility drugs, which created a variety of bizarre side effects. And every month she'd had her period, regular and painful and bloody, making her feel as if she were being emptied out.

Perry had wanted to stop. "It's not worth it," he'd say, or "We can always adopt." Intellectually she'd understood him, she'd even agreed with him. It made no difference: She had to keep on trying.

And one day she was pregnant, and nine frantic months later Ashley Anne was born. The perfect baby, the answer to every dream, and not for one moment what Hannah had thought she would be.

Ashley, whose every smile was a miracle, whose every act was a discovery and a terror. Ashley, the repository of the family's moods. When Perry and Hannah fought—even if it was in the middle of the night, quietly, with the door of their room shut tight—the next day Ashley would silently take their hands and draw them together. When one of them had had a bad day at work, Ashley would cry and try very hard to be good. When they were more worried than usual about money—even if they'd been meticulous about not letting her know—she'd bring her piggy bank and empty it on their bed.

Ashley hadn't wanted to move. She didn't like change. It frightened her. She said something awful was going to happen. But now that they were here she seemed the member of the family most taken by the house. On bright days, when sunshine streamed through the leaded-glass windows, Ashley sparkled and danced. At night she, like the house, closed in on herself.

Ashley was truly happy here. Hannah wouldn't spoil that. Hush! Ashley will hear! It had become a kind of chant, or prayer, and served only to make both her and Perry more incensed.

* * *

In the years before the house was hers, Hannah had never seen people living there, although there had been signs of habitation—lights on at night, the lawn mowed, for a while a fierce black Doberman leaping at the wrought-iron fence. Then the house was empty for a long time, and a "For Sale" sign sat at the bottom of the hill, well away from the house itself.

When Perry sold a series of paintings for more money than they'd ever imagined, they bought the house on the hill. Just like that. It took less than a month from Hannah's first incredulous call to the Realtor until closing. Everything progressed with an almost eerie ease: They sold their squat, cozy little house to the first couple who looked at it; their loan application was processed faster than the agent had even seen; they toured the house on the hill one time and everyone in the family—even Ashley—felt at once that it was theirs. It was as if the house, with its elegance, its concentrated energy, had reached out and claimed them, like a new mother counting her infant's fingers and toes. After that tour Hannah found she couldn't remember details—exactly how the rooms converged, what color the wallpaper was—but she remembered the feel of the place, the atmosphere, the sense that she had no choice but to accept the claim of that house.

"Why has it been on the market for so long?" Perry had thought to ask, adding lamely, "It's a wonderful house."

The Realtor, a cool young woman with long eyelashes and expensive clothes, had smiled. "Who knows? Maybe it was just waiting for you."

Indeed, there was such a sense of relief and completeness about the house now that Hannah felt as if she were part of an organic process. Sternly she told herself that this was foolish anthropomorphizing, to which she was prone anyway; when they'd moved out of their old house she'd stood in the empty living room after all the others had left and aloud she had said, "Good-bye," and "Thank you."

But the sensation was inescapable. Struggling with the sticky front gate after a long day at work while she balanced her heavy briefcase in the other hand; reading the Sunday paper in the quiet parlor while elsewhere in the house Ashley and Perry watched "Doctor Who"; eating breakfast at the sunny kitchen table (she'd always wanted a kitchen with a breakfast nook, but it had seemed such a silly criterion for house-buying that she hadn't mentioned it to anyone; now here it was)—in a dozen intimate little ways every day Hannah felt the house growing around her, into her, like an oyster with a grain of sand, she and the house taking on aspects of each other and becoming something new.

Now, scarcely a month after moving into the house, Hannah heard herself shrieking outrageous and cruel things at Perry that she didn't think she meant, and then frantically studying his reaction for something familiar. As she whispered, "I love you," and took him inside her, her mind ejected another phrase like a many-layered pearl for her to see: "He's not the man I married." She didn't know what it meant.

Hannah was a social worker, and she was very tired. After ten conscientious years, it was now abruptly clear to her that she didn't understand human nature, that no one did, that human nature was not accessible to human understanding. That troubled her like a betrayal. She remembered as if it were a youthful foible, slightly embarrassing and endearing at the same time, how much she'd wanted to be a social worker, how she'd never even considered another profession. Things weren't fair and she was going to change them. But once she'd entered the field, it was not what she had expected. It was almost as if by wanting it so much, pursuing it so single-mindedly, she'd changed it. The longer she worked the more keenly she saw the occupational hazards: hypocrisy, arrogance, disrespect, confusion. Coming home at night, especially to the house on the hill with its darkness enveloping the lights inside, was an intense relief, even though almost every night she bruised her hand on the front-gate latch.

Hannah was clinical director for a program serving the non-institutionalized chronically mentally ill. Over the years she'd worked with other groups—elderly in nursing homes, battered women, alcoholics, families of delinquent teenagers. Every time she'd changed specialties she'd been excited at first, eager to learn and to see what difference she could make. Every time the boredom, the sense of déjà vu returned sooner than before.

She saw now that the characteristic common to all these people was disappointment: Having gotten exactly what they'd wanted, it was not what they wanted anymore. The old man near the end of his life, the wife beaten by a man she could not leave, the drinker in search of the perfect high, the parents whose children were not what they intended them to be—all of them disappointed. As in all the cruel old fairy tales about the dangers of wishing, the thing had changed to become something evil and monstrously familiar.

The schizophrenics were the most unsettling, because much of the time you couldn't tell the patients from the staff. Their psychosis was only an elaboration of the way everyone else lived, yet they seemed unable to perform even the simplest daily tasks without running full tilt into the truth that, more and more, seemed to Hannah the central fact of human existence: Things are not what they seem.

Sometimes when she came home at night she'd see the patients staring at her out of the shadows that clung to the odd corners of the house, stubborn shadows that would not leave even when she replaced all the light bulbs with ones of higher wattage. Their eyes and voices, the way they held their hands, seemed haunted, possessed. She was seeing that same look now in her husband. The look of those who cannot believe their eyes.

Many of the patients could feel it coming on. "I'm going to be crazy," they'd say, and then the staff would alter medications or set up more structure, or just watch, helpless to provide more than the most minimal protection against the outside world. "Out of touch with reality," it said on the charts. Lately Hannah sometimes found herself all but incapacitated by confusion over who was out of touch with what.

"I'm going to be crazy." Hannah sat in the clawfoot bathtub late at night and said it aloud to see how the syllables would feel in her mouth. She found them almost comforting.

* * *

"Mom," said Ashley seriously one day when she came home from school. "Are there ghosts in our house?"

Ashley was eight. In the last month or so she'd undergone one of those growth spurts that so disorient parents. There were moments when Hannah barely recognized her.

"Why do you ask? Have you seen something?"

"All my friends say this is a haunted house. It *looks* like a haunted house."

Ashley was a poetic child, aware at a distressingly early age that frequently things are not what they seem. Knowing she wouldn't be reassured by a mother's simplistic protest that ghosts aren't real, Hannah explained matter-of-factly: "If a house is haunted, Ashley, it's only by the spirits of people who've lived there. Other people who've loved our house the way we do. There's nothing to be afraid of in that."

Ashley's blue eyes widened with interest. "Oh, Mom, then do our spirits haunt this house, too?"

"I think so," Hannah told her. "In a way." Hannah suddenly felt distressed, wondering what it was she was teaching her child.

Perry was the only one of the family who hadn't immediately felt at home in the new house, who didn't seem to have a natural place here. Wonderful as the house was, there were a number of things to be done to it, and Hannah understood that most of that responsibility fell to Perry: He was the handyman. What she did not understand was his need to get everything done so quickly, even at the expense of his painting. Nearly every waking moment he was doing something to the house. Often he didn't come when

she called him for meals, and she was afraid to call
him twice, though having the family scattered at
mealtime felt to her like a potentially fatal flaw.

"I don't know what it is," he told her, "but I just
can't do the work until things feel right around here,
and they don't feel right just yet."

Hannah worried. Always before, he'd been able to
paint even at the most awkward times. When they
went on vacation, even on overnight trips, Perry took
an easel and paints along and worked, sometimes until dawn if he felt particularly inspired. Hannah had
not been jealous; to deny the need to paint would be
to deny Perry himself. Now it was as if something
had altered Perry's personality, and she was afraid
she didn't know him anymore.

He erected all the bookcases, replaced the broken
windows, reattached separating wallpaper. She ap-
preciated all that. His artist's hands also were remarkably skilled at manual labor. But then he started
making "improvements." He decided to finish their
enormous attic. "For guest rooms," he explained,
"and you may want your own office someday." He
repainted both stairwells. Suddenly one day he decided to add a redwood deck on the south side of the
house.

"See how much better the house looks," he said.
"It'll be happier this way."

"It?"

"Sure. The house needs things." She desperately
wished he would smile. He used to give her a playful
smile when he talked like this. "Just as you and I need
things."

"But what do you need right *now*, Perry? Your
painting . . ."

He cut her off with a wave of his hand. "I'm doing fine. Just let me finish a few more things around here."

One day when Hannah came home from work she found him up on a ladder repainting the eaves a glossy black.

"Why are you doing that now? Can't it wait till summer?"

"It has to be done sometime," he said between clenched teeth. Hannah realized she was afraid to talk to him; he'd seemed to be angry with her all the time lately. But she wanted to make him stop; she wanted him to be happy.

"I really don't mind if you'd like to do that later, Perry. I don't think it's a high priority."

He jerked his head around so suddenly she was terrified he'd fall. The ladder rocked, and he grabbed at the soffit. She saw that his feet were on the step above the little sign that said: DANGER: DO NOT STAND ABOVE THIS STEP. She wanted to make him stop, but he was glaring at her, and she backed off.

Perry had always been terrified of heights. She didn't understand.

Every time they had an argument Hannah waited for Perry to say, "I don't love you," or "I'm leaving." He never did. He said he never would.

She woke up in the middle of the night. She felt around the edges of their bed in the darkness. Alone. She got up quickly and almost stumbled out the door. "Perry," she whispered. She could hear Ashley snoring lightly from across the hall. It was pitch-dark in the hallway; there wasn't a light fixture there, and Hannah was afraid that Ashley would tumble down the stairs. But she was more afraid of asking Perry to do something else to the house.

The odd narrowness of the second-floor windows and the thick, lenslike ornamental panes did strange things to the light from the streetlamps. The shadow of her flowing gown rippled the flocked wallpaper, as if she were passing through a distortion in the architecture of the house. "Perry." The whisper would not carry.

Every old house has noises—in their previous home they could hear almost everything that happened anywhere in the house—but this one seemed to have far fewer than most. There was a hush in this house. There was the sound of the huge gas-forced-air furnace coming on, and the pipes creaking as the dust inside them slowly heated up. But nothing else. She couldn't even hear her own footsteps because of the thick carpeting in the hallway. Sound did not carry in the house, and she had liked that. Even the real estate agent had commented on it.

But now that feature disturbed her. As if the house were suppressing even the smallest of disturbances. Hannah didn't think she liked that very much, the house holding things down, muffling her family. She wanted to know where Perry was right now. And this house wouldn't let her hear him.

When she reached the end of the hall, she saw the sliver of light under Perry's studio door. He hadn't been in there since they'd moved. He hadn't even made the improvements he needed in order to paint. The light was inadequate, there was only one outlet, and he hadn't yet built the cabinet for storing his paints. When she'd told him she thought he should make the studio his first priority, he'd just shrugged it off. "I'll get to it," he said. They'd been using it as a storage room; boxes were stacked shoulder-high.

When she opened the door he was sitting before his easel, jammed between walls of boxes. She felt a momentary elation, until she noticed that he was cutting long slits in the canvas with a utility knife.

"Perry?"

He stared at the canvas, jabbing at it playfully with the knife.

She came to his side. From what she could see between the numerous vertical tears and holes he had made, it was a dark, smudged canvas, with a streak of red near the middle. Incredibly amateurish; Hannah had never known him to paint so badly.

"Perry, what are you doing?"

He looked at her. She was sure he hadn't had those lines in his face before. "Playing. Just playing." He looked at the knife. "You know . . . I want to paint, Hannah. I *need* to paint."

"I know." She touched his shoulders. They were trembling.

"But I can't. Something's not right, and I don't know what it is. I do everything I can think of, but I can't seem to make it right. *I can't paint*, Hannah."

"It's just a bad spell. It'll get better. You'll see. You paint very well, you *know* that."

"It's never been this bad." He looked back up at her. "Sometimes you want something so bad you poison it. It's like you haunt it, drive it crazy, make it something cheap and negative, and it's never the same again. I'm . . ." He looked down at his hands, the hands that Hannah so dearly loved. He was holding the knife. For a moment she was afraid he might cut those, too. "I'm not making any sense."

Hannah looked around at the shabby room, dim and filled with boxes, and tried to imagine the rest of the house beyond it, her wonderful dream house. No clear images came. She rubbed Perry's shoulders. "No, you make perfect sense," she finally said. And wondered wearily what they were talking about.

Every night Hannah came home from work exhausted from the senseless task of trying to make sense out of things. The house welcomed her, and her relief at coming home to it approached a lover's passion. The longer she lived there the better she came to understand its little idiosyncracies: The front gate opened easily now to let her in, but stuck the other way as if reluctant to let her out. She didn't dare mention it to Perry. He would fix it, and she didn't want him to. She was beginning to think they shouldn't be imposing their will on this house.

Ashley had become an obsessive housekeeper. She was forever polishing the wooden floors, vacuuming the red-carpeted stairs, scurrying to pick up the smallest bit of litter in the yard. They'd figured out that her room, fittingly—the small back bedroom at the top of the narrow winding stairs that the Realtor had called "the servants' stairway"—had probably been the maid's room.

When Hannah caught her in the midst of a flurry of housekeeping and pulled her into her lap, Ashley wouldn't look at her. She fidgeted, played with her hair, even struggled to get down. That wasn't like her. It worried Hannah, made her angry, and she pressed. "Ashley, what's all this about? You've been acting strange since we moved. Don't you like our new house?"

Ashley's eyes widened in surprise. Seen from the side, they seemed to bulge a little. "I *love* our house!" she protested. "I love it just the way it is!"

"Then what's going on?"

"Nothing."

"Ashley." Hannah felt a sudden flash of anger, almost rage. Her hands tightened around the child's upper arms until she was sure it hurt, but Ashley didn't flinch, and she, to her own dismay, didn't loosen her grip. Instead she shook the girl, until Ashley's small head lolled. *Tell me what's wrong.*

Abruptly Ashley turned to her and cried, "Mommy, our house is haunted and I can't find the ghosts!"

Hannah caught her breath. In that split second of laxness her daughter slid out of her lap and ran hysterically up the steps, slamming the door to her room. It was a very muffled sound, without echoes.

"I'll bet there's a secret passageway somewhere in this house," the Realtor had told them. At the time, knowing it was part of the sales pitch and completely unnecessary, Hannah hadn't taken it seriously. But there were signs. The house had been remodeled many times—Perry discovered the evidence everywhere. Too many times to suit Hannah.

Beside the basement stairs was a cubbyhole that extended three feet back under the foundation for no apparent reason and then just stopped. In a dark recessed corner of the laundry room Perry had come upon a thin false wall with a tall, empty space behind it.

Under the flowered rug in Ashley's room was a sealed trapdoor. Its edges were so neatly nailed and painted that it was almost indiscernible, but Ashley had discovered it and hadn't told anybody until Hannah noticed the uneven way she'd replaced the rug. Even then she'd lied, insisting fearfully that she knew nothing about it. Finally Hannah—who abhorred physical violence and had never used it with her child —spanked her, and then Ashley confessed. "I was looking for the ghosts!" she sobbed. "I thought maybe the ghosts lived down there!"

Frustrated, guilt-ridden, Hannah had shouted at her: "Now you listen to me! There's no such thing as ghosts!" But Ashley, of course, did not believe her, and would not take comfort in her arms.

She'd hardly seen Perry for several days. He was up before she was, off somewhere making God knew what alterations to their house. And he was up long after her, working at this or that. She never could figure out exactly what, and was afraid to ask. He made almost no noise, no more than the noises the house might normally make by itself: the creakings, the tiny scrapes, the soft and distant thuds, the resettlings. She sat up in bed sometimes, late into the night, listening for him, trying to distinguish his sounds from the house sounds. Sometimes she'd wake up suddenly in the middle of the night, as if something had awakened her, and find him missing from the bed. Then she'd try to hear the sound that had awakened her from sleep, the sound that might have been him working in the house somewhere, changing their house, altering it until it no longer resembled the house she had coveted so long, her dream house. But that telling sound was no longer present. It had disappeared, just as Perry had seemed to disappear, somewhere into the too-vast shadowed corners of the house.

When Perry did come down for meals, he came reluctantly, obviously displeased by the interruption. He'd serve himself in silence and then stare glumly at his food. His agent had called three times asking about commissioned works. Hannah had taken the calls because she couldn't find Perry in the house. The first time, she spoke to him about it, but he yelled at her to mind her own business, and after that she left him notes, which he did not acknowledge.

Now she could hear Perry coming down the main staircase for dinner, almost half an hour after everyone else had sat down. The third message from his agent was by the telephone in the hall. She glanced at Ashley, who looked tense and drawn, jabbing at her food with a fork that trembled visibly. The child knew everything. Hannah's heart went out to her. It was all too much. This life wasn't safe enough for her little girl, and she couldn't make it better.

Something slammed into the wall out in the hall. Ashley jumped as if struck, crying. A face so pale Hannah barely recognized it appeared at the dining room door. The eyes were pinkish, the hair dark and flat against the skull—darker than it should have been, as if filthy with the dust of ages.

"I can't eat today, Hannah," Perry said.

"Don't worry about your agent," Hannah began. "I'll—"

"You won't do anything," he said coldly. "I just can't eat today!"

There was almost a growl in his voice. Hannah looked immediately at Ashley, who was sobbing now.

And suddenly Hannah felt an uncontrollable anger as well. "Don't do it, Perry. Not *now!*"

"I've got work!"

"You have to eat! *Look at you!*"

Hannah saw Perry draw back his fist and thought he was going to strike her for the first time. He was going to beat her, maybe go on beating her until he had killed her. Perry, who had been visibly shaken when Ashley had had a mere touch of fever.

But the fist struck the dining room wall instead, several times, sending plaster and torn wallpaper cascading to the floor. Hannah thought the fist seemed to float in the air by itself, as if it had nothing to do with Perry. She felt drunk or drugged. She wondered if she might be hallucinating.

Ashley was on her feet, screaming. If it had not taken Hannah a few moments to grasp what was happening, she might have taken her beautiful little girl, her dream child, into her arms right then, comforted her, calmed her down, made her safe again. Stopped the worst from happening.

Ashley was hysterical. "You've hurt the house! First you changed it so it's not the same anymore! Now you've *hurt* it!"

"Ashley, honey . . ." Hannah felt herself pull out of the chair.

"You've done it, too! You've *poisoned* things, Mommy!"

Hannah stopped, rigid. Her hand was out to her daughter, but Ashley was already running toward the stairs. Hannah glanced at Perry—something had broken in his face, and he was looking at her, and she knew that her husband was back with them for a time.

But what about Ashley?

"Ashley! Darling, it's all right now!"

But Ashley didn't answer. Perry looked panic-stricken. "Listen!" he said.

Door after door closed upstairs, one after another as if following the progression of Ashley's flight, her escape into the safety of the house. Finally the slamming stopped, but not before Hannah realized that there had been far more slams than there were doors in the house.

She couldn't find Ashley. She wandered through the house day after day, like a wraith herself, looking in all the hidden places she knew, trying to imagine if there were more. Perry was desperate, and blaming himself the way the old Perry would have, tearing out all his improvements, trying to find the extra doors they had both heard that day. He was convinced he had accidentally covered some of them up in his remodeling, and yet Ashley had still found a way through to the original house.

Hannah lifted the rug in the child's room and dug at the edges of the old trapdoor with a putty knife and a screwdriver, but it was still wedged tight. She went outside, into the gray night air of the city that was never still, and called her daughter's name. Her voice echoed against the walls of the house and stopped.

Sometimes at night Hannah would awaken, and again Perry would be gone from their bed. But now she knew he was busy searching, and she felt guilty because she had taken a rest. She could hear him walking through the rooms, pounding on the walls, looking for hollow places, whispering his daughter's name. She could hear everything now.

"Give my baby back to me," she whispered, but the house refused to answer.

Perry thought the mirror on the bathroom wall might hide a passageway, so together they spent hours trying to remove it. The house gripped it tightly as if it were part of its own skin. At last they collapsed into each other's arms, crying softly, staring into the mirror from the floor. Hannah thought their images in the mirror were too faded and pale to be real. Two malevolent spirits haunting this wonderful old house, haunting the little girl who lived here.

The sounds rose and fell outside the bathroom door. Hannah could not distinguish individual strains in the tide. She listened for a very long time.

"I'm going to be crazy now," she whispered to the house. And whispered it through the rooms for years.

But sometimes it grew quiet and there were other sounds, soft footsteps and a child's laughter, the sound of someone happy in her house of dreams.

The Servitor

Janet Fox

Tepid air flowing through the truck's open window ruffled Dyann's sandy hair but did nothing to evaporate the sweat on her face. She could feel the makeup melting and trickling down till she was sure she looked like something out of a horror movie. The old man who drove had pale eyes, almost lost in folds and wrinkles cast by years in the sun; from time to time his eyes left the featureless road and looked curiously in her direction, moving away as she looked back. He hadn't said more than the "Hop in" he'd begrudged her when the truck had slewed to a stop in roadside gravel, and the "How far ya goin'?" after they'd begun to move again. Midsummer's heat had leached all color from the pastures on either side of the highway; a desultory wind wagged the dry grass as if something sinister moved hidden in it.

She let her head droop over the suitcase she held on her lap, remembering the almost insane haste with which she'd packed it several days before, running from bureau to closet and returning with armloads of clothes, rejecting this or that garment at the last minute and flinging it out. The urge to run had hit her when she had been cleaning the medicine cabinet and opened a prescription bottle to find a roll of bills. It had suddenly occurred to her that this was the chance she'd been hoping for all these months, and she was in the bedroom, packing like a crazy woman before she even knew she'd made a decision. She had planned to leave after the first beating, but that had been almost a year ago. She had planned to turn him in to the police after the second, but then had thought better of it. After all, she *knew* him, and the cops didn't. Whatever temporary shelter they might devise, Vic would just bide his time and put on his "wronged husband" act, and then no matter where she was, he would come after her.

She knew he was probably coming after her now, for that matter, but with the money, she had been able to put a lot of distance between them.

The car had ground to a stop along the road about fifteen miles back, whining and leaking a plume of smoke from beneath its hood, and it would have been a clear indication of her trail, except that she had cleaned out the glove box, taken off the plates and stowed them in her suitcase. It was just another abandoned wreck now, would probably be towed off by the highway patrol.

The driver hit his brakes, causing her to jerk forward in the seat. "Here's the turnoff . . . you sure?"

"I'm sure. You said the Wrede house was still there."

"It's still there, what's left of it." It occurred to her that if this *were* a horror movie, he would be obliged to say something like, "Don't go to that place, miss, it's haunted," but he only leaned out the driver's side window to spit a wad of phlegm.

Her sweat-sodden skirt adhered to the truck's vinyl seat as she slid out of the truck, baring her legs to mid-thigh. The driver's pale eyes took this in with no change in expression. She lifted the suitcase and began to walk down the gravel road, not looking back to see the truck dwindle with distance along the gray curl of highway.

Her face felt hot and gritty a half hour later as she stood in the driveway of the old Wrede house. It was only a narrow opening between trees, two deeply etched ruts in the dry ground. As she entered it, thorny creepers caught at her ankles, and a spiderweb broke across her face with a tickling sensation, a frail barrier that seemed to stand between a world of midday and one of twilight, for close-grown trees and foliage here created a pocket of coolness, a sanctuary of gold-shot green as sunlight spangled down through thickly leaved branches.

The outlines of Simon Wrede's house were blurred by the tide of foliage that washed against it. In a break in the greenness she saw here a dormer window, here an expanse of gray sun-blistered wood. Gradually she could make out its entirety, but though it had kept its shape, there was a fragility to it, the feeling that, if disturbed, it might come crashing in upon itself. She found herself surprised, maybe even disappointed, that she now saw it as just an old house, long abandoned and soon to fall to its own internal decay.

Simon Wrede, usually called Uncle Simon, though he was related to no one in town, had been the town wacko. Dyann supposed that every little town had its eccentric and reclusive resident about whom it was almost mandatory to make up stories. Simon was supposed to have killed cats and dogs in secret "witch" ceremonies, and when some local calamity occurred, older residents would look knowingly in the direction of the Wrede place. It hadn't dimmed his glory in the least when the old man had succumbed to a commonplace heart attack a year before Dyann left town. And here was the house, still standing, every window still intact, though filmed over and discolored by grime, cloudy as blind eyes.

True, it stood at some distance from Sawtelle, but Dyann remembered that hadn't stopped her and her friends from making the occasional pilgrimage to Old Man Wrede's on a Halloween night. She stepped up on the porch every bit as cautiously as she had on those occasions when they'd sneaked up to knock on the door and run away, but this time it was because the weakness of the old wood gave her a queasy feeling as she stepped on it. There had been the most delicious scary feeling as they'd stood before the door, as if it would open wide and there the old wizard would be. Of course that never really happened, Dyann thought, because he was nothing but a frail old recluse. Nobody in town missed him for weeks after his death, and the only reason they investigated was that someone said they'd seen a layer of houseflies clinging to his screen door.

She pushed back the warped screen and tried the door. It swung inward at her touch in a way that made her uneasy, but when she went inside, all was innocent and quiet—a moldering divan leaking cotton, a coffee cup with dark rings of corrosion inside, and two wasps gluing their gray paper to a window-sill. She dropped her suitcase and moved through the other rooms, not daring the rickety stairs that led upward. The rest of the house was as empty as this room was, as full of echoes. She rubbed her sun-blistering face, thirst beginning to torment her. Like a memory, it occurred to her that there was a creek running behind the house at a little distance, and she went out to look for it.

The unmistakable sound of running water drew her through a tangle of brush, and she saw water cascading over flat yellow rocks into a sinkhole. She dropped to the ground to drink and then peeled away the layers of sweaty clothing and slipped into deeper water.

Feeling better, she was still puzzled a little because she didn't think she had been familiar enough with the Wrede house to have known about the creek. Strange how memories you didn't know you had could pop into your head. *But I did need the water,* she told herself, *so I'm glad it was there.*

Darkness was falling fast, and she had no light, so she hurried back to the house. The divan sighed beneath her weight as she lay down, enveloping her in its musty smell. A broken spring pressed its shape into her hip, but she was soon asleep.

She was walking again, interminably through intense sunlight, red patterns forming and breaking up behind her closed eyelids. Suddenly she found herself in a small, enclosed space with Vic standing before her as clearly as she'd ever seen him, the well-cut expensive suit, perfectly groomed blond hair, face expressive and mobile, the lips sensual—all important to his image—only the eyes were expressionless, the color of slate. Dyann had soon learned that it was only around the eyes that you could detect what a crazy bastard he was, though of course she hadn't known that at first. She had actually considered herself very lucky. Later, after their marriage, she always knew by watching his eyes when he was getting the idea of knocking her around for a while. They almost always ended up in bed at the end of it. He probably couldn't get it up any other way these days, she supposed.

"I've been looking for you," he said. "Do you remember what I told you I'd do if you ever tried to get away from me?"

He had once told her, at length, in loving detail. Remembering, she wondered now if she wasn't a little crazy herself to have tried to escape. By the cool intensity of his voice she had known he had meant every word. That he would probably be enjoying himself the whole time.

"Now I'm going to make good on my promise," he said, and taking a step closer he had reached out to grasp her roughly. His fingers melted through her flesh until she could feel his hands gripping the bones in her arms.

She struggled upright, stifling a scream. Darkness and an overwhelming scent of decay were all around her, and at first she didn't know where she was—bizarre possibilities ran through her mind for a moment, then she remembered. The silence was not quite complete; she thought she heard the faint scrape of someone's foot on the floor. She froze. Something had awakened her from the dream, and if he'd managed, by some miracle, to trace her here, this was the kind of game he'd enjoy. At any moment she might feel his hands on her, and—

She leaped to her feet and began to flail around the room blindly.

At last she stopped, panting and exhausted, feeling foolish and yet safe since she'd blundered all about the room and found nothing. *But I'm safe here only for a little while,* she told herself. *I've got to get out of here before he shows up, and to do that, I've got to have more money.*

Though a new storefront glittered here and there, Sawtelle was the same grimy collection of buildings clustered along one narrow main street. Dyann thanked the teenager who'd given her a lift in his glorified jeep and got out in front of the Citizens Bank, straightening the skirt of the red dress that Vic had said was sexy in the days of their courtship. Considering what Bernie Bauer had been like, it was odds on that Eliot was stuck in his old teller's job in this hick bank.

She remembered acres of marble, bars on the tellers' windows, shiny tiles on the floor, and a deer head on the wall, but now there were glass doors, green carpeting, new improved windows for the tellers. When she looked up, she saw that the deer head was still there, quietly moldering.

"I'm looking for Eliot Bauer," she said, approaching the nearest teller.

"The bank president? Do you have an appointment?"

"I think he'll see me. I'm an old friend. Tell him Dyann Landry."

She was shown inside one of the stuffy offices in

back, and to her surprise there was Eliot sitting behind the desk that used to belong to Old Man Bauer. She could remember catching glimpses of him sitting back there puffing on an immense cigar. Eliot didn't look like his father, but he didn't look as she remembered him either. He'd been quarterback his junior and senior years, and leanly muscled; now his paunch almost touched the desk he sat behind. The muscles of his face were lax as well, and he had a mournful look, like a basset hound, she thought. There was also something odd about the shape of his hairline. Eliot wearing a rug? she thought, and almost laughed aloud, but didn't when she remembered her own haggard face in the mirror the day she decided to split from Vic. Now without makeup, without even a mirror to help her rearrange her hair, she was probably no beauty herself.

"I didn't know you were back in town," said Eliot, his eyes and voice steady but his fingers idly flicking a pen against the blotter on his desk. "I'd heard you got married."

"I heard the same about you."

"I, uh, have quite a bit to do this morning—" he said.

"I can get right to the point. I need some money . . . to help me get out of town. Maybe you'd even like me to leave."

"You've come to me for money? For . . . blackmail money?"

"Why not? You've got an image to maintain—wife, kids, the neighbors. People you might not want to know about our little secret. I don't mind keeping it a little longer."

Dyann felt suddenly ashamed, as if she were bringing up some sordid chapter of her life before a total stranger. The Eliot here and now didn't have much in common with that handsome, confident boy she'd met after the winning game with Claridge High. But she forced herself to go on. She needed the money. "We don't have to play games about this, do we?"

"You can't just waltz in here off the street and bring up a lot of . . . painful things I thought were forgotten. My dad paid for you to—"

"He paid to keep the Landrys out of his precious family tree. He paid off before to have our baby murdered—why not again? Why can't you keep paying over and over again? Somebody should pay for it!" She heard her own voice with a feeling of shock. She hadn't meant to lose control.

Eliot's hand moved to the receiver of the phone on his desk. "I don't intend to pay blackmail to a whore like you. Do you know that I can make one phone call and have you thrown into jail—that's who I am in this town now!"

She took a step backward, realizing that it wasn't bluster. Bernard Bauer had pulled the strings in Sawtelle, but now he was dead; those strings still had to lead somewhere. "Okay, I'll go. You don't have to flex your big-man-in-a-small-town muscles."

I was nuts to come back here, Dyann thought as she trudged back toward the Wrede house. *I had big dreams, I was going to come back here someday in a fancy car, a fur coat, maybe to show 'em all that I was somebody.*

The coolness of the foliage washed over her, and she felt almost as if she'd come home as she came back into the abandoned house. She'd forgotten that it'd been some time since she last ate, and she felt ravenously hungry. But she couldn't buy even a hamburger with no money. She heard a faint thump from overhead. There was a pause and then two more noises as something hit the roof. She ran outside just in time to see an apple come bouncing off the roof and roll into the overgrown grass of the yard.

She saw that a huge apple tree overspread the house, its branches heavy with fruit. Several more apples fell as she watched, and she hurried to find them where they lay in the grass. The fruit was small, with a purple-red skin, and when she bit into it, she tasted a sharp, winy tang. Three of them took the edge off her hunger. *I wouldn't want to have to eat these for every meal, but—* she thought, *I'm glad they showed up when I needed them.* She found it odd she hadn't noticed the apples before, and mid-summer didn't seem the time for fruit to ripen. Still, who knew what sort of varieties Old Simon had planted. Maybe there was even an overgrown garden out back. *A person could be self-sufficient here. Maybe the house has everything I need—even money.*

The rumors that had circulated about Simon always contained a few hints that he was a miser as well as a wizard, and the children who dared come out here often speculated on the fortune he might have hidden in the house. She supposed that the house had been thoroughly searched by officials after Simon's death, but if there really was money, and he had been clever about hiding it, it might still be here.

It was approaching evening again when she decided to try looking on the second floor. She'd found a few greasy black candles hidden under the floorboards in the kitchen, and she lit one now, wrinkling her nose at the awful smell of the thing. Stressed wood complained under her feet as she climbed. Shadows sent pseudopods of darkness toward her, only to be driven back again as the candle flickered. She moved along the walls in what had probably been a bedroom, and stopped as she felt a draft, as of a wind blowing through some door that had been left open. Inspecting the wall more closely, she saw a faint outline under the peeling wallpaper's garish pattern, as if someone had papered over a door. She tore excitedly at the paper with her nails; the dry stuff flaked away easily until she had exposed a crack through which she'd felt the draft earlier. There was a hole where a doorknob had once been. She gripped it and pulled outward as hard as she could. It gave with a groan and a haze of plaster dust.

There was only darkness beyond the open door, and it was a moment before she could force herself to enter, light from the candle picking out this or that detail in irregular spasms—a shelf of bottles and jars, some broken, some half filled with cloudy liquids, some with rotted organic forms, now unrecognizable, lying at the bottom. Symbols scrawled in yellow chalk on the oily dark boards of the wall. The skull of some small animal, possibly a cat, pale and fragile as ivory sculpture.

And on the back wall a cross on which was nailed a dry, dark body, the unsteady light making it still seem to twist in agony. Dyann's hand fluttered to her stomach and she had opened her mouth to scream when she recognized the body as that of a frog. She had thought at first it had been a fetus and her imagination had made it seem that she had felt the touch of tentative fingers deep within her womb.

Everything was draped in a shroud of cobwebs and

dust, having been long abandoned. The wagging tongues of the townspeople hadn't been wrong with their talk of witchcraft. Simon Wrede had been only a senile old fool playing his games, she had thought, someone to be pitied more than feared. And yet she wondered why he should have sealed off this room.

The creak of a floorboard made her turn around in panic. Shadows lay thick in the tiny room. A distorted one, vaguely anthropomorphic, lay across the floor at her feet. As she watched, it began to slide farther into the room. It kept coming and coming until it had reached the ceiling, though there appeared to be no solid shape behind it. A coldness washed over her again, that directionless draft as if somewhere a door had been left ajar.

She was certain she wasn't alone.

"Who are you? . . . What?" she amended hastily and stood frozen in the midst of her own echoes, hair prickling at the back of her neck.

The voice was a harsh-textured whisper—there and gone, so rapidly she couldn't even be sure she had heard it, as she scrambled from the room, dropping and extinguishing the candle in her haste. But she would always remember what it said.

"I serve."

The next morning Dyann felt as if she had been drunk; her head throbbed, her eyes ached. At one moment she had herself firmly convinced that she had heard nothing, the next she was ready to run screaming out of the house, never to return. Since without the house she'd have neither food nor shelter, she finally managed to get herself to return to the small room.

By daylight it was only a dusty closet, Simon's witch paraphernalia only a ludicrous collection of junk. She was silent for a long time, afraid that in disturbing the silence she might disturb something else, something that Simon had stirred up with his sundown services and that, for whatever reason, was still linked with this place, though Simon had been dead for years.

Believing and not believing, she stood in the middle of the cluttered room and said loudly, "I want them punished. Eliot and all the rest of the bastards who always spit on me and told me I wasn't good enough. The ones who murdered my baby. I want them to lose everything."

Nothing happened.

"Yeah? I thought so." Feeling foolish, but relieved all the same, she returned downstairs and went back to the overgrown garden, where she found some strawberries growing wild. She gorged herself, popping them into her mouth one after another until red juice ran down her chin.

The days blurred a little after that. It seemed to her that summer was interminable, the sun high and hot just beyond the trees that held the old house in their umbral coolness. She could not have said whether it was three days or two weeks when she heard the crunch of tires in the rutted driveway outside. She had been in this place of safety so long that thoughts of Vic weren't the first ones to occur to her, but when she looked out and saw the shiny low-slung car, her hands gripped the sill till they were white-knuckled. At that moment it didn't occur to her to run, even if there had been any place to run to. She only stood staring as Vic swung long legs out of the car and stood up, stretching his muscles in a controlled way, as if he'd been on the road a long time.

He had been wearing sunglasses and now removed them in the dimness cast by the trees, looking at the old place. With the confident air she'd grown to know and hate, he moved up onto the porch. Distant sunlight outlined him just outside the door, and she thought, *A gun. I should have bought a gun.* Thoughts of a weapon made her look quickly around the room; there was only a thin board with a rusty nail sticking through it, but she picked it up and held it behind her back as Vic confronted her, smiling casually, as if it had been the easiest thing in the world to find her here. Dyann knew that to anyone not looking at his eyes he'd make a pleasant appearance; unfortunately she was looking at his eyes, and she knew he was beyond reasoning with, beyond begging.

"Pathetic," he said. "You couldn't stop talking about the hick town you came from; you were always going to go back. You were going to show them. I knew you'd go back there like a rat to its hole, and the funny thing about people in a small town, they know everything that's going on. Ever notice that?"

As he talked, he had been coming closer.

"Then they'll know you came out here."

"I'll just have to clean things up afterwards, that's all. Nobody ever comes to this place. In town they called it haunted or something. This place suits you, Dyann. Pathetic."

His last syllable was drawn out as she swung the board, and his hand shot out to grab her wrist, but her aim was only spoiled enough to make the nail rake along the side of his face, leaving a groove that turned first white and then red, as blood began to seep. When his hand went to his face, she pulled free and ran for the stairway, hoping it might hold her weight but not his. She felt the stairs sway as she climbed; plaster was coming down in a shower, but she made it to the top just ahead of him. She knew she wasn't thinking when she ran into the closet because once there, there was no place else to run.

When she saw his shape fill the doorway, she went down on her knees before the crucifix. "Whatever you are, if you are, I want him to die, just make him die before he touches me." Vic had paused in the doorway, she supposed in surprise at her crazy behavior. She knew just how crazy it really was because she realized it was about the closest she'd ever come to saying a prayer, and knew that in the next moment Vic's hand was going to come down on her shoulder.

In the intensity of feeling she had closed her eyes tight, and when no touch came, she opened them. The room was swimming in shadow, though daylight still streamed in through the door. Vic swayed in the doorway. His eyes were dilated, beginning to bulge out of their sockets, and his mouth worked, bubbles of foam forming there and sliding down his chin. A dark flush, almost blue, was climbing into his face, and his features were now contorted beyond what one normally thought of as human. He began to curl forward, his chest caving in. When he fell it was in a fetal posture right below the crucifix, his face suffused with liver-colored darkness. His feet scuffled at the floor in a last spasm and he was still.

Dyann didn't dare go near him for a long time. He had had a seizure of some kind, she reasoned, yet she never remembered anything like it happening in the time she'd known him. It was as if, she thought, his lungs had collapsed inside him, or as if someone had grabbed a double handful of lung and . . . squeezed. She knew it wasn't sane to be thinking of things like that, but ever since she'd heard the words, "I serve," she'd had the impression of some sort of presence left here by Simon's occult experiments—something mindless and bumbling, maybe, like a big old dog looking for someone to obey. She knew it hadn't been enough just to ask; it had to be something she wanted with her whole being, like Vic's death.

Finally coming closer to the body, she forced herself to put her fingers on his neck to check for a pulse. There was none.

She remembered that he usually carried his money in a money belt around his waist, and she tore open his shirt. She undid the buckle and felt a satisfying weight in the belt. She found the car keys in his pocket. With this money and the car, she could go anywhere. Remembering that people in town had known Vic came out here, she knew she needed to get the body out of sight.

It took several hours of tugging and pulling, dragging the body down two sets of stairs with the head bumping down each riser in a sickening way, but at last she had the body poised above the old cistern in the backyard (she didn't care that the memory of where it was just suddenly came to her).

Reflections off oily water far below cast moving patterns on rock walls coated with slimy green algae; there was a dank smell. Vic's eyes, pale cloudy marbles in the darkness of his face, stared upward at nothing. She had a momentary doubt that he was really dead; maybe he'd sit up with a ghoulish grin on his face. This thought made her strain to push the torso over the edge, the weight carrying the whole body in. After a moment there was a splash, light patterns moving crazily upward. *Gone*, she thought, levering the rock that covered the cistern back into place. *And that's what I'm going to be, too. Gone!*

It took little time to repack her suitcase and to hide the traces of her habitation. She didn't look back at the house as she got into the car, started the engine, and pulled out of the drive. Full sunlight seemed almost painful to her eyes and skin as she came out of the shelter of the trees. A dry summer had parched the pastures to a uniform white-gold. Eventually, she knew, someone would come and tear down the old house, not knowing what Simon had left there, not knowing the possibilities of it. And then . . . ? Then, she supposed, it would be gone, scattered to the winds.

Her foot moved to the brake, stopping the car so suddenly it slewed sideways. If she left now she would never really know what those possibilities were, what sort of power was in the house or how it could be controlled.

It would go down in local history as the year of the blight, the year the bank failed, though history, as a whole, would be unmindful of it. Dyann sat looking out a second-story window at the cool greenness of the trees that moved subtly, though there was no wind. Whenever she left the place (though she didn't leave it often now; the sun was too painful) she noted how outside a roughly spherical area the drought had curled the leaves, withered the grass. She liked to sit here in the midst of this greenness and turn things over in her mind, as a child will turn a sticky bit of candy over and over with his tongue. She remembered Main Street, the boarded-up windows, debris gathering at the curbs, the telltale signs of abandonment. A fly-specked sign, shakily hand-lettered, was still in the bank's window. "Closed." She had stood gloating over that sign until she'd caught sight of her own face distorted by the glass, the skin darkened and blotched, weathered close to the bone, the eyes deep-socketed as if receding from light that was too strong.

It was growing dark as she looked out, flowers in the untended garden becoming blurs of violet. Past triumphs were good to remember, but she had felt herself growing restless. Her mind played idly with the thought that now, her enemies dealt with, it was possible to have the child she once gave up, but her mind kept veering away. Who really knew how something like that would turn out, and bending time seemed like a dangerous thing to do since her identity was so rooted in the here and now. After a while she felt herself slipping off into a doze.

Just beyond the stand of wild-grown flowers was the cistern, and she noticed that a wedge of darkness lay alongside the rock that covered it. She hardly knew what she had been thinking of—something about the past.

Shadows by the cistern had deepened; something seemed to be rearing itself upright above it. Something that didn't seem meant for movement was attempting to walk. Patches of phosphorescent mold gleamed on the matted fabric of the suit, the body beneath no longer giving it a man's shape, but of something shriveled, bent— As the figure staggered forward, some rotting fragment fell off.

With growing panic, she watched the shape cross the lawn. She realized that she had been thinking of one of her few decent times with Vic, before she'd realized what he was really like. His lips and hands on her skin in the darkness, then his lean, hard-muscled body moving against hers.

She could no longer see the thing, but could hear it moving blindly along one wall of the house. When she realized that her desire had called it, she tried to break free of dreams, but drowsiness clung to her. She could hear sounds on the staircase, a harsh scrape as of one foot dragging, and then an unsteady step, scrape, and step, as it pulled itself up the stairs. She could imagine fingers moving along her flesh, leaking the slime of corruption, a body whose contours shifted liquidly against hers, disintegrating in her arms.

Her own scream reverberated through the house, awakening her. She found herself still in her chair, her body slick with sweat, the yard innocent under fading light. Pale flowers nodded over a slab of stone.

It would have been more comforting to have considered it all a dream, but in the morning she forced herself to go out by the cistern, and she saw on the ground a patch of flaking scalp with a lock of discolored blond hair.

She knew if she stayed in the house her loneliness would waken desire. This was no house for idle wishes.

"So, whatever-you-are, if you really are here at all . . ." She spoke aloud, her own voice sounding dry and cracking, as if the physical change she'd seen reflected in the bank window were continuing. "So now that I'm Cinderella and all my wishes come true, tell me this. Why haven't I been happy, not even for one minute?"

There was no answer, and she heard her own dry laughter, like a mark of her insanity to think that any of this was more than just her own crazy imagination. Then something like a gentle fingertip touched her, this time inside her skull. *Because, of course, happiness is only a temporary and accidental hormonal balance between body and mind,* she told herself, and wondered if that was really her own thought, just before light began to fall through the shifting tree branches above in the most gorgeous prismatic patterns. The day was more beautiful and perfect than anything she could ever remember.

Dyann walked back toward the house after a leisurely swim. Sunlight and the gentlest wind touched her bare skin. The sight of the old house with its wreathing foliage made her feel a sudden surge of contentment and joy. How simple it was, just to take each day as it came, just to be happy. She smiled secretively. And this state of happiness need not end; it could be forever. She shivered in delight at the thought.

She entered the house confidently, but in the next moment she was aware that the day's sunshine was hidden under clouds, and the smell of the house rose around her, rank, corrupt, moldering.

"What's wrong?" Her voice rose, plaintive as a child's. "I want my happiness!"

She felt the familiar sensation of a door opening, somewhere, leaking that alien radiance, threatening to draw out all of this world's warmth and light. She drew in her breath as a fleeting burst of joy trailed through her mind like a promise—or a reward. It seemed that within her chest idle fingers were curling around her heart.

"Now," came the fast-fading whisper. "Serve Me."

Blanca

Thomas Tessier

When I told a few close friends that I was going to Blanca, their reaction was about what I had expected. "Why?" they asked. "There's nothing to see in Blanca. Nothing to do except disappear." Sly smiles. "Watch out you don't disappear." "Maybe that's why I chose it," I said with a smile of my own. "It might be nice to disappear for a while."

For a travel writer who has been on the job ten years, as I have, it isn't so easy to escape. The good places have been done, the mediocre ones too. You name it and I've probably been there, evaluating the hotels, sampling the cuisine, checking out the facilities and amenities, chatting up the locals. It's a great job, but I was tired of the regular world. What I needed was a therapeutic getaway, to spend a couple of weeks in an obscure backwater doing nothing more than sipping cold beer on a terrace and reading a good book.

I knew people in the business who'd been to

Blanca. It's boring, they told me. Miles and miles of rolling plains and rangeland. There's a dead volcano somewhere in Blanca, but it isn't worth climbing. Yes, the towns are neat and the people are pleasant enough. There's never any difficulty getting a clean room and bed for the night. But nothing happens, there's nothing to do. No monuments or ancient ruins. No carnival, no festivals or feasts. The night life is said to be fairly low-key, so if you're looking for that kind of action, which I wasn't, there are much better places to go. Blanca was cattle country, and the only good thing I ever heard about it was that the steaks were excellent.

Blanca is not a nation but a territory, overlapping several borders in that region of the world. The native Indians were crushed nearly two centuries ago. They survive, a sullen minority now thoroughly domesticated by generations of servitude as cheap labor cowhands, meat packers, and household help. The European settlers tried to create Blanca as an independent state, but numerous rebellions failed and it was eventually carved up by its larger neighbors. But Blanca is Blanca, they still say there, regardless of the boundaries that appear on maps.

Because Blanca has comparatively little to offer the visitor, it is not on any of the main routes. I had to catch two flights, the second of which stopped at so many featureless outposts along the way that it seemed like days before I finally reached Oranien. With a population of nearly one hundred thousand it is easily the largest city in Blanca.

I checked into the Hotel des Vacances, which was within walking distance of the central district but just far enough away to escape the noise. My room was large and airy and had a small balcony that over-looked two residential streets and a park. It was comfortable, and not at all like a modern luxury hotel.

I slept for nearly eleven hours that first night, had steak and eggs for brunch, and then took a lazy walk around the center of Oranien. The narrow side streets had a certain pioneer charm—the original hard-clay tiles had never been paved over and remained neatly in place. But the most remarkable feature of the city was its state of cleanliness. I began to look for a piece of litter and couldn't find so much as a discarded cigarette butt. It reminded me of parts of Switzerland, or Singapore.

On the top floor of a department store I caught a view of the southern part of the city, a vast stretch of stockyards, abattoirs, and railroad tracks. All the beef in Blanca passed through Oranien on its way to the outside world. I'd come to a dusty, three-story cowtown, and it was the tidiest, best-scrubbed place I'd ever seen.

But then I'd heard stories about the police in Blanca. They *were* the law, and if you had any sense at all you never challenged them. Littering ranked close to treason by their way of thinking, and while that might seem harsh to some, I had no problem with it. I've seen immaculate places and I've seen squalor; on the whole, I prefer the former. Besides, it had nothing to do with me. I was on vacation, recovering from a personal mess, exorcising old demons (including a wife). The first few days I was in Oranien the only cops I saw were chubby little men in silly uniforms, directing traffic. They looked like extras in some Ruritanian operetta.

"Not them," Basma said quietly. "The ones you

must worry about are the ones you can't see. The men in plainclothes. They are everywhere."

"Even here?" I asked, amused but intrigued.

"Yes, surely."

We were in the small but very pleasant beer garden behind the Hotel des Vacances. There were perhaps two dozen other people scattered about the umbrella-topped tables in the late afternoon sun. A few neighborhood regulars, the rest visitors and hotel guests like myself, passing through. Everyone looked happy and relaxed.

My companion was both a foreigner and a local resident. Basma had taken it upon himself to join me at my table the day before, when I had just discovered the beer garden and was settling into *The Thirteenth Simenon Omnibus*. At first I resented the intrusion and tried to ignore the man, but he would not be denied. Finally I gave in and closed my book.

We spent two hours or more drinking and chatting, with Basma carrying most of the load. But he was easy company. A middle-aged Lebanese, he had reluctantly fled Beirut while he still had a cache of foreign currency. The city had become unbearable, impossible, and he believed he was a target of both the Christians ("Because I am a Muslim") and the Shiites ("Because they think all international businessmen are working for the CIA."). Besides, business had pretty much dried up. Basma had been in Oranien for the best part of three years, doing the odd bit of trade and otherwise depleting his capital. He was eager to move on to more fertile ground, but had not yet decided where that might be. By then I was tired and tipsy and went to bed early. But we agreed to meet again the next day and have dinner in town, which is how we came to be discussing the police.

"Who, for instance?" I asked.

"Let's not be looking around and staring," Basma said softly. "But that couple at the table by the wall on your right. I've seen them many times and wondered about them."

A handsome man and a beautiful woman, both in their late twenties. He wore a linen suit, a white shirt, and no tie. He had dark hair and a strong, unmarked face. She was dressed in a smart, obviously foreign outfit—skirt, matching jacket, and a stylish blouse. I imagined her to be the daughter of a local big shot; she had that air of privilege and hauteur. They made me feel old, or perhaps just envious of their youth and good looks.

"I don't care," I said. "I'm just passing through. All I want to do is relax for a couple of weeks."

"Of course." Basma smiled indulgently.

So that night he gave me the grand tour of Oranien, such as it is. After the mandatory steak dinner we strolled through the main shopping arcade, which was full of the latest European fashions and Asian electronic equipment, all carrying steep price tags. We took in a couple of bars, briefly surveyed a dance hall that doubled as an economy-class dating service, and then stopped for a while at a neon-riddled disco called Marlene's, where the crowd was somewhat interesting. There the sons and daughters of local wealth came to dance, flirt, play their social games, and get blitzed. Basma called them second-raters, because the brightest of their generation and class were away in America or England, studying at the best private schools and universities.

By the time we'd squandered some money at a posh gaming club and had a frightening glimpse of a very discreet place where you could do whatever you wanted with girls (or boys) as young as thirteen, I'd seen enough for one night. Oranien's dull and orderly exterior masked the usual wanton tendencies. It didn't bother me, but it didn't interest me.

Back in my room, I poured one last nightcap from my bottle of duty-free bourbon and lit a cigarette. I'd had a lot to drink, but it had been spaced out over many hours, with a meal thrown in somewhere along the line. I wasn't drunk, just tired, reasonably buzzed. I know this for sure, because whenever I have gotten drunk in the past I've never dreamed, or at least I've never remembered it. That night I did have a dream, and it was one I would not forget.

I was sleeping in my bed, there in the Hotel des Vacances. It was the middle of the night. Suddenly I was awakened by a loud clattering noise. I jumped out of bed. I was at the window, looking out on what seemed to be a historical costume pageant. It confused me, and I couldn't move. The street below, brightly lit by a three-quarters moon, was full of soldiers on horseback. They carried torches or waved swords. The horses continued to make a dreadful racket, stamping their hooves on the clay tiles. Every house in sight remained dark, but the soldiers went to several different doors, roused the inhabitants, and seized eight or ten people altogether. They were thrown into horse-drawn carts already crowded with prisoners. The night was full of terrible sounds— soldiers shouting, men arguing or pleading in vain, women and children wailing, a ghastly pandemonium. It seemed they had finished and were about to move on when one of the soldiers, obviously an officer, turned and looked up directly at me. I was standing out on the little balcony, gripping the wrought-iron railing tightly. The officer spoke to one of his comrades, who also looked in my direction. The officer raised his sword, pointing to me. I knew his face—but I had no idea who he was. A group of soldiers, apparently responding to instructions, hurried across the street to the hotel. Still, I couldn't move. A terrible fear came over me as I realized they would take me away with the others. The rest is sensation—the twisting, falling, hideous sweetness we all dream more often than we would like before it actually happens—dying.

I slept late—it was becoming a welcome habit—and woke up feeling remarkably cheerful and energetic. I remembered the dream, I thought about it through my shower, over brunch, and during my walk to the newsstand for the most recent *Herald Tribune.* I sat outdoors at a café, drank two cups of coffee, smoked cigarettes, and read about Darryl Strawberry's 525-foot home run in distant Montreal.

It was great to be alive. Any sense of menace or fear had dissolved out of the dream. It had already become a kind of mental curio that I carried around with me. Maybe I was happy simply because I knew I could never have had that nightmare in New York. What it seemed to say to me in the light of day was: "Now you know you're in Blanca."

"It's local history," Basma agreed when we met in the beer garden later that afternoon and I told him about the dream. "You must have known about it before you came here."

"Sure. Well, vaguely." I lit a cigarette while the waitress delivered our second round of beers. "I've heard the jokes about people being taken away in the dead of night and never seen again."

"Yes, but they are not jokes. What you dreamed is exactly how it used to happen—and by the way, it still does, from time to time."

"Really?"

"Of course."

"Well, that's politics, which never interested me. I'd just as soon get back to dreaming about sex."

"Aha." Basma smiled broadly. "No need just to dream about it, you know."

"It'll do for now."

Basma shrugged sadly. I knew I was doing a bad job of living up to his mental image of American tourists as people hell-bent on having an extravagantly good time. We had a light dinner together and then I disappointed him further by deciding to make an early evening of it. I was still a bit tired from our night out on the town, and I wanted nothing more than to read in bed for a while and then get about twelve hours of sleep. I had it in mind to rent a car the next day and see a bit of the nearby countryside, however flat and dull it might be.

Simenon worked his usual magic. I was soon transported to rainy Paris (even in the sweltering heat of August, Simenon's Paris seems rainy), where Inspector Maigret had another nasty murder to unravel. It was bliss, but unfortunately I drifted off to sleep sooner than I expected. I woke up a little after four in the morning, the paperback in my hand. I dropped the book to the floor and crawled under the covers. But it was no good. Finally I sat up and groaned, realizing that I would not be able to get back to sleep. For a while I simply stayed there, lying still.

I got out of bed when I noticed a strange flickering of light reflected on the half-open window. It came from the street below, a lamppost or car headlights most likely. But when I stepped onto the balcony and looked down, I was paralyzed by what I saw. They were all there again. The horses, the carts, the soldiers with their swords and torches, the pitiful souls being dragged from their homes, the mothers and wives, the children. It was a repeat performance of the grim nightmare I'd had only twenty-four hours ago, but this time I was wide-awake. I forced myself to be sure: I took note of the cold, harsh wrought iron beneath my bare feet, I sucked in huge breaths of chilly night air, and I looked over my shoulder into the hotel room to reassure myself in some way. But when I turned back to the street below they were still there; the scene continued to play itself out. I was awake, and it was happening.

I realized there were certain differences. Noise—there was none. The horses stamped, the soldiers shouted, the men argued, and their families sobbed, but I heard none of this; I could only see it taking place. Silence ruled the night. And then there was the officer, the one in charge, who had pointed his sword at me in the dream. I spotted him again and he still looked familiar to me, but I didn't know who he was. This time he never once glanced in my direction. He and his troops went about their business as if I didn't exist, though they could hardly fail to notice me standing there on the second-floor balcony, the room lit up behind me. The fact that they didn't may account for the other difference, the lack of fear in me.

The scene had a terrible fascination, I was transfixed by it, but at the same time I felt detached from it, uninvolved. I didn't know what to make of it. I felt puzzled rather than threatened.

Finally I did something sensible. I looked up the street, away from the scene, and sure enough, I saw the usual line of parked cars that I knew belonged there. It was a comforting sight. But then, when I turned back, the dream drama was still just visible. The soldiers and the carts had formed a wavy line and were marching away from me toward the main road, a hundred yards or so in the distance. I watched them until they reached the intersection with that broad avenue, at which point my eyes could make out nothing more than the bobbing, meandering flow of torch flames.

It took another few minutes for me to realize that what I was looking at was a stream of headlights. Then I became aware of the sound of that traffic; the silence was broken. The early shift, I told myself. Hundreds of workers on their way to the abattoirs, stockyards, and packing plants on the south side of the city. The news agents, short-order cooks, and bus drivers. All the people who open up the city before dawn every morning. Any city. I stepped back into the room, sat on my bed, and lit a cigarette, wondering how yesterday's nightmare could turn into today's hallucination.

"Do you take drugs?" Basma asked me casually.

We were walking through the park, toward a bar I'd never been to in my life. It was about five that afternoon, and I'd blurted out the story of the hallucination—which was what I still took it to be—as soon as we met for our daily drink and chat.

I laughed. "No, it's been a few years since I did any drugs, and even then it wasn't much."

"You are quite certain that you were fully awake when you saw this—whatever it was?"

"Yes."

"And you were awake *before* you saw it?"

"Definitely. I was lying there, feeling sorry for myself for waking up so early. I saw the orange light flickering on the window—it's a glass door, actually, to the balcony."

"Yes, yes," Basma said impatiently.

"Well, as I told you, I sat up, went to the window, stepped out onto the balcony, and there it was."

"I see."

Basma didn't speak again until we reached the bar, a workers' grogshop that offered only the locally brewed beer, Bolero. Once we got our drinks and I had lit a cigarette, Basma returned to the subject.

"You think it was hallucination."

"Yes, of course," I said. "What else would it be?"

"Ghosts." Basma smiled, but not as if he were joking. "Perhaps you saw some ghosts from history."

"Oh, I doubt that very much."

"Why? It makes perfect sense. What is more, I think you may have been awake the first time you saw them, two nights ago. You only thought it was a dream; you were less certain because it was the first time and you had been drinking more—yes?"

"Yes, I had been drinking more, but I still think that I was dreaming. It ended in a panic and I was lost in sleep in an instant—no sensation of getting back into bed or thinking about it." I stubbed out my cigarette and lit another. I didn't like disappointing Basma again, he seemed as eager as a child to believe in ghosts. "Besides, even if I had been awake, that doesn't mean it was not a hallucination."

"The same hallucination, two nights in a row." Basma gave this some thought. "And you have some medical history of this?"

"No, not at all," I had to admit.

"Then why do you think it should suddenly start happening to you now?"

I shrugged. "The stories I'd heard about Blanca. The emotional distress resulting from the breakup of my marriage. Throw in the mild despair I sometimes feel at the approach of my fortieth birthday." I finished the beer and looked around for a waitress—a mistake in that bar. Then I realized how self-pitying I sounded, and it annoyed me very much. "To tell you the truth, I really have no idea at all why this kind of thing should be happening to me."

"Hallucination?" Basma asked again, quietly.

"That makes a lot more sense than an army of ghosts."

"As long as it makes sense to you."

It didn't, in fact, but I was fed up with talking about it, fed up with even thinking about it, so I fetched two more Bolero beers and then changed the subject. I told Basma about my day trip. I'd hired an Opel Rekord that morning and driven past miles and miles of cattle ranches, through small but impeccable villages, in a wide looping route north of Oranien. Altogether, I was out of the city for about five hours, and I'd seen quite enough of the countryside. There was nothing wrong with it—it was agreeably unspoiled rangeland—but it was bland, featureless, utterly lacking in charm or interest. Just as I'd been told.

"Yes." Basma nodded. "I have heard that once you leave the city it's much the same in every direction, for hundreds of miles. Although I've never seen for myself."

"You've never left Oranien, since you got here?"

"Why should I? There's nothing to see." His smile broadened into a grin. "Is there?"

"Well, no."

"Do you still have the car?"

"Yes, until tomorrow noon," I told him. "It's parked back near the hotel."

"Good. If you don't mind driving, I would like to show you something. Not exactly a tourist attraction, but I think you'll find it worthwhile."

He wouldn't tell me where we were going, but there was still plenty of daylight left when we drove away a few minutes later. I followed his directions, and it was soon obvious that we were heading toward the south end of the city.

"The stockyards?" I guessed.

"Ah, you've seen them."

"Only from a distance." I told Basma about the view from the department store.

"Now you will see it all close up."

I was mildly curious. We passed through the commercial district and then a residential area not unlike the one in which I was staying. The houses and apartment buildings became shabbier and more dilapidated the farther we went from the center of the city; the middle class in-town neighborhood gave way to the worker-Indian tenements on the outskirts. I wanted to drive slowly so that I could see as much as possible, and in fact I had to because there were so many people out on the streets. Kids playing games and ignoring the traffic, grown-ups talking in small groups (men to men, women to women, mostly), and the old folks sitting stoically wherever they could find a quiet spot. Most of the social life, including the cooking and eating of food, seemed to take place outdoors.

Almost before I realized it, we were there. The industry and the workers' lodgings had sprung up together over the years, without benefit of design or long-term planning. There were row houses right up to the open doors of an abattoir, apartment buildings wedged between a canning factory and a processing plant, and a vast maze of corrals holding thousands of cattle bumping against dozens of tiny backyards. After we had cruised around for a while, I began to understand that these people literally lived in their workplaces: you would go home when your shift was finished, but home was hardly any different. The interminable stupid bawling of the cattle, the mingled stench of blood, raw meat, and cowshit, the constant rattling of trains, the drumming vibrations of the factories—everything here, everything you saw or heard or felt or smelled was about decay and death. You could taste it in the air.

We reached the worst of it, a mean stretch where finally the people themselves seemed only marginally alive. They stood or sat about in front of their shacks looking dazed. The streets, no longer paved, became increasingly difficult to navigate. Ditches ran along both sides, and they ran red with blood from the slaughterhouses. In the absence of traffic and other human noises, the shriek of power saws carving animal flesh was piercingly clear. At every pile of garbage vicious cats and scarred dogs competed with huge brown roaches and gangs of rats for whatever was going. It was getting dark fast.

"I hope you know the way back."

"Yes, of course."

Basma gave me a series of directions, and it wasn't too long before we were on a better road. Neither of us had spoken much in the course of our slumming tour. As soon as I caught a glimpse of the lights in the center of the city my stomach began to relax. I've been to some of the worst refugee camps in the world and never felt so tense. But refugee camps are at least theoretically temporary, and there is always the hope, however slim, of eventual movement. The people I had just seen were never going anywhere.

"I suppose I've had Blanca beef many times, in all my travels," I said, just to say something.

"I'm sure you have," Basma agreed promptly. "They ship it out in every form. Brains, tongue, heart, kidneys, liver, as well as all the usual cuts, prime rib, steaks and so on, all the way down to hot dogs and Vienna sausages. If it isn't tinned or wrapped in plastic, it's frozen."

We began to joke about becoming vegetarians, describing the best salads we could remember having, and we kept at it until we were comfortably settled with drinks in Number One, which was supposedly the better of Oranien's two topless joints. It was expensive but otherwise all right. That kind of bar, where the music was loud and the women occasionally distracting, was just what Basma and I needed, since our excursion into the south end had left us in no mood for serious conversation. We drank until the place closed, by which time we were both unfit to drive, so we left the rental car parked where it was and hired a taxi.

I wasn't surprised when Basma got out of the cab with me at the hotel. I didn't know exactly where he lived but I assumed it was in the neighborhood because we'd met in the beer garden and we always said good night outside the hotel.

"Would you like to have a nightcap in my room?" he asked me as the taxi pulled away.

"No, thank you very much. I couldn't take one more drink."

"Are you sure? I have a bottle of Teachers, pretty good stuff, and I live right there, across the street." Basma pointed vaguely to the first or second building on the opposite corner. "Come on, one more."

"No, really, thanks, but I'm going to fall down and pass out, and I'd rather do that in my bed than on your floor."

Basma shrugged. "Okay. See you tomorrow."

"Sure, good night." I turned away, but then stopped and looked back at him. "Hey, you know what? Your building is one of the ones those ghost soldiers raided."

"Don't be telling me such things," he said from the middle of the street. "I don't want to know that."

"Why? It's just ghosts, and history. Right?"

"Never mind that."

Basma wagged a finger at me and kept going. I made it upstairs, locked my door, and even managed to get my clothes off before spinning dizzily into sleep. It was nearly noon when I opened my eyes again. The first thing that came to me was how nice it felt not to have another hallucination, nightmare, or ghostly apparition to brood about. I'd been truly out of it, and I'd slept straight through, unbothered.

On the negative side, however, I felt terrible the moment I stood up. I took a long shower, which made me feel cleaner but did nothing for my head, and I was going to get some food when I remembered the rental car. I didn't want to pay another day's charges but it was already late. When I got to the car I found a parking ticket under the wiper blade. I shoved it in my pocket, wondering if I could safely tear it up or if the vaunted Oranien police would catch up with me before I flew out next week.

The car rental agency wanted me to pay for the second full day, naturally, since I was well over an hour past the deadline when I finally got there. I had no luck arguing until I pulled out my *Vogue* credentials, at which point the manager suddenly became obsequious and sympathetic. No problem: no extra charges.

Then I got some much-needed food into my stomach. I went back to my hotel room, tore up the parking ticket, and fell asleep again on the bed while trying to read the *Herald Tribune*. It was after four when I dragged myself down to the beer garden. I held off on the alcohol, cautiously sipping mineral water while I waited for Basma. An hour later I began to wonder if I was wrong. We *had* agreed to meet in the usual place at the usual time, hadn't we? Maybe he had business to attend to elsewhere and I'd misunderstood him in the boozy fog last night. I wasn't disappointed or annoyed, because I really wanted a break from Basma's company, for one evening anyway. I stayed a little longer, out of courtesy, and then returned to my room. He'd know where to find me if he turned up later. But he didn't, and I had a very welcome early night.

The next day I felt great, and I did what I had really wanted to do all along. I sat in the shade in the beer garden, reading Simenon. I had breakfast there, followed later by more coffee, then lunch, and, in the middle of the afternoon, lemonade and a plate of watermelon chunks. By five o'clock I'd knocked off both Maigret novels in the volume, and I allowed myself a glass of cold Bolero beer. It was a very pale lager, but I was beginning to develop a taste for it.

Where was Basma? I had a sudden guilty flashback to our drunken parting. I'd teased him about the ghost soldiers, as he thought of them, and now it occurred to me that I might have annoyed him. Perhaps that was why he was staying away. What you do when you're drunk always seems much worse when you reconstruct it later. I was tired of sitting there, but once again I stayed on for another hour or so, until it was obvious that my Lebanese friend was not going to put in an appearance.

I went looking for him a little while later. I started with the corner building diagonally opposite the hotel. Inside the unlocked screen door was a small entry foyer with a tile floor and a rickety wooden table. The inner door was locked, so I rang the bell, and kept ringing it for nearly five minutes before a heavyset, middle-aged woman answered.

"I'm looking for Mr. Basma," I told her.

"He go."

"When do you expect him back?" She shrugged and shook her head at this. "Well, can I leave a message for him?" I took out a pen and a piece of paper I'd brought for that purpose. But the woman continued to shake her head.

"He go," she repeated emphatically.

"Isn't he coming back?"

"Men come. He go with men."

Simple enough, and the end of the story as far as she was concerned. I wasn't ready to give up, however.

"What about his things?"

"What?"

"Things. Clothes, belongings." Most people in Blanca can speak English because the local dialect is one of those clotted, homegrown curiosities of limited use, like Afrikaans. But this creature's English seemed marginal at best. "His possessions, his personal—his *things,* dammit."

"Gone."

"When did he go?"

"Yesterday."

"Can I see his room?"

"Room?"

"Yes. Basma's room. Please."

"Yes, yes. Come."

It took a while to get there, because the woman moved only with difficulty. She showed me into the front room on the first floor. It was a dreary little place with a couch, a couple of chairs, a table, a hideous wardrobe, and a single bed. There was a small bathroom and, behind a plastic curtain, an even smaller galley kitchen. The few items of furniture were old and worn, the walls faded and unadorned, the carpeting thin as paper. I went to the window and looked out at the park and the quiet streets. I looked at the balcony and window of my room in the hotel across the way.

"Nice view," the woman said.

I nodded absently. There was no doubt in my mind that Basma was gone for good. The room had been completely stripped of all personal items. What was there was what you got when you rented a very modest furnished room.

"Three hundred crown," the woman said.

"What?"

"Three hundred crown. One month." She waved her hand in a gesture commending the room to me. "One hundred U.S. dollar."

"No." I hurried away.

That night I slept by the balcony window in my room. I used the big armchair, and stretched my legs out on the coffee table. It was not a comfortable arrangement, but it wasn't unbearable, and I wanted to be there. It seemed important not to miss the apparition, if it should occur again.

I tried to read for a while, but I could no longer keep my mind on the words. Basma wouldn't have left so suddenly without saying good-bye, I told myself. From what the woman had said in her skeletal English, he had been taken—and that surely meant taken against his will. But by whom, and why? It seemed highly unlikely that his Lebanese enemies would come such a distance to exact revenge, and he'd been so insistent in cautioning me about the Blanca police that I couldn't imagine he'd ever set a foot wrong here. Certainly not in the realm of politics. But Basma was an entrepreneur, so it was not impossible that he'd gotten involved in some shady deal that had landed him in trouble with the authorities.

Could I help him in any way? He had been good company, a friend. He hadn't tried to con me. He'd been a useful guide to the city. It seemed wrong just to shrug it off mentally and forget about him. But I couldn't think of anything to do, other than ask the police about him—and I was reluctant to do that.

It was dawn when I awoke to the sound of car doors slamming. The first thing I saw was a silver Mercedes with black-tinted windows, parked at the corner across from my hotel. The car's yellow hazard lights were flashing. Four men wearing sunglasses and linen suits entered Basma's building. While they were inside, a van with the similarly darkened windows pulled up behind the Mercedes and waited. A moment later the four men reappeared, with a fifth man in their custody—he wasn't even handcuffed, but it was obvious he was their prisoner. I stood up, swung the window open, and stepped out onto the balcony.

"Basma."

I had spoken to myself, barely whispering the name in stunned disbelief. But the five of them stopped immediately and looked up at me. Basma looked terrified. I thought I recognized one of the other men. I was so shocked and frightened, however, that I took a step back involuntarily and stumbled. I had to grab the window frame to catch my balance. Then the scene was finished, gone as if it had never happened, and I was looking down at an empty street corner.

I sat on the bed and lit a cigarette. My hands shook, my head clamored. The smoke was like ground glass in my throat, but I sucked it in deeply, as if trying to make a point with my own pain. I'd been so many miles, seen so much of the world, the best and the worst and the endless in between, but now for the first time in my life I felt lost.

Then I became angry with myself. My feelings didn't matter in this situation. Basma was the one in trouble, and I had to try to help, or at least find out what was happening to him. For all I knew, I was the only friend he had in Blanca. I didn't want to—it scared the shit out of me to think about it—but I had to do something. And now I knew where to start.

They came into the beer garden at four o'clock that afternoon, as they had several times during the past week. The woman was beautiful as ever, cool and formidable. The kind of woman you would fear falling in love with, but love to watch. It was her man, however, who fascinated me. The man in the linen suit. Basma had warned me about them. I was pretty sure the man was the officer on horseback I had seen twice. I *knew* he was one of the men I had seen take Basma away.

Dreams, nightmares, hallucinations, ghosts. Take your pick. But maybe the simplest, truest explanation was that I was in the middle of a breakdown, caused by the collapse of my marriage and my abrupt flight to this miserable place. It made sense, and I hesitated, clinging to my own weakness. But I was there, Basma was gone, and that man in the linen suit was very real. I got up at last and approached him.

"Excuse me," I said. "I'm sorry to intrude, but I wonder if I could speak to you for a moment."

"Yes. Please."

He gestured for me to take a seat. They looked as if

they had just been waiting for me to come, which made me feel even more uncomfortable.

"I've seen you around here almost every day since I arrived—I'm on vacation—and the thing is, I can't find a friend of mine. He seems to have disappeared. His name is Basma, he's Lebanese, and he was living in the corner building across the street. Do you know him?"

"I don't think so."

"Can you suggest how I might find out about him?"

"Go to the police."

They seemed to regard me with an impossible mixture of curiosity and disinterest. I was getting nowhere.

"He seemed to think you were a policeman."

At last, something. The barest flicker of an eyebrow, then the man smiled, as if at some silly misunderstanding. The woman was keenly attentive now, and it was hard not to return the all-consuming look in her eyes.

"I work in the government," the man said. "I am not a policeman. But you are a visitor here. Let me ask some people I know about your friend for you. Of course, I cannot promise you anything."

"I understand."

"Are you staying here?"

"Yes." I gave him my name and room number and told him I would be staying five more days. "Thank you for your help. I'm sorry to trouble you."

"No trouble."

Later I felt disgusted at how deferential I'd been, all but groveling for a scrap of information. The man knew Basma, knew the whole story far better than I did; he was a primary player. "Thank you for your help." But how else could I have handled it? It would have been crazy to confront the man and accuse him of arresting Basma. It would have been absurd to tell him that history replays itself every morning on that street corner, and that I'd seen what he and his colleagues had done.

So the possibilities for action on my part were extremely limited. I'd done what I could. I began to think that I should let it go, that it was just one more thing in my life to put behind me. Basma was rotting in some filthy jail cell, if he wasn't already a ghost. In any event, nothing I could do would make the least difference. I might try to write about Basma and Blanca, something political with teeth in it—but not here, not until I was safely back in New York. I'd never done anything like that before.

I slept well that night and did very little the next day. I took a couple of short walks, but mostly hung around the hotel, reading and relaxing. The government man and his beautiful woman did not put in an appearance. Then I enjoyed another peaceful night, free of dreams and ghosts. It was so pleasant to idle away afternoons in the beer garden, sipping iced tea and nibbling slivers of cold melon. I was glad that the man in the linen suit failed to show up for the second day in a row.

I did think about Basma at odd moments, but in my line of work I meet so many people, all over the world. Already he was slipping away from me. And I had calmed down enough to realize I would never write that article. I wasn't equipped to do that kind of thing properly. Tourism was my beat, not politics or ghosts or disappearances. To hell with Blanca. Maybe it was a surrender of sorts, but by admitting these things to myself I felt I was on the way to a full mental recovery, and that had been the whole purpose of the trip in the first place.

That evening I intended to find a new restaurant, have anything but steak for dinner, and then scout a few bars. I was in the mood for serious female contact at last. It was a little past seven when I stepped out of the hotel. At that instant the silver Mercedes braked sharply to a halt and the man in the linen suit jumped out. He came right at me. I was determined not to let this nasty little hood intimidate me anymore.

"Do you want to see your friend?"

"Yes. Where is he?"

"I will take you." He gestured toward the open car door. "Please. It is still light."

I was aware that the other people on the street all stood motionless, watching. Calmly, at my own pace, I walked to the car and sat down inside. I was in the backseat, between the man I knew and another fellow, who ignored me warily. I was not surprised to see the beautiful young woman in the front seat, along with the driver. She glanced at me once, then looked away. We raced through the center of the city. We were heading south, I knew that much. I asked a few questions, but the only answers I got were vague and unsatisfactory.

The driver never slowed down. If anything, he pushed the car a little faster when we reached the crowded working-class district. People and animals sometimes had to jump out of the way at the last second to save themselves. I could sense the others in the car trying not to smile. We passed the factories, the slaughterhouses, the tenements, the stockyards, the grim processing, canning, and freezing plants. We ripped through the sprawling shantytown and continued beyond the point where Basma and I had ended our exploration. Finally we were on a dirt road, crossing a vast scrubby wasteland. We had gone a couple of miles when I saw that we were approaching a cluster of vehicles parked with their headlights on, pointing in the same direction.

They walked me to the edge of a long ditch, about eight feet deep. It was dusk, not yet too dark to see, but spotlights had been hooked up to a generator to illuminate the scene. It was all so bright it hurt my eyes. Perhaps a dozen other men stood about, smoking, talking quietly, taking notes and photographs. When my eyes adjusted, I forced myself to look carefully.

There were a lot of bodies in the ditch, I would say at least twenty. All the same: hands tied behind the back, the back of the head partially blown away, bloating features. I noticed the swarming insects, the ferocious smell. I stood there for a while, staring, but so help me I could not put together a single thought. A couple of men wearing goggles and masks were getting ready to spray the ditch with some chemical.

"Can you identify that person?" the man in the linen suit asked me, pointing to a particular corpse. "There."

"Yes, that's him." In spite of the puffed face, parts of which had already been nibbled at by animals, I had no difficulty picking out my late friend. "That's Basma."

"I am so sorry," he said casually. "A terrible way to die."

As if there were any good ones.

"Why did this happen to him?" I asked. "He was a harmless little man, a foreign guest in this country. Why should they"—I almost said "you" but managed to avoid it—"do this to him?"

"Come here, please."

He led me back to the car, where the young woman waited. She looked smart as ever, this time in a tropical pantsuit with a white blouse open three buttons deep. The man nodded to her. She reached into a briefcase I hadn't noticed and handed him something. He held it up for me to see.

"Did you do this?"

I could feel the blood vacating my cheeks, then rushing back as I tried to muster a sense of embarrassed contempt. He had a large rectangle of cardboard, on which were pasted all the torn pieces of my parking ticket.

"Yes, we do that all the time back in New York. I hope it's not a felony here. I'm willing to pay the fine, whatever it is, and I'll pay it now, if you like."

"Did you refuse to pay a late fee to Bolero Rent-a-Car, and did you threaten to write negative comments about that agency in your travel articles?"

I took a deep breath, exhaled slowly. "I was about an hour late, but I explained the situation to them and they seemed to be satisfied. If they're not, then I'd be glad to pay the fee."

"May I have your passport."

I gave it to him. "Why?"

"You can get in the car now. An officer will drive you back to your hotel. Thank you for your help."

"I need my passport," I told him. "I'm flying home in three days. Sunday afternoon."

"I know," he replied. "We will contact you."

I tried to talk to the driver on the journey back into town, but he ignored me. I was furious, but frightened as well. The whole thing was a grotesque charade. They didn't need me to identify Basma, but they made me go through with it, knowing that I wouldn't have the courage to accuse them of his murder. Take a good look in that ditch, they were saying to me, this is the kind of thing we can do. They were toying with me, because it's their nature to toy with people.

What, if anything, could Basma have done to bring about his own destruction at the hands of these people? Had he been involved in some way with a radical faction in Lebanon? Did the authorities here think they were eliminating a Muslim terrorist? Was he a crook or a smuggler, a charming criminal who had escaped from Beirut only to run out of luck in Blanca? To me he seemed a pleasant, fairly idle fellow with an agreeable manner and a taste for godless liquor. But, in fairness, I hardly knew him. We had a few dinners together, a lot of drinks, that's all. It was a brief acquaintance. Our backgrounds and our circumstances were totally different. They couldn't do *that* to me.

Common sense told me I had nothing to fear. The parking ticket and the rental agency were trivial matters that could be settled with a little cash. I was an American, a travel writer for a major international magazine. They might push me around, but they wouldn't hurt me.

All the same, I decided to take certain precautions. The next morning I tried to contact the nearest American consulate, which was some four hundred miles away. At first the operator of the hotel switchboard told me that all long-distance lines out of Oranien were engaged. After an hour of fruitless attempts she said she had learned that they were "down," and that she had no idea how long it would be before they were working again. So I went to the central post office and tried their telephones, but with the same result.

I tried to rent another car—at a different agency. I'm not sure what I intended to do with it, but I was refused one because I could not produce my passport.

I didn't bother with lunch. I drank a couple of beers and smoked a lot of cigarettes. I wandered around until I found the railroad station. I bought a ticket on the next departing train, although I wasn't even sure where it was going. Then a uniformed policeman confiscated the ticket, smiling.

"We don't want you to disappear on us, sir."

Of course. They got the parking ticket from the wastebasket in my room. They'd talked with the rental agency about me. They'd been watching and following me all the time. It was pointless to wonder why. I went back to the hotel and, as calmly as possible, I wrote a letter to my lawyer in New York, telling him where I was, that I had a problem with the authorities, and that if he hadn't heard from me—my voice on the telephone—by the time he got the letter, he was to do whatever it took to get me out of Blanca —press conferences, congressmen, the State Department, the works. I wrote more or less the same thing to my editor. I used hotel stationery and did not write my name on the envelopes. The hotel was unsafe and so were the streets, but I thought my chances were a little better outdoors. I went for a walk and slipped the letters into the mailbox on the corner as inconspicuously as possible. I crossed into the park and sat on a bench for a while, smoking. Nothing happened. I got back to my room just in time to look out the window and see a silver Mercedes pull away from the mailbox.

This is my last night in Blanca. Tomorrow I am supposed to be on the noon flight out of here. I still have that ticket. I do not have my passport. For two days and two nights I have waited. Nothing happens. I am waiting. There's nowhere to go, nothing to do, except smoke and drink and wait.

I think of them all the time, the handsome man in the linen suit and the beautiful young woman. Mostly I think of her, with her blouse open three buttons deep. Her breasts are not large because I saw no cleavage, but I know they are perfect. Her skin finely tanned with the faintest trace of sun-bleached down. I would like to have her, to lick her, but she is impossible to touch. You can only look at a woman like that and wonder what it would be like to fuck death.

Tonight when I ask at the desk for a wake-up call they smile and say yes, of course, and smile some more. No one writes it down. The porter says I don't look well. Would I like dinner in my room? Some company? Clean, he adds encouragingly.

It'll be over long before noon. Around four or five in the morning the silver Mercedes will arrive, the van right behind. The men in the van are there to strip the room of my possessions after I'm gone. Some morning in the future you can look out one of these windows and see how it happened, too late for me—and for you.

I hope I'm not alone, I hope there are others. Many will be arguing, begging, screaming, shitting their pants, but some will walk unaided, with quiet dignity. If I have to, that's what I want to do.

Not that it matters.

I crush out a cigarette. I open another bottle of beer, reach for another cigarette. I don't have to go to the window to see what is happening outside. There is light in the sky.

Look for me.

Nine Gables

James Howard Kunstler

 In the late winter of that year our marriage was not going well. So as couples in trouble often do, we cooked up a desperate scheme to save it and bought Nine Gables.

It stood off Route 28 outside Minerva, an impressive heap of carpenter Gothic tracery, gingerbread fretwork, and fancy shingling surrounded by dark, hulking cedars that grew so close as to appear to be feeding on it. The eponymous nine gables were overstated. Two steep ones faced the road—divided by a queer narrow pediment in the Greek style—but the other seven were just little dormers set along the roof. It had functioned as a hotel for half a century, the last decade haphazardly, until shutting down for good some three years before we came along.

Marion and I were on our way home from a poisonous weekend at Tupper, where we'd gone to cross-country ski. A freak February heat wave drove the mercury to 53, accompanied by rains that turned the trails into something like a piña colada, marooning us in the lodge with our resentments. There was nothing to do but read and drink too much of the bad house wine, and early Sunday morning we left.

We drove south for miles without talking. Then, as though out of nowhere, Marion said, "It's this life of ours."

"Huh? Our life?"

"In the city. We've got to get out of the city."

This idea had the force of an epiphany. Yes, of course, the city was ruining our marriage, our lives. The mean, vicious, frantic, insidious, never-ending grind of it. We were into our thirties, and New York was wearing us down to the bone. Still, I'd never seriously considered leaving the city, only thought of it in fleeting moments of disgust, like when you are riding the subway on one of those June days when the air underground is like warm, smelly glue and the car is filled with sullen, miserable foreigners, and you think there must be something else—you know good and goddamn well there are lots of better places—but five minutes later you are standing on the corner of 59th Street and Fifth Avenue, by the park with the horse-drawn cabs lined up along the curb, and you think, God, this is *it*.

Anyway, as we drove away from Tupper, a plan rapidly took shape as though it had sprung full-blown with an independent life of its own. Marion was a partner in a catering service. I ran the foreign investment desk at one of the newer Wall Street firms and had plenty of confidence in my business abilities. We knew we could run an inn better than the one we'd just spent a miserable weekend at, and soon we were excitedly spouting ideas about it. As we motored southward, we passed any number of properties with

Realtors' signs planted along the slushy roadside. Finally we came upon Nine Gables. It was the only place we actually got out of the car to look at, and we tramped all around it before scribbling the Realtor's number on the road map.

Events rushed us forward after that as though some great force of nature, like a wave, were carrying us helplessly toward a strange destiny. We returned upstate the next weekend to inspect the inside of Nine Gables and some of the ninety acres that went with it. We made the purchase offer, put our West Side co-op up for sale, and broke the news to our circle of friends. April 20 we closed, and on the first of May we moved to the mountains, astonished and rather frightened to find ourselves so drastically transplanted.

That first year we worked like mad to transform the old derelict into a warm, cheerful inn. We were open for business in time for Christmas and operated very successfully through the winter sports season. Unfortunately, our marriage was not so easily rehabilitated. For months we'd been too preoccupied with hammers and paintbrushes to notice. Then the following spring, when we had a little breathing room, and the blackflies kept tourists out of the mountains, I realized with a certain shock that very little had actually changed between us.

Marion appeared quite content in her new life, above all busy. But late at night our bed was like a frontier between two small countries existing uneasily side by side, speaking two entirely different languages. When we made love, which was infrequent, it was quick and furious, like a border brawl. It was passion without tenderness. I despaired silently, afraid to bring the subject out into the open, for now we were more than husband and wife, we were business partners, and I was afraid that we had made a terrible mistake. Then, in late June, Hazel Brett appeared.

She arrived the first afternoon of true summery heat—which was killing off the last blackflies. She was a petite, golden girl, around thirty, with buttery hair and an excellent figure, dressed in baggy khaki shorts and a plain white cotton blouse. She wore nail polish but nothing on her lips, which were a natural, very subtle, and handsome shade of pink. I had the distinct impression that she belonged in a different era, the 1940s. She had turned up without a reservation, but that was all right because it was just before the busy season. I offered to help get the rest of her baggage from her car, but she said she had no car.

"How'd you get here?"

"Train."

There was only one train that I knew of that still ran into the Adirondacks and this was a special excursion out of Schenectady for railroad buffs. The only place it stopped was North Creek, where it reversed direction for the return trip, and it ran only on weekends. This was a Monday.

"How did you get over from the station?"

"Taxi," she said with a sunny smile.

"How long will you be staying?"

"I don't know," she said.

Back in New York you could see dozens of gorgeous women just walking to lunch. But I'd been away from the city for more than a year now, and so the anxiety of being faced by such a stunning creature prompted a number of strange reactions in me. I

tried to act as businesslike as possible, as though I
didn't notice how attractive she was. On the other
hand, I didn't want her to think I was blind, or a
fairy, so I volunteered as how Marion and I had just
acquired the old place and fixed it all up—so she'd
know I was married. Ms. Brett took all this in with
apparent interest, but didn't ask any questions. Then,
on the stairway, carrying her single small suitcase, I
couldn't resist telling her that I'd been an investment
banker, so she'd know that I had done more substantial things in the world than tote people's luggage.

"My father was a banker too," she said in a voice
that rang musically. Her accent wasn't quite British,
but fancier than upper-crust American—something
like a stage accent. "I think he felt that it was a dreadful bore."

"It was," I said as we stood before the door to her
room. "I mean, it was for me." She wore a tantalizing
perfume. "Ah, here we are. Room Eleven."

"It's adorable," she said. "I'm sure I shall be very
happy here."

"Supper is at seven. Casual dress. Well, 'bye now."

The food was Marion's domain. Always an excellent cook, she seemed to have thrown herself into a
creative frenzy since we'd opened up Nine Gables, really going all out even when we ran at low occu-
pancy. Her obsession with cooking grew in an inverse
ratio to our declining love life. Acutely sensitive
about whether the guests were pleased or not, she hid
out in the kitchen during meals, leaving me to preside
in what we called the Public Room. There was a small
bar, two long tables and several smaller round ones.
Meals were served buffet style.

To my disappointment, though, Ms. Brett did not

come down to supper. Afterward I took a tray up to her room and knocked. She came to the door wearing a flannel robe.

"I thought you might have slept through suppertime."

"How sweet of you," she said, taking the tray from me. "I was so awfully tired. It's very restful here."

"This is veal."

"How lovely."

"In a Chinese sauce. My, uh, wife likes to experiment."

She just stood there holding the tray, listening attentively as I babbled on. I yearned to come in and sit with her, to watch her eat, but the idea was absurd. Instead I blurted, "I'd be happy to show you the Pinnacle Hill trail tomorrow. It's a sort of nature walk we blazed through the woods."

"That would be very nice."

"Say eleven o'clock?"

"Fine."

Ms. Brett did not come down to breakfast either. But promptly at eleven she appeared in the front parlor, where the desk is. I ducked into the kitchen to tell Marion I was taking some guests on a hike (partial lie), and then we set out. Our little trail led two miles through the woods and then up the aforesaid promontory, a hill with a good view of Schroon Lake and Vanderwacker Mountain. I pointed out the various trees, mushrooms, and wildflowers along the way, increasingly unable to take my eyes off Ms. Brett. She, too, had a rapt way of paying attention to every word I uttered. It was both complimentary and very alluring. I grew more intoxicated by her with each step we took away from the inn.

We reached the top of the hill about one o'clock. I took a wool plaid throw blanket out of my day pack and spread it on the flattest patch of rock. I'd packed some lunch: a hunk of cheese, some pears, and a half loaf of the fine crusty bread Marion baked with such dedication each night. Also a bottle of California red. Ms. Brett reclined as though it were the most natural thing in the world, propping her head on an elbow.

"What brings you up to these mountains?" I couldn't help asking.

"I was hoping to meet a handsome, clean-living, hardworking man," she said with a wry smile, which I took to denote she was ribbing. "An ex-banker. Someone like yourself, Mr. Otis."

"Call me Carey. May I call you Hazel?"

"Yes. Let's be reckless."

Her smile faded. She gazed at me now with a look that sent alternating waves of fire and ice down my spine and yet that drew me helplessly closer to her until it seemed that her intentions were unmistakable: She wanted to be kissed. The lunch was never eaten, the wine bottle never opened. Physically, she revealed herself as completely as a secret shouted in a meadow. But when it was time to go, I knew nothing more about her life or who she really was. "We must be careful," I said on the way back, as though to reassure myself. "Very, very careful."

A week passed, then another, and Hazel Brett remained with us at Nine Gables. Some days she left early in the morning, alone, and returned in the afternoon, going where I had no idea. She was "a solitary sojourner," she said. She did not once come to the Public Room for breakfast or supper. And though she never requested it, I brought her a tray each night.

She ate like a bird. I would watch her pick at a few morsels, and then the two of us would be hungrily upon each other, while down below Marion got things set up for the next morning's breakfast in her maniacal, obsessive way.

Of Hazel Brett's personal life, I learned precious little more except that she had gone to California to be an actress—a *screen* actress, as she put it—and that she had returned to the East in deep disappointment. I supposed that Nine Gables was a place of exile for her, a place to examine her aspirations, salve her ego, and quietly plan her future. I liked to think that I was respecting her privacy by not pushing for more information. But the truth was I didn't want her to have any existence beyond the present life she shared with me. And though the arrangement was making me a nervous wreck, I could not face the prospect of her eventual, inevitable departure.

That Marion might find out about us both terrified and exhilarated me. But through some odd combination of circumstances, the two of them never so much as crossed paths in the hallway. Then, one day after she'd squared away the breakfast things, Marion was out at the desk leafing through the registration book. The desk was *my* domain.

"What are you doing?" I asked.

"Just looking," she said, taken aback. "D'you mind?"

"No. Of course not. Sorry."

"Who is this Hazel Brett, anyway? I don't believe I've laid eyes on the woman."

"She's middle-aged. Fat. Divorced," I dissembled wildly. "Came up here to have a nervous breakdown. Ha ha."

Marion gaped at me. "Well, I hope she's not bother-ing the other guests."

"No, no, no." I tried to keep joking. "It's a very *quiet* breakdown."

We went on another week, another week of stolen passion, mystery, and trepidation. Then one morning I blew a radiator hose while driving back from the hardware store in Warrensburg. By the time I re-turned, it was after three o'clock. Now, in mid-July, we were entering the peak of the summer season. Marion, in her cooking apron, was foraging through the registration book again.

"What's this all about, Carey?" she said irritably. "This Hazel Brett hasn't paid a dime since she ar-rived."

"An oversight," I said lamely.

Marion must have been in exceptionally foul and turbulent spirits. Maybe a cake she was baking fell that morning. Who knows. In any event, without even discussing the matter further with me, she charged upstairs to Room Eleven. I followed, natu-rally. She knocked on the door several times.

"Ms. Brett walks a lot," I said. "By herself."

This hardly discouraged Marion. She threw open the door and marched right into the room. It was spotless. Our two chambermaids, local girls, were good, but from the looks of it you wouldn't have thought the room was even occupied. Marion stalked over to the closet and opened it. Inside was nothing but a white blouse.

"I think this Ms. Brett has cut out and stiffed us," Marion said, bracing her hands on her ample hips. "I wish you'd pay more attention to things around here." She jerked the blouse from the closet and all but flung it at me. It was still full of her perfume. "Give this to Dawn," Marion snarled, meaning the slimmer of our two cleaning girls.

I was heartsick—no, devastated. It was a busy Friday, with waves of new arrivals, seven couples in all, but the petty details of checking them in did not deflect the blow of losing Hazel so unexpectedly. In bed that night Marion said, "You're miserable."

"I have good days."

"This wasn't one of them."

"No. You?"

"I'm too busy to be miserable. If I stopped what I was doing in the kitchen for five minutes, I might discover how I feel. I'm happy with my pots and pans."

"I envy you."

I felt the bed shake and thought she was chuckling, but when I turned to look, I saw tears fall in a damp trail down the side of Marion's face into the wilderness of her brown hair, and I realized we were both lost.

A week later, just as I was about to repair to the Public Room to mix cocktails for the dinner crowd, a woman appeared in front of the desk as soundlessly as if she'd been deposited there by a breeze. She looked to be in her mid thirties, auburn-haired, with the broad shoulders of an athlete, dressed in pleated whipcord slacks and a checked shirt of the type that would have been considered country casual wear in my mother's day. She carried only one suitcase and said she'd taken a taxi from the airport in Placid. Though she didn't look anything like Hazel Brett, she possessed a similar inner glow, a radiance as enchanting as a summer night in the mountains. She registered under the name of Helen Denning.

"You're a ghost," I whispered as she dotted the *i* in her name.

She laughed in a beguiling way that suggested something more than sheer amusement. Then she placed a warm palm against my cheek. "Do I feel like one?" she said.

"I wouldn't know," I said, trying to hide the tumultuous emotions that churned inside me. Then I showed her up to Room Eleven, which seemed to please her.

The next day I drove to the library in Warrensburg and searched through volumes of reference books until I came upon an entry in the *American Biographical Dictionary:*

Helen S(impson) Denning. Professional golfer. 1912–1978. Wife of Great Lakes shipping millionaire Miles Denning. Divorced, 1942. Although among the leading players of the 1930s, Helen Denning won only a single major tournament in her professional career, the Women's P. G. A. 1936.

In time, Helen proved to be an adequate replacement for Hazel Brett. She had a sense of humor much like my own and seemed to enjoy referring to what subsequently went on between us as "our strange predicament." That I had gone quietly crazy seemed a stark possibility, and yet an acceptable one, because I was happy. At the same time it did not escape me that all this was terribly unfair to Marion, who returned to our loveless bed in exhaustion each night after her long day of culinary heroics. I came to admire her tremendously, though I no longer felt any desire for her.

Hence, it was a pleasing surprise to come in from a day of stacking cordwood in October to find Marion at the desk registering a tall, dapper, cheerful man in tweeds, with a wide snapbrim hat boyishly pushed back on his head. He had a neatly trimmed mustache and wielded a briar pipe with a curved stem as he spoke animatedly of his love for the rugged mountain life. His speech had the archaic innocence of a less jaded era, and the aroma of his tobacco powerfully evoked times past, as only smells can. Marion appeared mesmerized by him. I glanced at the book. The name Rex Alvord was unknown to me then, but since that afternoon I've seen most of the dozen-odd movies he made for Warner Bros. between 1936 and 1942, when his ship was sent to the bottom of the South Atlantic by a German torpedo.

Now Marion and I have rooms of our own. Our existence at Nine Gables could not be more satisfactory. I would go so far as to call it perfect. The guests come and go, and we have our favorites. Sometimes on quiet winter afternoons, when an icy stillness grips Nine Gables, I notice the clock ticking away what we prosaically call the moments of our lives, and my heart floods with gratitude for a world so generous, so tender, and so full of mystery.

The Last Cowboy Song

Charles L. Grant

I saw her first in the fog. She wore a long pale dress the moon washed of its color, and her hair, never very long, played games with a breeze hiding in the apple tree by the garage. I was washing the dishes, not an easy thing for me these days, and I'm afraid I dropped a tumbler into the sink. The sound of its breaking made me put a startled hand to my chest; the sight of her out there, a wisp among wisps, made me lean against the sink so hard I could feel the sharp edge of my buckle.

I looked down, sure I'd cut myself on the glass, and when I looked up again, through the window cluttered with sun catchers, the fog had risen. And she was gone.

"You're dreaming awake, old son," I told myself. I stared. "Dreaming."

And that night I had a dream that woke me at dawn, old tears on an old face, and an old obstruction in my throat that no amount of coughing could clear.

I dressed as quickly as I could then—pants that are

never snug enough, shirt that never quite hangs right from my shoulders, socks that fall and shoes whose laces have more knots than my fingers on rainy days. I ate quickly too, and after scrabbling through my closet for a coat that wouldn't mark my age so clearly to those who watched me, I locked the back door and hurried down to the park.

Kory Finn was there, and Marv Laibor, and over by the grass oval near the Civil War monument, Ollie Paise had already staked out his place near the statue's pedestal, a large brown bag of seed in his hands. Waiting for the pigeons. He always waited for the pigeons. Every day. And none of us ever told him the pigeons were gone.

"You look like hell, Will," Kory said as I sat beside him and stretched out my legs.

"Not a good night."

Marv snorted. "When's the last time you had a good one, Will? You can't remember, that's when. It's the curse. Damn. It's the curse." He flattened his black bow tie with a palm, brushed off his lapels, and crossed his spindly legs at the knees. His shoes were black patent leather. He polished them every night. Just as he brushed the tuxedo jacket he wore in the sun. He doesn't dance anymore. None of us, now, know the words to his music.

Kory looked at him with a smile that would have terrified a baby. "Sing, Marv, or shut up."

"Too early."

"Then shut up."

Marv huffed and took out his comb. Stared at it. Put it away. He'd forgotten what it was like to use it and feel the pull and the sweep and the patting in place.

"I think I need some help," I said, ten minutes later when the first of the day's pedestrians wandered by.

"Bah," said Kory. "The day you need help is the day I hang it up, go live in a shack by the tracks."

I smiled. "You have a house bought and paid for. Why would you live in a shack?"

"Sympathy," he answered. "You can't get sympathy at our age if you're not dirt poor." His mustache was a ghost twenty years white, his eyes too dark. He never wore anything but a moth-ravaged cardigan over a white shirt. When it got too cold, he stayed home. The only coat he owns he's saving for his funeral. "You should talk, by the way."

"I do, or so you tell me."

"Constantly." He lit a cigarette.

Ollie scattered some seed and whistled softly.

"She was in the yard," I said at last, scratching at my neck until my fingers felt the skin pull away. My hand dropped into my lap. I didn't look at it. It wasn't mine.

Kory turned toward me, right arm propped against the back of the bench. "You're kidding."

"Saw her clear as day."

"At night?"

"Full moon."

"Loonies," said Marv. "Full moon means loonies."

"I'm not crazy."

"Just old," Kory said.

"Younger than you." I nodded. Younger by five days. It makes a difference.

"What are you going to do about it?"

"I don't know. She scared the hell out of me, that much I can tell you."

"She always scared me too."

I laughed. Kathryn scared everyone. She always had. Never one to hide her mind, never worried what others would think. They called her nuts and rude and vicious and uncaring, and those who didn't love her never bothered to return. She always told me that the first minute she laid eyes on me she knew we were meant for each other. I took that to mean that I didn't know it but I didn't have a chance; she agreed. But when I tried to tell her that I had felt the same, that day in the lobby of the hotel in Denver, she only laughed and hugged me and called me an old fool who'd say anything to keep from being tickled to death. That was true. But so was the other.

Marv took out a pitch pipe and blew on it. One note. He hummed. It was perfect.

I almost ran then. I felt myself tensing to get off the bench and charge as fast as I could through the park. I have no idea where I would have gone, but I wouldn't have been here.

Then Kory put a hand on my arm, leaned close, and whispered, "Don't worry. He's only warming up. It always takes him a couple of days to warm up."

"Does not," Marv said. "I can sing anytime I want to."

"Then sing, you old crock."

"Don't want to."

"Then shut up."

Ollie spread another handful of seed.

And that night I ate in the luncheonette on the corner.

I do that sometimes. I'm not a great cook, my food usually tastes like the cardboard it comes in, and so once in a while I give myself a treat. The waitress knows me, calls me by name, even flirts with me now and then until her boyfriend comes by. I don't think he likes me every much. He gives me the look that says, "Act your age, Pop, and stay in the corner." I always smile then because it makes him mad and makes him feel guilty.

She wasn't working that night.

Kathryn was.

I spotted her reflection in the mirror over the counter, and when I turned, she was standing by the rear booth, taking someone's order. She knew I was looking. She always could tell. Her hand would take up a strand or two of hair and twirl it a bit, pull it over her cheek, let it go. A second time. Then there'd be a sideways glance, a twitch at the corner of her mouth, and a slight cock of her hip.

She did it all now.

I turned away and finished my coffee, dropped two bills on the table, and walked out. I didn't want to see her, not while she was working, and not while my heart was trying to decide which way to run. By the time I reached my front porch, I was sweating; by the time I had the key in the lock, I was shivering; by the time I was inside and flopped on the couch, my mouth was so dry I couldn't swallow.

I fell asleep there.

I woke there.

I heard her in the kitchen, slapping the toaster because it never worked until she hit it.

Though it was early October, the sun was hot on my back, and I concentrated on it, feeling it bake through my coat, through my shirt, through my skin. Then I concentrated on my left leg, which had fallen asleep. I reached down and massaged it, wincing at the needles that seemed not to stay down there but move up across my chest and into my eyes. Finally I stood and took off the coat, dropped it on the floor as I crept-walked into the hall and looked down to the right.

The kitchen was empty.

But I could smell burnt toast.

"Awake or not, you're still dreaming," I said to fill the house, reclaim it, and went upstairs to take a shower. My back ached, I smelled like a racehorse, and I needed the thunder to keep me from thinking.

It came anyway: You're crazy, Hawking, you've finally gone crazy after all these years.

"But you're not," Kory insisted when I told him that afternoon. "Christ, you live alone like that, you idiot, you're bound to start seeing things."

I reminded him that I've been alone for nearly a decade.

"That's only because you're too damned stubborn to go crazy sooner. Like Ollie." He punched my arm as we strolled along the main street, checking the prices in the windows and complaining, just like old men. "At least you don't wear them damned boots anymore."

I looked down at my shoes. "No, I guess not."

"Can't pull them on, right?"

"Well, yeah, they do tend to get a little stiff these days," I admitted.

He punched me again. "Tex Ritter rides again." He laughed, blew a kiss to a little girl hiding and giggling behind her mother, and pulled me into the bookstore. "Let's see if they have any porn."

They didn't. The clerk looked shocked, and glared at me as if it were my fault. The price of notoriety, I guess. When I had the energy, I made a lot of pretty loud noises in this town—about freedoms, big government, the individual, things like that. Young man stuff. Easy to say when you don't think you're old enough to die.

We stopped at the church for a moment, waiting for a wedding to clear the pavement. Rice all over the place. The minister standing at the entrance. A limousine with tin cans tied to the rear bumper just pulling away from the curb. A large woman in pink cried on the shoulder of a tall, red-faced man. He was holding his breath. I knew he was. I had done it myself when my daughter was married, and I did it again when she never made her first anniversary.

"Will, let's—" Kory stopped.

I frowned, suddenly worried. He sounded as if he were going to pass out, and I was too thin to hold him, to keep him from falling.

"Kory?"

He grabbed my arm tightly, squinting up at the church steps, trembling.

I looked, saw the minister in white, saw Kathryn in a white suit, holding a bouquet of violets, tilting her head so she could listen to what he was saying.

Kory dragged me through the guests still waiting on the sidewalk, not to the steps but to the corner and around it. Almost running. I was breathing so hard I found myself putting my feet in time. I protested loudly, tried to stop him, and finally at least slowed him a block later.

He dropped his hand and looked at me. "I don't get it."

"Tell me about it."

He yanked a handkerchief from his hip pocket and mopped his face several times. He looked at it. He looked at me. "You talk too much, that's all. If you were in love with Marilyn Monroe, I'd see her too."

I nudged him into motion again, toward the park. "Kory," I said, "I haven't said her name in almost five years."

He nodded, but not at what I said. "We'll talk to Ollie. He'll know what to do."

"What? Ollie's crazy!"

He looked at me. "And we're not?"

We didn't talk to Ollie, and Marv wasn't there. By five o'clock it was dusk and I was tired of listening to Kory babble about psychic phenomena and walking dreams and senile dementia and the contents of every doctor's office medical magazine he'd read in the last twenty years. I left him alone, sitting under a park lamp, staring at his hands and watching them knit themselves into a nightmare.

The kitchen smelled of macaroni and cheese casserole.

Enough, I thought, is enough.

I walked in and said, "Kory has decided we have to put ourselves in a home."

Kathryn, apron about her waist, hair tied back in a bun, looked up from the stove and said, "He's nuts."

I laughed. "So am I."

"Yes, but I don't love him, I love you."

I ate well that night, slept well, and spent the next week dragging old clothes out of old closets, tossing some in bags for charities, piling others for the dry cleaners. I vacuumed, dusted, polished, washed the windows, washed the car I used once a week to drive to the doctor's office. Kory called once, to see how I was, did I have a heart attack or what, and sounded terrified when I told him what I was doing; Ollie called to tell me about the pigeon he'd seen the day before, a beautiful brown and white one; and Marv called on Friday, to tell me that he was ready to sing the next day, if I was interested.

I wasn't.

I was.

Kathryn stood in the bedroom doorway while I dressed, her arms loose across her chest, a cockeyed grin on her lips. "Surely you're not going to wear that stuff, Will."

I looked up at her. God, she was beautiful.

"I have to, Kat."

I zipped up the jeans, buttoned the warm plaid shirt, and sat on the edge of the bed and held a black boot in my hands. My feet in their socks were scrawny. Chicken claws. Ankles narrow enough to cause envy in a Victorian maiden. I didn't think I could do it; I thought I'd fall, break a hip, a rib, and die without knowing how the sun looked again.

I tugged one on.

The other one came easy.

Then I took a deep breath and stood.

And, oh, God, I felt tall. My stomach was flat again, my chest not so concave, and the heels on the hardwood floor were drumbeats that warned the villains Will Hawking was back in town. I deliberately avoided passing a mirror; foolish I may have looked, but I felt, for the first time in years, as if I were something more than a man whose years had been stored in a trunk.

In the spare room was a chest of drawers in which I kept all those things I had that I had no one to give to, those worn and useless mementos of a time when there were people who cared, and people who visited, and people who remembered that I hated being called Willy. In the middle drawer was a belt, a brown leather belt I'd bought in Georgia on a business trip, but I didn't care about that—it was the buckle. A winged eagle Kathryn had given me for our first anniversary. Or a birthday. Or Christmas. It didn't matter when; what mattered was that it was.

I threaded the belt through its loops.

I polished the eagle with my palm.

Then I went downstairs and into the kitchen.

She was in the backyard. By the apple tree. Where I had buried our rings after I had buried her.

I stood in the doorway and turned slowly around, grinning like an idiot, hands on my hips, a mock scowl on my face.

"This town," I said, "is too big for the both of us."

"Then come with me, Will," she said, "where we can both clean up the bad guys."

I tipped a ghost hat to her, and made myself something to eat. For some reason I was hungrier than I could remember, and it was more than an hour before I left the house and walked through the October afternoon to the park. The leaves had changed, the neighborhood smelled of woodsmoke, and the edge to the air for the first time in years didn't make me wish for a seat by the furnace.

Ollie was whistling when I sat on the bench. Seed in one hand. Seed on the ground at his feet.

Kory stood behind the bench, frowning. "This is stupid," he said. He was furious. "This is the damnedest thing I've ever heard of."

Marv stood in the middle of the path, a small crowd already gathering. They always did when he sang. His voice belonged to a man who had scores left, not months, and when he finished, he never passed a hat. The applause was genuine, the smiles and the tears unfeigned, and the cries for more were always met with a shy smile that told them, "Next time, maybe next time."

He looked at me. "You got your boots on."

"Break your goddamn neck," Kory muttered.

A young couple in jeans and shirts like mine glanced over and were puzzled. A quartet of tellers from the bank passed a Styrofoam cup of coffee around, clearly impatient, clearly anxious. Some kids from the grade school. Word got around when Marvin stood up in his tuxedo.

And just as they were about to get restless, to think about going back to work or to their shopping, he sang, nodding to himself, one shoe tapping to give him the time, eyes closed though you could see them moving if you looked hard enough. I don't know which songs he performed for the first fifteen minutes, but I did know that he got a couple of laughs, a lot of applause, and a few friendly whistles when he started singing about ranches and mountains and home on the range where there weren't any trucks and there wasn't any smog and a man could show a woman how the stars really looked when there was no light to blind them.

I didn't move.

I was cold.

For the first time since I've known him, I let myself know why he sang the way he did, and it scared me.

And more when he looked at me with that way he had, the one that said "Good-bye" and "So long" and "Jesus, I'll miss you" and said, "Will, this is for you 'cause you're my pal and you never laughed at me all these years."

"What is it?" I said, not knowing my voice.

He shrugged. "Don't know. I'll make it up. The last cowboy song I'll ever sing."

Colder, as the words pleased his listeners and stuck me like nails; colder, as a blond child began dancing; colder, as Kory put his hand on my shoulder, took it away, and when I looked, was lost under the trees whose leaves began to drift to the ground.

Colder, as I stood, not wanting to go.

Colder, as I walked out of the park, Marv singing behind me.

I don't know why, but instead of going home, I went first to the pet shop and bought a canary and asked them to send it to the house where Ollie lived.

Then I went to the church and stared at the steps and the carved doors and the spire and the announcement board and wondered what had happened to all the rice.

Only then did I head for home.

Come with me, she said as I stepped onto the porch.

I can't, I thought, turning the knob, walking inside.

A man knows his time, she whispered.

I touched the old clock in the hall, the old coat in the closet, the centerpiece of dried flowers on the old dining room table. "I can't," I told her then. "This is wrong, it's not time at all."

I whirled and raced into the kitchen, which smelled of old floor wax and linoleum and coffee grounds and burnt food on the stove and damp paint on the walls, and I said, "No."

Yes.

"Forget it, Kathryn. I'm crazy."

Yes, but it's time.

I laughed angrily. "The hell with that! Kory was right—"

Kory said good-bye.

"—this is stupid. I love you, you know that, I always have. But I'm not ready and I'm not going anywhere."

"No," she said as she came through the fog and the song and the screaming, *but I am.*

I held her then, and I kissed her, and I told her again how much I loved her, how much I loved her still, but when I asked her who'd be left after me, she only put her head on my shoulder.

And I knew the answer to that one too.

Oh, Lord, I love her.

But, oh, Lord, I'm so scared.

The Ring of Truth

Thomas F. Monteleone

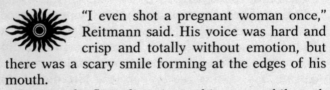 "I even shot a pregnant woman once," Reitmann said. His voice was hard and crisp and totally without emotion, but there was a scary smile forming at the edges of his mouth.

I sat on the floor, listening to his story, while rock music filled in the dead spots. My three roommates and I were all half drunk, but the wine did nothing to dispel the palpable sense of dread, the stench of a triumphant evil that pervaded the room.

The lights from our Christmas tree colored each of our faces in various hues of horror and revulsion, but nobody told Reitmann to stop—especially after he told us about the "Ring of Truth."

Denny Reitmann was one of those guys you meet in college and you just know he isn't going to be around for the commencement exercises. At least *I* knew it.

Ex-high school jock—but not the quarterback or shortstop type; Denny was your basic offensive guard or maybe a catcher. In high school he was the guy who could never get the experiments to come out right in chem lab, who was always clowning that he'd cut off his fingers in metal shop. He was the one who could eat fifteen hot dogs at the Spring Fever Fair, and cut the loudest farts during P.E.

And when a guy like Denny Reitmann went to college, it was only because there was nothing better to do at the time.

Then it seemed like all of a sudden there was a shitty little "military action" going on in Central America, but most people didn't care about places like El Salvador or Honduras or Nicaragua. The stock market was fluctuating as usual, interest rates were rising, and the import wars were getting pretty fierce. A lot of the second-level nations like Mexico and Brazil had stopped paying even the interest on their billions-plus loans to the United States, and a nasty recession was getting ready to take a bite out of the country's hind parts. As a result the poor minorities were being ground up in society's gears pretty good.

But if you were twenty years old, white, and going to a monstrous diploma factory like the University of Maryland, everything seemed to be just fine.

Denny Reitmann roomed in my dormitory on the College Park campus, and although you couldn't say that he was my friend or that I hung around with the guy, I guess I knew him as well as anybody did. He didn't seem to have any real close buddies. Oh, sure, everybody laughed at his crude jokes, and we all shook our heads when he would proudly announce his abysmal grades, but none of us was really tight with him.

It was like all the guys could sense Denny's true

"essence"—a kind of bleakness. A void where his feelings should have been is probably the best way to describe it. I mean, you could look into Reitmann's eyes and not be completely sure there was anything behind them.

It was right after Christmas vacation in my sophomore year, and everybody was piling back into their rooms to start boning up for the end-of-the-semester grind—the finals.

Everybody, that is, except Reitmann. He came back with the rest of us, but only to clean out his dresser drawers, desk, and closet.

"I'm packin' it in, you guys," he told anyone who would listen. "I figured it out, and even if I ace all my finals, I'm still gonna flunk out, so what the fuck, huh?"

I guess a few of us tried to talk him out of it in a half-assed kind of way, and some of the other guys took him down to the Rendezvous for a farewell drunk, but the overall reaction to Denny Reitmann's departure from academe's fair grove was a big ho hum.

Besides, there wasn't really much time to mourn the dead; those finals were always a bitch, right?

I made out all right with all of them, even Organic Chemistry—the only one that really had me sweating. I knew that without decent numbers in Organic, not even that semi-bogus med school in Grenada would let me through the door. Thus triumphant, when semester break finally arrived, I went off with my roommate, Bob, to ski in western Massachusetts at this great slope called Brody Mountain.

When we came back to the dorm to begin the spring semester, there was the usual joking and back-slapping and glad-handing. Everybody seemed keyed up for the start of the long haul into summer. So it wasn't until a bunch of us were getting ready to make the hike to the dining hall that somebody noticed the postcard tacked to the bulletin board by the door to the lounge. Postmarked at Fort Benning, Georgia, the card bore a short note, which read:

Hey Guys,
   I was getting board, so I joined the Marines. They shore do make things rough on us down here, but I think its going to be O.K. I like the rough stuff. Study hard and (smile) don't be like me.
                          Denny Reitmann

"Jeez," someone said. "The asshole joined the Marines, can you believe it?"

"With Reitmann, I'd believe anything," I said.

"I guess that's what happens when you get B-O-A-R-D," said my roommate, pulling the card off the corkboard and tossing it in the trash can.

Everybody had a quick laugh, and we piled out the door, on our way to get some overcooked vegetables and the day's Mystery-Meat Special. By the time we entered the dining hall, the conversation had become fixated upon the perfectly shaped ass of a blond girl standing several places ahead of us in the line. I don't think anybody gave Denny Reitmann another thought until he came back from a place everybody started calling "the 'Dor" . . .

. . . right before Christmas a year later. I was almost midway through my junior year. Bob and I had taken an apartment with two other guys from the dorm, and we were having a great time playing the sophisticated-young-man game.

A lot can happen in a year. I had discovered Mahler and Beethoven, French wines like Puligny-Montrachet and Cabernet, the irrefutable logic of Bertrand Russell, the lyrical essays of Loren Eiseley, and —well, I think you get the point. I was becoming enlightened and enriched and all that shit.

I was also becoming terrified of the El Salvador war.

They say that everything that goes around comes around, and goddamn if this wasn't the whole Vietnam mess all over again. The radio was daily talking about Sandinista body counts versus GI casualties— as if we were talking about sporting events instead of people killing each other. The network evening news looked like an old Sam Peckinpah film, and I kept thinking about how close we all were to being part of the horror show.

The horror show crept a little closer the day the apartment phone rang five or six times before anybody bothered to answer it.

"Hello," I said.

"Jack, is that you?"

"Yeah, who's this?"

"It's Reitmann! It's me, Jack. How ya doin', man?"

I did a mental double-take, realizing at last with whom I was speaking. *Reitmann,* for God's sake! Talk about the last guy I'd expect to hear from . . .

"Yeah, right . . . well, how are you, Denny? Where are you? What've you been doing?" I found myself saying the semi-automatic greetings, asking questions I didn't really care to have answered.

"I'm back on leave . . . from the 'Dor, man. They

were lettin' us finish up our hitch a little early 'cause-a Christmas—you know how that goes . . ."

"Yeah, right," I said, at a total loss as to what to say next. What the hell did he want, calling me? How did he find the number? And most important, why me?

"Listen, I'm at my mom's place, and it's gettin' kinda beat around here, and I was wonderin' if I could stop over for a little while, huh?"

"Jeez, Denny, I don't know . . . we're all getting ready to study for some exams."

"Your mom gave me the address," he said as though not hearing me. "And guess what? Your apartment's pretty close to my mom's, so it's no hassle, man. I'll see you around eight, okay?"

Before I could say anything, he'd hung up. I told Bob and Mike and Jay we were going to have company, and received a mixture of reactions. Of which, Mike's was the best: "Well, at least he can tell us some war stories . . ."

And he certainly did.

"A *pregnant* woman . . ." said Jay. "Christ, Denny . . . why?"

"Because she was a fuckin' beaner, that's why!" Reitmann's eyes were like tiny steel balls, like a rat's or maybe a raven's. "They all carry grenades, and shit, man, they all want to kill themselves an American. And besides, it was my job . . . I was a sniper."

"What do you mean?" I asked.

Mike passed me the Chianti bottle, and I poured another glass. I was already blitzed pretty good, and this last one was just icing. I had been amazed at how the Marines had changed Reitmann in such a short time. His playful, kind of dumb, but almost likable mannerisms had been sawed-off along all the edges, filed down until there was only a crude undercarriage left. And on that raw frame, the jar-heads had constructed their killing machine—a guy full of hate and poison and a belief that everybody in the world was ultimately out to get him. Reitmann looked at me as I exhaled.

"A sniper, man! Don't you know what a sniper is?" His voice had turned suddenly acidic, condescending.

"Yeah, I guess, but maybe you should clarify any misconceptions we might have."

Reitmann explained that snipers were specially trained "gyrenes" who spent upward of thirty days at a clip out in the jungle, alone, playing a crazy survivalist game, eating whatever they could find, and shooting whatever moved. After a month or so like that, they would report back to their base for a few days' R and R, and then back into the bush for more grub-eating and beaner-popping.

Denny smiled that half-crazy smile as he nodded. "Yeah. You see, we were special, my squad. You had to be special to be picked for the Black Aces platoon . . . that's what they called the snipers—the Black Aces."

"Why?" asked Bob.

Reitmann shrugged. "Don't know. They just did. My sergeant had these special decks of cards. I don't know where he got 'em, but it was a deck of nothin' but aces of spades, you know? And when we first got to Usulutan, he passed out a deck to each of us snipers."

"What for?" asked Jay.

Reitmann smiled, chuckled a bit. "That was the neat part, man. See, each time we zapped a beaner, we were supposed to leave one of them aces on 'em. It was like a sign that all the Sandies knew about—they all knew the snipers were real bad-asses, you know?"

"Kind of like a calling card," said Jay.

"Yeah, I guess." Reitmann was looking far off, as though reliving moments in the past. Again that weird smile was starting to form at the corners of his mouth. "I used to use their own knives or bayonets and stick my aces to their chests—ain't no way they'd miss it that way."

"I guess not," I said.

"Hey, they were scared shitless of the guys in my squad! Especially after my sergeant started the 'Ring of Truth.'" Denny Reitmann smiled and nodded to himself. There was a cold shine in his eyes that gave me a chill.

"The 'ring of truth'?" asked Jay. "What was that?"

"Check this out," said Denny, as he jumped limberly to his feet. His hand lifted his bulky sweater above his waist to reveal a brass ring attached to a leather harness. The harness slipped over his wide belt.

"Here it is," said Reitmann. The ring was perhaps four inches in diameter. It looked awkward and uncomfortable.

"I don't get it," I said. "What're you talking about?"

"We used 'em to carry our ears, man," said Denny. "That's how we earned early leave on our hitches."

"Your ears?" Bob started giggling. He was pretty drunk.

Reitmann looked at him with cold black eyes. "Yeah, man. You see, every time we sniped somebody, we'd cut off their right ear and put it on our ring. When we'd come back to base every thirty days or so, we'd turn in our ears and get credits toward an early out."

"Kinda like savings coupons," said Mike. He looked as repulsed as the rest of us, and had not been trying to be funny.

Reitmann grinned, then chuckled. "Yeah! Yeah, I never thought of it like that! Coupons . . . I like that." He paused, his ball-bearing eyes turreting about the room. "You see, with them ears, there wasn't any bullshit about how many beaners you plinked. Great system, huh?"

"Yeah, just great," I said, perhaps a little too sarcastically. Some things never changed, and I wasn't really surprised to hear the Marines were still using such incentive programs.

Reitmann's expression shifted as he glared at me. Teeth bared like fangs, jaw muscles taut, the flesh about his eyes all pinched inward.

"You don't like that, Jack?" he said tauntingly. "A little too strong for you, huh?"

Jay cleared his throat. "Let's face it, Denny . . . it's a little strong for anybody, don't you think?"

"Christ," said Mike. "How'd you keep them from rotting? Didn't they start to stink after a while?"

"Yeah, they stunk a little, but it wasn't as bad as you might think. After you been out in the bush for a couple weeks, everything smells like it's dead." Denny chuckled at this small jest. "But most of us used to carry a mess-canister of formaldehyde. I'd stick 'em in there for a couple days, then dry 'em out on a flat rock in the sun. After that they'd usually hold up till you got back to base anyway."

The conversation deteriorated from that point onward, and as the effects of the wine wore off, everybody had had about enough of Denny Reitmann. I think it was right when he told us that he planned to carry a .45-caliber automatic on his person for the rest of his life (so that he could "waste anybody who fucked with him") that I announced I had to get up for an eight o'clock class.

Everybody else picked up the suggestion, and suddenly Reitmann was being escorted to the door. He paused and looked at us for a moment, then he smiled.

"You buncha pussies think you got it good, don't you? Well, I'm tellin' you . . . your turn's gonna come. You'll see what it's like to finally be a man."

Mike grinned. "I don't think so, Denny. I told the board I was a fag."

We all laughed, and Denny appeared insulted, perhaps a bit angered. I didn't think it was a good idea to intimidate this poor asshole.

"You can laugh all you want, but just remember that it's men like me that's protectin' all the wimpies like you guys. That's why I'm goin' back . . ."

"What?" I said. I couldn't help myself. "Why?"

Denny's ball-bearing eyes gleamed. "'Cuz I got a score to settle with a couple more wetbacks . . . for the guys in my squad that didn't make it."

"Jeez, Denny, that's nuts," said Bob.

"Do you know what the Sandies do when they catch a sniper?"

Before any of us could answer, he continued:

"They always cut his dick off and stuff it in his mouth." Reitmann grinned crazily. "Yeah. That's the way I found two of my buddies."

Nobody spoke for a moment, and the silence grew quickly awkward, painful.

"Good night, Denny," I said. "Be careful. When you go back . . ."

He grinned that crazy grin for the last time that night and slapped my arm extremely hard. "You too, Jack . . . all of you. And who knows, when you guys get down there, I might be the guy waitin' to greet you when you get outta the chopper!"

"I wouldn't be surprised," said Jay.

And then we shut him out into the night, into the void where our thoughts never ventured. I can remember a great sense of relief passing over me, as though I'd been told a great plague had finally ended.

"That sucker's stone crazy," said Mike.

"I feel sorry for him," said Jay. "They've turned him into a monster."

"He's a fucking psychopath," I said. "I don't ever want to see the son-of-a-bitch again. He gives me the creeps. Did you look into his eyes?"

"Can you believe he's going back?" asked Bob.

"I hope he stays there," I said. "Him and his 'Ring of Truth' . . ."

Five years later people were still dying in Central America, and the newest President (God, how I loathed the man!) was trying to get the country out of the whole mess "honorably." It was a joke, but nobody was laughing.

Especially me.

The year I finished medical school, the draft lottery pulled my birthday up as number 9. Very, very bad. But I had already started my first year of residency at Johns Hopkins, specializing in laser microsurgery on the nerves and capillaries. Since this was a fairly new field, the Army decided that I could be very useful in saving severed, or partially severed, limbs.

And so even though I was drafted, they gave me a commission and, after boot camp, shipped me off to a V.A. hospital in Philadelphia for some experience before giving me a free ticket to the San Salvador Base Hospital and a chance to save a few GIs' extremities.

We had a ward in Philly for 'Dor vets who came back in such bad shape they'd never been able to leave. Para- and quadriplegics; the Johnny-got-his-gun basket cases; men with half their skulls and brains and faces blown away; guys with so many organs missing they had to stay forever hooked up to a series of artificial support machines; and the Section Eights, the Funny Farmers.

Of course, that's where I saw Denny Reitmann again.

It's funny, but I had almost been expecting it on an unconscious level. I had tried to forget about the night he showed us the brass ring on his belt, but I knew it would shamble through the back corridors of my memory forever.

Denny Reitmann and his Ring of Truth.

I knew, even back then, that both of them would be part of that psychic baggage I would always carry with me. And when I first entered the part of the hospital known as the "Permanent" Ward, walking down the rows of beds which contained every horror and abomination committed to human bodies you could ever imagine, I had an odd feeling pass through me. It was like those times when you can sense someone watching you, usually in a crowded public place, and you turn around and bang, there he or she is—caught, staring right at you. I experienced a kind of psychic preemptive strike as I accompanied Dr. Barahmi on his rounds. In an instant I *knew* that I would see Reitmann in one of the beds up ahead. It was an unshakable certainty, an absolute knowledge, and it caused my knees to go weak for just a moment.

Catching myself on the rail of the nearest bed, I paused and shook my head, as if to clear it. Please, I thought. Not Reitmann. Anybody but him.

But I found myself walking past the beds, scanning the faces of the doomed souls within them, actually searching for the familiar features I knew I was going to see.

"Jack!" Reitmann's voice was raspy. "Jack Marchetti!"

Turning to the right, I saw him waving his arms frantically. His complexion was pallid under the fluorescent light; his eyes, like single spheres of birdshot, were sunk into his skull. There was no impish grin about to appear at the corners of his mouth, there was no pinched sneer. His face was a design for panic and fear and despair. Reitmann looked hideous to me —a specter from a past I wanted to forget.

"Hello, Denny," I said softly, my voice shattering. I reached out and shook his hand.

"You know this man?" asked Dr. Barahmi.

I nodded, fighting a lump in my throat. I thought I might actually faint, or maybe heave my guts out.

Denny appeared anxious, as if there were a terrible fear inside just waiting to break free. He wouldn't let go of my hand. "You a doctor now, Jack? You come to get me out of here?"

I could only nod, then shake my head, confused.

Denny burst into tears as he tried to speak. "All you guys tried to forget about me . . . everybody wanted to forget about me . . . everybody but you, Jack. I knew you were different from the rest of them . . ."

I swallowed with difficulty. "I'm . . . I'm no different, Denny." I'm probably worse, I thought.

Dr. Barahmi patted my shoulder and backed away to give us a private moment. It was at that point that I noticed the absence under Denny's sheets. Picking up the covers, I could see that he had lost both limbs just below the knee. Denny suddenly stopped his crying.

"Mine," he said in a terrible, raspy whisper. "Got me on my third day back, the motherfucker . . ."

"You shouldn't have gone back. You'd made it, you were safe."

He shook his head. "None of us are ever safe, Marchetti. Not even guys like you."

There was something about the way Reitmann intoned that last sentence that made me recall his calling us pussies for dodging the draft any way we could. Ducking the pain and the horror had been a double-edged sword. A part of me was, of course, glad I hadn't been maimed or crippled, but there was another part of me that carried a shapeless guilt for not taking my chances like all the poor bastards in the ward that surrounded me. This was not a subject I liked to dwell upon or even think about, but there was something about Reitmann that was bringing it to the surface.

"You've been here since the last time I saw you?" I covered up the stumps of his legs, tried to look into his spooky eyes.

"That's the ticket, man. Right after New Year's my legs bought the farm, and they skied me outta there. Been here ever since."

"Why? You look like you could have prosthetics

with no problems. A little therapy and you could be walking all over the place."

He chuckled inappropriately. "Even with new legs, I couldn't get away from them . . ."

"What? Away from who?"

"So I figure why bother?"

"Denny, what're you talking about?"

He looked up at me and started laughing. "Didn't they tell you, Jack?" His throat filled with a hyenalike cackling, and he threw his head back against his pillow. "I'm as crazy as a shithouse rat!"

Dr. Barahmi appeared soundlessly by my side and tapped my shoulder. "I am sorry. You could not have possibly known. Come. Perhaps we should leave now."

Numb, I must have nodded my head and allowed the Chief Surgeon to guide me to the exit from the ward and out into the antiseptic nothingness of the central corridor. But even out there, I could hear the lunatic laughter of Denny Reitmann. As we entered the elevators, the cackling seemed to change into a windswept wailing, a preternatural banshee's scream. The sound echoed in my skull even as the doors closed and we began our descent. It was at that moment that I knew I must try to help Denny Reitmann.

Spending a few hours in the medical records library told me all there was to know about him. After stepping on the mine, he lost a lot of blood before the medics could get to him. After suffering from severe shock, he lapsed into a coma for almost a month. When he woke up on the hospital ship to find his legs gone, whatever was left of his mind—whatever part the Marine Corps had not already ravaged—caved in. For the better part of the next three years Denny exhibited all the symptoms of catatonia. Gradually he began to respond mimetically to the most routine stimuli, and, after a visit from a member of his sniper squad, he finally started showing signs of a possible recovery. He made an effort to locate the others in his squad, and this desire for contact was very helpful to Denny in regaining his verbal abilities. For the next two years the entries in his file were the expected kinds of progress notes on a recovering schizophrenic. His chemotherapy, originally high doses of Prolyxin, had been tempered over time to include the usual spectrum of antihallucinogenics like Haldol, Mellaril, and finally the old standby: Thorazine. He responded well in both group and individual therapy, and the notes on that period of his treatment were encouraging. Denny's prognosis changed from "guarded" to outright optimistic until . . . he learned that the other members of his squad were dying off, one at a time, but quickly and inexorably.

When Denny learned that the last cohort from his Black Aces squad had died, his condition deteriorated rapidly. His file noted increases in chlorpromazine therapy, his repeated mentions of "visions, voices, and sounds in the night." His hallucinations increased, and he became extremely paranoid and fearful of each coming night.

It all sounded rather typical to me, but not having had any psychiatric work since the survey stuff at med school, I figured the best thing to do would be to check with Denny's therapist, Dr. Michelle Jordan.

Her face was vaguely familiar to me when we met in her office. I guess I'd seen her in the halls or in the elevators, but, prior to finding Reitmann, I wouldn't have had much reason to talk to her. Dr. Jordan looked very good for a woman in her early forties, and she seemed pleased to see me take an interest in her patient. Which was fine with me. Some of the more insecure types feel very threatened when another doc tries to study one of their guinea pigs.

"To be honest with you," I said softly, "in my thoroughly unprofessional opinion, Denny didn't seem very crazy to me."

Jordan fired up a Winston. On her desk lay a huge ceramic ashtray from the occupational therapy shop (I recognized the mold) overflowing with butts. "No, he doesn't show any symptoms unless you get him on the subject of his squad."

"Are they all dead but him?"

She nodded, took a deep drag.

"How the hell did he find out?"

"Denny became a prolific letter hack. He had managed to keep in touch with each one—there were only eight of them, actually."

"And they're all dead. Seems pretty weird, don't you think?"

Jordan shrugged, dragged.

"You know how they all died?"

"A variety of things. A couple from diseases. The rest were accidental."

That struck me as very weird, very strange. "Foul play suspected in any of them?"

Dr. Jordan smiled. " 'Foul play,' doctor? Do you read a lot of English mystery novels?"

I smiled, maybe blushed a little. "What I meant was do you think any of them might have been killed? You know—murder?"

"You know, I've never really given it any thought. Why do you ask?"

I shrugged. "I don't know, really. What's he afraid of at night?"

"He won't tell me," said Dr. Jordan. "If I could find out, I could maybe help him work past it."

"Maybe he'll tell me," I said, getting up. The room was so rank from the cigarette smoke, I had to make tracks.

"They want this," said Denny as he reached into the drawer of his bed stand, fumbling around for something.

I had visited him just before nightfall and had closed off the bed's privacy curtains to suggest that we were more alone than we were. I hoped he might open up to me.

"Who's 'they,' Denny?"

Ignoring my question, he kept rooting around in the drawerful of junk until he found the object he was looking for. He held it up for me to see.

"This is it. You remember what it is, don't you, Jack?"

Even in the dim light the brass ring seemed to glow with an eerie warmth, a power. It was a talisman of evil, a magnet that could draw the darkness to it. I felt a tightening in my throat as I looked at the ring. My eyes felt as if they might start watering.

"Yes," I croaked. "I remember it."

Denny laughed, his eyes beading up like Timkin bearings and staring off into space. "It ain't really the ring they want, Jack . . . it's these . . ."

Denny gestured along the ring, and I knew immediately that he was seeing things I could not see. And I knew now who "they" must certainly be . . .

It was funny, but it was right at that moment that I

realized how wrong I had been about poor Reitmann. I thought back over how I had consigned him to humanity's trash heap, how I'd condemned him for being such a soulless bastard, for letting the jar-heads turn him into a fucking monster. But now, as I sat there watching him twitch and leer and squirm in his bed, I knew that the guilt was writhing and twisting through him like a swarm of maggots feasting on a fresh kill. It was eating him alive like a cancer, a leprosy of the soul.

Looking at Denny was like looking into a mirror. That's the way it is whenever we really take the time to look at anybody else, I guess.

"I'm the only one left," said Denny. "They got everybody but me."

"Why would they leave you till last?" I said almost in a whisper.

He chuckled, pointed at the flat sheets below his knees. "Because I'm the easiest . . . I'm not going anywhere."

It seemed as good an answer as any, and I nodded but said nothing. I couldn't think of anything to say. How do you tell a guy with grooves of terror etched permanently into his face that there's no such thing as the boogeyman? How do you explain that the embodiment of guilt can assume many shapes and guises? That we all create prisons of our own device?

No. That's all bullshit to somebody who's been standing on the edge of the pit, who's been hearing the demon cries and the flap of the leathery wings of madness.

"Help me, Jack . . ."

"What can I do?" I looked at him and for an instant he appeared to be a little boy, propped up on a fluffy pillow, waiting for a bedtime story. There was a simple pleading in his features, and for the first time a sadness in his eyes.

"Stay with me . . . when they come, if you're here, maybe it will help."

I looked out beyond the privacy curtain to the nearest window—a black rectangle where night tapped upon its pane. A tomblike quiet pervaded the ward, as though it waited collectively, expectant like a crowd at a public execution.

"Will you, Jack?"

"What?" I looked back and the little boy was gone. Denny was again the steel-eyed, twisted wretch. He was just a piece of litter tossed out the window while we all careened down hell's highway. My mind was wandering. I hoped I didn't appear to be ignoring him.

"I said will you stay with me, Jack?"

The thought of sitting by his bedside until he fell asleep should not have freaked me the way it did. My gut reaction was to say no and simply slip away into the night. Denny Reitmann was waiting for something, and I didn't want to hang around to find out what it was.

But I tapped his shoulder reassuringly and forced a smile to my face. "Sure, Denny. I'll stay."

Some of the anxiety seemed to go out of him after that. He smiled, closed his eyes, and nodded. I thought about giving him a shot to put him out for the night and get me off the hook, but I just couldn't do it to the guy.

In addition, there was a part of me that wanted to know what he was so damned afraid of. If he thought his victims were coming back to reclaim their ears, I wanted to be there to help him get through the trauma.

I owed him that, at least.

Crazy or twisted or whatever—Denny Reitmann had sacrificed his legs. I'd never even given up anything for Lent.

And so I sat there in the darkness watching him lie on his back, eyes closed, chest rising and falling. Starlight and the albedo of a half-moon spilled through the nearby window, giving everything a whitish-blue cast. The air was tinged with medicinal smells, such as ether and iodine, punctuated by the night rattles of labored breathing, of troubled sleepers coughing and rasping through their dreams.

I don't know how long I sat there, listening to night sounds, but at some point I must have slipped into a half sleep, because my neck jerked up, snapping back to reluctant consciousness. For a moment I didn't remember where I was, and the disorientation startled me. Responding to some atavistic stimulus, my heart began hammering, and I was instantly awake. I looked at my patient, who slept calmly.

Then suddenly he opened his eyes, wide-awake. It was weird the way he just came awake like that.

"What is it, Jack?" Reitmann's voice reached out in the darkness.

I looked at him, just as a draft of cold air passed over us.

"What do you mean, Denny?"

"Did you feel it, just then?"

I couldn't bullshit him. "The cold . . . ? Yeah, I felt it."

"They're comin', man. It's tonight. I can feel it."

His face had become drawn and pale, his eyes jittering around, blinking furiously.

"Take it easy, Denny. Why would they wait until now, after all this time? Why would they . . . do it . . . when *I'm* here? Don't you think that would be too much of a coincidence?" I tried to smile casually.

"Maybe they've been waitin' for *you*, Jack . . . maybe you owe them too?"

Reitmann's voice had a fragile edge on it, but his words still cut me. What the hell was he talking about?

"Listen!" Reitmann half-whispered.

"I'm sorry, Denny, but I don't—"

I stopped in midsentence. I *did* hear something: footsteps, bare feet, slapping on the cold tile of the outer corridor, growing louder, getting closer. There was no rhythm, no pattern to the sounds. A cacophony of uneven slaps and drags and shuffles.

"Aw, jeeziz . . . ! It's *them*, Jack! I know it is!" Denny screamed and his voice seemed to resonate through the ward, as though we were inside a vast cavern.

The sounds of advancing feet grew louder, thicker. Whoever it was shambling up the hall, they made up quite a crowd.

Standing up, I started away from the bed, and Reitmann reached out to grab my arm. His palm was cool, but slippery with sweat. "No, don't go!"

"Denny, I just—"

Looking out into the ward, I blinked my eyes, lost my voice.

The ward was gone.

A low, animal-like ground fog was boiling up like dry ice on a stage. All around us the fog rolled in like waves on a beach. The double row of beds had vanished. The walls, windows, bed tables, everything . . . was *gone.*

"What the hell?" There was a piece of me that desperately wanted to believe that this was one hell of a nightmare, that I'd better make myself wake up now because things were getting out of hand.

But there was no waking up from this one.

Denny must have seen them before I did because he started screaming, pulling himself out of the bed with his hands.

There was movement in the fog. Shapes coalesced slowly, like the ghosted images on a snowy television screen. The uneven cadence of their approach grew more distinct, and I could see the point men, the van, homing in on us.

Some of them were stick-figures, bone and tendon animated by the whirling, karmic forces that turn the gears of Eternity. Others, lean and brown-skinned, were more whole, but none of them had any ears. . . .

Reitmann had pulled himself up against the headboard of his bed, teetering on his stumps. The drawer to the bed table rattled open, and he thrashed around the contents frantically.

"I got it! I got it right here! I got it!" He repeated the words over and over like a litany, and without turning around, I knew what Reitmann was looking for.

There was no way to tell how many of them were there, but I saw women and children among the ranks of soldiers. Some of them were so far gone, though, that you couldn't tell male from female. . . .

Oddly enough, the initial jolt of panic left me when I realized that I couldn't run, that there was no place to hide. I accepted this and waited for whatever was to come.

The first wave of them reached the end of the bed, splitting their formation and swarming around both sides of it. I could smell their foulness, the corruption that steamed off them in acrid sheets. The air was thick with the sting of their hate, and I began to suffocate. They surged all around me, pressing me into the soft decay of their flesh.

Reitmann had descended into babbling madness. A pitiful wailing escaped him as they surrounded him, absorbing him into their mass as a cancer would devour a healthy cell. He threw the ring at them, and it disappeared in their midst. Reitmann continued to scream, but I could no longer see him. I was overcome by a paralysis that also had a calming effect on my mind. I watched everything with the detachment of an only mildly interested spectator.

Abruptly the screaming stopped, as though choked off. There was a finality about the silence that enveloped me as totally as the crush of putrid bodies. I could see their heads all turning, heads with new right ears. Slowly, silently, they turreted about until the eyed and eyeless alike were all looking at me . . .

. . . Orderlies found me the next morning, sagged in my bedside chair. Reitmann had died during the night, leaving us with a bug-eyed, lip-peeled expression engraved into his waxy face. One of the orderlies said Denny looked as if he'd opened the cellar door to hell, and I wanted to tell him how close to the truth he might have been.

But I remained silent, waiting for them to gurney his legless corpse off the ward. My memories of what had happened were painfully crisp, having none of the ragged edges of a nightmare. But I also had the feeling there was a segment of the whole experience still missing. Something else had taken place last night, I was certain, but I didn't remember until much later in the day, when evening crept up to windowsills on stalking-cat feet.

I was in the hospital cafeteria standing in line. Ahead of me were several medics—part of a class receiving emergency field surgical training—and as I stared at their uniforms, a vision passed through me like a wide, cold blade.

Like an epiphany, I had a flash of memory that filled in the dead space. I suddenly knew what I had so obviously repressed.

"Are you all right, doctor?" asked a nurse who had been standing behind me. Looking down, I saw the contents of my tray littering the floor. I felt as though I were emerging from a time fugue.

"I don't know . . ." I said, and staggered from the line, feeling the stares of others in the room as I turned in slow circles. I wanted to escape, but there was no place to run.

Then, remembering:

They had taken me to their battlefield. A vast, featureless plain where time melted and ran like lava, where light and shadow danced eternally at the limits of your peripheral vision. The ground was thick with their bodies. Stacked and jammed like endless cords of kindling wood, the arrangement of battle corpses stretched off to the dim horizon in all directions. But there lay some who still lived, who still twitched and shook in the depths of the charnel field, and it was for them that I had been brought. Down all the hours of the tunneled night, I pushed back entrails into ruptured bellies, pulled shrapnel from slivered torsos, sutured severed legs and arms . . . and ears. I washed myself in the equitable blood of revenge. There was no end to the carnage, no end to the tuneless song of their pain.

But it was not this knowledge that had so stunned me, as much as the certainty that they would be coming back for me—*tonight and every other night.*

For as long as the hate burned like the heart of a star.

Forever.

Eyes of the Swordmaker

Gordon Linzner

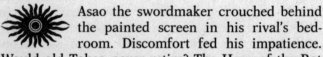 Asao the swordmaker crouched behind the painted screen in his rival's bedroom. Discomfort fed his impatience. Would old Takeo never retire? The Hour of the Rat was half fled, and Asao had stolen into the room well before midnight.

He shifted his leg to ease a muscle cramp. The unaccustomed weight of a *daito*, a long sword, kept pulling him off-balance. Black cotton draped him from head to toe, including a cloth that covered his face, except his eyes. The disguise had been inspired by rumors of the shogun's ninja agents. He wondered how the assassins breathed through these masks. Perhaps they'd never worked in Kyoto; the city's valley location made summers hot and sticky.

Surely the old craftsman was not still reading, by so vile a light as that cast by the vegetable-wax candle! Could he have fallen asleep without extinguishing it?

Asao dared not look around the screen to check, for fear of meeting Takeo's unearthly steel-gray eyes.

Ah! Those eyes!

Their unnatural color was attributed by some Kyotans to an unknown *gaijin* ancestor, a Hollander or Portugese gone astray before the country was closed to foreigners in the early seventeenth century. Others claimed it was a gift from Inari the rice god, protector of blacksmiths, the metallic color indicating Takeo's affinity for his trade. All agreed their gaze was unsettling, belonging to a world beyond that of Tokugawa Japan.

If Takeo turned those eyes his way, Asao could neither proceed nor explain his presence.

Rain pattered on the wooden rooftop, gusted across the outer veranda to splash the shutters. The *tsuyu*, the rainy season, had begun. Asao wriggled his toes in still-damp socks; his sandals were tied to his obi. He had chosen this night because the storm would obscure signs of his passage, and the drum of June rain would conceal his shallow breathing. Unfortunately, it also hid from his ears any sound of Takeo's activities.

The room went black.

Asao caught his breath, willed his leg not to tremble. He had to allow Takeo time to fall asleep.

Asao bore no personal ill will toward the elder swordmaker. He did not like the fellow, but neither did anyone else in Kyoto. Takeo was a glum little man who took little pleasure in his status as Kyoto's —and therefore Japan's—greatest living swordmaker. Edo might have been the seat of power of the Tokugawa Shogunate for the past two centuries, but thousand-year-old Kyoto was the cultural center, and home to the emperor.

Indeed, Takeo often spoke of his skill as a curse. He

was wary of his customers and hostile to his colleagues.

Asao counted himself the opposite, always ready to exchange a cup of sake and a bawdy tale, despite several reverses in the past year. His wife had drowned in a boating accident on Lake Biwa just that spring. Their only child moved to her new husband's village on the Kanto Plain. Dowry and funeral expenses had devoured the bulk of his savings. He'd had to dismiss all the servants except old, ill-tempered Morie.

Takeo's famed skill made it impossible for Asao to recover. Those warriors who could afford the younger man's prices preferred to wait on Takeo's list for the best. Asao's most able apprentice, disappointed by the lack of work, successfully petitioned for a release from his contract, leaving only the unpromising Wasabe to assist on those few commissions that came his way.

Asao was not the only *kaji* in Kyoto to feel the pinch. Without Takeo, there would be more work for all in the swordmakers' quarter, from even the fussiest samurai. Asao was the most desperate of them, though, and had the least to lose.

A harsh snore cut through the thrumming rain. Takeo's. Time to act.

Asao's palm felt slick against the *tsuka*—the hilt so newly fashioned that the wood was not even wrapped with ray skin. He drew the weapon and eased from behind the screen.

The darkness was relieved by a dim veranda lantern just outside the partly shuttered window. Takeo lay on his back on sleeping mats in the center of the room, head braced on the wooden pillow, thick lips fluttering. His pale green kimono rose and fell with each breath.

How easily Asao could slit that temptingly exposed throat!

He scowled at the thought. Asao was no murderer. He came not to kill Takeo, only to blind him. Was that so bad? The older man took so little joy in his work, surely he would not miss it; just as surely, Takeo was already so rich that he did not need to work.

The man in black could take away Takeo's livelihood, but not his life.

Asao knelt beside the master swordsmith. He fumbled with the blade, searching for the grip that would give him the cleanest stroke, to inflict as little pain as possible. Never before had he wielded a sword; like Takeo, he'd only made them for others. This angle, perhaps . . . or maybe that one. . . .

How little he knew of the uses of his creations! Asao could hardly imagine how it would feel when the keen edge bit through living flesh. Perhaps he should leave and try again another night, when he'd thought things out more fully.

Gusting wind rattled the shutters, waking Takeo. His eyes stared up at the black-clad stranger with a calm fear, as if Asao were an expected, overdue, though unwelcome guest. Whatever the orbs' origins, their glint made a perfect target.

The blade fell.

Takeo cried out. Hands scrabbled at his blood-gouting face. Crimson splashed his green sleeping kimono.

Asao also shouted, horrified by his own act. The cloth muffled his voice.

Footsteps echoed in the interior passageway of the

house. In another moment the room would be crowded with servants and apprentices.

Asao slipped out onto the veranda and plunged into the storm, stockinged feet sliding in the mud, half-blind from his own tears. Rain melted his footprints, confounding his pursuers. It also washed the blood from the unsheathed sword.

But the heavy drops could not purge the evil deed from his heart.

"You promised my sword would be ready today!" blustered the samurai Yumata. His thick eyebrows writhed like caterpillars.

"And it was," Asao replied, dabbing at his forehead. Behind him, young Wasabe stoked the workshop fire. "Alas! At the last minute a flaw was found in the metal. The weapon would serve you well ninety-nine times out of a hundred, but that hundredth time . . ."

Asao had in fact buried the last shard an hour before Yumata came to claim it, after first scratching his signature from the tang. It pained him to destroy a fine piece of work, but he dared not sell a dishonored weapon.

What madness had made him use a commissioned weapon for his foul deed? How could he have imagined a warrior would not know if a blade had tasted blood? He'd taken a loss he could ill afford.

Yumata spat past Asao's shoulder, into the newly birthed flames. "Bah! I hired you out of need for haste, because that fool retainer lost my *daito*. Otherwise I'd have put my name on Takeo's waiting list."

"Lord Matsuyama's troops are still forming. Will one more week make such a difference? Wasabe and myself will work day and night—"

Yumata snorted. "Yes, yes, if it can't be helped. I'll practice with my *wakizashi* a little longer, though a medium-length sword is hardly the same thing. You may take your extra week."

"Thank you, Yumata-san."

"I could not get a Takeo sword now, in any case."

Asao wiped his lips. Putting on a cat show, feigning innocence, proved a greater strain than he'd thought. "Eh?"

"Haven't you heard? Some villain broke into the old man's home last night and put out his eyes."

"How dreadful! No, this one has spent the morning in prayer, purifying himself to reforge your sword. These burglars become bolder every day. May the magistrate capture the criminal soon!"

"Some question whether it *was* a burglar. The servants say nothing was taken." An eyebrow arched.

Asao wiped a hand on his thigh. "The thief must have been frightened off after stabbing Takeo. What other motive could there be?"

"What, indeed?" The samurai winked. "A stroke of luck for you, eh? I expect you'll receive some lucrative commissions in the next few weeks."

Asao gasped, perhaps too loud. "Indeed, fortune and misfortune are like twisted strands of rope. Every swordmaker in Kyoto will benefit, but none of my acquaintance would have wished for this."

"A fair answer." Yumata stroked his chin. "Lesser men may be less kind."

"Never fear. This one shall give your blade priority."

The samurai nodded. "I return in seven days. Do not fail me again, swordmaker. My medium sword bites deep enough."

The samurai Naketoshi approached on the following day, as the swordmaker took a break from the forge. Asao had slipped off his ceremonial garb and sat clad in only a loincloth. Perspiration glistened on his wiry body.

"My regrets, noble warrior," Asao began, wiping his brow. "This one cannot take on new work until my present task is completed. You might try—"

Naketoshi sniffed. "You mistake my intentions, swordmaker. I already own a most excellent weapon, one of Takeo's last." He patted the hilt at his side. The blade shook in its scabbard.

"Wasabe!" Asao called. "Tell Morie to bring tea for our guest."

"Another time, perhaps," the samurai replied. "There are other calls to make before sunset. I stopped to advise you that several of Takeo's customers, myself included, have collected almost a hundred ryo. We offer it in exchange for information leading to the identity of the thief who blinded him."

"Our swordmakers' guild has done likewise, though not to such impressive effect." Every smith contributed handsomely to defer suspicion from himself— but not so handsomely as to awaken it anew. Asao alone could be certain none of his neighbors had done the deed.

"What about you, smith? Did you hear anything unusual that night?"

Asao licked his lips. "Alas, this one dreamed soundly." Indeed, the incident now seemed as unreal as a dream.

"Pity. If you remember something, please communicate with any samurai."

"This one shall do so." The quivering scabbard engaged his eye. Naketoshi must have a nervous tic in his hip.

A strange compulsion overcame Asao.

"Excuse me, but this one has not seen a Takeo blade up close in many years. Would it be possible . . . ?"

Naketoshi frowned in reflex, then shrugged. He slipped the sheath from his sash and partially withdrew the sword to expose a hand's breadth of steel. To unsheath the entire blade, as if facing an enemy, would be rude.

"Beautiful," Asao whispered. "What kind of man would destroy the skill that fashioned this?" He reached forward hesitantly. "May this one presume . . . ?"

The samurai smiled indulgently. "Considering your profession, why not?"

Asao meant only to brush his fingers along the blunt edge, but, as he touched the metal, it seemed to leap and twist. The cutting edge slashed his palm.

"Careful!" Naketoshi cried.

Asao sucked at the wound. "My clumsiness entirely. Think nothing of it. This one thanks you for your kindness."

The samurai replaced his sword. "You'd better tend to that gash at once."

Asao nodded.

"Don't forget the hundred ryos, if you hear anything of Takeo's attacker."

"This one will remember." Asao watched the samurai depart, ignoring the crimson that dripped on his thigh. The blade again rattled its scabbard, as if in frustration, although scabbards were designed to fit tight. Naketoshi seemed not to notice.

The warriors might never discover Takeo's attacker, but the swords, Takeo's children, already knew him.

One week later Asao sat on his heels, sucking his metal-tipped bamboo pipe and contemplating the new sword with satisfaction. Never had he worked so quickly, and never, he felt, had he produced a finer blade. Perhaps the pressure of a short deadline brought out the best in him. It was not perfect—to create perfection was to challenge the gods—but it came as close as one dared.

Sandals scraped the dirt road outside his workshop. Asao smiled, anticipating Yumata's astonishment when he found the work completed half a day early. He turned slowly, savoring the moment.

The smile vanished. The sandals were only those of Wasabe, who shuffled forward with uncharacteristic somberness.

"What is it, lad? You were to fetch Yumata."

"News," the boy said. "The guild's again collecting for Takeo."

"Sweetening the pot? Surely a witness would have spoken up by now! I can't spare another copper."

"Not a larger reward, master. This is to pay for Takeo's memorial stone."

Asao wept with genuine grief to hear of Takeo's passing. Who could have guessed that a killing infection would take root in the ruined eye sockets, or that it could spread so quickly?

No Kyoto swordmaker worked the day of Takeo's funeral. Asao did not view the morning cremation, but he could not avoid the noonday ceremony on

Swordmakers' Hill, a cemetery reserved for the city's greatest smiths. He added his own silent prayer to that of the priest, as Takeo's ashes were placed beneath the memorial stone paid for by the guild.

Afterward Asao sat cross-legged on his veranda, overlooking the interior garden. He tempered his melancholy thoughts by sipping green tea as he contemplated the finely wrought miniature landscape, with its perfectly scaled mountains and streams. A thin, loose-fitting *yukata* kept him comfortable in the still, hot air of a summer afternoon. Ominous clouds gathered in the west. Few streaks of sunlight broke their cover to penetrate cool shadows now, as evening approached.

His gaze rested on a particularly smooth and pleasing stone, one he'd picked up years earlier on a pilgrimage to Mount Fuji. Large as a half fist, it held a place of honor in front of Asao's favorite resting spot, despite his gardener's claim that it spoiled the natural beauty he worked so hard to create.

A shiny steel-gray circle appeared in the center of the stone. It winked at him.

Asao leaned forward, blinking, his hands cold as ice. He would have stood and walked to the stone, but his legs would not unbend.

"Wasabe!"

The boy shuffled noisily along the veranda's wooden planks. "Yes, master?"

"The stone. The Fuji stone. See anything odd about it?"

The boy smiled nervously. Plainly, he was considering what answer would most please the swordmaker. "It is unusually handsome," he offered.

"I don't mean that, idiot! Any strange markings? Discolorations?"

"No, master. It is as pure as the day you brought it here."

"Fawning pup," Asao said with a sneer. "How would you know? You were still suckling your mother's breast then, if not inside her belly! Look again. I saw . . . a glimmer . . . on its surface."

"A trick of the fading light?" Wasabe offered hesitantly.

Asao mulled over this suggestion; the boy's eyes widened with surprise. "No," he decided at last. "This had definite shape: a spot of shining gray against the ebon stone."

"Gray, you say? Gray-green, perhaps?"

Asao shrugged.

Wasabe smiled. "Why, it must have been Old Baku raising his head. He rarely displays such energy; no wonder you did not recognize him."

"Hai! Of course. The tortoise."

"Shall I fetch him out for you?"

"No. That will be all."

"Yes, master. Oh. Morie wishes to know about dinner."

Asao sighed. "I'm not very hungry. I'll speak to her presently."

Wasabe bowed respectfully and exited through the sliding door at the end of the veranda. A moment later Asao got to his feet and followed. He paused at the panel for a last soothing look at his twilit garden.

Near his feet a curve of gray-green tortoise shell protruded from the veranda's edge. Asao's chill returned.

Not even as Young Baku could the reptile have moved so far, so quickly.

"Bean-curd soup and a single bowl of rice!" Morie complained, banging a pot against the charcoal brazier. "I might as well not cook at all!"

"Shh," Wasabe urged. "He can hear you."

"Don't think he hasn't heard worse, my boy. Weren't you fetching well water, or do I wash up in my own urine?"

In the adjoining room Asao idly poked in his cloudy miso soup for one of the slivers of fish Morie added to her recipe. His lips twisted in a rueful smile. Normally he enjoyed eavesdropping on the bickering between his cook-housekeeper and the young apprentice. Tonight the pair merely sounded pathetic.

His chopsticks found an object the size and shape of his thumb. What little appetite Asao had immediately fled.

With trembling fingers, Asao drew out the chopsticks. His grip failed at the first glimpse of steel-gray; the thing rolled, with a splash, back into the beige liquid. Moaning, Asao poured out the bowl's contents. The liquid seeped between wooden floor planks, leaving behind thin scraps of white fish meat and green seaweed.

"What's this?" Morie cried. "How am I to keep this place clean?"

"I did not call," Asao snapped.

"I heard a moan. I thought you were ill. I can brew licorice tea."

"Leave me alone!" Asao thrust his utensils into the bowl of rice.

"What *have* you done?"

The swordmaker fled to his own room and thence from the house. Morie was right to be distressed by the sight of chopsticks sticking up in the bowl of rice. That was how one offered rice to the dead.

Asao paused beside a paper street lantern at the foot of the Shichijo-dori bridge, which spanned the Kamo River. His knees quivered; his empty stomach churned acid. Perspiration soaked his thin *yukata,* to chill him as it dried in a quickening river breeze.

To calm himself, Asao concentrated on the water rushing beneath him and the songs of cicadas along the river's banks. Was it only two months since he'd stood here to admire the cherry blossoms?

Asao carried his pipe and pouch of high-quality Kokubu tobacco, brought north from Satsuma province on Kyoshu. The very thing for soothing abused nerves! He'd forgotten his firebox, but the street lantern could provide the flame.

A quick look around assured him he was alone; to foul the air in the vicinity of a warrior, who might want to test a new sword, was inadvisable. The foreign-born addiction claimed some samurai, but by no means all. Asao drew aside the badger netsuke that held the pouch strings shut, and began shaking fresh tobacco into the long-stemmed pipe's bowl.

His trembling hand spilled a miniature Fuji of expensive weed at his feet.

From the shallow bowl peered a steel-gray orb.

"You're so tense!" Omomo—Peach—observed as she massaged Asao's shoulders. "You've been working too hard."

"That might explain it," the swordmaker acknowledged without enthusiasm.

Asao had waited for more than an hour in the common room of the licensed brothel, after crossing the Kamo River to reach the Miyagawa-cho district. He'd had to sip sake he did not want, keeping his eyes closed lest they spy something nestled at the bottom of the cup. This had not helped his nerves.

Still, a *yujo*—woman of pleasure—of Omomo's quality was worth the wait, even though this was not a high-class geisha house such as the Gion or Pontocho. The acknowledged star of the establishment was an expert in the forty-eight positions, and knew such secrets as the use of dried sea slug rings to prolong an erection. Though he could ill afford the expense, Asao felt that only Omomo could drive tonight's horrors from his mind. The lower-class amateurs in their temporary shacks along the riverbank would not suffice.

"Have you any special request?" Omomo asked, her fingers digging lower.

"Well . . . there is that touching of mouths. . . ."

"Ah. *Seppun.*"

"A barbarian custom, I know, but . . ." His words were cut short as Omomo cupped his cheeks in cool hands and kissed him languorously.

"Now," she said, tugging loose his *yukata*, "lie down and let Omomo do the work. Does that feel good?"

Asao nodded, smiling.

"And that?"

Asao sighed.

"What a good boy you are! I see you won't need any charred newts, eels, or lotus root tonight."

"No," Asao agreed. Terror, it seemed, could be aphrodisiac enough.

Her orange silk kimono slid with a whisper to the polished floor. She wore no undergarment to spoil the garment's line. Balancing on the balls of her feet, Omomo knelt before Asao. Her thighs parted demurely. The pubic hair was carefully trimmed and plucked, a testament to Omomo's sexual skill.

Asao stared at the heavenly gate in anticipation.

It opened and stared back.

Well into the Hour of the Rat, Asao entered the cemetery in which Takeo's ashes were buried. A damp wind swooped down the hill, building swiftly to near storm pitch, tugging at his clothes. Loose sleeves flapped stingingly against his arms. The heavy aroma of fresh-turned soil filled his nostrils.

Asao had stopped at his workshop long enough to pick up a small oil lamp, but in this wind it would not stay lit; he set it down near the gate. It was no great trick to find the top of the hill, even on so dark and starless a night. It was no joy, either, but the swordmaker saw no alternative. He'd go mad if he had to be haunted the rest of his life by the man he'd killed.

A fat raindrop slapped at his cheek. The storm was about to break. As he looked up, clouds parted to allow a sliver of moonlight to touch the newly scarred ground around the grave marker he'd helped pay for, not fifty paces ahead.

A glowing blue mist began to congeal there.

Asao was expected.

As he'd feared.

Rain fell steadily now, turning the hillside to mud

as Asao trudged up it. The blue mist did not waver; if anything, it grew more solid. Asao stopped within ten paces. The mist clearly resembled Takeo from head to ankles, which floated in the air where a living person's feet would have been.

Two dark hollows in the haggard, translucent face fixed on Asao. A frozen expression betrayed nothing.

"You know me, Takeo," the swordmaker began. "Asao. I live down the road from where you, ah, used to, ah . . ."

The luminescent form nodded. Boneless fingers urged Asao to continue.

"I, ah, I was the man in black that night. I am your murderer." He laughed nervously. "Of course, you know that, or you wouldn't be haunting me."

Another nod.

"You have every right to wish me ill. Mine was an evil and unjustifiable act. Yet I swear by Inari that I never meant for you to die."

The figure shrugged.

"I know, intentions count for little against deeds. Still I dare come here to beg your forgiveness. Please tell me how I may atone."

The ghost shook its head.

Asao moaned in hopelessness. "Then slay me now and be avenged!"

A shiver passed through the form. Takeo's ghost turned his head, focusing eyeless orbs over his own shoulder. Asao followed his gaze reluctantly. His mouth filled with cotton.

Behind Takeo floated *another* eyeless ghost, of more transparent shape. This one's face turned toward still another shape, almost invisible in the rain-streaked night. This last also looked behind. Asao saw no farther. He could only guess, as the marrow of his bones froze, how many more marchers might make up this grotesque night parade—marchers that were beyond the ken of mortal eyes.

The last ghost seemed to pluck something from the air beyond. Limp fingers offered the object to the one in front, who solemnly passed it on to Takeo. Takeo in turn held his hand out to Asao.

The swordmaker reached forward unwillingly. He'd thought himself outside Takeo's reach; obviously, he was wrong.

Two cold, hard orbs were pressed into his sweating palm.

A flash of lightning overhead startled Asao. He instinctively clapped his outstretched hand across his eyes.

The thunderclap that followed segued into Asao's moan. The ghosts echoed, in empathy or mockery, his pain. He collapsed in the graveyard mud, *yukata* plastered to his thin frame.

When Asao looked up again, the world had a glistening, metallic sheen. Before him stood not three ghosts, but a score or more, melting away one by one as though dissolved by sheets of rain.

Takeo was the last to vanish.

One cool day in September, after the Bon Festival crowds had come and gone, Wasabe tugged at his master's sleeve. "A visitor," he said.

Asao looked up from the white paper he was cutting into strips for his ritual *gohei* hangings. He made a bitter face when he saw Yumata at his workshop door. "Only three months, and already in need of a new sword?" he snapped.

"On the contrary, swordmaker," the samurai replied. He fingered the hilt at his sash. "Your weapon served me exceptionally well in battle. I paused in Kyoto, on my way home, to tell you of my appreciation."

Asao made a sour grunt.

"Your skill," Yumata continued, "has been greatly underrated. You are now the finest swordmaker in Kyoto. I would advise any warrior to come to you."

Asao dropped the white paper strips. They scattered like fresh snow. One hand covered his eyes. With a sob, he pushed past the warrior and crouched, miserable, in the dust outside.

"Has some demon possessed Asao?" he heard Yumata ask. "He looked like a crab with its claws torn off."

"My master has always been moody," Wasabe explained.

"I never had that impression."

"You do not work for him, sir. He's been soured by those many years that his work had been overshadowed by Takeo, just as Takeo's own skill—according to my grandmother—had once been obscured by that of the great Kamagura."

"Yes, I heard that story last time. The innkeeper remarked on the coincidence that Kamagura also died after being blinded. Yet I remember Asao as a cheerful man, and he took Takeo's death hard." The samurai was surely puzzled, Asao thought, to debate the matter with a mere apprentice.

"Perhaps, sir. This humble one can only observe that my master, unlike other craftsmen, takes little pleasure in his work. Some days he treats everyone he meets as a potential assassin, even myself. Getting more work might be bringing out that aspect of his character lately, but he's always had that moodiness in his personality."

"Indeed?" encouraged Yumata. His tone indicated he was more amused than annoyed by the boy's insolence.

"Certainly. You might as well claim that his eyes have not always been that unearthly steel-gray color."

Asao's tears seared his cheeks like molten iron.

The Guide

Ramsey Campbell

The used bookshops seemed to be just as useless. In the first, Kew felt as if he had committed a gaffe by asking for the wrong James or even by asking for a book. The woman who was minding the next bookshop, her lap draped in black knitting so voluminous that she appeared to be mending a skirt she had on, assured him that the bookseller would find him something in the storeroom. "He's got lots of books in the back," she confided to Kew, and as he leaned on his stick and leafed through an annual he'd read seventy years ago, she kept up a commentary: "Fond of books, are you? I've read some books, books I'd *call* books. Make you sneeze, though, some of these old books. Break your toes, some of these books, if you're not careful. I don't know what people want with such big books. It's like having a stone slab on top of you, reading one of those books . . ." As Kew sidled toward the door, she said ominously, "He wouldn't want you going before he found you your books."

"My family will be wondering what's become of me," Kew offered, and fled.

Holidaymakers were driving away from the beach, along the narrow street of shops and small houses encrusted with pebbles and seashells. Some of the shops were already closing. He made for the newsagent's, in the hope that though all the horror books had looked too disgusting to touch, something more like literature might have found its way unnoticed onto one of the shelves, and then he realized that what he'd taken for a booklover's front room, unusually full of books, was in fact a shop. The sill inside the window was crowded with potted plants and cacti. Beyond them an antique till gleamed on a desk, and closer to the window, poking out of the end of a shelf, was a book by M. R. James.

The door admitted him readily and tunefully. He limped quickly to the shelf, and sighed. The book was indeed by James: Montague Rhodes James, O. M., Litt. D., F. B. A., F. S. A., Provost of Eton. It was a guide to Suffolk and Norfolk.

The shopkeeper appeared through the bead curtain of the doorway behind the desk. "That's a lovely book, my dear," she croaked smokily, pointing with her cigarette, "and cheap."

Kew glanced at the price penciled on the flyleaf. Not bad for a fiver, he had to admit, and only today he'd been complaining that although this was James country there wasn't a single book of his to be seen. He leafed through the guide, and the first page he came to bore a drawing of a bench end, carved with a doglike figure from whose grin a severed head dangled by the hair. "I'll chance it," he murmured, and dug his wallet out of the pocket of his purple cardigan.

The shopkeeper must have been too polite or too eager for a sale to mention that it was closing time, for as soon as Kew was on the pavement he heard her bolt the door. As he made his way to the path down to the beach, a wind from the sea fluttered the brightly striped paper in which she'd wrapped the volume. Laura and her husband, Frank, were shaking towels and rolling them up while their eight-year-olds kicked sand at each other. "Stop that, you two, or else," Laura cried.

"I did say you should drop me and go on somewhere," Kew said as he reached them.

"We wouldn't dream of leaving you by yourself, Teddy," Frank said, brushing sand from his bristling gingery torso.

"He means we'd rather stay with you," Laura said, yanking at her swimsuit top, which Kew could see she hadn't been wearing.

"Of course that's what I meant, old feller," Frank shouted as if Kew were deaf.

They were trying to do their best for him, insisting that he come with them on this holiday—the first he'd taken since Laura's mother had died—but why couldn't they accept that he wanted to be by himself? "Granddad's bought a present," Bruno shouted.

"Is it for us?" Virginia demanded.

"I'm afraid it isn't the kind of book you would like."

"We would if it's horrible," she assured him. "Mum and Dad don't mind."

"It's a book about this part of the country. I rather think you'd be bored."

She shook back her hair, making her earrings jangle, and screwed up her face. "I already am."

"If you make faces like that no boys will be wanting you tonight at the disco," Frank said, and gathered up the towels and the beach toys, trotted to the car, which he'd parked six inches short of a garden fence near the top of the path, hoisted his armful with one hand while he unlocked the hatchback with the other, dumped his burden in, and pushed the family one by one into the car. "Your granddad's got his leg," he rumbled when the children complained about having to sit in the backseat, and Kew felt more of a nuisance than ever.

They drove along the tortuous coast road to Cromer, and Kew went up to his room. Soon Laura knocked on his door to ask whether he was coming down for an apéritif. He would have invited her to sit with him so that they could reminisce about her mother, but Frank shouted, "Come on, old feller, give yourself an appetite. We don't want you fading away on us."

Kew would have had more of an appetite if the children hadn't swapped horrific jokes throughout the meal. "That's enough, now," Laura kept saying. Afterward coffee was served in the lounge, and Kew tried to take refuge in his book.

It was more the M. R. James he remembered nostalgically than he would have dared hope. Comic and macabre images lay low amid the graceful sentences. Here was "that mysterious being Sir John Shorne," Rector of North Marston, who "was invoked against ague; but his only known act was to conjure the devil into a boot, the occasion and sequelae of this being alike unknown." Here were the St. Albans monks, who bought two of St. Margaret's fingers; but who, Kew wondered, were the Crouched Friars, who had "one little house, at Great Whelnetham"? Then there were "the three kings or young knights who are out hunting and pass a churchyard, where they meet three terrible corpses, hideous with the ravages of death, who say to them, 'As we are, so will you be' "— a popular subject for decorating churches, apparently. Other references were factual, or at least were presented as such: not only a rector named Blastus Godly, but a merman caught at Orford in the thirteenth century, who "could not be induced to take an interest in the services of the church, nor indeed to speak." Kew's grunt of amusement at this attracted the children, who had finished reading the horror comics they'd persuaded their father to buy them. "Can we see?" Virginia said.

Kew showed them the sketch of the bench end with the severed head, and thought of ingratiating himself further with them by pointing out a passage referring to the tradition that St. Erasmus had had his entrails wound out of him on a windlass, the kind of thing the children's parents tried halfheartedly to prevent them from watching on videocassettes. Rebuking himself silently, he leafed in search of more acceptably macabre anecdotes, and then he stared. "Granddad," Bruno said as if Kew needed to be told, "someone's been writing in your book."

A sentence at the end of the penultimate chapter— "It is almost always worth while to halt and look into a Norfolk church"—had been ringed in grayish ink, and a line as shaky as the circumscription led to a scribbled paragraph that filled the lower half of the page. "I hope they knocked a few quid off the price

for that, old feller," Frank said. "If they didn't I'd take
it back."

"Remember when you smacked me," Laura said to
Kew, "for drawing in one of Mummy's books?"

Frank gave him a conspiratorial look which Kew
found so disturbing that he could feel himself losing
control, unable to restrain himself from telling Laura
that Virginia shouldn't be dressed so provocatively,
that the children should be in bed instead of staying
up for the disco, that he was glad Laura's mother
wasn't here to see how they were developing. . . . He
made his excuses and rushed himself up to his room.

He should sleep before the dull sounds of the disco
made that impossible, but he couldn't resist poring
over the scribbled paragraph. After a few minutes he
succeeded in deciphering the first phrase, which was
underlined. "Best left out," it said.

If the annotation described something better than
the book included, Kew would like to know what it
was. Studying the phrase had given him a headache,
which the disco was liable to worsen. He got ready
for bed and lay in the dark, improvising a kind of
silent lullaby out of the names of places he'd read in
the guidebook:

> Bungay, Chipley, Creeting St Mary,
> Herringfleet, Rumburgh, Snape;
> Great Snoring, Blickling,
> Bradfield Combust, Weeting;
> Breckles, Rattlesden, Diss . . .

Almost asleep, too much so to be troubled by the
draft that he could hear rustling paper near his bed,
he wondered if the scribbled phrase could mean that

the omission had been advisable. In that case, why note it at such length?

He slept, and dreamed of walking from church to church, the length and breadth of East Anglia, no longer needing his stick. He found the church he was looking for, though he couldn't have said what his criteria were, and lay down beneath the ribbed vault that somehow reminded him of himself. Laura and the children came to visit him, and he sat up. "As I am, so will you be," he said in a voice whose unfamiliarity dismayed him. They hadn't come to visit but to view him, he thought, terrified of doing so himself. It seemed he had no choice, for his body was audibly withering, a process which dragged his head down to show him what had become of him. Barely in time, his cry wakened him.

If the dream meant anything, it confirmed that he needed time by himself. He lay willing his heartbeat to slacken its pace; his eardrums felt close to bursting. He slept uneasily and woke at dawn. When he limped to the toilet, his leg almost let him down. He hawked, splashed cold water on his face, massaged his hands for several minutes before opening the book. If he couldn't read James's ghost stories, then viewing a location that had suggested one of them might be as much of an experience.

The book fell open at the scribbled page, and he saw that the line beneath the phrase he'd read last night wasn't underlining after all. It led from the next word, which was "map," across the page and onto the fore edge. Rubbing together his fingers and thumb, which felt dusty, he opened the book where the line ended, at a map of Norfolk.

The line led like the first thread of a cobweb to a

blotch on the Norfolk coast, where the map identified nothing in particular, showing only beach and fields for miles. The next scribbled phrase, however, was easily read: "churchyard on the cliff—my old parish." It sounded irresistibly Jamesian, and not to his family's taste at all.

In the hotel lounge before breakfast he read on: "There was a man so versed in the black arts that he was able to bide his time until the elements should open his grave . . ." Either Kew was becoming used to the scrawl or it grew increasingly legible as it progressed. He might have read more if the family hadn't come looking for him. "We're going to give Granddad a good day out today, aren't we?" Frank declared.

"We said so," Bruno muttered.

Virginia frowned reprovingly at him. "You have to say where we're going," she told her grandfather with a faintly martyred air.

"How about to breakfast?"

At the table Kew said to the children, "I expect you'd like to go to Hunstanton, wouldn't you? I understand there are dodgems and roller coasters and all sorts of other things to make you sick."

"Yes, yes, yes," the children began to chant, until Laura shushed them.

"That doesn't sound like you, Daddy," she said.

"You can drop me off on your way. I've found somewhere I want to walk to, that wouldn't have anything to offer you youngsters."

"I used to like walking with you and Mummy," Laura said, and turned on her son. "That's disgusting, Bruno. Stop doing that with your egg."

Kew thought of inviting her to walk to the church with him, but he'd seen how intent Frank and the children had become when she'd hinted at accompanying him. "Maybe we'll have time for a stroll another day," he said.

He sat obediently in the front seat of the car, and clutched his book and his stick while Frank drove eastward along the coast road. Whenever he spoke, Frank and Laura answered him so competitively that before long he shut up. As the road swung away from the coast, the towns and villages grew fewer. A steam train paced the car for a few hundred yards as if it were ushering them into James's era. A sea wind rustled across the flat land, under a sky from which gulls sailed down like flakes of the unbroken cloud. On the side of the road toward the coast, the stooped grass looked pale with salt and sand.

Apart from the occasional fishmonger's stall at the roadside, the miles between the dwindling villages were deserted. By the time the car arrived at the stretch of road that bordered the unnamed area that the blotch of grayish ink marked on the map, Bruno and Virginia had begun to yawn at the monotonousness of the landscape. Where a signpost pointed inland along a road, an inn stood by itself, and beyond it Kew saw an unmarked footpath that led toward the sea. "This'll do me. Let me out here," he said.

"Thirsty, old feller? This one's on me."

Kew felt both dismayed by the idea of being distracted from the loneliness of the setting and ashamed of his feelings. "They'll be open in a few minutes," Laura said.

"Boring, boring," the children started chanting, and Kew took the opportunity to climb out and close the door firmly. "Don't spoil the children's day on my account," he said, "or mine will be spoiled as well."

Now he'd made it sound as if they were ruining his holiday. He patted Laura's cheek awkwardly, and then Virginia's, and leaned back from the open window. "Five o'clock here suit you?" Frank said. "If we're late, there's always the pub."

Kew agreed, and watched the car race away. The children waved without turning their heads, but Laura kept him in sight as long as she could. Just as the car reached the first bend, Kew wanted to wave his stick urgently, to call out to Frank that he'd changed his mind. Six hours out here seemed a more generous helping of solitude than even he needed. Then the car was gone, and he told himself that the family deserved a break from him.

He sat on a rustic bench outside the building striped with timber, and turned to the scribbled page while he waited for the door to be unlocked. He found he was able to read straight on to the end, not least because the ink appeared darker.

There was a man so versed in the black arts that he was able to bide his time until the elements should open his grave; only the passage of so many years, and the stresses to which the falling away of the land subjected the grave, twisted not only the coffin almost beyond recognition but also what laired within. Imagine, if you will, a spider in human form with only four limbs, a spider both enraged and made ungainly by the loss, especially since the remaining limbs are by no means evenly distributed. If anything other than simple malevolence let him walk, it was the knowledge that whoever died of the sight of him would be bound to him.

Kew shivered and grinned at himself. So he could still derive a frisson from that kind of writing, all the more pleasurable when he remembered that James had never believed in his ghosts. Was it really possible that Kew was holding in his hands an unpublished episode by James? He didn't know what else to think. He gazed along the path through the swaying grass and wondered what it led to that had produced the description he'd just read, until the sound of bolts being slid back made him jump.

The landlord, a hairy bespectacled man whose ruddiness and girth suggested that he enjoyed his beer, looked out at Kew and then at the book. "Bit out of your way if you're walking, aren't you?" he said, so heartily that it served as a welcome. "Come in and wet your whistle, my lad."

A bar bristling with decorated handles and thick as a castle parapet marked off a quarter of the L-shaped room, beyond which were a few small tables draped with cloths, and a staircase guarded by a visitors' book. The landlord hauled on the nearest handle and gave Kew a pint of murky beer. "I was driven here," Kew explained. "I'm just about to start walking."

"Are you not using that book?"

"Why, do you know it?"

"I know all of that man's work that's set around this countryside. He had the touch, and no mistake." The landlord pulled himself a pint and drank half of it in one gulp. "But he didn't find anything round here that he wanted to write about."

Kew thought of showing the landlord the annotation but wasn't quite sure of himself. "Do you know if he ever came this way?"

"I should say so. He signed the book."

Excitement made Kew grip the handle of his tankard. "Could I see?"

"Certainly, if I can dig it out. Were you thinking of eating?" When Kew said that he better had, the landlord served him bread and cheese before unlocking a cupboard beside the stairs. Kew glanced at the handwritten paragraph to remind himself what the writing looked like, and then watched the landlord pull out visitors' book after visitors' book and scan the dates. Eventually he brought a volume to Kew's table. "Here he is."

Kew saw the date first: 1890. "He hadn't written any of his stories then, had he?"

"Not one."

Kew ran his gaze down the column of faded signatures and almost didn't see the name he was searching for. As he came back to it, he saw why he had passed over it: The signature bore no resemblance to the handwriting in the guidebook. He sighed and then sucked in a breath. The signature directly beneath James's was in that handwriting.

Was the signature "A. Fellows"? He touched it with his fingertip and tried to rub the cobwebby feel of it off his finger with his thumb. "Who was this, do you know?"

"Whoever came after Monty James."

The landlord seemed to be trying not to grin, and Kew gazed at him until he went on. "You'd think these East Anglians would be proud to have James write about their countryside," the landlord said, "but they don't like to talk about his kind of stories. Maybe they believe in that kind of thing more than he did. The chap who ran this place was on his deathbed when he told my father about that signature. It seems nobody saw who made it. It's like one of Monty's own yarns."

"Have you any idea where James had been that day?"

"Some old ruin on the cliff," the landlord said, and seemed to wish he had been less specific.

"Along the path outside?"

"If it was, there's even less there now, and you'll have noticed that he didn't think it had any place in his book."

The annotator had believed otherwise, and Kew thought that was a mystery worth investigating. He finished his lunch and drained his tankard, and was at the door when the landlord said, "I wouldn't stray too far from the road if I were you. Remember we're open till three."

This felt so like the protectiveness Kew had escaped earlier that he made straight for the path. Didn't anyone think he was capable of taking care of himself? He'd fought in the war against Hitler, he'd been a partner in an accountancy firm, he'd run every year in the London marathon until his leg had crippled him, he'd tended Laura's mother during her last years and had confined himself to places where he could wheel her in her chair, and after all that, he wasn't to be trusted to go off the road by himself? James had followed the path, and it didn't seem to have done him any harm. Kew stuffed the book under one arm and tramped toward the sea, cutting at the ragged grassy edges of the path with his stick.

The fields of pale grass stretched into the distance on both sides of him. The low cloud, featureless except for the infrequent swerving gull, glared dully above him. After twenty minutes' walking he felt he had scarcely moved, until he glanced back and found that the inn was out of sight. He was alone, as far as he could see, though the grass of the fields came up to his shoulder now. A chilly wind rustled through the fields, and he limped fast to keep warm, faster when he saw a building ahead.

At least, he thought it was a building until he was able to see through its broken windows. It was the front wall of a cottage, all that remained of the house. As he came abreast of it he saw other cottages farther on, and a backward look showed him foundations under the grass. He'd been walking through a ruined village without realizing it. One building, however, appeared still to be intact: the church, ahead at the edge of the ruins.

The church was squat and blackened, with narrow windows and a rudimentary tower. Kew had to admit that it didn't look very distinguished—hardly worth singling out for the guidebook—though wasn't there a large gargoyle above one of the windows that over-looked the wide gray sea? In any case, the sight of the church, alone on the cliff top amid the fringe of nodding grass, seemed worth the walk. He threw his shoulders back and breathed deep of the sea air, and strode toward the church.

He needn't have been quite so vigorous; there was nobody to show off for. He had to laugh at himself, for in his haste he dug his stick into a hole in the overgrown pavement and almost overbalanced. Rather than risk tearing the paper jacket by trying to hold onto the guidebook, he let the book fall on the grass, where it fell open at the scribbled page.

He frowned at the handwriting as he stooped carefully, gripping the stick, and wondered if exposure to sunlight had affected the ink. The first lines appeared blurred, so much so that he couldn't read the words "best left out" at all. Perhaps the dead light was affecting his eyes, because now as he peered toward the church he saw that there was no gargoyle. He could only assume that the wind had pushed forward the withered shrub which he glimpsed swaying out of sight around the corner closest to the sea, and a trick of perspective had made it look as if it were protruding from high up on the wall.

The church door was ajar. As Kew limped in the direction of the cliff edge, to see how stable the foundations of the building were, he discerned pews and an altar in the gloomy interior, and a figure in black moving back and forth in front of the glimmering altar. Could the church still be in use? Perhaps the priest was another sightseer.

Kew picked his way alongside the building, over illegibly weathered gravestones whose cracks looked cemented with moss, to the jagged brink, and then he shoved the book under the arm that held the stick and grabbed the cold church wall to support himself. Apart from the slabs he'd walked on, the graveyard had vanished; it must have fallen to the beach as the centuries passed. The church itself stood at the very edge of the sheer cliff now, its exposed foundations sprouting weeds that rustled in the sandy wind. But it wasn't the precariousness of the building that had made Kew feel suddenly shaky, in need of support; it was that there was no shrub beside the church, nothing like the distorted shrunken brownish shape he'd glimpsed as it withdrew from sight. Beside that corner of the church, the cliff fell steeply to the beach.

He clutched the wall, bruising his fingertips, while

he tried to persuade himself that the shrub and the portion of ground on which it stood had just lost their hold on the cliff, and then he shoved himself away from the wall, away from the crumbling edge. As he did so, he heard a scrabbling above him, on the roof. A chunk of moss, too large to have been dislodged by a bird, dropped on the grass in front of him. He clapped his free hand to his chest, which felt as if his heart were beating its way to the surface, and fled to the entrance to the church.

The priest was still by the altar. Kew could see the blotch of darkness that was his robe, and the whitish glint of his collar. Thoughts were falling over one another in Kew's head: the guidebook was a late edition, and so the scribbled annotation must have been made decades later than the signature at the inn, yet the handwriting hadn't aged at all, and couldn't the words in the visitors' book which Kew had taken for a signature have been "A Follower"? The only thought he was able to grasp was how far he would have to run across the deserted land from the church to the inn—too far for him to be able to keep up the pace for more than a few minutes. He dodged into the gloomy church, his stick knocking against a pew, and heard a larger movement overhead. "Please," he gasped, stumbling down the aisle into the dimness.

He hardly knew what he was saying or doing, but where else could he go for help except to the priest? He wished he could see the man's face, though rather less fervently once the priest spoke. "It brought you," he said.

It wasn't just his words but also his voice that disturbed Kew. Perhaps it was an echo that made it sound so hollow, but why was its tone so eager? "You mean the book," Kew stammered.

"We mean what you read."

Kew was almost at the altar now. As his eyes adjusted, he saw that what he'd taken to be dimness draping the pews and the altar was a mass of dust and cobwebs. More than the tone and timbre of the voice, its forced quality was beginning to unnerve him. "Your friend James thought it, but he didn't write it," the voice said. "We inspired him, and then I had to write it for him."

If James had used the handwritten paragraph in one of his tales and identified the setting as he tended to, Kew thought with the clarity of utter panic, more people would have visited this church. He was backing toward the door when he heard something clamber down from the roof and land just outside the doorway with a sound like the fall of a bundle of sticks and leather. "James nearly saw, but he didn't believe," said the figure by the altar, and stepped into the light that seeped through a pinched grimy window. "But you will," it said out of the hole that was most of its face.

Kew closed his eyes tight. His panic had isolated a single thought at the center of him: that those who died of seeing would be bound to what they saw. He felt the guidebook slip out of his hands, he heard its echoes clatter back and forth between the walls, and then it gave way to another sound, of something that scuttled lopsidedly into the church and halted to wait for him. He heard the priest's feet, bare of more than clothing, begin to drag across the floor toward him. He turned, frantically tapping the pews with his stick, and shuffled in the direction of the door. Beyond it was the path, the inn, his family at five o'clock, further than his mind could grasp. If he had to die, please let it not be here! What terrified him most, as he swung the stick in front of him and prayed that it would ward off any contact, was what might be done to him to try and make him look.

Getting Back

P.W. Sinclair

1

The tornado that cut a wandering path across southeastern Wisconsin on the night of my homecoming never came very near my parents' farm, yet in a way it was the start of everything. A symbolic beginning, if nothing else. A harbinger.

My father was the best weather forecaster I knew. He didn't need meteorologists' reports; he didn't rely on homilies about red skies in the morning; he didn't feel anything in his bones. He just knew what signs to look for and how to read them. So that night, while the radio issued warnings about seeking immediate shelter, my father laughed.

"That storm's not gonna hit here," he said. "Look at the sky. Might veer just to the south, maybe, but she's not coming here."

The four of us—my mother, father, grandmother, and I—sat on the screened front porch in the muggy twilight, drinking beer. Bursts of thunderstorm static cut through the damage reports from neighboring counties on Dad's transistor. Lightning slashed the

sky at long intervals, while it rained gently, relent-
lessly.

My grandmother, at one time the best storyteller I'd
ever met, talked about past storms. She talked about
the North Atlantic hurricane that almost sank the
ship bringing her parents from Germany to New
York, and about the Great Lakes gale that had threatened the schooner carrying them to Milwaukee. My
father nodded at various parts of the tales, interject-
ing a comment or two and laughing at the appropri-
ate points.

My mother was strangely quiet. She'd inherited a
great many things from her mother, among them a
healthy dose of the tale spinner's art. But that night
she had nothing to offer. She sat in her wicker chair,
a few feet apart from the rest of us, nursing her beer
but not finishing it, her eyes focused on a point somewhere beyond the porch. I watched her for a long
time while Grandma rambled on, and finally I leaned
over to whisper to my father.

"Is Mom all right? She's so quiet."

He turned a long, slow gaze on me and said, "You
had yourself a long drive today, didn't you?"

"I . . . yeah, I guess so. Yeah, it *was* a long drive."

He nodded and took a swallow from his bottle. "I
could tell. You showed it when you pulled up. A long,
hard drive."

I sighed. "It was a long, hard *year.*"

"Oh? I thought you wanted to be a teacher."

"I do. I just think my choice of . . . Look. Can we
talk about this later? Tomorrow, maybe?"

"Sure, son, whatever you want."

"Now what about Mom?"

Again he gave me that long, languid gaze. Then he

turned away, and by that time my grandmother had launched another story and my opportunity was gone.

The wind picked up as the night went by, and the sky above the barn was lit more and more often by vivid electrical streaks. Still, Dad's prediction seemed to be on the mark, for while we continued to hear about downed power lines, fallen trees, and damaged homes in an area that stretched from Madison to Milwaukee and south to the Illinois border, we were never directly threatened.

It was sometime after ten when my grandmother fell asleep in her chair. Mom had gone in without a word almost half an hour earlier, and the night was now silent except for the sounds of rain, thunder, and wind. I faced my father again.

"You didn't tell me about—"

"I think we'll be lucky with the corn this year. The spring was just right, and the summer looks good."

I slammed my open palm on the arm of the chair. "Dammit, Dad, I—"

"She started her chemotherapy again, Pete." His voice was small and tight, strangled.

I stared at him. His face was crisscrossed and distorted by shadows. A fifty-three-year-old man who looked aged and ageless at the same time.

I didn't know what to say, and when I found something at last it was juvenile, utterly useless, stupidly shallow.

"You're kidding."

"No, I ain't."

"But—"

"She took sick in the Red Owl two weeks ago. Fell down, took a whole display of canned peas down with her. Finally admitted she'd had the pain again since March."

"Oh, Jesus. I thought the doctor said she was in remission."

He shook his head slowly. "That was three years ago, Pete."

The voice on the radio was saying something about a new funnel cloud sighting in an area not far distant from the farm. Perhaps that cyclone, churning along several miles away, was responsible for the distant roaring in my ears, but I didn't think so.

"I . . . I really thought . . . Oh, shit."

"Now, Pete—"

But I'd stopped listening. I rose like a stiff, mechanical doll and went outside. The jungle humidity swept over me, and the rain came with it. The wind, ripping across the yard, tore at my hair and clothes.

"Pete, the storm—" my father called from the porch, but his voice already sounded distant, unreal.

I hurried toward the barn, but didn't stop when I got there. I turned right, cut between the twin hulks of the equipment sheds, and entered the field we'd always called the north pasture. It was planted in timothy that year, as it almost always was, and already it was going on shin-high, ready for the season's first cutting in a week or two.

The sky was still charged with electricity, but I went on anyway, not caring that being out there in the middle of that field was one of the more foolhardy things I'd ever done. My mother was dying. The cancer was back. Three years of relief and the blackness had returned to the horizon. The past year—my first of full-time teaching—had been one mighty kick in the gut. And now, coming home for the summer to recoup and recover, I had just been kicked again.

It took me forever to cross the field. Several times lightning stroked toward the ground less than a half-mile away. My shirt and pants were drenched, my hair dripping, hanging across my forehead like a lunatic's wig. Still I went on until I'd reached the property line at the back of the north pasture.

Here was a gap-toothed row of box elders and Norway maples my father had planted twenty or twenty-five years earlier. They were swaying wildly in the wind, and the rush of air through their branches made a sighing, whistling chorus of eerie pain. Running just behind the trees was a barbed-wire fence, then a stretch of overgrown no-man's land that separated the property from the north-south highway.

Standing there, looking through one of the gaps in the tree line, gazing down the highway toward the south, I heard another rumbling sound in my ears, this one much louder than before. It was a sound very much like a long, powerful freight train. A sound like a million running feet. It shook me to the roots of my teeth and the center of my bones.

And then I saw it, perhaps seven miles off, distinguishable in the night only as a darker patch of blackness. A roiling, churning, whirling swatch of midnight. A funnel cloud.

It was moving away from our land, away from the highway on a southwest-northeast line. I thought about running but didn't. It was moving away and I was fascinated. Watching it vanish across flat farmland, hearing that roar in my ears and feeling the steady vibration beneath my feet, I felt chilled. The power of that swarming darkness made me shiver; I felt a slow gnawing of primitive fear in my belly.

"God is angry today," my mother would say when we were little and tornado warnings would force us to take shelter in the farmhouse cellar.

Now, as I saw an honest-to-God funnel for the first time in my life, that didn't seem far off the mark at all.

I watched until the cloud had blended with the night and the roar had faded, until the ground had stopped shaking. Then I realized just how wet I was.

Soaked for life, I thought crazily. And on the heels of that: God is angry today.

I shook my head and turned back toward home. The wind had become a knife against my skin.

"Mister?"

I stopped in midstep. Literally. One foot was halfway to the ground. Then I whirled around to face the trees and the place where the little boy had spoken.

I wiped the rainwater from my eyes but still saw nothing beyond swaying branches, blowing leaves snapping back and forth like tiny pennants.

"Mister, please . . ."

I took a step forward. The voice was small, plaintive, very real. But I couldn't see the boy anywhere.

"Who is it?" I called, the words torn from my lips by a vicious gust of wind.

"Mister?"

"Where are you?"

"Mister?"

It was then that I had what I'm sure was a premonition, the first and last time I've ever experienced such a thing. I'm not positive that "premonition" is the right word, but in that instant I *knew* that I had to get out of there. I *knew* something terrible was sweeping down on me. Then it felt as though a great hand were turning me around again, pushing me away.

"Mister?" Soft and small, lost and pleading. "Mister?"

I ran, heading for home, fleeing on the strength of the wind and the raw, horrible power of that black sensation . . . that fear . . . that premonition.

"Mist—"

The little boy's voice was swallowed by a shattering, splintering crash as one of the largest box elders in the row toppled to earth, sending branches and wood shards flying.

I only looked back for an instant, never breaking stride.

The wind howled at my heels.

2

The next morning was bright and sunwashed, a bit cooler. My mother's mood was considerably better; she sat at the breakfast table chatting twice as much as the rest of us, Grandma included. Her son was home, she must have said three times, and nothing could make her happier. When Debbie got back from college at the end of the week, we'd be a real family again. That phrase—real family—troubled me, but it was worth it to see Mom feeling fine.

My father said nothing about the night before, for which I was grateful. I'd been a fool, running on gut emotion into the teeth of a wild storm and then— alone, frightened by the funnel—suffering aural hallucinations. I saw no need to have any of that brought up.

"When's Debbie getting here?" I asked, keeping the conversation on safe ground.

Mom smiled. "Friday afternoon. She called last week, said her last exam's Thursday night, and she'll drive up the next morning. You two . . . let's see . . . sweet Jesus, you haven't seen each other in almost two years!"

I nodded. "The last time was just after I entered the master's program. But we write every week and talk on the phone a couple times a month."

"Still, it shows that you don't come home enough, not nearly enough. Not at Christmas or Thanksgiving, not at Easter. You'd think you were ashamed of us, or something. You'd think—"

"Faye," my father said, "the boy just got up. Don't start on him now."

I cringed at the use of "boy"—which I'd always considered a pejorative—but was thankful for his defense nonetheless. Mom, though, wasn't quite ready to give up.

"I know he just got up, Reuben. But he's a member of this family and he ought to act like it. It couldn't hurt. The Manse family sticks together. They celebrate their holidays together." She looked at me, and now I saw with relief that the lecture was a gentle one. Her words were harsh, but her eyes betrayed a soft good humor.

"Don't get me wrong, Peter. I'm so glad to have you home this summer, you wouldn't believe. I just think we ought to see you more often."

I shrugged, looking into my Rice Krispies. "I've been busy."

Grandma snorted. "Education," she said sagely, "is a dangerous thing."

And at that we all laughed; the tense atmosphere shattered and blew away.

After breakfast my father pulled on his gloves and headed for the equipment shed. I went after him, wanting to ask more about Mom. We paused just outside while he lit a cigarette and adjusted his Trojan Seed cap. He studied me with an unreadable gaze.

"Wind took down a tree last night."

I swallowed. Had he already been out to the property line? Or had he followed me last night, staying a few yards behind, to make sure I'd be okay? I said nothing, but offered a tiny nod.

"I was sorry to see her go," he continued, "remembering the way you used to play in her and all. You and Stevie had a treehouse there for a couple, three years, remember?"

"Treehouse?"

"Sure. In the big oak down at the foot of the drive. You remember that treehouse, don't you? You fellas used all them old Burma Shave signs we had piled in the barn."

I relaxed. He didn't know about the box elder at the back of the north pasture.

"I remember," I said with a smile. "Burma Shave signs and rusty, bent nails from the old chicken coop."

Dad laughed. "You fellas were a couple of regular carpenters, all right." He started toward the shed again. "Gotta move along, Pete. Stop by later and meet the new hired men. We're rebuilding the engine on the Deere, be there most of the day."

I still wanted to ask about Mom but decided it could wait. I told him I'd pop in later, and I watched him walk away, his head lowered and the small stoop in his shoulders—a stoop he'd had as long as I could remember—just a little more pronounced than it had been when I was last home.

I stood in the yard for a long time, looking around at the house, the freshly painted barn (white with green trim, green aluminum roof, the words "MANSE FARM 1923" in black above the long sliding doors), the adjacent stone silo, the equipment sheds, the dog kennel, the poultry pen and coop. A million scents assailed me, each one bringing a rush of memories. I smelled manure and damp earth, cut grass, gasoline, paint, and old wood. I thought of an entirely different set of aromas—pencil shavings, paper and books, chalk dust—and wondered for the first time in a long time if I'd made the right decision.

Not knowing what else to do, I headed for the barn, cutting across the lawn and climbing the driveway's slight incline to the upper floor.

Inside it was cool and dim. I could hear the cows downstairs stirring restlessly, lowing, anxious to be let out to pasture. Up here was the old hayloft, seldom used in my lifetime, and a series of large grain rooms to the right and left that had been full constantly when I was little but had been replaced by concrete cribs outside when I was in high school. The place was now used mainly for storage. The loft and grain rooms were loaded with unwanted household items: old battered beds, sea trunks with broken locks and missing hinges, backless chairs, couches minus their stuffing. The center section of the barn was used for parking. My Escort sat next to the family pickup. In the corner were two Lawn Boy push mowers, a Wheel Horse garden tractor, and a rack of grass shears and hedge clippers, all of which would only be in the way in the equipment sheds.

I stood next to my car and looked up the length of the rotting ladder that led to the loft. I remembered Debbie, Stephen, and me playing up there, endless summer afternoons. Games of pirates and cowboys and secret agents, the kinds of games kids never seem to play anymore. Games of big city hospital and oceangoing cruise ship and hidden underground laboratory.

I remembered Stephen, two years younger than me, so much quicker, more agile, going up the now-dangerous ladder like a little monkey, taking the rungs two at a time and laughing at his brother and sister for being so slow. I remembered Stephen always creating new games, keeping things interesting. I remembered Stephen . . .

. . . Stephen screaming . . .

. . . Stephen crushed beneath the old Allis Chalmers . . .

. . . Stephen's life ebbing, spilling out onto the bare earth of the east acreage . . .

. . . Stephen . . .

I stood there in the barn and cried, hard and long. I'd cried at the time, of course, but not often enough in the seven years since.

. . . Stephen . . . Steve . . . Stevie . . .

It felt damn good to stand there crying like that. Frankly, I don't care what that sounds like. I'll say it again. It felt damn good to be in the barn where we'd played so often, crying for my dead brother.

* * *

As Mom had been quick to point out, it had been a long time since I'd been home. Three years, to be precise, ever since my graduation from the University of Wisconsin and my entrance into the graduate program there to earn a master's in education. My room, therefore, hadn't changed since schooldays. A rabid sports fan then; my walls showed it. They were covered with pennants—Badgers, Packers, Brewers, even the old Milwaukee Braves—and with wonderful clippings and posters from the Green Bay glory years. My high school diploma was mounted above my desk, where I'd hung it before going off to Madison. My senior year required reading still lined the bookshelves at the foot of the bed, Salinger cheek-to-cheek with Dickens.

After a hamburger and potato salad lunch with the family and the two hired men (a short, stocky grouch named David Falkner and a peach-fuzzed kid named Tommy Scheinholt), I said I was going to my room for a nap. My grandmother and mother flashed concerned looks as I left the table. My father mumbled something about Milquetoast teachers, but grinned as I passed his chair.

In my room I gazed out the window at the fields beyond. The north pasture and its timothy could be seen only from the other side of the house, but from here I could see the southern acreage. It was divided into three neat sections, green wheat, very young corn, and a crop that looked like sweet peas, although they might have been beets; it was a little early to tell. It was a beautiful sight, all that fertile land, and since it seemed to be the day for it, I gave into the rush of old memories and new fears.

I'd loved the farm life as a child but had chilled to it

in high school when the playtime decreased and the workload went up. In that period, when normal adolescent rebellion runs rampant anyway, I determined to go to college and see if there was a better way before I committed myself to keeping the Manse Farm going. The death of my younger brother in a tractor accident two weeks before my eighteenth birthday had wiped out that wait-and-see policy. The farm was not—absolutely, certainly, without a doubt in the world—for me. It was a stinking place. A horrible, boring, backbreaking, viciously dangerous, and cruel place. It was the life-style of the past. It was outdated, fit only for dull-witted rednecks and their ugly, graying wives.

So I was a teacher, in a small northern Michigan town. My first year on the job had been an eye-opening journey through small-time hell, and my first day back on the farm brought with it so many incredible sights and smells that I was utterly bewildered for the first time since the tenth grade.

What in the hell *did* I want, anyway? And was the rush of hatred for this life that had spilled out of me as Stephen's blood had spilled onto the ground still relevant seven years later? Somehow I didn't think so. If anything, crying for him in the barn today had been a release from that sort of thinking.

"Shit," I said, leaving the window and throwing myself on the bed.

My mother was dying.

Did that fit into the equation somehow? And if so, where?

Debbie was going to the University of Illinois, thinking about art school after graduation. When Mom was gone, my father would be alone. And he was no spring chicken, although by no means old. With Debbie and me gone, there were no more Manses to carry on the farm that my father's father had begun. I'd never looked at that as a duty before, but perhaps it was . . . perhaps it was.

Thinking all those crazy thoughts, I fell asleep facedown in the pillow and dreamed. Stephen was not in the dream, nor was Debbie. My parents weren't in the dream. I was all alone there, wandering through a dark house filled with closed doors, and each door was a vital decision I was unable and unwilling to make.

3

I awoke in darkness to the touch of a cool hand on my forehead and the strong smell of fried chicken in the air. I'd overslept, missed dinner, and my mother had brought a plate for me, was now trying to wake me up.

But as I blinked rapidly and struggled toward alertness, the cool, small hand moved down my cheek to the side of my neck. That was a strange way to wake—

My vision cleared and I looked up into the face of a child. A small boy with fine, delicate features, china-white skin, blond hair in a rough bowl cut. His lips looked extremely red against his pale skin; they were drawn back in a wide, trembling bow of agony or fear.

I sat up like a shot, slapping the hand away, trying to get out of bed.

The child stumbled backward, and I noticed for the

first time that he was crying. Several teardrops were frozen on his face, as if in a painting.

"Fanny," he said in a high, quavering voice. "W-where's Fanny?"

The air in the room grew suddenly, terribly cold, and then the child was gone.

Terrified, I fumbled for the light on the nightstand and clicked it on.

I was alone.

There was indeed a plate of food—fried chicken, mashed potatoes, string beans—sitting on my desk, a glass of reddish fruit punch beside it, but my door was shut, my window closed.

There wasn't another soul in sight.

4

Debbie was even more beautiful than I remembered, more beautiful than the picture of her I kept on my bedroom dresser in Michigan, more beautiful than the every-boy's-cheerleader-fantasy-come-to-life of her high school days. The last three years had matured her, softened her, added a certain measure of peace to her smooth, lovely face.

Good Lord, how I had adored this girl as we'd grown up. And how I'd missed her since we'd been apart.

She wheeled her car into the driveway on Friday afternoon, leaped out and ran toward me seconds after putting it in park.

"Peter! It's true! You *did* come home! Jesus Christ, it's good to see you!"

We met halfway between her car and the house,

embracing while Dad waited on the porch and smiled.

"Put her in the barn, Deb," he told her, "next to Pete's little Ford. I don't want you blocking the drive."

She rolled her eyes in mock disgust and tugged my arm. I clambered into the passenger's seat while she got in, gunned the engine, and headed into the barn.

"Like the wheels?" she said, grinning.

"Yeah, not too shabby. You didn't tell me you'd bought—"

"Actually, it belongs to my roommate, but she's taking classes this summer and working on campus, so she said I could use it. Pretty damn neat, huh?"

I laughed, thinking that look of peace had been a thin illusion. She was still the same—the frantic enthusiasm was still there, undampened.

She pulled in beside my Escort and shut off the engine. Then she turned to me and shook her head sadly. I knew what she was saying. It had been far too long.

"So," she said after a moment. "How are you, big brother?"

I shrugged. "I've been better. You, on the other hand, look fabulous. Looks like Champaign agrees with you."

"Yeah, I've always had a taste for the bubbly stuff."

"I meant the town, pea brain, and you know it."

They were silly jokes, but we dissolved in laughter.

That night we sat next to each other at dinner and relived enough old times to bore even Grandma. After that we sat on the porch, as we had on the night of my own homecoming. This time with the whole family there (the *real* family, as Mom had called it), I felt secure enough to bring up the subject that had been bothering me for two full days.

When the talk and laughter had dwindled, I took a deep breath and said, "Hey, Dad, who bought the old Purliss place, anyway?"

He gave me a strange look. "The Purliss Farm? Whaddya mean?"

I was referring to our nearest neighbors, almost a mile down the road, and I said so.

"I don't know what you mean, Pete. The Purlisses ain't even had it up for sale."

"You mean Old Man Purliss still—"

"And old *Missus* Purliss," my grandmother said. "The bitch."

"You mean they still live there?" I found it hard to believe. The Purlisses had seemed old when I was a kid, ancient by the time I'd left home.

"Sure do," Dad said. "He still raises his smelly chickens, and she still chucks rocks at any kid who rides by on a bike. Why?"

"Oh . . . no reason." I grinned sheepishly. "I . . . I was just wondering if there were any new kids in the neighborhood. I've seen a few around the farm the last couple of days."

My father's eyes narrowed. He leaned over the arm of his chair so that his face was just inches away from mine. "Kids? Around the farm?"

Very sorry now that I'd brought it up, I tried to wave it away. "Probably just kids from across the highway, playing around in the north pasture."

"There haven't been any children here since you and Debbie went off to school. And since the Berrand boy joined the Air Force." This came from my mother. "Are you sure?"

"I thought so," I said, with a laugh that I hoped sounded casual. "Guess I was seeing things, huh?"

Nobody else was laughing. "Seeing things," Dad repeated thoughtfully. "Maybe. But I'll keep my eyes open. Maybe the Arlettes have their grandkids for the summer. Helen always says she wants them to visit."

I shifted uneasily. Part of it was because of the way I'd just made myself look foolish, but a much larger part of my unease came from remembering the voice in the storm, the cool touch on my forehead and neck, the tortured face with the frozen teardrops highlighted on bone-china cheeks. Luckily Debbie noticed my discomfort and came to the rescue, asking in the snidest possible tone if I'd seen the way the Illini had clobbered the Badgers in football the year before.

When the rest of the family had gone to bed, I lingered on the porch, staring through the screens at the yard. The house was dark and quiet. I almost screamed when Debbie came up behind me and touched my shoulder.

"You okay, kid?"

I tried to smile. "Who're you calling kid, kid?"

"Seriously. Are you all right?"

"I'm fine. Sure."

She came around and perched on the arm of my chair. We were silent for a long time; the only sounds were the chirr of crickets outside, the muted ticktock of the antique wall clock in the entryway behind us.

"What's this about kids on the farm?" she said at last.

I sighed. "Nothing. Like Dad said, it's probably just Helen Arlette's grandchildren. They can probably use the help with their farm, don't you think?"

She stared at me. Her lovely blue eyes seemed suddenly dark, almost frightening.

"It's something else, isn't it? You didn't tell us everything." I opened my mouth to protest, but she cut me off. "Dammit, Peter, tell me! What's wrong? What'd you see?"

A cool hand on my forehead . . . a child's tortured face, there and then gone . . .

"Peter."

I smiled. "Me no see nothink, *señora.* Me just a poor peasant who—"

"Peter, please . . . what's wrong?"

Once more I sighed. "Look, Debbie, believe me. I didn't see anything. And if I did, I couldn't tell you right now. If you want to know the truth, I'm not convinced that what I saw wasn't just a bad dream."

She frowned. "I don't understand."

"I didn't have a very good rookie year. Of course, you know that already."

She nodded. "You wrote about some of it. And while we were making dinner, Mom mentioned that you were in a rotten mood when you got home the other day."

"Yeah. Well. I think the things I was talking about tonight might be the result of that. You know, I had every single illusion shattered. I'd always thought the city schools were the bad ones, the inner ghettos were the hot spots. I knew all about crime and threatened teachers. I knew about the dropouts and unteachables. I knew about lousy board politics. I just didn't expect to find that in a small town. I mean, my God, I wasn't there a week before some shop class degenerate pulled a hunting knife on me in lit class! He was actually going to stab me, I think. And this is in a school of four hundred and fifty in a town of twenty-five hundred! I saw almost as many unteachables there as in my student teaching in Chicago. And I couldn't seem to stay on the right side of that nepotistic joke they call a Board of Education. Let's just say that I had a lot of false hopes stolen and a lot of expectations ruined."

"And your dream?"

I shook my head. "Whatever it was, I think it was an after-effect of the last nine months. I . . . I really don't know. It was frightening, but it was also two days ago. If it was a dream, I think I finally got it out of my system."

She patted my hand. It was a contrived, motherly gesture that nevertheless comforted me a bit. "Whatever you say. But don't forget that pact we made when we were kids, you, me, and Steve. You want to talk, you talk. You got a problem, I'm there to listen. Got it?"

I smiled and kissed her on the cheek. "Thanks, Deb. Really. But I think I'm okay now. I really do."

5

I woke up the next morning when a dog began barking outside my window. For a moment, lying there groggy and heavy-lidded, my mind not yet functioning, I had the uncanny sensation of being transported back in time. When I was ten, we'd owned four dogs—two collies, a springer spaniel, and a mutt. The last of them, the mutt, had died in my junior year of high school. My parents hadn't owned a dog since, and the kennel by the equipment sheds, like the grain rooms in the barn, was now used for storage.

The barking went on and on, and when I finally came to enough to realize that I wasn't ten anymore, it began to fade.

I scrambled out of bed and went to the window, yanking on the cord and sending the shade rattling up on its roller. The sun was very bright; it almost knocked me back, like a physical blow to the face. When I was able to focus, I saw it. Saw them.

A large dog was running across the yard, heading for the fifty acres of young corn. It was a huge beast, a Great Dane by the look of it, and the way it was frisking and frolicking, tossing its head and barking at the sky, seemed almost ridiculous for its size.

A dog, running away.

And at its heels, charging along pell-mell after it, trying mightily to keep up, was a small boy in coarse woolen overalls, white shirt, and old-fashioned, honest-to-God suspenders.

A dog, running away.

And at its heels the little boy who'd awakened me from my nap on my second day home, touching me with an icy hand, crying as though he'd just lost the best friend he'd ever had.

A boy and his dog, a dog and his boy, running away.

I turned from the window, burying my face in my hands and telling myself it was another stupid dream, another nightmare brought on somehow—inexplicably—by the experiences I'd had in my first year of teaching.

It was getting harder all the time to believe that.

* * *

"I can't figure it, Reuben," David Falkner was saying to my father as I entered the kitchen. "I checked everything."

"Did you—"

"Every-frigging-thing, Reuben. The carb's fine, the filters 're clean, the fuel line's wide open, the pump's dandy-great."

My father shook his head. "And she's still not getting gas?"

"Not enough. She starts up, runs a second or two, and chokes out. I mean, shit, we ground the heads and changed the rings. She's got brand-new plugs. What's wrong?"

"I don't know, Dave. Tell you what. I'll be out in a minute to look at her. If we still can't get it running, I'll call Mike Hoff over to the dealership. Maybe he could take a look."

Falkner, cheery as always, growled something profane and stomped out of the house.

I crossed the kitchen and poured a cup of coffee. "Problems, Dad?"

"Your father needs a new tractor," Grandma said from her place at the table.

"Can it, Eva. I *don't* need a new tractor."

"Is something wrong with the Deere?" I asked.

He nodded. "We just finished a two-week rebuild on her and she won't run. Even before the rebuild, we could keep the engine going." He sighed, fingering the buttons on his denim shirt. "Dave Falkner's one of the best damn mechanics in Washington County. I just don't understand it."

"Your father needs—"

"Eva!"

My grandmother only laughed at the edge in his voice.

"I don't need a new tractor. What I need is this one running before we cut the north pasture next week."

He paused and looked at me closely, as though realizing for the first time I was there.

"You slept in," he said. "Breakfast's been over for an hour. Your mom and sister drove into Milwaukee for the day."

"I was up. I was just . . . just sitting in my room. Thinking."

He mumbled something, already distracted again by the problem of the John Deere. A moment later he'd gone outside and I was left to scrounge my meal in the company of my mother's mother.

I thought briefly of asking her about local children, but decided against it. She'd been there the night before when I'd brought it up and hadn't volunteered anything then. I ate my toast and cold cereal as quickly as I could and went outside.

Heading for the north pasture, I decided that I had to get some kind of fix on this thing. Whatever you wanted to call it—waking dream, hallucination, mental effects of a bad year, *whatever*—it was just crazy enough to be frightening.

After that first night it had been a vague kind of fright, disjointed, detached. The kind of fright you feel watching the nightly news and seeing a disturbing thirty-second film clip from a distant country. Bothersome. Soon forgotten. The chill I'd gotten watching the funnel cloud had been much worse than the chill of the sad little voice, the falling tree.

The next day had been worse. Being awakened by the hand on my forehead and seeing that face, hear-

ing that voice—"Fanny. W-where's Fanny?"—had
brought an emotional kind of fear, as though I had,
for just a quick moment, been cursed with the ability
to look into my own grave. I'd seen something impossible, been touched by someone who couldn't be
there. Was that, then, a fear of ghosts? A fear of the
unknown? I wasn't sure, but it had pressed on my
heart in a way I'd never experienced before.

Now this morning—the dog and the boy. What kind
of fear had I felt then?

I thought I knew.

It was the fear of the unknown again, yes. Fear of
something that really couldn't be. But more signifi-
cantly, it was fear for my own mind.

I was seeing things. Somehow, in some way. Creating pictures, inventing scenes.

The fear I felt realizing that was the fear of a slipping grip. It was the fear of a crumbling foothold.

Say it! I had to tell myself.

It was, simply, fear of insanity.

Ten minutes later, kneeling at the base of the fallen
tree, I temporarily forgot about fear and hallucinations and shaky footholds on reality. I was struck by
something I think few twenty-five-year-olds ever are
—pure, childlike wonder.

The box elder that had gone over in the storm had
literally been ripped from the earth. Its root system
stretched toward the sky like the arms of thirty or
forty religious supplicants. Large, gnarled, trunklike
roots went off in every direction, narrowing to spi-
dery, dirt-clotted capillaries that stirred gently in the
morning breeze.

The ground around the tree was littered with wood

chips and pieces of bark ranging from tiny to huge. Broken branches were lying as far as ten feet away, their leaves still green.

Most amazing of all was the crater.

Where the tree had been rooted was a gaping hole in the landscape, three feet deep, at least, more than three feet across. The inside was littered with more wood chips and shreds of root that had been left behind. The earth was gravelly—no fine topsoil here—and only a few slugs and earthworms moved through it.

It was the crater that put me in awe. Like the unleashed power of the funnel cloud, it left me a bit weak-kneed. To think of a wind powerful enough not only to crack a tree this size, or to split and topple it, but actually to seize it and *rip* it whole from the earth . . .

God was angry, a part of my mind whispered.

And you were there to see it, another part whispered back.

Once again I felt the tremor I'd felt that night, the tremor that'd been caused only in part by the passing tornado, the vibration of the ground beneath my feet.

And then the sun caught something small and bright inside the crater, sending a finger of light right at me. I squinted and bent over, scrabbling in the stony soil until my fingers closed on a tiny metal object. I tugged, coming away with a small, scarred medallion. Its tarnished fine-link chain came after it, slithering out of the ground like a snake.

I held the medallion up, brushing away a few loose particles, tilting it this way and that, looking at it.

It was the size of a half-dollar. Etched on its surface was the profile of an animal—a lamb, most likely—

and below it were the words THE LORD IS MY SHEP-
HERD. Actually, a good-sized nick had taken away the
last half of the word "shepherd," but the meaning was
clear enough. I turned it over.

The back was rough and had but one word engraved on it, the name JASON.

A religious medallion, given as a gift, perhaps, for
Christmas or baptism or confirmation. I had no way
of knowing how old it was, nor did I want to hazard a
guess. It was in awfully good shape, considering
where it had been. There were the few small nicks,
the larger flaw that blotted the word "shepherd," and
now I noticed that the chain that had once held it
around Jason's neck was broken. Still, considering
the fact that it had been buried here for God knew
how long, it was close to mint.

I stood and slipped it into the back pocket of my
jeans, then knelt and rummaged in the dirt again.
Perhaps I would find something else buried here,
something lost by someone long ago that would give a
clue to the medallion's age or Jason's identity. I didn't
find anything, yet still found the work absorbing, an
indication, I suppose, that something Stephen had always said to me was true: Small things amuse small
minds.

During the next twenty or thirty minutes, I worked
my way around the edge of the crater, manually turning the earth in search of history. I'd already decided
to make a complete circuit of the rim before stepping
down inside the hole, and I was close to finishing
with the perimeter when the scream shattered the air
like a rifle shot.

"Siegfried! No!"

I spun around, almost losing my balance and toppling into the pit.

"*SIEGFRIEEEEEEEEEEED!*"

In that instant I felt a panic I'd felt only once before, when that student in my lovable small-town school had pulled his deer-gutting knife on me, had pushed me to the wall next to the chalkboard and held it to my chest.

The dog I'd seen that morning frolicking in the yard was no more than thirty feet away across the north pasture, and he wasn't frolicking anymore. Not by any stretch of the imagination. That massive beast was charging straight at me, hackles raised, teeth bared in a terrifyingly vivid snarl. The boy was at its heels, trying to call the dog back, trying to stop it before it could kill me, but right then there seemed to be little doubt about who would reach me first. That dog was so much quicker, more powerful than the boy.

"Siegfried! Stop now! Noooooo!"

There was nowhere I could run, trapped as I was at the edge of the pit alongside the treeline and the barbed-wire fence, so I did the only thing I could. I raised my hands to ward the animal off, a foolishly weak gesture that to an outsider might have seemed comical if the situation hadn't been so deadly. I think I cried the word "no" myself, but I'm not sure if I said it or only wanted to say it. The dog was less than fifteen feet away now, and its pace had not slowed.

And then the impossible happened. The young boy leaped forward and snagged his dog around the neck, catching fur and flesh and hanging on, screaming at the beast to stop, to leave me alone. The animal's momentum carried it forward a few more feet before it came to a reluctant stop five feet from where I stood. With its owner still clinging to its neck, it planted its forefeet in a combative stance and growled at me, a low, eerie sound that came from deep in the back of its throat.

"Bad Siegfried!" the boy scolded. "Bad, bad dog. Bad boy."

The dog didn't seem chastened in the least, but it did stop growling and relaxed its position a little. After a long, silent moment the boy released his grip. The threat appeared to be over.

The boy hurried to my side, looking up at me with wide, frightened eyes. And yes, it was the boy who couldn't exist, the boy who'd awakened me with a cool touch, the boy who'd frolicked across the yard that very morning. It was the phantom boy, the ghost boy.

"You all right, mister? You all right?"

I spoke without thinking. "Yes. I'm okay, Jason. Thank you."

At the sound of his master's name, Siegfried uttered a short growl, but made no menacing moves.

"You know my name," Jason said. "How do ya know my name, mister?"

I reached into my pocket and pulled out the medallion. I held it out to him and he opened his small, pale hand to take it from me. He turned it over and over, staring at it without saying a word. Over and over, like a magician practicing a trick.

"That is yours, isn't it, son?"

"Yes, mister. Yessir, it is. You found my medal. Lord-golly, you really found my medal! Where?"

I made a vague gesture at the pit behind me, and then, aware that this was a kind of magical moment, an impossible conversation that could end abruptly at any instant, I said, "Son . . . who are you?"

The boy frowned, gripping his medallion tightly and holding it to his chest.

"I'm not going to hurt you, boy. Who are you?"

"Jason Widder," he said in a small, weak voice.

"And who's Fanny? Is Fanny your sister?"

Clearly, I'd said the wrong thing. The boy's expression changed in a flash from one of shy interest to one of hot panic. He leaped forward, grabbing on to the front of my shirt, letting the medallion fall to the ground.

"Where's Fanny? You've seen her? Where is she? Where is—"

"Whoa, Jason, hang on." I extricated myself from his grip, stepping aside. Siegfried growled again but remained where he was. "I haven't seen Fanny. I just want to know who she is. Is she your sister?"

He stared at me for a long moment, and I could almost see the wheels rapidly turning inside that small blond head. He was debating whether or not to believe me, whether or not to trust me with any information beyond his name. I stared back at him, trying to make my expression both firm and kind. I tried not to let the fact that I was standing in the north pasture holding a conversation with a ghost—for surely that's what was happening—enter my thinking at all. I was very afraid of what I'd do if I thought about that too much. I was scared that if I allowed myself to admit that I was speaking to a phantom, I might run screaming into the field.

"She's my sister," Jason said at last. "But I haven't seen her in . . . in a long time. I'm scared, mister. I think my papa might've gotten her."

Puzzled, I said, "Your father? Is he around?"

" 'Course he is! And he wants to hurt Fanny and me." He stepped closer again and dropped his voice to a husky whisper. "He tried to kill us, both of us."

"But, son . . . Jason . . . aren't you . . . oh, Jesus . . . aren't you already dead? Aren't you already—" I stopped in mid-sentence, because the boy's expression had changed yet again. I knew right away that by asking him that question I had ruined the magical moment myself. It was going to end very soon, and my words had ended it. The boy and the dog began to flicker in front of me like an image on a piece of extremely bad film. Frightened, not ready to let go, I reached out and tried to hang on to him, but he was fading, fading oh, so fast, and my hand closed on an insubstantial form, closed on nothing but air.

"Jason, no! Stay here, son, I'm sorry! I'm sorry, Jason, but don't—"

Again I stopped. It was too late. I was alone in the field, hard against the edge of the gaping crater, with nothing to show for the incredible thing that'd just taken place. I had no boy and no dog, no answers to my hundreds—thousands—of questions. Nothing. Even the medallion was gone.

"Jason, please come back," I said, without much hope. My only answer was the rumble of traffic on the highway a half mile away.

"Jason?" I said again, loudly. "Please?"

A gentle breeze stirred my hair, and I could feel my heart breaking when after five minutes no one had come to join me in the field.

6

Mom and Debbie didn't get back from the city until just before suppertime, and by the time they did I'd had plenty of opportunity to think about what had happened to me at the back of the north pasture that morning.

I believed it all by then. Quite frankly, it didn't seem I had any choice. First of all, I didn't know a lot about psychology—one of my worst courses in college—or the various manifestations of unstable, failing minds, so I had nothing to do but resort to that old line—I know what I saw, therefore it had to be true.

With that simple realization came a sort of peace. At least I no longer felt the fear I'd felt before. Whether or not I should be scared that there were ghosts haunting my parents' property—haunting *me* —I didn't know, but they seemed harmless enough, almost powerless. Good Lord, Jason didn't even seem to know what he was. It was as if he didn't understand that he was dead, that the world was different now than when he'd been alive. He was still looking for a sister who'd been dead for maybe one hundred years, running from a father gone nearly as long.

So I was no longer worried for my sanity or safety, at least at that moment. But I was still troubled, this time by the horrendous sense of loss I'd felt when the boy and his dog had vanished. I'd thought at the time that my heart had broken when they'd left me alone, and even later that didn't seem far from the mark. And I couldn't say why.

It might have been losing a chance to complete my "interview," which was, I had to admit, the opportunity of a lifetime. Yes, it might have been that, but I thought there was something else working at me too. Without understanding, I felt an even greater opportunity had vanished along with Jason and Siegfried. Without knowing what or why or how, I sensed that some mighty chance had been just millimeters away from my fingertips, a chance that had evaporated like the morning mist that lay over the farm before sunrise each day.

After dinner Debbie and I left the family on the porch and took a walk around the property, skirting the barn and going out to the head of the driveway, along the road. We sat on the remains of the fallen tree where Steve and I had once had our treehouse and talked a lot about a lot of things. I wanted desperately to tell her what had happened that morning, but couldn't. Maybe it was because I didn't have the vocabulary to describe what was happening to me. Or maybe it was because I was just too damned confused to risk embarrassing myself in front of my younger sister, the girl I'd spent my entire life idolizing.

"You still seem kinda tired," she said at one point, "worn out. Did you have those . . . *dreams* . . . again last night?"

I forced a phony smile, at the same time feeling awful about lying to her. "No dreams," I said. "I slept like a baby."

That wasn't precisely a lie, but I knew that sleep wasn't the issue and that my answer was only artful sidestepping.

She reminded me again that she was a good listener, invoking the childhood pact between us and our dead brother, and so she wouldn't feel mistrusted or neglected, I talked to her. But not about Jason.

Instead I dredged out all the tales of my rookie year as a teacher, giving her the chance she craved to feel motherly, to provide aid and comfort.

It was much later on, when I went to bed, that I came to understand what was still bothering me about that morning. Like something Biblical, the answers showed up in a dream.

"Hey, Peter, you c'mon outta there right now!" Stephen said to me. "You c'mon out and we'll talk, man to man! Just me and my big brother!"

I was hiding in a familiar place, behind the mountain of bales in the lower barn, wedged between scratchy hay and baling wire and cold stone walls. Stephen knew I was there, because I'd always been there as a kid. It was that lack of originality that made me "it" a lot in our three-way games of hide-and-seek.

"C'mon, Peter, I know where you are, so just show yourself. Let's have a little talk, just the two of us, whaddya say?"

Slowly I stood up and came around the edge of the hay, flashing a sheepish grin.

"You always knew where I hid, dammit. Always."

Stephen grinned.

He looked the way I wanted him to look, the way I've always chosen to remember him. Younger than me, he'd nevertheless been taller, with a more muscular, athletic build. More handsome, too. Not a sixteen-year-old Adonis, exactly; that would be an exaggeration. But it wouldn't be untruthful to say that he'd had more success with girls before his death than I've had at my age.

"Yeah, I always knew," he said now. "Just like I always knew what was on your mind. I could tell you right now what you're thinking."

"Oh? What am I thinking?"

"You're thinking how good I look for someone who's been dead so long." He laughed. "You were worried that when you came out from your spot there, I'd be all bloody and banged up, like if the Allis had just rolled over on me. You thought it'd be closed-casket time all over again."

Wincing, I said, "You're right. You always could tell what I was thinking."

His lips stretched back in a long, sly grin. "I know what else you're thinking, Peter. You're thinking about that little kid, Jason, the one with the dog." Another laugh. "Siegfried . . . a Nazi dog, or something. I'm right, aren't I? You're thinking about the kid with the Nazi dog."

I nodded, aware for the first time that this had to be a dream. Usually, discovering a dream in its middle is a fun experience—it means you're okay, safe, free to do anything you damned well want. Somehow, it wasn't like that this time. I knew I was in my bed, that Stephen and I weren't standing in the lower barn. I knew that everything was a product of my sleeping subconscious, and yet it was still a humbling, awesome experience. I was so glad to see my dead brother that I wanted to throw my arms around him and hug him close, but I couldn't. God help me, but I was afraid. Of him, of myself, of the discovery I felt barreling at me from just around some mental corner.

"Yeah," Stephen said then. "Jason. He died a long time ago, you know."

"I know. But he doesn't know he's dead. At least

. . . at least I don't think so. Talking to him was strange. It—"

"Hey, Peter, I was there," Stephen told me. "I saw the whole thing. You had a million questions to ask him."

I wanted to deny it, absurdly embarrassed that my brother, the ghost, had seen me talking to another ghost. But of course I couldn't deny a thing.

"You wanted to ask him how he died. And about that sister of his, Fanny, or whatever her name is. You wanted to ask about his father. You wanted to know what it's like over here on this side, and you wanted to know about me. You were older than me, yeah, but not a helluva lot smarter. I could always figure out what was really on your mind. You wanted to know if the kid'd seen me . . . you thought if *he* could come back, maybe I could, too."

And that was really the end of the dream, for although I know it went on some time longer, that surreal conversation stretching out for several more minutes through Stephen's questions, Stephen's observations, and my meek acknowledgments, the important part of it passed right then.

He was right. That was why the conversation in the north pasture had seemed so important, and why I'd been heartbroken when it had ended. Jason was my key to the mystery of Stephen's death. My brother had died young and so had Jason. Jason came and went from the other side and so might my brother.

I awoke in the dark, sharp and alert from the moment my eyes opened. A thin ribbon of sweat was trickling past my right eye; I swept it away and climbed out of bed, got dressed without turning on the light. It was several moments before I realized I was talking to myself in a husky whisper as I zipped my jeans and tied my sneakers.

"That's it," I was saying over and over. "Go find Jason. Drag him over to this side. That's it. Get the answers. Yeah. That's it. Get the answers."

I shut my mouth as soon as I heard what I was saying.

The house was lit by moonlight coming through the windows as I made my way down the steps, through the kitchen and outside. My mind was spinning out of control. The dream had made me think about a lot of things—Stephen for one, my mother's cancer for another, and there were more—all of which were rushing at me now, all in a jumble, demanding to be considered and debated, pushing to have their say.

I stopped at the edge of the gravel, where the front lawn of the farmhouse met the driveway. The moon was even brighter out here, lighting the barn like a floodlight; the shadow the huge building cast looked distorted, monstrous. I swallowed and took a long, slow breath, exhaled, took another, and sighed. I wasn't completely in control, but obviously the edgy, caffeine-like high I was on now was as relaxed as I was going to get.

Answers.

That seemed like the single most important word in the universe as I crossed the lawn heading for the north pasture.

7

I stood at the bottom of the box elder crater for the first time. It was even bigger than I remembered;

when I tried to look over the rim, I had to crane my head back and up before I could see the bases of the other trees, the barbed-wire fence they masked. I couldn't see the passing headlights on the highway at all.

My walk through the timothy had done a little bit to sober me up, and now, twenty minutes after getting out of bed, I was reaching a point of some rationality. That is, I was beginning to wonder what I was doing there.

It was two o'clock in the morning and I was alone at the edge of my father's property, ready to conjure up the ghost of a little boy who'd been killed by his father a long, long time ago. Why? So that the little boy—who didn't even realize what he was, mind you —could point the way to the other side, could tell me, perhaps, how to bring my dead brother back, how to stop my mother's cancer before it killed her, or maybe how to turn back the clock to a time when a swelling tumor and a tractor rollover were unheard of, could possibly be averted.

Magic, I thought. That's what I'm after. Simple magic. Impossible magic.

I sighed again and thought of something a teacher had said to me just before Christmas of the last year. He was a twelve-year veteran of the school that was killing me, and he'd taken me aside in the faculty lounge, smiling and saying, "I know what your problem is, Manse. You had your head in the clouds. Small town, north woods, rural consolidated school. You were thinking heaven and roses. Shit, Peter, nothing's heaven and roses. Put your feet on the ground and you'll see it's not that bad, though. Look at it a little realistically and you might get to like it. But for God's sake, stop dreaming."

Hearing those words in my mind, I wondered if that's what I was doing now—looking for roses again, heaven and roses. I wondered if my head was back in the clouds.

"Jason?"

The name escaped my lips before I even knew I was preparing to say it. It startled me, and I broke out in gooseflesh.

"Jason? Jason Widder?"

A truck rumbled by on the highway. When that intrusion passed, I heard footsteps coming toward me in the dark. No longer afraid of ghosts, as I had been when that cool touch had awakened me in the dark, I was nonetheless afraid of deeper things. The soft approaching footsteps made my breath catch in my throat. I felt a band of cold pressure seal itself around my heart and begin to tighten.

"Jason? I'm here, Jason, where I found your medallion."

The footsteps came closer, moving like a whisper through the timothy. Soft . . . like a stealthy animal . . . soft . . . like a spirit moving before a gentle breeze.

"I'm here, Jason," I said. My voice had dropped to a rough whisper.

The footsteps paused, moved forward again, then stopped entirely. I was opening my mouth to speak the boy's name once more, but what came out instead was a scream—the sound of shock and pent-up frustration—when Debbie spoke to me.

"Who the hell're you talking to, Peter? Who's Jason?

And what're you doing out here in the middle of the night?"

8

She had followed me easily, hearing me on the stairs and dogging my path like a spy as I crossed the yard and the pasture. Embarrassed, I allowed myself to be led back to the house but refused to go in. We sat instead on the porch steps, our backs to the screen door, our knees touching, the only sounds for a very long time the constant chirr of crickets and the distant barking of the Arlettes' dog, more than a mile down the road.

Finally: "Another bad dream, big brother?"

I laughed. It was so like her, going for even a small laugh in the face of what, to her, must have seemed an insanity.

"Actually, it wasn't all that bad. I dreamed about Steve this time."

Even in the dark I could feel her gaze sharpen. "What about Steve?"

"I dreamed . . . no, I *found* a way to change everything. To bring Stephen back. To maybe get rid of Mom's cancer. I don't know . . . but I think I found a way to make everything better again. To give me another chance at the decision. You know. To let me take over the farm, work with Dad, anyway, until he'd be ready to turn it over to Steve and me."

I stopped the rush of words as abruptly as I'd started them, felt my skin go hot and crimson. None of that was true—it was nothing but fantasy—and it was certainly nothing to be telling Debbie, whom I'd always loved and admired, whose admiration I'd craved in return.

Savagely, I wondered what was happening to me. Talking to spirits, running into pastures in the middle of the night, fantasizing things that could never be. And worse, talking about all of it.

Debbie was still giving me that hard stare. I didn't respond, pretending to be interested in the worn spots on the knees of my jeans.

"Peter?"

I still didn't answer. Jesus, I'd said enough already.

"Peter, what's wrong? Good Lord, was the teaching really *that* bad? What did they do to you in that hick town?"

This time I responded, but it was just a mumbled word: "Nothing."

"Are you serious about staying here, on the farm? My God, don't you remember how we worked? Don't you remember how important school became to us after the accident? How it was the only way out? And we got out! Both of us! This is supposed to be our last summer here. . . . I didn't tell them yet, but it is. Next summer I'm going East with a friend, going to take classes at an art school near Cape Cod, a workshop thing. And by next year you should be really settled . . . somewhere.

"Peter . . . look at me . . . tell me you're not seriously thinking about staying on the farm."

I turned to face her for the first time since my outburst. I felt another one coming on, but managed to keep it simple. "Debbie, this farm is haunted. There are ghosts here."

Her mouth opened, working soundlessly for a moment. Then she began to cry. "Oh, Peter, dammit!"

She got up and fled into the house, the screen door slamming behind her, loud enough to wake the dead.

I stayed on the steps for a while, looking out across the moonstruck yard, seeing Stephen, Jason, and Siegfried in every shadow. There was my brother, leaning against the open barn doors, grinning at me, his teeth dazzling, his posture casual. There was the dead boy, with his dog, near the base of the silo, crouched and watching, as though wanting to approach but not wanting me to ruin everything again by telling him he was dead.

Close to dawn I went inside and back to my room, pausing long enough outside my parents' bedroom to look in and see them in their twin beds. I felt a tear roll down my cheek as I stared at my mother's curled and sleeping form.

Dammit.

I'd ruined it for Jason. I'd ruined it for Debbie. My own mind was a tempest. And yet I hadn't meant any harm. I just wanted to make it all better. A simple thing. I just wanted everything to be fine, the way it had been a long time ago.

9

I heard them talking about me as I came down for breakfast later that morning. I heard my mother protesting something Debbie had just said, heard my father grunt in surprise, heard Debbie rush on, mentioning something about professional help, a doctor. I paused only long enough to hear that before making my entrance.

I knew I looked a wreck—fifteen minutes in the

shower and ten in front of the bathroom mirror had done nothing to erase the effects of the night. My eyes were narrowed and bloodshot, my cheeks surprisingly sunken. Combing my hair had been a worthless endeavor since it was as dry as straw, flying away in several directions at once.

"G' morning."

My father grunted again as I came around the corner. Debbie let out a small cry. My grandmother muttered, "Shit." Only my mother remained calm and tried to act normal, although I could tell by the way she was looking at me that Debbie had told them everything I'd said and done in the middle of the night.

"I hear we lost a tree out at the property line," Dad said then, confirming what I'd suspected. "I guess it went down in that storm."

"I guess so," I said. And then: "Deb? I really need to talk to you. Will you take a walk with me?"

What came next frightened me more than anything else that had happened—more than the storm or the voice in the night, more than the cool touch on my cheek or the vicious charge of the phantom dog. What happened was that Debbie didn't answer me right away. Instead she looked at Mom and Dad, at my grandmother, with a pleading expression in her eyes, a look that said plainly: "Get me out of this. I don't want to be near Peter because he's crazy."

My sister. My own little sister.

Nothing, even the dim and oh-so-distant possibility of recapturing the past, was worth that.

"Please, Deb? Give me a half hour, will you? I don't think that's asking much."

She flashed me a very forced smile and said, "All

right, but only a half hour. Mom and I are going shopping again this morning."

"Debbie—" my mother said, but was cut off as my sister repeated, "Mom and I are going shopping again this morning."

The firmness in her voice as she restated the lie made me want to weep.

The talk didn't do any good. I tried, but in the end it was worthless.

I took her out to the box elder crater where she'd found me in the night and told her the entire story. At one point I had to reach out, grasp her wrist to keep her from hurrying away. She listened to the rest, shaking her head sadly throughout, and when I tried to get Jason to appear to us, she backed away several steps, watching with horrified fascination, certain, I'm sure, that the last of her brother's sanity had fled.

Jason didn't appear. Wouldn't appear. Not even the damned dog would show up. At last Debbie said she'd seen enough and returned to the house, leaving me sitting on the edge of the hole with my head in my hands.

He was my own personal spirit, I supposed. I didn't know why, but for some reason he had appeared to me and me alone, and now would be with me the rest of my life.

I looked up, knowing what I'd see.

Jason and Siegfried were standing just a few feet away, looking at me with concern.

"What's wrong, mister? You hurt?"

I nodded.

"You need help? I'd get my ma, but I can't find her.

Still, you gave my medal back and all, so if I can help you, you just say the word."

I tried to tell him to leave. That's what I wanted very badly to say to him—Go away, dammit, just go away, you're dead—but the words that came out when I spoke were much different.

"Who are you, Jason? Tell me about yourself."

He looked surprised. I had to prompt him again for the story, which was finally told. He started speaking slowly, cautiously, but gradually gained confidence and speed. I don't believe it took more than ten minutes to hear about his life.

He was eight years old, he told me, and lived nearby (here he motioned with a small hand to the subdivision across the highway, which had been privately owned farmland when I was a child). His mama and papa worked nearly twenty acres, grew a great deal of corn and oats, raised chickens and pigs. They had one cow and one horse. The pride of the farm was a new four-row plow that had been purchased recently.

His papa, it seemed, was a man taken with the holy word of God. It was he who'd given Jason the medallion, had given a smaller but similar one to Jason's sister Fanny. He was a strong man, a good man, but unfortunately was taken with drink almost as much as he was with the power of the Scriptures. With his drinking bouts came episodes of surliness, which served only to warn the family that an outbreak of horrible violence was soon to follow. Jason's papa had, in the past, broken some of his mother's fine china; he had smashed a kitchen chair against a doorframe; he had beaten the cow and kicked the chickens and attacked the pigs with a pitchfork. On several occasions he had physically beaten Jason and Fanny, once so badly that Jason had needed a rushed trip to Dr. Grumbacher, who lived more than five miles away.

His mama—"the best person in the world"—tried to control these episodes, and more often than not received a few licks of her own as compensation. In the end, the only good she could ever do was to help the children *after* their beatings, by holding and hugging them, by crooning lullabies while they fell asleep in the single bed they shared in the loft.

One day—Jason couldn't remember how long ago now—his papa had been even more taken with the drink than usual. It had been a very, very long time between bouts, and the children had allowed themselves to believe the drinking might be over for good, that their papa's promises to cure himself had finally come true. But now they realized that the time between episodes hadn't meant anything at all, in fact had served only to make the next attack worse.

On that final day Jason's papa actually killed the horse and several of the chickens. Then he came after Jason with anything and everything he could find: a shovel, a hand rake, the awful pitchfork, his own belt and boots. Jason remembered being battered very badly, remembered Siefried trying to come to his defense but being beaten back, and after that he became confused. He recalled fainting and then waking up in a world where everything was different—"It smells different, sounds different . . . it *feels* different"— and where he couldn't find his way home.

He had been wandering the area for an indeterminate time, often through a fog that he described as "a dreadful mist" and often in total darkness "even in the heat of noon," trying to find his way back across the wide road to home, trying to locate his mama so that she could help soothe him as always, and trying to find his beloved sister Fanny, who, he feared, might have been hurt very badly in their papa's last fiery burst of drinking violence.

"But it's different," he repeated in conclusion. His voice was beginning to quaver. Siegfried hovered over him protectively. "I know where I am, mister, really. I know I live just over there. But I can't *get* there, try as I might! I can't find the house or the barn. I call for my mama and she doesn't come. And I can't find F-Fanny anywhere!"

Now the tears exploded from inside him, and I got up and moved to his side, cradling the little ghost boy in my arms, hugging his phantom but nevertheless very real body, stroking his dead but oh-so-tangible hair. I crooned words to him that I imagined his mama might croon, if they could somehow find each other in the darkness one hundred years after their deaths.

"I just wanna go home," he murmured against my shoulder.

"I know," I whispered in his ear, as my own tears started to come. "Believe me, Jason, I know, I know."

10

They found me about twenty minutes later. My father. My mother. My grandmother. Debbie. I must have been a helluva sight to them, sitting there alone on the edge of the crater, crying, shivering, speaking to the dead.

They got me back to the house, where I promptly succumbed to what my doctor later called a batch-illness. "Exhaustion," he told my parents, "and influenza and a bronchial infection that's damned near pneumonia." I was treated there in the farmhouse, had to stay on my back in my childhood room for almost two weeks. During that time I was visited often, both by my doctor and by another doctor, who was introduced as a colleague doing a paper for a prestigious medical journal on the treatment of upper respiratory ailments. I didn't find out until much later that this second man was a psychiatrist.

When I recovered, Debbie and I went to Madison for a weekend together. I looked up old college buddies, showed Deb the places of what I referred to as my flaming youth, ate a lot of pizza, drank a fair amount of beer. We saw three movies, a bad rock concert by two local groups, and a summer stock version of *Charley's Aunt* featuring a fading soap opera star whose name I've forgotten. In short, we crammed more into two and a half days than I ever had before or have since.

When we went back to the farm, I began the letters and phone calls, the newspaper scouring and cashing in of old debts that make up the search for a new teaching job.

All that was nearly five years ago. In the time between then and now my grandmother passed away quietly in her sleep. My mother went into remission a second time, finally relapsed, and died just before Christmas last year. My father, burdened like all farmers by rising costs and diminishing prices, sold the property after my mother's death and is living in a Florida condominium where he dabbles in rock collecting, photography, and God knows what else. He wrote to me recently and said that he is happy, though I wonder how a man born and raised on a farm, who made his living from the land for so long, can really be happy in the land of grapefruit and polyester. Debbie graduated from U of I and has a fine job teaching art at a private New England college. She has never given up her own painting, and recently had a show at a Boston gallery. Unknown to her, I have clippings from the Boston papers, good reviews of her work. I keep those clippings on my desk, where I can look at them whenever I feel the need and think of her.

Myself, I'm living in northern California, teaching high school in a largish consolidated district and loving it most of the time. I have learned, as that veteran Michigan teacher once counseled, not to set my sights so high. I no longer search for heaven and roses. Bad students exist, obviously, but so do many good ones, even a few great ones. For every industrial arts animal who sulks in the back of the room, there is a literature lover in the front row, with his or her hand eagerly raised. No one has pulled a deer-gutting knife on me recently. I am active in board politics, and currently am helping design a new curriculum package for the next school year.

In the last five years I've dreamed of Steve only once. In the dream I was sitting at my desk, grading essays on—what else?—*The Catcher in the Rye* and listening to Prokofiev on the stereo. I glanced up and saw him standing in the doorway, leaning against the frame, young and healthy as always, casually relaxed.

He didn't speak. But he smiled at me. It wasn't his hell-raising rogue's smile but rather something more calm. A little more sedate. Wise. Almost beatific.

As though he approved.

I have a good life now. There really isn't a better way to describe it than that. It's not perfect, surely, but it's comfortable. On bad days I am able to look ahead, and on good days it's difficult to imagine that there was a time when I wanted something more, something so very much different.

But there are times when I awake in the middle of the night and imagine I hear a tractor chugging away in the distance, or hear a screen door slamming and Steve's footsteps racing down the front walk, or hear my mother whistling bad Big Band music as she bakes in the kitchen. I hear those things and my eyes fill and I wonder what if . . . what if I could have . . . if I could . . .

At those times I also hear another sound, one that fills my heart and mind with a longing so intense that it's quite simply beyond words.

I hear the sound of a large dog barking as it races past the house, the sound of a lost young boy following behind, calling its German name over and over and over again.

I hear that and wonder if he, alone among all the creatures who ever walked the earth, has managed to find his way back.

Walkie-Talkie

Donald R. Burleson

The house stood gaunt and bleak in the falling snow, a quarter of a mile from its nearest neighbors. Truthfully, Ken had expected no cheer upon seeing the place again, he had, in fact, rather dreaded it, and now that the Victorian frame loomed before him against the evening sky like some stiff-backed old recluse in the swirling gray-white flakes, he had an unpleasant taste in his mouth, looking at the shuttered bay windows and winter-dusted gables. An unpleasant taste, and his feelings were too muddled even to tell exactly why.

He pulled the car into the driveway and got out, stood for a moment, turning his collar up and trying to collect his thoughts. The house wasn't officially on the market yet, but he had had people at the real estate office looking in on it for him—being sure the furnace was operating at least at a low level to keep the pipes from freezing, that sort of thing. And now that he had finally had an opportunity to come up from Connecticut and see to matters, the house would be listed for sale soon, as soon as he could sort out his parents' things and take care of whatever else had to be done. Somehow now the place looked pathetically dependent on him, a once-strong companion come down to helplessness and solitude, a once-reverberant arena now silent.

Trudging across the front yard, he glanced at his mother's snow-crusted rhododendrons flanking the bottom of the porch steps like two squat multiheaded gargoyles; Mom would have covered them, of course, before the first frost if she had had the chance. As he creaked up the steps onto the porch, he noticed his father's snow shovel leaning against the wall by the door, in the shelter of the porch; it had always been one of Dad's gentle little foibles that he left the shovel there for most of the year instead of putting it away down in the cellar. In the winter Mom would caution him about shoveling snow for more than a few minutes at a time, a man his age, bad for the heart. Well, it had required no snowstorm-induced heart attack to take Dad to the grave—just some drunken imbecile, driving full-tilt at him on the wrong side of Route 101. Mom too; both of them dead-on-arrival in the ambulance. No more snow shoveling now, no more rhododendrons.

Ken unlocked the front door, stepped into the house, stamping snow off his shoes, closed the door softly behind him, and switched on the light. The utilities were all still connected; he had had the bills mailed to him in New Haven.

He surveyed the living room. Odd, how much dust could settle on everything in only a few months. He would have come up to manage the sale of the house earlier if his affairs had permitted; now the place would need a thorough cleaning before it could be shown to anyone. The dust seemed to blanket everything, softening all the corners, making details indistinct. Bookcases, end tables, sofa, chairs protruded mutely from the muffling dust like frozen pieces of old conversation, fossil memories, awkward and absurd remnants, of what was once life. This was all it came to, then.

He hadn't entered the house at the time of the funeral, back in early October, and rather wished he hadn't done so now. A motel in town for a few days would have been expensive, but now it seemed odd that he had let that persuade him to stay here in the house. There must have been other, less conscious reasons, he thought; maybe he had really needed to return to the little piece of New Hampshire where he had spent his childhood, to look at the house once again before it passed out of the family forever, look at it and see if—what? He didn't know, couldn't quite formulate his motives. But here he was, in any case, standing in an ossuary of family relics, looking at the now meaningless jumble of objects around him, objects no longer animated by the presence of the life they had been a part of, dust-drifted objects standing in quietly sardonic assembly. They seemed to say: We never sang in the church choir or planted shrubs or ran a business or raised a son or read poetry aloud or twinkled with consciousness and intelligence, but we survive; the world abounds with irony, does it not, young friend?

Young? God, it seemed like a long, long time ago that he'd been a child in this house.

Maybe that's because I haven't been back here very often since, he thought, flipping the pages of a telephone book on the little table by the door to the dining room and watching it send up a wheezing little cloud of dust. Outside, the wind gathered in a forlorn-sounding moan at the shuttered windows, and a little eddy of cold ash stirred vaguely in the depths of the chimney's yawning black mouth. More often, he reflected, Mom and Dad had come down to New Haven for a visit, especially after his divorce nine years ago; Melinda and his folks had never gotten along. Had he been selfish, making them travel to see him rather than the other way around? In any event, childhood in this house—the dog, the Christmases, the red bicycle, Judy, the swimming and picnic trips to Greenfield State Park—all these things felt more like images half-remembered from some book than real memories.

Why had he thought of Judy?

He walked through the dining room to the kitchen, where the ivory-colored stove and refrigerator looked like angular dinosaurs projected at him through shrouds of dust. Fortunately, on his way in he had eaten at some fast-food place at the edge of town, and would eat out in the morning, but he might well have to think of doing some cooking here if his stay lasted for very many days. Not that he wanted to. There was something almost ghoulish about the thought of using his mother's kitchen when she— He was going to have to get hold of himself; there was work to be done in the days ahead, things that had to be handled with a clear mind. Enough of idle and pointless woolgathering.

He returned to the front of the house and started climbing the stairs, flipping the switch to the stairwell light only to see the bulb up there brighten and go out, leaving the upward regions cavernously dark. Climbing, he felt the muscles pulling painfully in the small of his back, threatening the trouble he sometimes had; distant, indeed, were the memories of bounding up and down these stairs as a spry schoolboy. At the top he was relieved to find that the upstairs hall light did snap on to wash a pale but adequate illumination over the worn carpeting and faded Victorian wallpaper. There was a musty smell everywhere. Avoiding his parents' bedroom for the moment—plenty of time later to go through their things —he proceeded to the second door and opened it. The hinges creaked, stirring dust-softened echoes. He entered his old room and turned on the overhead light.

All was unchanged—the dilapidated bed, the battered and several-times refinished bureau, the nightstand, the rickety bookcase, the window with the chipped pane that Judy had broken, countless years ago, tossing up a rock to summon his face to the window. Now another face leaned suddenly at him from behind the window, a face contorted into saurian folds of sable flesh. It was his own, older now, and rippled into odd strata by the closed black shutters beyond the panes. He stared at the reflection that the panes, the shutters gave back into the lighted room, stared at the ancient chipped glass.

Judy.

Pushing the thought to the back of his mind, he opened the closet and surveyed its superficial contents—a nondescript jumble of hanging clothes, several cardboard boxes on the floor, and a litter of miscellaneous things on the shelf above the clothing. He would have to go through all this, along with the contents of the rest of the house. Some of the cardboard boxes exuded an odor of mildew and must have been moved up from storage in the cellar at some point, perhaps to save them from further dampness; he wondered what might be in them. But he had more immediate concerns; his luggage was still in the car, and the shutters on all these windows could at least be opened and latched back. He had arranged to have them closed to protect the windows while the house sat empty, but he had to have them open now—the house was enough like a tomb already.

At the door of his room he switched off the light, but stood for a moment looking back into the room in the wan light from the hall. What was in those boxes? The past; jumbled little jigsaw-puzzle pieces of himself. No, he was sure there weren't even any pictures of Judy. Nothing left of her, except in the mind.

He descended the musty stairwell, hearing the wind sighing all around against the house. Outside, the snow was falling harder.

By the time he had brought up his luggage and gone around seeing to all the shutters (lingering only as briefly as possible in his parents' silent bedroom), it was well past eleven o'clock, but he wasn't sleepy. Back up in his room (*his* room, for a man in his early forties, in a house about to be sold and walked away from forever?) he switched on the bedside lamp and lifted one of the mildewy cardboard boxes out of the closet and onto the bed. He tore at the masking tape, opened the carton, and started piling the contents to one side on the bed. He had to be careful; if he bent over the bed too long at a time, his lower back sent up brittle slivers of pain, and it was difficult to straighten up. He peered at the mounting heap on the bed—old posters, folded up; school yearbooks; a woolen cap with a large hole; spiral notebooks; baseball cards bound up in rubber bands; a framed perfect-attendance award from the ninth grade; two packages of brown shoelaces; an envelope full of old coins; a pair of gritty-looking sunglasses; pencils; a watercolor paint set rusted shut; a Boy Scout handbook; a pocketknife rusted shut; a Duncan yoyo with string still attached; a magnifying glass; more pencils; and, near the bottom, a small oblong object wrapped in a dishtowel. The windowpanes creaked coldly in the wind, and somehow now he felt he would have been more comfortable if he had left at least these shutters closed against the night.

Sitting down on the bed (a sharp back pain, quickly subsiding), he began to unroll the dishtowel, wondering what the object inside it was. And wondering why the thought of it, the vague feel of it through the cloth, made him nervous when he didn't even know yet what it was. Or did he?

Yes—God, from that Christmas morning unimaginable years ago. Odd, to hold the thing again, turning it over in his hands as he must have turned it over in smaller hands that first time. Now, though, the feeling was different. No seasonal family chatter this time, no candle glow and tinsel and laughter, no eggnog, no boyish thrill. Just a silent house, just an older mind burdened with a restless litany of memories threatening to writhe awake.

The walkie-talkie unit was still in good condition, at least to the eye; its hard black plastic casing was a little dulled but nowhere cracked or chipped. It didn't feel as heavy as he remembered it. "Press to transmit" was still legible in tiny raised letters beside a button, and on the back the little panel slid open easily to reveal a space for two flashlight batteries, empty now. A sorry mess it would have been by now if batteries had been left inside; he had been only twelve that Christmas and had never used the set past that following summer. Judy had been twelve, too.

He slid the battery cover closed again with a snap and set the unit on the nightstand beside the bed. There had been, of course, another identical unit; he could still remember how the pair of them had looked, side by side in the box, when he first opened the package that far-off morning—shiny twin bundles of promise appealing instantly, joyously, to a wide-eyed, Christmas-intoxicated boy too old for Santa Claus myths, too young for the trials that were to come.

He had entrusted Judy with the other walkie-talkie unit the next day. Judy down the street, Judy with the sometimes roguish, sometimes pensive face, with the cat-green eyes that sometimes twinkled with mirth but sometimes held pond-bottom depths of mystery—Judy whose straw-blond hair blew free in the wind, whose tomboy face was turning pretty. Gone all these years now, stirrable only in the gray ash of memory.

Kenny-me-boy, she had called him. He could almost recall now the first edge of excitement he had felt as they tried the units out, he on his front porch, she a few hundred yards away behind her own house, the unit in his hand crackling into life. "Kenny-me-boy. Can you hear me?" He had pressed the transmit button and answered. Even now he remembered that he had thought of replying in kind by calling her Judy-me-girl, but something in his pubescent mind had been reluctant, reluctant to imply that she might be "his girl." It was different; her epithet for him didn't imply "boyfriend," he thought, though he hadn't been sure. He called her Judy, and said yes, he could hear her. And they talked back and forth, laughing, until some of the novelty of the thing wore off. He let her keep the other unit, not even accepting it back after he could have done so.

How strange and ambivalent life had been at that age. A rough-and-tumble playmate known since kindergarten suddenly began awakening into young womanhood, rather in advance of his own awakening, and a long-known pair of green eyes began to shine, at times, with a quality unfamiliar and a little disconcerting. Sometimes more than a little. She seemed impatient for him to develop a parallel to the urges stirring within her own frame, and at times he caught her looking at him with an expression whose meaning he was afraid to explore too honestly. But mostly things went on as usual, and he looked forward to hearing, after school, the walkie-talkie come to life ("Kenny-me-boy"), anticipated it with only a slight twinge of apprehension, heard it with only a partial understanding that a voice could change and take on new tonal undercurrents just as a pair of eyes could glimmer with newfound meanings.

Then that one afternoon in Phillips Park she fixed him with a stare only partly incongruous in so young a girl's face, and said, "Kiss me." He did, a desultory peck that she seemed to interpret as a little victory for herself, but only a little one; clearly, she had expected more, would expect more in time. And however normal an adult he had grown up to be, his twelve-year-old self hadn't been ready for her, for the depths in those eyes.

A sharp little sound at the window brought him back to the present.

Standing too suddenly, he winced at the clutch of pain in his back and walked, half-stooped, to the icy windowpanes. It had been a broken branch flung by the wind against the glass, of course. What else could it have been? His back slowly allowed him to straighten up, and he tried to look out the window, but the reflection of the room was too bright. Snapping off the lamp, he peered out into the night. The sky fell fragmented in countless shards of white, blanketing the shrubs, the fence, the yard below; down the way, the streetlamp was a solitary wan urchin standing at a loss in the storm. Nothing moved but the wind. He pulled the yellowed curtains closed.

Later, in his old bed, he slept poorly. In his dreams he thought he saw the walkie-talkie, the *other* unit, buried in trash and garbage in a dump yard, its black plastic case cracked and soiled. An obscured figure rooted in the foul refuse heap to dig it out and clutch it in what seemed more like a paw than a hand.

He slept much later than he had intended, rising headachy and tired. By the time he had dressed and showered and shoveled the driveway and gone downtown for something to eat, it was almost noon. He spent the afternoon at the real estate office on the town common, arranging to have the house listed for sale, and later stopped to buy some groceries, absently picking up a package of flashlight batteries at the checkout counter. He returned to the house to begin sorting out his parents' effects, bagging up a quantity of clothes for the Salvation Army bins and picking among the books downstairs to decide which ones to keep. By five o'clock it was quite dark outside and beginning to snow again.

He cooked himself pork chops and potatoes and made some coffee. Eating his cheerless meal at the kitchen table, he felt strange; too quiet in here, too many memories. As he was finishing his coffee, a sort of rattle sounded from just outside the house. He pulled on his overcoat in the living room, then stepped out onto the porch in a swirl of wind and snow. Something white and angular and hissing scuttered at him from the top of the steps. He uttered a little cry and shrank back against the door, sending the snow shovel thumping onto the porch. His assailant had been a sheet of newspaper tossed by the wind. Shuddering and pulling his coat collar tighter to his throat, he trudged around to the side of the house, toward the sound.

It was the wooden trellis that extended on that wall from the ground to just below his bedroom window, banging and clattering now in the wind. His father had built the latticework structure many years ago for his mother to grow creeping vines on, and he could just make out, wormlike here and there in the wet snow, the winter-blasted corpses of some of those vines in the pale radiance of the streetlight. The trellis was fairly sturdy, and on occasion Judy had climbed it to tap at his window, he remembered. Limned now in snow, it looked like an arrangement of thick, square white mouths all moaning in unison with the wind. He went back inside and busied himself with sorting out more books.

By ten o'clock he ascended the stairs very tired and went to his room. After undressing and getting into his robe, he placed on the nightstand the book he had brought up from the living room, and turned down the sheets on the bed. He was tired but somehow not sleepy now, and he found himself staring at the black plastic object beside the book on the nightstand. Going to his coat on the back of the chair, he retrieved the flashlight batteries from the pocket and sat back down on the bed to snap them into their compartment in the walkie-talkie.

He extended the whip antenna and clicked the unit on.

It hissed a constant crackling hiss, a radio receiver tuned to no station.

Hhhh-hhhhhhhh.

The sound of it was vaguely disquieting to him. Undead memories again. He smiled wanly at the absurdity of the thought that there could be anything to hear. He pressed the transmit button, not speaking into the microphone, of course, and released the button. The hissing surged up again.

Hhh-hhhhhhh—Khhh.

The formless sound was being modulated by the wind.

Khhh-hhhhh-hhn.

It was eerie, somehow, the way random radio noise could almost—

Khh-hhhn-nnn.

—could almost seem to shape itself into speech.

Khhh-nnnnn.

Dry, rasping, like spiderwebs made into sound.

He stared vacantly at the unit, which went on hissing its empty night sound. He thought of Judy, Judy never to grow further into womanhood, Judy dead all these years. When she had fallen ill, that summer following the Christmas of the walkie-talkie, he had visited her once in the hospital, and even there, even then, in her sedation, her now sunken green eyes had seemed to penetrate him with silent questions, expectations. *That little peck wasn't the kind of kiss I meant,* they seemed to say—but this surely had been his imagination. He had never quite come to terms with just why he had never visited her again. Maybe he simply couldn't bear to see her that way, maybe he didn't want to have to sort out his feelings, maybe he was just afraid to face her again. In any case, she was gone a week later, and it was a long time before he could walk past her house or linger near that bench in Phillips Park.

Khhh-hnnnn-hhhhh.

Lost in thought, he hadn't been listening. Had the sound—

Khhn-hhhee-mmmh-bhh-hhoi.

No, surely to God; enough of this. Outside, the wind had risen to a howl and was dashing wet puffs of snow against the windowpanes. He quietly rebuked himself for being so silly as to let the place, the house, the memories, the storm get on his nerves to this extent.

Khhn-hheee! Whispering, dry, toneless.

He pressed the button to transmit, feeling very foolish, and spoke into the mike: "Is someone transmitting? Hello. Anybody there?" He released the button.

Ch-hhhhhoo-dhheeee.

Certainly not; certainly he had not heard that. But when he involuntarily leaned too suddenly forward and felt the muscles tense in his lower back, he realized that the pain was subtly interlaced with cold little tendrils of something else altogether. Before he knew what he was doing, he had the transmitter button down again. "Is someone out there?"

Khhhhn-hheeeee—*hhhh-hhhhhh—CH-HHOO-DHE-EEEEEEE.*

He felt a drop of perspiration sneak down his face. Button down again, he said hoarsely: "What do you want?" This was crazy; there couldn't be anybody—

Khh— a gust of wind covered over the sound.

"What?"

Ksssss!

At the same moment there was a sharp cracking sound at the window, and he jumped up off the bed, his back clutching him with a cruel grip of pain. Incredulously, he stared at the window.

There was now another small chip in one of the panes.

Hhhhhhh—KHH-HNNN-HHEEE. And now another sound, from below, outside. It took his mind a moment to register that it was the ivy trellis again, clacking in the wind against the wall. If somebody was out there trying to play some sort of—but in a snowstorm? And who even knew he was here?

He switched the lamp off; the room filled with a darkness that was like some sable fluid aswish with sound—the ululation of the wind, the creaking of the trellis below the window, the nasty hissing of the walkie-talkie, the pounding of his own heart. Leaving the unit on the bed, he went to the window and dropped onto his knees in front of the chilly panes. He immediately regretted doing so, for his back spasm swelled to a miserable chorus of agony. But he had to look.

Below, out of his line of sight, the trellis rattled a strange cadence against the wall, a clattering clearly audible above the wind. Through the wheeling wet snowflakes he could see the white-blanketed yard below, faintly illumined in the peripheral glow of the streetlamp. Surely those were not footprints; the wind, it must be the wind scattering the snow.

Behind him, in the musty dark of the room, the walkie-talkie sang idiotically to itself in dry tonelessness.

Khhn-hee-hmee-hhh-hhoi.

Just below the level of vision, below the window, the trellis creaked louder than before. The wind—dear God, let it be only the wind! In his fear he tried to get up to look out, to see farther down the wall, but his back was locked in a vise of pain; he couldn't stand, couldn't move, could only stay on his knees before the window.

The pain must be affecting his mind, because to his eyes the swirling snow seemed from moment to moment to part, revealing an unclear form emerging into view from below, at the window now, nodding closer. Like some feverish lantern show, the blurred outlines of the thing darkened, lightened, darkened as the snow shifted and eddied in the uncertain light. In those quick moments of increased light it looked chalky, an osseous blossom growing out of the night. It was the storm, the wavering light, the wind, of course, making the snow seem to coalesce into solid patterns. The wind, the wind, oh, God, please, the wind.

But how could the wind seem to rattle with brittle fingers at the panes?

KHHHNN-HHEEEEEEE!

And how could the wind slowly, fumblingly begin to raise the window to send a tumult of snow into the room, stinging his face with cold? No—he could deny it no longer.

Whimpering, he looked into those cavernous eyes as the dry hissing went on and on, looked at the maggotlike writhing of that unthinkable mouth leaning to him as a fetid exhalation out of the storm.

And he understood perfectly well that this time she was going to get the kiss she had really wanted.

Major Prevue Here Tonite

William F. Nolan

The trees were burning.

That's how they appeared to ex-Californian Hubbard Rockwell—blazing around him in furnace reds and shades of dazzling orange and flickered sunbursts of yellow. A gusting wind aided the illusion, releasing flurries of brittle, flame-colored leaves that blew like sparks of fire across the black asphalt in front of Rockwell's moving car.

Connecticut in the fall. Everything Hub Rockwell had hoped it would be: an endless lariat of red-barn roads, looping through loam-rich October woods, broken by clear-running creeks, dipping into quiet valleys with small towns curled like sleeping cats in the cool shadows of easy-rolling hills.

No wonder so many business people commuted each day to their jobs in the roaring steel-and-concrete maelstrom of New York. It was worth the effort. As he built his sales career, he'd be able to afford a home here in Connecticut. It was certainly a goal worth working toward.

Hub was ending his second month on the job and considered himself lucky to have found a downtown bachelor apartment complete with cockroaches (no escaping them in the Big Apple), wall cracks, and a puce-green plaster-bulged ceiling that threatened to collapse on his head. By California standards (he'd grown up in Riverside), the rent was outrageous, but he had expected that. At least the job held solid promise.

These relaxed weekend drives, when he could be alone and free, were balm to his city-stressed soul; they provided Hub Rockwell with an alternate reality. The shrouding gray cinder smoke of New York gave way to the clear blue sky of Connecticut. He valued these unhurried trips as personal therapy, a way to keep sane after five days in the crazed sprawl of Manhattan.

Milly would love it out here in these woods, he told himself. Millicent Therese Kelly, a Fresno girl just out of college, ambitious and strong-minded, with an Irish temper that had flared up once too often to sustain their fragile relationship. After they'd lived together, tempestuously, for a year, she had finally split away from him on a tide of bitter accusations. Some of which were true. He *had* been seeing another woman on occasion, but it wasn't anything serious. Not to him, at least. Milly thought otherwise. Too bad; they might have had a life together. Their relationship was the closest he'd come to marriage in his twenty-five years.

Once she had talked of touring New England in the fall "to see all the trees burning." Her phrase—and he thought about her words now as he drove through these flame-bright, wind-tossed woods. He missed her. Maybe he'd give her a call when he got back to New York on Monday, just to establish contact again. Perhaps a bit of what they'd shared could be salvaged. Friendship in place of passion? No, probably not, since Milly was at her best in bed. Phoning her was a lousy idea. Wouldn't accomplish anything.

He'd met a girl at work (Sandra) who reminded him of Milly. Same sensual mouth and heated blue eyes. Something might ignite between them. Hub smiled. The fires of October . . .

He had a thick steak and some good wine at the Brookville Inn; then he took a post-dinner stroll along the quiet sidewalk, looking for the theater. There was always a local movie house along the main street in these small Connecticut towns—but, one by one, the theaters had gone under in the competitive wake of television and home video.

The Roxy in Brookville was no exception. It had obviously been out of business for some while now, with a hand-lettered sign in the dusty box office reading: SORRY, WE'RE CLOSED. THANK YOU FOR PAST PATRONAGE.

Hub looked at a faded lobby card behind cracked glass, advertising the last film shown here: Julie Andrews, at the top of a tall green hill, arms raised, her mouth wide in joyous song. From *The Sound of Music*. But there was no longer any music inside the Roxy—just dust and silence. Sad, thought Hubbard Rockwell. That was the word for it. Each closed theater seemed to drain life from the heart of the towns. He always felt angry, standing in front of these boarded-over relics of yesterday. A damn shame, really.

He walked back to his parked car, turning up the collar of his coat. It was getting chilly. The wind had risen as the afternoon lengthened, and the sky was bulked and swollen with storm clouds. Looked like rain for sure.

He'd had fine clear weather since Friday night when he'd left New York; it was Sunday now, and time to be heading back to the city. At least the rain hadn't spoiled his weekend.

Rainstorms always managed to depress him. As if the skies were weeping. Milly thought rain was romantic—but then women were like that. They built romance into everything.

It was almost dark as Hub unlocked the door of his metallic-silver Mazda. The rain was suddenly here; as he eased behind the wheel it made flat, spatting sounds on the windshield and roof. Well, in a couple of hours he'd be safe and dry in his apartment, ready to launch a fresh assault on his job tomorrow.

That's what you have to do in sales—mount aggressive campaigns. Push, push, push. And Hub Rockwell knew how to push. Which had become a problem in his relationship with Milly. She accused him of amorality, but you can't afford to worry about morals in business. Not if you expect to reach the top. And he had total confidence in himself. In the next five years Hub fully expected to be vice president of sales, and in ten years he'd be running the firm. *And* have his house in Connecticut. Just a matter of pushing to the edge of the envelope.

The storm turned into a bitch. The wind kept getting stronger as he drove the black strip of highway, unwinding in front of his low beams like the shining back of a snake.

Rain volleyed the windows, and he felt the wind thumping the side of his Mazda with hard-knuckled blows. He had to keep adjusting the wheel to compensate for these sudden gusts. His windshield wipers struggled to clear the swimming glass, forcing him to cut his speed to a crawl. Too dangerous, going any faster. Hell, at this rate, he'd be driving half the night to reach New York!

Then, as he breasted a low-sloping hill, he saw the lights.

Hub squinted, pressing his face closer to the windshield. Through the blowing curtain of rain he could make out a distant, flickering glow ahead of him at the bottom of the hill. A town. It didn't make sense. He'd studied the latest map for this area, and the next town was a good twenty miles farther.

The rain was abruptly sliced off as he entered a long covered wooden bridge spanning a swirl of muddy water. As he bumped across, his tires banged dull echoes from the weathered boards.

The town lay just beyond the bridge, with a sign identifying it as: EDGEFIELD. He'd never heard of it. Must be no more than a village.

The storm resumed its assault as Hub eased the Mazda down the main street. The sidewalks were deserted; no surprise on such a hellish night. All the shops were closed and lightless; the glow that had beckoned him emanated from the far end of the street. Neons. Tubes of raw color blinking red, yellow, and blue through the down-slash of rain.

A theater! A local movie house, by God! Hub could make out the name as he drove closer: Styx. And on its marquee, in bold black letters: MAJOR PREVUE HERE TONITE.

Why would any studio wish to preview their film out here on a rainy Sunday night in the dead-smack middle of nowhere? Somebody's head was going to roll in the publicity department. Stupid. Pointless.

Yet here it was.

Hub stopped his car in the loading zone directly facing the box office. There was a small parking lot next to the theater. The lot was empty. And no other cars were parked along the street. Then who was inside the place?

He could make out a ticket seller perched on a stool behind the fogged glass of the box office. A little bald-headed man with a thin face, just sitting there staring out into the rain. He didn't seem to notice the silver Mazda parked at the curb.

Inside his car, with the engine pulsing and the wipers ticktacking steadily, Hub Rockwell grinned to himself. Why not? Why not buy a ticket and get inside out of this damn rain? Maybe in another couple of hours the storm would die out and he'd have a clear run into New York. The latest radio report had indicated an upcoming break in the weather. Besides, he was always complaining about these local movie houses being closed down and here was one going full-blast, wide open for business. And showing a brand-new film in the bargain. Then don't just sit here gawking, he told himself. Support the natives. Keep movie theaters alive in America. Get your ass in there!

He got out of the Mazda, locking it. A plastic trash barrel bumped his leg, then rolled on across the lot, propelled by the wind. Hunched against the cold rain, Hub walked rapidly to the theater.

A large gray tom was crouched under the sheltering edge of the marquee—a rag-tail stray with smoky yellow eyes. Ears flattened along its skull, the animal opened a fanged mouth to hiss at Rockwell as he came around the corner of the brick building. A feral odor drifted up from the gray cat. Hub kicked at the animal, but it dodged away, still hissing. He'd never liked cats and couldn't understand people who did. The Chinese had the right idea: Cook 'em for soup!

Rockwell was impressed by the theater's Art Deco facade. The lobby was shining black and silver under the blaze of lights. Two female water nymphs, painted in gold leaf, embraced at each side of the box office, creating a mildly erotic effect.

Now the thin-faced little man inside the booth was looking through the glass at Rockwell with flat, impassive eyes. Well, at least I've caught the fellow's attention, thought Hub, with a trace of annoyance. He should be grateful to see me. On a foul night like this he's lucky anybody stops here. Lucky to have a job. A miracle the place is still open in a town this small. Maybe teenagers come here. Somewhere to go on a date.

Hub glanced at his wristwatch. It was almost 9:00 P.M. Which meant the film had probably started.

"What's the title of this picture?" he asked, getting out his wallet.

"We don't give the title. Not for our sneak previews." The little man's voice was as flat as his eyes. "But you're right on time. It hasn't started yet."

"Good," said Rockwell, pushing a new five-dollar bill across the box office counter. Along with his ticket, he got back a dollar and a half in change. The small red pasteboard was pretorn. Meaning that Baldie was cashier *and* ticket taker. It figured, given the low profit margin of a place like this.

"I'm sure you'll enjoy the show," said the little man —and his bloodless lips curved into a faint smile.

Hub entered the inside lobby. Again he was impressed. A wine-dark rug cushioned his steps, and the walls were ornately decorated in a scrolled silver-and-gold motif. Sea nymphs capered with long-necked swans across the ceiling.

The candy counter was surfaced in beveled mirror glass and outlined in blinking red neon. It seemed amply supplied with a variety of sweets, ice cream, and soft drinks. An old-fashioned popcorn machine was working busily behind the counter, fresh corn bubbling from a silver urn and spilling against the steamed glass.

But no one was there to sell anything.

Hub thought about getting a Coke and a Snickers bar, but he knew he'd have to tap on the door of the booth to get the ticket seller out to the candy counter, and he wasn't that hungry. Also, there was something unsettling about the little man. Hub experienced a distinct sense of unease when he thought of listening to that flat voice again. Ridiculous, actually. An over-reaction—but there nonetheless.

Rockwell parted a fold of hanging velvet, pushed open an inner door, and entered the main auditorium. He paused at the head of the aisle. The screen was curtained and the overhead lights were on. Hub had a clear view of the seats, row on row, two hundred or more. They were empty. All empty. He was alone here.

No wonder these hick theaters were closing. Weekend night with a brand-new film to be screened and nobody shows up. One ticket sold. To Hubbard Rockwell. What a lousy place to hold a sneak preview!

Should he leave, go back to his car, forget the whole thing? An outside rumble of thunder reminded him of the storm. Dumb to go back out there. No, he'd stay for the movie. A private showing, just for ol' Hub.

Now that he looked it over, the auditorium was even grander than the lobby—with ornate, intricately carved ceiling decorations and superbly executed wall paintings of vast flowered gardens. Angelic forms floated through the gardens, their outspread wings reflected in painted pools of shimmering purple. The wall scenes were designed to soothe and pacify: soft yellows, gentle greens, muted earth browns.

All wasted, thought Hub. Wasted on a town that didn't give a damn about Art Deco or unique craftsmanship. No doubt about it, the era of the local movie palace had definitely ended.

Rockwell walked to a row of seats halfway down the aisle, entered the row and moved to the exact center seat. And sat down.

The instant he was settled the house lights dimmed and the spangled velvet curtain drew back with a creaking rustle to reveal the wide white screen.

A strident blast of music swelled from high wall speakers. The screen darkened to black. Night black. Sky black. Now the sound of a heavily gusting wind filled the auditorium and rain silvered down; thunder cracked and rumbled.

A car, silver like the rain, breasted a hill, wipers working vigorously against the storm. The car paused there, then began a slow descent, headlights probing the rainy darkness.

Hub shifted in his seat, wondering when the credits were going to roll. But the action continued without them. Not so unusual. Many current films begin with a dramatic prologue, establishing a mood prior to the picture's title. Hub settled against the thickly cushioned seat and watched the silver car bump its way across a covered wooden bridge, a twin to the one just outside of town. Not many of these old antiques left in Connecticut. By daylight, on a clear and sunny afternoon, they exerted a nostalgic charm. By night, during a storm, they seemed squat and ugly, almost *dangerous* to cross.

The car paused again on the other side of the bridge. From the driver's point of view, the screen revealed the single main street of a small town, with a rain-hazed glow of lights at the far end.

The car rolled slowly forward, past tight-closed shops and dark storefronts, stopping again at the end of the street. Near the lights. *Neon* lights.

Hub drew in a sharp breath when the camera panned up to the bright-lit marquee of a movie theater, to black display letters spelling out: MAJOR PREVUE HERE TONITE.

He was now rigid in his seat, hands gripping the armrests. What was happening? The onscreen theater looked *exactly* like this one. Was he watching some kind of documentary filmed in this town during another stormy night?

The film continued. Hub watched in cold shock as the driver parked his car in the lot *(precisely where I parked mine!)* and walked toward the front of the building. The man had his coat collar up, and Hub couldn't see his face. A gray tomcat hissed at the stranger as he approached the box office.

Hub felt beading sweat on his flesh; he was chilled. The muscles along his cheeks were ridged with tension. His eyes were locked to the screen.

Now the camera observed the man from behind as he talked to the ticket seller. Hub knew what the dialogue would be, what they would say to one another. He anticipated every word of it.

"What's the title of this picture?"

"We don't give the title. Not for our sneak previews. But you're right on time. It hasn't started yet."

"Good," whispered Hubbard Rockwell numbly in the darkness.

"Good," said the stranger onscreen.

"I'm sure you'll enjoy the show."

And the man walked inside.

Of course Hub knew who the stranger was. Rockwell watched Rockwell enter the main auditorium *(this auditorium!)* and select a seat halfway down the aisle *(this seat!)*.

But how had it been done? Obviously, he had been filmed from the moment his car topped the hill into Edgefield. Cameras had tracked him as he drove into town. But how could this footage have been processed and screened? How was it possible for him to be sitting here *watching* it all?

Now the situation became truly insane as Hub realized that the film being unreeled on the screen of the theater within the picture was the *same* film he was watching!

But then the action changed. Hub saw the man in the film suddenly leap from his seat and run for the lobby. When he reached the exit door it was locked.

He banged a fist against it, jerking at the inside release bar. The camera swung to the rear box office door which was flung open—and Hub saw the pale, bald little man emerge to race like a spider across the lobby. In a horrific, fluid thrust, the little man plunged a long-bladed kitchen knife into the stranger.

The victim stumbled back, clutching at the knife handle, which protruded obscenely from his chest. Then he toppled to the rug.

The little man turned away from the body. He looked directly into the camera and smiled. "I'm free," he said.

And disappeared.

The screen went black.

The house lights were full on when Hub Rockwell, in shocked panic, bolted from his seat and ran up the aisle into the lobby.

Everything was changed. Grotesquely changed. The walls were scabrous, damp with mold. A single raw bulb near the ceiling cast twisting shadows. The water nymphs were headless, gilt paint flaking from their cracked-plaster flesh. The candy counter was draped in a gray lacework of cobwebs. A red-eyed rat scuttled, chittering, between Rockwell's feet, and the sour smell of wet cats befouled the air.

The dust-filmed glass exit door leading to the night street was nailed shut, boarded with heavy planking —as Hub pulled frantically at the rusted release bar. He tried to smash his fist through the glass. To no avail.

He was clawing at the splintered boards with bleeding fingers when the rear door of the box office abruptly popped open and the little man swept out, eyes wild, a glittering kitchen knife in his right hand.

He closed swiftly on Rockwell—who let out a small choked gasping sound as the little man drove the blade deeply into Rockwell's chest.

With both hands clutching at the handle of the knife, Hub sprawled onto the faded, time-rotted lobby rug, lying on his back, his breath bubbling in his throat, his eyes dimming rapidly. And just before total, utter darkness possessed him, he heard the ticket seller deliver the final line of dialogue: "I'm free."

And the little man was gone.

Fade to black.

Outside, the rain is over. The thunder is silent. A full moon slides out from massed clouds to bathe the Styx in a wash of pale yellow. The building is in sorry disrepair. Its neons are dark, crusted with soot, and its grimed lobby is trash filled, smelling sharply of decay. A dead rat, partially decomposed, lies in front of the boarded-over box office amid fragments of broken glass. Several of the curled black display letters have fallen from the theater's cracked marquee. Those remaining spell out: MA OR PR V E HE   TON   E.

A storm-racked night exactly one year later.

A building in Edgefield, Connecticut, pulses into glowing life.

A car motors slowly through the rain along the main street. Stops before the neon dazzle of light. The Styx. With its marquee brightly announcing: MAJOR PREVUE HERE TONITE.

A ticket seller waits inside the gleaming Art Deco box office.

The driver parks, gets out of his car, locks it. Walks up to the box office. Asks if he's too late for the preview. No, he's right on time.

Buys a ticket. Goes inside. Takes a seat halfway down the aisle. No one else is in the theater.

The house lights dim and the film begins.

In the box office, Hubbard Rockwell waits, staring into the rainy darkness, his ghost-white fingers convulsively gripping the handle of a long-bladed kitchen knife.

His bloodless lips curve into a faint smile.

It's time for the exchange.

He will soon be free.

The Brush
of Soft Wings

Melissa Mia Hall

The face first appeared on a Sunday: eyes, nose, mouth, a wavering image in the corner of her bedroom window. Ceciley pulled the shade down and closed the curtains, her breath coming in great gulps and gasps. It took three cups of tea and a handful of cookies before she calmed down. One of the kids in the neighborhood was playing a trick on her. One of the brats wanted to scare the old lady to death. She washed up the cup and saucer and avoided looking out the window over the sink. The neighborhood running downhill right into a sinking cesspool of trash and nothing she could do about it except survive. Nobody with any class lived on this street anymore, just the dead-end kind. There were too many untidy, sprawling families with kids nobody looked after proper, both parents working or both parents not, lurching from day to day on welfare, not like it was in her day. A few old people like herself, on rightfully earned social security, tried to keep appearances up, but without any help from young people, what could you expect? Colored people and white trash, Mexicans, slant-eyes, it didn't matter what nationality, nobody cared anymore. Yards going to weeds and garbage, homes that used to be respectable and presentable allowed to run down due to neglect from landlords and families too tired or too lazy to fight the disease of poverty.

Sometimes she felt a sort of pity for everyone, even the unsupervised children and the Mexican family next door who could hardly speak English and were always opening their doors to another member of an ever-extending family. Ceciley could never figure out exactly who the head of the family was, it changed from week to week. She didn't think the face belonged to them. It was too pale, the eyes with dark circles, the hair yellow or white, young hair, young face. She thought it belonged to the white trash down the street, the house with five or six screaming, mewling kids, the wild kind that run the streets day and night. Blondes or redheads, you could hardly tell, their hair was always dirty.

She walked down the hallway to her bedroom. She cast an apprehensive glance toward the window. Her throat felt tight. Ought to be something on TV. She fiddled with the knobs and frowned at the color TV that needed adjusting. The man kissing the girl looked too green. It figured that it was out of whack because her son had given it to her the week before he left Texas for California, taking his wife and her two grandkids away from her just like that. Not that she really cared. She never much liked her son, a wimp who always did what his wife wanted. Well, she

didn't need them, any of them. At seventy-eight she
was still self-sufficient and gloriously independent.

But she didn't need that face either. She didn't de-
serve it. She minded her own business and never
caused trouble for anyone. Maybe an occasional call
to the authorities when things got out of hand, like
when that boy was beating up on that little Spanish
girl or when the bozos down the street wouldn't keep
their pit bull tied up good enough and it chased Mrs.
Zimmerman for a good five blocks. What were they
doing owning one of them dogs anyway?

That face. It had a way of showing up at twilight or
late afternoon, sometimes in the early morning
hours, usually in the bedroom windows, but once in
the glass panes in the back door, and one time in the
kitchen window while she was cleaning the sink out
with Ajax. Watching her like a hawk, staring, face
working soundless-like words she didn't understand
or flat couldn't hear. It didn't appear in any of the
other windows and she never looked at it long
enough to see if it was attached to anything, although
it was bound to be. Sometimes it scared her, it made
her want to scream, and a cold chill would take hold
and shake her around. All her bones rattled with it.
Especially when the face seemed in torment, little
mouth open, the colorless eyes in pain, eyebrows a *V*
of anguish. Often she expected crying to accompany
the visitation, standing stock-still, she'd wait for the
crying to come after she had run from the face to
hide herself behind doors, walls, curtains. She'd hold
her arthritic hands over her ears, waiting.

It never came, for three months: August, September, October. The face would come, but no scream.
The regularity of the visitations began to dissipate her

fear. Or the fear mutated into something else. It got to where she'd stand by the window and wait for it to come. She'd look at it longer now, and the bodyless apparition now assumed more substantial proportions. By December she could stare at it. The face would implore her, the mouth moving, saying something she couldn't rightly hear. It was a her; she had decided that, because the hair was long and the lips a delicate seashell pink. The child wasn't a ghost, though; she'd tap on the glass. At first it didn't bother Ceciley, but then the tapping became irritating. She began to hate it. "Leave me alone!" She would hiss at the face and tap back at the glass. "Do you hear me!" The little hands would reach up and keep tapping. Finally, on a Friday, Ceciley heard what she was saying. "Let me in—" plaintive, shrill, begging, thin.

She'd been right at the beginning. It was merely a mistreated child. It had never been a ghost. That was a strange disappointment. A ghost held a bit of glamour, magic.

Cold December outside, damp and dreary. She made herself look back outside at the face, narrow like a fox, a button nose red with cold. The dark blond hair hung down in straggly wisps across the wide, luminous forehead. Her high cheekbones were strong like an Indian's but the white-gray eyes were unnaturally large with albino lashes. "Let me in—"

Peering down through her thick glasses, Ceciley finally allowed herself to see the sticklike body, the torn T-shirt, the sweater riddled with ragged holes, the tattered jeans, the sockless ankles, the run-over shoes. The light from the backyard glowed around her. She couldn't really see the ankles or the shoes, but she expected them to be as she imagined.

It was against her better judgment. It had to be a trick of some kind. But the face seemed so pitiful and young—six, seven, a malnourished ten? She thought of the beef stew bubbling in the kitchen. As if the face heard her, the thin voice wavered through the glass, "I'm hungry," and Ceciley felt a flush spread across her own face, carrying its rosy heat down her neck and down into her bosom. Her stomach growled. "I'm hungry, too," she whispered and went around to the back door.

Twilight had dipped into darkness. It was totally insane to let in an urchin; it was unsafe and foolish. The kid could be a clever thief. Still she found herself undoing the latches down to the chain. She pulled the door open and peeked out above the chain. A hand shot through the space and grabbed at her, a cold hand, fingers grasping. "Let me in—I'm cold," the thin voice whistled in.

Against her better judgment, Ceciley undid the chain, stepped aside, and watched the child come in. Instead of run-over shoes, she wore torn sneakers, the old-fashioned kind like Gene used to wear.

"Thank you," she said, carefully redoing the locks.

"Don't you have a family to look after you?"

The child looked at Ceciley with a blank expression.

"Got a name?"

"Do you?" she said cockily, taking Ceciley by surprise. She walked into the kitchen and hovered over the stew pot. "You got cornbread in the oven? I can smell it."

Ceciley stood in the doorway watching her. "No name, no food. My name is Mrs. Ceciley Smith, and I can't abide fools in my house."

"Me either. My name is Leona Anne. Call me Lannie. It's easier."

"Lannie. Okay. Where do you live—down the street?"

The small hands reached toward the bubbling pot. Ceciley shrieked, "Don't touch that pot! You want to burn yourself? Go sit down at the table—I'll bring it to you, Lannie—Leona."

The child turned away obediently and sat down at the kitchen table. She folded her hands primly. "If you prefer to call me Leona, that would be acceptable, too."

"Your hands clean?"

"I think so."

"Well, if you don't know for sure, maybe you'd better go to the bathroom and wash up."

"Yes, ma'am," she said, jumping up and heading for the bathroom with the fluid motion of someone who already knew where she was going. Ceciley felt a shiver snake up her spine.

When Leona returned, Ceciley put the stew and cornbread before her with a trembling hand. "You been here before?"

Leona blew on a dripping spoon. She shrugged noncommittally. "I don't think I believe in reincarnation."

Ceciley sat down, wincing at the ache in her knee joints. She buttered her cornbread methodically and carefully, cutting it with admirable smoothness, dropping nary a crumb in her lap. Leona crumbled hers in her bowl and mushed it around with her spoon. "It's good," she murmured.

"Yeah, I think so, but we were talking about how you knew where the bathroom was. Have you been here before?" She held the child's gaze for a few seconds. Leona was hard to read. Finally, Leona shook her head.

"Ceciley, are you all alone here?"

She looked to the drainboard where Bobbie sat in his birdcage. He danced on his perch, squawking and fussing. "No, I got the bird there."

"I mean, all by yourself with nobody."

"What's it matter, missy?"

"I don't know, I was just talking."

"Eat and let me do some of the talking." Leona obliged her with a satisfying slurp. "Eat like a lady."

Leona wiped her face with the cloth napkin. "It's real nice for you to finally let me in. I was beginning to think you never would. It's awful cold outside."

A draft curled around Ceciley's ankles. "It's not exactly warm in here. I have to be careful because of the bills. I usually eat in front of the TV in my bedroom during the winter." She pointed her spoon in the direction of the parlor. "I just close off the parlor and the dining room with that plastic curtain there."

"That's real smart."

"What say we take the bird and our stuff into the bedroom. I got some nice trays I like to use. I just sit 'em on my lap, see? It's mighty convenient."

"I'm all done."

"Well, go look in the cookie jar. I reckon there's some cookies in there. I like cookies, don't you?"

"I sure do."

When they were settled in front of the TV, Ceciley kept talking; it was like a river out of control at flood stage. She hadn't had a good jaw session in weeks. She told Leona about her family out in California, pointed out Johnny and Kate's latest school photographs on the wall, and told all about her last eye operation. Leona was a good listener, but Ceciley was having a time trying to find out about the kid's own family. Most likely she was ashamed of them. Probably a passle of no-account deadbeats. It was eight-thirty P.M. How could they let their little girl run wild?

"Don't you think you'd better call your parents and let them know where you are? It's getting late. You've got school in the morning, don't you?"

"I'm okay. They know where I am."

Ceciley *tsked* under her breath and thought how terrible it was that they obviously condoned their own child's going around begging for food. "You got brothers and sisters?"

Leona nodded. Ceciley wondered if she had lice. "Don't you get enough to eat at home?"

"Not really."

"Don't your folks get food stamps? I'm not too proud to use them. I mean, if you don't have any other choice."

Bobbie screeched from his perch, hitting the bell suspended from the top of his cage. He ruffled his feathers and hopped about wildly. "You think you're so smart!" Ceciley told him.

"How old is he?"

"Pretty old, like me. How do you know he's a he?"

"I dunno."

"How old are you?"

"Old enough."

Leona turned and surveyed Ceciley thoughtfully—or was it blankly? Ceciley felt a shadow of the old fear brush her skin. The child was too pale, unearthly, sickly. She expected Leona to cough up blood sud-

denly, to keel over in a faint. Ceciley went to her
dressing table to rummage around for an old sweater
the child could wrap up in. "I got this sweater you can
have." She straightened up and turned to hand it to
Leona, but she was gone.

"Leona?" She hurried to the kitchen and saw the
back door standing open. The cold white winter
moon peeked through the naked branches of her old
pecan trees. She couldn't see hide nor hair of Leona.
She could hear some soft Spanish music coming from
the radio next door. She smelled their spicy, fragrant
cooking.

"Grandma señora—you eat yet?" one of them hollered, hanging out on their stoop.

"Yes, thank you," Ceciley hollered. She glimpsed a
toothy white smile.

"Good night, Grandma señora."

Ceciley shut the door and sighed.

Now that the face had become Leona, she no longer
feared it. Ceciley wanted the child to come more
often, but she didn't come back until Christmas Eve.
In the time before then, Ceciley kept busy. She went
on the bus downtown and bought a few gifts at Mon-
nig's for Gene and his family, not much but a little
remembrance, panties for Kate and Gene's wife,
Sarah (she bought Sarah's a size too small just to be
mean), and underwear for Gene and Johnny as well.
She threw in a small box of Stover's candy too.

At night she watched TV and dreamed about the
past. Mainly Jeff. That was Gene's daddy, a real man,
tall and strong. He rode the rodeo, was real good at
calf roping when he was young. They went to Mexico
once, and Omaha, Nebraska. He died too young, be-

fore they'd got done loving. She'd been married twice after, but both marriages had been dad-blame, god-awful flops. She couldn't even remember their faces. But Jeff's face she could touch with her fingers. And at night, at night, yes, when he hovered over her, she could touch other things. Time could blur things, make things softer and better than maybe they had been in reality, but if that's all you had . . . Women of certain ages still needed certain things. It always made her mad to see how the media tried to turn old women into old children with brittle voices and stupid outfits, like those dumb nets over tightly curled hair.

Gene had called and made a halfhearted offer to fly her out to California, that place of movie stars and suntans. He couldn't really afford it, and she didn't want to be a burden to anyone.

She didn't have a Christmas tree, but she had a Christmas card arrangement in the parlor. She'd look at it from time to time, marveling at the waste of postage.

The child came back, bearing a luxuriant sprig of mistletoe.

"Where you been, Leonie?" She'd added the "ie" out of sheer impulsiveness. When she was a girl she'd had a best friend named Fannie. It just sounded festive and right.

Leonie smiled. "Around. Merry Christmas!" She hugged Ceciley and held up her cheek for a kiss. Her skin was like frosty glass, almost burning Ceciley's lips.

"I got dinner all ready. Are you hungry?"

"I'm always hungry," Leonie sighed, going to the stove to warm her hands.

"I see you got a new coat." She approved of the clean red car coat. Leonie had on a new pair of jeans, too. And she'd gained weight and her hair was clean. "You look real nice."

"The Goodwill store and Sears."

Ceciley had fried chicken, peas, yams, all sorts of good food, even fudge and a pecan pie. She dished up two brimming plates. "You want some milk? Fix it yourself."

"That'd be great." Leonie took the two plates and carried them to the bedroom. "I'll get the milk later."

When they finally got settled, Leona attacked her food as if she were starving, licking her fingers and chewing noisily. She polished off a leg and looked at Ceciley. Her eyes, formerly so pale, had taken on a faint shade of blue. "I think I should move in here for a while."

Taken aback by this sudden pronouncement, Ceciley looked away. "I don't know if your parents would approve of that."

"Ha! They'd approve of anything. They don't care what I do."

"Maybe I'd better talk to them."

"No, they can't. I mean, they don't have a phone or anything. They don't care."

Ceciley's heart bothered her, or maybe it was gas. She swallowed and coughed into her napkin. "Okay, but you have to live by my rules. And I don't have any money, you know."

"I know." Leona's eyes were turning bluer by the minute. Her blond hair was also turning darker, a golden brown, shiny and healthy. Ceciley wondered if it was the same little girl at all. Leona had finished eating. Now she was playing with Ceciley's crochet bag. "I prefer knitting needles," she said, pointing a crochet needle at Ceciley. "Don't you? Especially the colored kinds, metallic-like, long and cold—click, click. Could you teach me how to crochet?"

"I don't do it much anymore. But, sure, I suppose."

"Can I clean out Bobbie's cage?"

"When it's warm enough maybe I'll let you bathe him."

"Birds take baths? Isn't that dangerous?"

"Not necessarily, not if you're careful."

Leona lay down on her stomach and looked into Bobbie's cage. Bobbie squawked and flew down from his perch to his food. He pecked at the grains nervously. He didn't like a big face looming over him. "Wouldn't he fly around the room, maybe get outside somehow?"

"I've only lost one bird that way. Parakeets can't survive outdoors, you know—not pet birds. You have to be careful."

"Why?"

"Bluejays and such; they'd eat 'em alive. Parakeets are fragile."

"So are people," Leona said, stretching. "Hey, let's watch TV."

The child stayed for a few long weeks. Ceciley watched her eat an inordinate amount of food, watched her sleep beside Ceciley in the big four-poster bed, flat on her back, her delicate hands folded across her stomach. Ceciley was always pulling the quilts over her, anxious that she not catch cold. She came and went with the breeziness of any child, coltish legs and arms akimbo, running instead of walking. Sometimes Ceciley brushed her hair. Leonie never cried out when her brush came upon a tough tangle.

Leonie didn't talk much. She just stayed at the house when she wasn't at school or off playing with her friends. Leastways, that's where Ceciley thought she went. Or maybe down to the parents who never called to check on her. She stayed with Ceciley. They watered the houseplants, they played dominoes, they worked at crochet, Ceciley squinting and trying to be patient with Leonie's clumsy fingers. They cleaned the bird cage. They watched TV. Once Leonie asked her to help her with her arithmetic. Ceciley tried to help her.

Leonie liked to draw. She'd show Ceciley her artwork—lots of bare trees and mountain ranges. She loved drawing mountain ranges. She tried to draw Ceciley. "You are too beautiful to draw," she said in exasperation, tearing the paper to shreds.

"I'm too ugly," Ceciley laughed.

"Why do you have to leave?" Ceciley asked her when the day came when Leona said she had to leave, gathering her few possessions into a paper sack from Piggly Wiggly.

"Other people need me, too."

That made Ceciley mad. "I don't need you; don't get that idea into your head, little missy. I was just trying to be nice. You've been company, don't get that wrong, but you got to lead your own life; I can't do that for you. That's what I told Gene when he married that girl. You got to live your own life. Yes, sir."

"When I come back, can we bathe Bobbie?"

Ceciley watched her go down the porch steps. "He's liable to be real dirty by then." Ceciley waved at the child running away down the street, the sun catching at her golden hair flapping in the February wind. The figure sparkled and faded, confusing Ceciley. Her gaze inspected both sides of the street, her hands shading her eyes in order to see clearly. The child had just vanished.

"Happy New Year!" an Oriental voice chirped in front of her.

Almost losing her balance, Ceciley stepped back and looked down at the black-haired boy right in front of her. "I didn't see you—"

He offered a covered dish to her. "Happy New Year!"

"A little late—" She paused, reflecting on the difference of their customs. It was nice of them to include her in their holiday. "Happy New Year—what year is this—the Rat?" The boy smiled and shook his head. He was bashful, ready to run across the street as soon as her back was turned. Might as well let him off easily. She turned, gripping the dish covered by tinfoil. It smelled all right, at any rate.

She ate the food in front of the TV, concentrating on an episode of *Simon and Simon*. A.J. looked like Gene. When she got done she opened the fortune cookie, eager for the fortune in spite of the little voice inside her telling her not to get too excited. The paper said: "You will find Monday an especially important day." Ceciley crumpled it and threw it in the wastebasket. Maybe Gene would call. Big deal. At least the egg rolls were tasty.

She kept waiting for the child to return. February gave way to March, and the air became delicious, most of the days balmy and sweet. The redbud trees were in full bloom, and the daffodils had pushed up through the soil. At night they almost glowed phosphorescently, nodding stars in the flower beds along the side of her house. It got to where she began talking about the child to her neighbors, but none of them could place her, not even Mrs. Zimmerman, who was supposed to know every person in a five-mile radius. They'd all give her those distant-sad looks when she talked about Leonie, like they thought she was getting daft and senile. They didn't think the child existed, but Ceciley knew she did. She'd touched her, kissed her, scolded her.

Ceciley was hanging out clothes in the backyard when the child returned, not on a Monday, but a Sunday, she recalled with a dash of regret. Jeff had always believed in fortune cookies. It was full daylight, around 11:00 A.M. Ceciley looked over to the Mendozas', hoping Juanita would be out and could see Leonie, standing beside her, pretty and bright, her hair in two pigtails tied with green ribbon.

"Hey, Ceciley, how you been doing? Miss me? I've come to wash Bobbie. I can't wait to hold him in my hand. He's so little and sweet."

Ceciley wiped her forehead with the edge of her apron. "It is warm enough, I do reckon. Come on—"

They went inside and got Bobbie's cage. They put it on the drainboard by the sink, laying out fresh newspapers. Leonie said she was scared to hold him, that she'd never held a bird in her hand before.

"There's nothing to it." Ceciley's big hand swooped into the cage and scooped up the tiny parakeet. His feathers were soft and his heart pulsed rapidly, a pinprick of life throbbing in fear. Leonie held out her palms, her wide eyes large with expectation. The faucet was already dribbling water into a cup. "I'm scared I'll hurt him," she said as Ceciley put Bobbie into her outstretched hands. Bobbie screamed and squawked, trying to get free. Leonie held on to him tightly. "He's so small," she whispered, looking into Ceciley's face. "Ooh—he's not moving. He's dead! He's dead! I've killed him! He's dead—"

"No—he's not; he can't be—" Ceciley's large hands took him away from Leonie's little hands. "Oh, God—"

Leonie's eyes were white like pearls, her lips curving into a half smile. "I felt it die."

"You can't hold a bird, you can't hold a bird," Ceciley said, half to herself, half to the face that shone up into hers tainted with an inexplicable ecstasy. Ceciley staggered to a kitchen chair, still holding the parakeet, crying and panting for breath. Leonie followed her, pushing and tugging for attention. "It was warm, so warm." She was climbing into Ceciley's lap, knocking the bird from her weak grasp. Her arms spread around Ceciley. "Let me hold you." Leonie's skin was smooth and soft, sliding against her rough skin. Leonie spilled tears on her arms and nuzzled closer. "I can feel your heart beat. Are you scared? Don't be. Don't be scared."

Ceciley's mouth worked but couldn't make sound. Her eyes bulged with shock as her chest caved in and the room spun about her, dancing with stars.

"I can bring you flowers and air, wonderful air that swims all around you and lifts you up high, higher than you've ever been before. I can make you fly with the wind. Be still now—"

"Let me go," Ceciley gasped. She tried to beat Leonie off, but the child had enormous strength. The

little hands held her closer, tight, the smell of her like
clinging honeysuckle and trailing geranium.

"I'm not holding you. You can't hold a bird," Leona
whispered into her ear. "It's a hard lesson to learn.
You don't hold something down that has wings. If you
do, it dies. Are you dying now, Miss Ceciley? It's okay
now. I can feel you dying. It's soft, warm." The cool
pink lips dashed across the aged forehead and
touched the silvery hairs still laced with black. "Good-
bye—good-bye—" Ceciley watched her own body go
lax and supple as the arms fell away. But the face
stone white and narrow, the eyes elfin and knowing
still hovered over her. She tried to scream once more
before the kitchen disappeared, before the wings
spread out for flight, but it was hopeless.

Brothers

David B. Silva

1

Some things that happen, it doesn't matter if anyone believes they happened or not. As long as you know in your heart. Like dying with a secret on the tip of your tongue. As long as you don't say it out loud, it's still a secret, and that's all that matters. I guess the only thing that matters now is that Dane is gone. Christ, I still miss him.

2

I was twelve years old that warm June morning when the thunderstorm somehow slid around the edges of the valley. The night before, on Channel 24, the weatherman had promised it to us. Dane had counted on it, and because he had, I guess I had too. He was the one most disappointed, though.

Dane had something special going with thunderstorms. He'd sit upstairs, on the sill of the bedroom window, looking out at the gray-black clouds rolling in over the mountain, the rain just starting to sprinkle, lightning flashes striking gold across the meadow behind the house, and it was always as if he were waiting for something. For as long as I could remember, he'd been waiting for something. I think that was the biggest secret he ever kept from me. We had been born two minutes and thirty-three seconds apart; Dane first, me second; him the strong, healthy one, me the runt—we'd spent every living minute of our twelve years together, and knew everything there was to know about each other. Except . . . except I had never understood his fascination with thunderstorms. And he had never told me what it was he was waiting for.

I guess the closest he ever came was in late May of that same year, just about a month before, when he called me over to the window where he was sitting. We were upstairs in the bedroom. For nearly an hour lightning had been zigzagging across the dark sky like shattered glass. You could feel the thunder rolling across the meadow, thick and heavy, slipping under the foundation of the house, climbing the walls like a shuddering after-shock.

"Look at it," Dane said.

An explosion of yellow-white light arced across the sky above the mountaintop like a magnificently electrified beast.

"You know what lightning is?"

"No," I said.

"It's this weird electrical charge that the clouds have to divvy up between themselves. That's how they stay alive, by passing around electricity. They feed it back and forth until it builds up a strong charge, then they toss off a little hot lightning and start all over again. In the end it makes them stronger." He had been staring out the window while he told me all this. And when he finished, he turned to me, his face as peaceful as I'd ever seen it, his eyes a summer-morning green, and he asked, "Does that make sense to you?"

"Sort of."

I'd wondered about it before, and suddenly I wondered again if I really looked like him, if I had that same conviction in my own face. Dane couldn't lie. When you looked into his eyes you always knew you were getting the truth from him.

"Nothing ever dies, Trey. Remember that. Things get tossed off, but that just makes them stronger. They never really die."

I didn't understand what he was trying to tell me then, but I knew it had something to do with his wait. Looking back, I think he was just trying to tell me that his waiting time was slowly drawing to a close. As it turned out, there wasn't much time left at all.

3

June had rolled around, and with it: warm summer mornings, long days, and cool nights.

The last morning of his wait, I woke up to find Dane sitting by the bedroom window again. There was something distinctly different about him, but I couldn't tell you what it was. Maybe it was nothing more than the way the sunshine seemed to create a soft orange-red aura around him. I don't know.

"About time," he said evenly, without even turning to look at me.

"What time is it?"

"Quarter to ten."

"Why didn't you get me up?" I felt something soft and warm expand inside me, then a yawn came climbing up my throat and escaped. In its place it left behind an odd sensation of emptiness. Completely unfamiliar. A little frightening. As if something inside me had quietly changed during the night. I didn't think much about it at the time, only that the feeling was new and strange.

"You're old enough to get up by yourself," Dane said.

"I know that, but now the day's half shot."

"You're old enough," he said again, almost a whisper. He didn't move an inch from the window while I got dressed.

"Looking for the thunderstorm?"

"The storm's not coming."

"That's great!" I pulled on my last tennis shoe, tying the long lace in a double knot. "At least we can do something outside today."

From downstairs Mom called up. "You finally awake, Trey?"

"Yeah."

"How about some breakfast?"

"Be down in a minute." Dane had suddenly shifted his gaze away from the window to where I was sitting on the edge of my bed. There was a reverent, weary expression etched into his face, as if something had weighed heavily on his mind during the night. "What?"

"Nothing."

"So what do you want to do today?"

"That's my question," Dane said.

"Then ask it."

"What do you want to do today?"

"I don't know. What do *you* want to do today?"

He grinned for the first time that morning, and it was genuine. "Put up the rope swing, that's what I want to do."

"Down at Sumner's Pond?"

"Yeah."

"Too cold," I said.

"What?"

"The water's too cold."

"No, it isn't."

"What are we going to use for a rope?"

"The hemp rope Dad uses on the dozer."

"To tie down the tarp?"

"Yeah."

"It won't hold."

"It'll hold."

"And what are we going to hang it from?"

"The old oak."

"I'm not climbing that tree."

"Then I will," Dane said.

"Mom'll never let you."

"Sure she will."

"Not if you were one of the great Wallendas and used two safety nets. Not in a million years, Dane."

"What if we don't tell her?"

4

Downstairs, Mom was standing over the stove, scrambling eggs. She looked up from the frying pan, and I could see in her face what she was thinking. Sometimes out of the corner of my eye I'd catch her watching me. Her dark eyes dilated into huge, sad things; her mouth drawn and tight with worry, and I'd realize she wasn't just watching me, she was watching *over* me. That's what she was doing that morning, watching *over* me, and thinking to herself: You eat a big breakfast, Trey; you're a growing boy, you need a big breakfast in the morning.

"Sleep well?" she asked.

"Well enough."

It had been cold the night before, below forty degrees, and the chill was still trapped inside the kitchen walls, insulated from the sunshine outside. I sat at the table, at the only place setting, where a warm swath of sunlight from the window over the sink had lit upon the tabletop. Dane sat across the table from me. "You already eat?" I whispered.

"No whispering at the table," Mom said.

"An hour ago," Dane whispered back. He had a mind all his own.

I always admired that about him, and I still think back to the time when we were in fourth grade at Brickston Valley Elementary. Miss Riley—she was our teacher that year, we called her Missus Ed because she had the hips of a horse, so wide there were mornings we didn't think she would make it through the classroom door—she caught us sneaking a smoke in back of the greenhouse that winter. It was a cold, damp morning, the grass thick with dew, and it was the first time I'd ever copped a drag off a cigarette.

Dane put me up to it.

If Mom had found out . . . cold Christ, she would have brought it all up again, about how sick I was supposed to be and how I'd never be as strong as other kids my own age. She never let up about that stuff. But this was one of those lucky times: Mom never found out, because Miss Riley never told her. I think Dane had something to do with that.

He took me out behind the greenhouse before school that morning. The school had put up the greenhouse the year before. It wasn't much to look at. Half a dozen parents had come down one weekend, sunk some four-by-four posts into the ground, rough-framed four walls and a roof, and covered the whole thing with sheets of thick, clear plastic. From the east wing of the school you couldn't tell if anyone was hiding out back or not.

"What's up?" I asked him.

Dane pulled a pack of Marlboros out from under his shirt. The pack had been crushed, but there were still a couple of cigarettes left. "I found them in Dad's desk drawer," he said, wrestling one of them free. It came out bent in the middle where he'd tucked the bottom half of the pack into his belt. "Try it."

"No way."

"Why not?"

"I just don't want to."

"One cigarette won't hurt you."

"I know that."

"Everything's a gamble," Dane said, somewhat coolly. "You never try, you never lose. But you never *win* either." His summer-green eyes smiled, and that was probably what did it for me. I always trusted those eyes.

"Just one."

He passed me the bent cigarette, filter first, holding it between his thumb and forefinger. Then he pulled a match out of his back pocket, struck it across the zip-

per of his jacket, and touched it to the tip of the cigarette. "Inhale."

I took a long, slow drag, managing somehow to get
the smoke all the way down to my lungs and hold it
there for a few counts. It wasn't what I'd expected.
You see people smoking and it always looks like
something you should try. But the taste was flat and
dry, and my stomach hitched right away, coughing
most of it up.

Dane grinned. "Think you'll live?"

"Longer than you," I said with surprising difficulty.

He laughed at that. But not in a way I was used to
hearing. There was something both sad and unfamiliar about it. As if I'd struck a hidden nerve and it was
everything he could do to keep from screaming out in
pain. I almost asked him what was wrong, but I never
quite got the chance. That was when we both noticed
a shadow moving on the other side of the greenhouse.

You couldn't actually see through those thick
plastic walls, at least not very clearly. Things were
always fuzzy and dark around the edges. But you
could make out enough to know when someone was
coming.

I guess I shouldn't have been surprised when Miss
Riley came trudging around the corner. She never let
much of anything slip by her. When you're ten, it's
easy to think of your teacher as being as old as the
crust of the earth and just about as brittle. But in
reality Miss Riley was only twenty-seven, and you
never put anything over on her.

"Trey?" she said, rounding the corner, her wide hips
swaying back and forth like the hind end of a horse,
her eyes all lit up with curiosity. "What are you doing
back here?"

"Nothing!" The cigarette dropped out of my fingers as if it had a mind of its own; it landed at my feet, and I tried to cover it with my right shoe.

"Smoking?" she said, surprised. She looked at Dane, her face tighter than I'd ever seen it, her eyes slit, but she didn't say a word in his direction.

She expects it from Dane, I thought.

"I'm going to have to tell your mother, Trey. You know that, don't you?"

"You don't *have* to tell her," Dane said in my defense.

"She needs to know."

"Why?" Dane asked quietly. I couldn't have asked that question. Never in a million years. But Dane did, and at that moment it was as if someone had sent a little jolt of electricity through Miss Riley's wide body. The rosy color bled out of her face, and she nearly tripped, backing up a step.

"It wouldn't be right for me to keep this from her," she said anxiously.

Something in the air had suddenly changed; it took me a moment before I realized it was the charge in the air, the static charge. Like on a warm summer afternoon when the humidity's thick and everything you touch gives off a shock. Only here, on this strange winter morning, the shock was Dane, and I guess Miss Riley must have instinctively known that, because what she was doing was making certain she didn't get too close to him. I could see a cold, white numbness seeping into her face. And I could smell the ozone in the air.

"She's not going to say anything," Dane said.

Holy, freezing Jesus, I thought, she's scared of him. Miss Riley's scared of Dane.

I looked to my brother. His green eyes were bright and fiery, as I'd never seen them before. For a brief moment I wasn't sure which one scared me the most . . . my teacher or my brother.

"I'm sorry, Miss Riley."

"You didn't do anything wrong," Dane said.

"I won't do it again," I added.

"What are you apologizing for?"

"You know cigarettes aren't good for you," Miss Riley said, her voice as smooth as she could make it. But she was still off-balance, still trying to play off the fear that had taken her by surprise. "They stunt your growth."

"Cigarettes?" Dane said with disgust. "You believe that?"

I glanced down at the Marlboro poking out from under my shoe. An empty, childish thought flashed through my mind: Maybe Mom had smoked cigarettes while she was pregnant? Maybe that was the reason I was so damn small? But then there was Dane. That wouldn't explain Dane, would it?

"Let's go." Dane grabbed me by the arm of my jacket; I felt his fist clench and draw the material into a tight wad. It felt as if someone had suddenly taken hold of my senses. He shoved me away from the greenhouse, back in the direction of the school. "She's talking nonsense."

"Where do you think you're going?" Miss Riley asked.

"Back to class," Dane said.

"Your mother, Trey! She'll have to know about this."

"Don't pay any attention to her."

"She's going to tell."

"No, she isn't."

I never looked back.

It took Miss Riley a few minutes to catch up with us in the classroom. She didn't say anything, not a word at first, just came in and sat down at her desk before finally opening the Social Studies book and trying to recover her smile.

Dane and I sat in the same seats we always occupied, I in the back near the window, he up front in the first row. From where I sat, Miss Riley wasn't the same woman who had caught me behind the greenhouse just a few minutes before, although I can't be certain how she had changed. On the flip side, I guess I wasn't the same boy. I'd learned that once in a while you have to try things just to see what they're like. And I'd also learned that sometimes people say things that they don't mean.

Dane had been right.

Miss Riley never did tell Mom about the cigarette.

5

"So what are you up to today?" Mom asked.

Dane looked across the breakfast table at me, his green eyes starting to cloud over, and that's all it took. He didn't have to say anything. The message that came into my mind was pure and simple: You don't have to tell her everything, Trey. Some things even Mom doesn't need to know. It was just that I hated keeping secrets from her.

"Going down to Sumner's Pond," I said quietly.

Dane shook his head. I think it was the first time I'd ever gone against his wishes.

"Oh, I don't know, Trey." Mom glanced over her shoulder at me, not quite as intently as I imagined she might; then she turned her attention back to the scrambled eggs. "It's dangerous down there."

"No, it isn't," Dane said.

"The water's twelve feet deep this time of year, still cold from the winter runoff; and you know, Trey, you aren't a strong swimmer."

"I can swim, Mom."

"He swims fine," Dane said.

"Maybe later in the summer. When the weather's warmer and the water's a little lower."

"See?" Dane whispered from across the table. I looked at him, surprised, because I'd never heard a "told-you-so" out of him before, and I had been half hoping he might offer me some help instead. But he didn't. "Some things you just don't share with her."

"Sorry."

"What?" Mom asked.

"Nothing."

"Tell her the way you feel," Dane said softly.

"But what if she—"

"You're whispering again, Trey. Always whispering," she said. She dragged the plastic spatula across the bottom of the frying pan, her mind utterly absorbed in getting the eggs scrambled just right. The years had caught up to her. I couldn't say when that had happened, only that that very moment was the first time I had noticed it. A soft, gray-white streak of hair had become visible in the back, looking something like the early morning frost that sometimes formed on the winter grass across the creek. I could almost see her walking ever so cautiously through the autumn of her life. Not unhappy with the way things had turned out. But not happy either. I think it was the first time in my life I had realized that my mother was a whole person, not just my mother. And that she wasn't that different from myself.

"I really want to go swimming down at Sumner's today, Mom."

"Trey—"

"I'm a good swimmer. Better than you think I am."

There was a strange period of silence, as if she had heard something in my voice that had never been there before. "Okay," she finally said, staring at me the same way I had just finished staring at her. As if she were seeing me for the very first time. "You go ahead and give it your damnedest and have a good time doing it. But I warned you. Don't say I didn't warn you."

"Really?"

"If you've a mind."

In the end I guess it was one of those things that no one could have prevented. The time was just right. Dane knew that somehow, and I guess in the back of her mind, in one of those intuitive areas, Mom knew it too.

6

"She's mad at you again," I said once we were outside. Above us, the sky was thinly cast with orange-tipped clouds. But in the distance, hovering over the mountains, there was a different sky. The clouds were angry gray-black oceans. A thunderstorm was building there. Like a giant rolling wave. Too faraway for Dane, perhaps; too close for me. In the back of my mind I had a sick, awful feeling about that storm. It was something like jealousy.

"I know," Dane said.

"She's always mad at you, Dane. How come?"

"Doesn't matter, does it?"

"It should. To *you*, it should."

"Well, it doesn't, so quit harping on it."

It had been more difficult than we'd thought it would be: untying the old hemp rope that held the winter tarp tightly against the dozer. I had slipped the last knot free, then Dane grabbed one end of the rope and started pulling. It unwound from the tarp like a huge earthworm, its head whipping back and forth, sliding helplessly backward through the eyelets until it was finally free. Then Dane had rewound it in short loops, hooking it first between the crook of his thumb and forefinger, then around his elbow, and back again, over and over. Now he was carrying it at his side, and when it brushed against his jeans it made a soft, whispering noise that sounded as if someone were saying: *come on . . . come on.* I was doing my best to keep up.

"Don't you ever get tired of it?" I finally asked.

"Of what?"

"Of Mom's ignoring you?"

Dane stopped. We had been walking along a dirt path, through a field of dying winter grass, but now we were standing still and I noticed that my tennis shoes were soaked from the dew. "You ever get tired of Mom ignoring *you?*" he asked. It didn't sound like a question, though. It sounded like an indictment.

"She doesn't ignore me."

"Never pays you much attention, either."

"Sure she does."

"No," he said, his voice softer than I'd ever heard it. Soft, but still firm. "She *worries* over you, Trey. That's not the same thing. She's scared for you. You're like a nightmare that keeps coming back. You remind her of something she doesn't want to remember. She's worried . . . and she's scared . . . but I don't think she cares. I don't think she ever will."

It felt as if a great abyss had opened the earth between us, the distance suddenly enormous. I started walking again. "You're wrong. She cares about me. She cares about both of us; she just doesn't know how to show it."

"Trey, she doesn't even know you. You aren't real to her. You died twelve years ago, in her womb, before you even had a chance to be introduced. Now you're like one of those envelopes with a window, the ones with the bills inside. All she has to do is look at you and she sees a debt she'll never be free of."

Miles away, over the ridge of the mountains, the sky lit up with a flash of lightning. The underbelly of the gray clouds turned a sharp yellowy-orange, then white, then gray again. The air was suddenly charged with electricity, and I thought for an incredible instant about that time behind the greenhouse when Miss Riley had been afraid to get too close to Dane because she knew—we *both* knew—he was giving off something that could hurt you.

Dane finally ran to catch up with me.

"You're jealous," I said.

He was breathing heavily, his green eyes bright. The tiniest hint of a frown pushed down on his mouth, then disappeared. But I had seen something behind it. Something plain and simple and honest. I don't think he'd meant for it to show.

"You *are!* You're jealous!"

"Maybe," he said evenly. "Then again, maybe I have good reason."

"What reason?"

Another bright flash of lightning lit up the distant sky, all yellow and orange and white. I watched until the golden streaks ran out, then I waited to hear what the thunder would sound like. It was the crack of a whip. A crisp slap against the sky. Followed by a long, throaty rumble that sounded something like fury.

Dane never did answer my question.

7

Sumner's Pond changed with the seasons.

During the winter months the runoff washed into Whiskey Creek from a hundred minor gulleys, raising the creek level and burying Sumner's Pond somewhere below the high-water mark. Come spring, though, the rains would slow, the creek level would drop a bit, and the pond would seem to form all over again. A rebirth of sorts. From caterpillar to cocoon. Sumner's Pond always came back again, from cocoon to butterfly, changed in subtle little ways, but always a thing of extraordinary beauty.

Dane dropped the rope at the edge of the sand.

Through the branches of the old oak tree, I saw a flash of distant lightning, its sharp colors shattering the skyline as if it were a broken mirror.

"Storm's growing stronger," I said.

There was a moment of absolute stillness, then slowly an angry roll of thunder began to build.

Dane glanced toward the mountains, his expression unreadable. Except for his eyes. It took a moment before I realized what had happened to them, then suddenly it seemed almost *too* apparent. They were dark now; the emerald-green fire had faded. It was as if the storm had begun to draw its energy from him, the way he'd told me it drew energy from itself. His eyes had become a reflection of the loss.

"Are you afraid to die, Trey?"

"What?"

"Are you afraid to die?"

"What kind of question is that?"

"Just answer it."

"Yeah, I guess. I never thought about it much."

The far bank was all blackberry vines that had been dormant during the winter and had only recently begun to show color and vitality again. The nearest bank was all sand and soft dirt, running up to the water's edge. The oak tree had rooted in the sand on the northern side of the pond. In places some of its thick roots had climbed above the surface and were exposed. They looked like ancient, mummified fingers.

Dane leaned up against the trunk of the oak, one foot resting on an exposed root. "Who's going up?"

"Not me."

He stared at me a moment, as if he were trying to decide what should come next. Finally he said, "It's not as bad as you think."

"Then you climb it."

"Not the climbing," he said. "The dying."

"I don't see how it could be all that good."

He smiled flatly, with a touch of visible disappointment. But more than that, I caught a glimpse of sadness behind his eyes. It wasn't there long, and after a moment he shaded his eyes and glanced toward the top of the oak tree. "You really don't want to climb it?"

"No way."

"Scared?"

"Yeah."

"Then that's why you should."

In the distance, over the mountain, the sky ignited in streaks of white-hot lightning.

"*You* do it," I said.

"You sure?"

"Better you than me."

He smiled again, with ease this time. "Maybe you're right." Then he picked the rope up out of the sand, looped it over his head, and started up the oak tree.

"I'm not afraid," I told him.

"I never thought you were."

"I'm not."

He shinnied up the trunk, past the first giant knot where the wind had torn the limb off two years before. I thought he might stop there for a breather, but he didn't.

Finally, I couldn't sit still any longer. "Wait up!"

Dane waited for me at the first solid limb, one foot shoved into the crook of the limb for support, one arm wrapped around the trunk of the tree for balance. More than once, the sky behind him exploded with lightning, and when he looked down at me he was a dark, faceless silhouette. A scarecrow of sorts.

When I caught up with him, we ended up sitting

side by side on the thick limb, about ten or twelve feet above the pond. The water was flowing lazily, quietly beneath us. I could see the gravelly silt bottom, the drifting tendrils of moss that had grown on an old, sunken log.

"Scared?" Dane asked.

"Not like I thought I'd be."

There was a crack of lightning in the distance, a stutterlike hesitation, then another shattering light show right behind it. I started counting off the seconds, vaguely aware that the storm seemed to be moving closer:

—one thousand one—

—one thousand two—

That was as far as I got before the enormous explosion of thunder hit.

It felt as if some immense force had taken hold of the tree and were shaking it with all its strength, as if it were trying to separate us—my brother and me—not only from the tree, but from each other.

I clamped down on the limb with both hands and held on tight.

Dane laughed above the sky's rumble. "Scared now?"

"No."

Then, quite naturally, the heavy thunder moved on. Across the field of winter grass. In the general direction of home. And I wondered briefly if Mom would be frightened by it.

"What was that?" I asked.

"Thunder."

"No, I've heard thunder before. I've seen lightning. A thousand times, maybe. Never like this, though. What's going on, Dane? How come everything feels so

. . . *wrong* today . . . like you're keeping something from me?"

Dane looked past me, toward the gray-black sky hovering over the mountains. There was something completely foreign in his expression, a strange combination of sadness and joy that seemed surprisingly compatible. "You've changed, Trey. Did you know that?"

"How?"

"In little ways . . . ways I don't think you even understand."

"Maybe you've changed too."

"Maybe."

"So what's the big deal?"

"No big deal. I just wanted you to keep that in mind. Things change in life. Sometimes suddenly. But life goes on, Trey. You draw as much energy as you can from your memories, because they'll make you stronger, then you go on."

"I can take care of myself."

"I know that," he said quietly. "That's the whole point."

Another explosion of lightning etched its deep electric lines into the distant sky.

—one thousand three—

Thunder followed.

Like a rolling quake of the earth.

Dane screamed with laughter.

But it was the thunderstorm's laughter I heard. And when the resounding wave of thunder finally rolled away from us, Dane's laughter sadly rolled away with it.

"It's time," he said, after a long period of eerie silence.

"Time for what?"

"(To go home.)"

I can't be certain that's what he said. It came out softly, like a whispered thought not meant for anyone else to hear. So maybe he didn't say it at all. Maybe it was just something my mind made up after the fact. Something to help me explain things. But he said something, then he started to climb the tree again.

"Dane?"

"What?"

"Are you okay?"

"I'm fine," he said, without looking down at me. It seemed as if suddenly he were in a hurry now. The rope was hanging from around his neck, swinging from side to side, as he used both hands to work his way higher up the tree.

The sky exploded with another splinter-run of lightning, and I realized for the first time that the sky overhead had fallen dark. As dark as Dane's eyes had fallen.

Eighteen, maybe nineteen or twenty feet up, Dane sat down on an overhanging limb and began to scoot his way out, over the water. Below him, Sumner's Pond was swirling with dark shadows. Directly above the pond, he stopped, unwound the rope from around his neck, and tied a quick slipknot in one end.

"You don't have to do this, Dane." I could smell a sharp, tangy fragrance in the air. Something similar to the smell that rises from a lit match. And I thought back to that day when Miss Riley had caught me smoking. And I thought back to all those times when Dane had sat on the windowsill and looked out at a faraway thunderstorm as if he were waiting for it to come take him home.

"Yes, I do," he said firmly, his hands working frantically all of a sudden.

"We can put it up some other time." The darkness overhead was brooding now, like the darkness of the pond below. Black somehow. Hiding secrets . . . maybe not from both of us . . . maybe not from Dane, but certainly from me. "Sometime when there's no storm," I said.

"There *is* no other time, Trey."

Then everything happened the way it often happens in a dream: with a distorted sense of time and place.

Dane tightened the knot, slipped the other end of the rope through, and gave it a pull.

The sky lit up again, like a fireball this time.

—one thousand—

A deafening explosion of thunder.

I looked up at Dane . . . he had slipped somehow and was falling . . . I saw his right foot drag across the bark of the tree, as if it were fighting to hold on . . . I saw it with such absolute clarity, so magnificently distinct . . . his hands reaching for the limb, stretching, coming up empty . . . his back arched like the back of a frightened cat . . . falling . . . falling away from the limb . . . toward the pond below . . . helpless . . .

"Dane!"

. . . and then a sudden echoing snap!

The slack of rope taken up.

Dane's body suspended in midair.

Swinging back and forth.

By his neck.

The only sound in the world the sound of the rope rubbing against the bark.

His eyes were still open, and somewhere in the

back of my mind I had a dream that he suddenly winked at me, then smiled, then screamed with laughter because he'd pulled a good one over on me. But it didn't happen like that. His body swung lazily back and forth at the end of the rope, each sweep of the arc a little shorter than the one before it.

Back and forth.

Another strike of lightning skittered across the murky sky.

I heard thunder, but it sounded faraway now.

Everything suddenly seemed faraway.

Dane was dead.

8

I spent the rest of the day sitting in the oak tree.

Within a few minutes of the accident the thunderstorm quietly disappeared.

So did Dane.

As if the storm had drawn away the last of his energy, his soul.

His body had swung freely back and forth, like a pendulum, driven by its own diminishing momentum. And it seemed as if each time he touched the outer edges of the arc a shade more of him disappeared into nothingness. By the time the rope had finally come to a rest, Dane was gone.

The thunderstorm quietly moved on.

The sky became bright again.

Later, it seemed, the brightness turned to evening.

Eventually I went home.

9

Mom was sitting on the back porch, waiting for me. The sun was setting above the mountains, the last trace of the storm gone, just an orange-pink sky left behind. I sat on the floor, next to her chair, my hands wrapped around the chair's arm, and for a long time I didn't know what to tell her.

After a while I gave up trying to find the right words and forced myself through whatever words came to mind. I told her about the rope swing, about being too scared to climb the tree, about the storm, about Dane's fall, even about the way he had . . . *disappeared.* It took me all of thirty minutes to get it out, a painfully long thirty minutes; and there wasn't a single moment when she stopped me to ask a question, or when I stopped talking long enough to see if she was still listening.

Night had fallen by the time I finished.

And Mom was crying softly.

"All these years," she said, after she'd had a chance to wipe her eyes on the Kleenex she kept tucked under the sleeve of her blouse. "All these years I was so afraid to say anything to you. You'd talk about Dane as if he were standing right next to you, and I'd look at you, this scrawny little kid who had—by the grace of God—just barely survived birth, and I'd want to shake my finger at you, Trey, because your brother was dead . . . Dane was *dead.*"

She was crying again.

I reached out and took hold of her hand.

"I don't know what I was thinking, Trey. I suppose I always hoped it would go away eventually, that one day you'd realize Dane wasn't really there and you wouldn't need him anymore. Sometimes that worry weighed heavy on my mind. And other times . . . other times I'd close my eyes and wish I could see him the way you saw him. I was always looking for him, half hoping he'd show up one day as if he'd never been gone. I guess that was silly of me."

"It doesn't sound silly."

"Yes, it does," she said, her face expressionless. She stared at me for a long time, then took in a deep breath that seemed to give her new strength. "He died, Trey. At birth. Somehow, the umbilical cord got tangled around his neck, and he strangled. Your brother was born dead, Trey. Two minutes and thirty-three seconds before you came into the world."

10

Some things that happen, it doesn't matter if anyone believes they happened or not. As long as you know in your heart.

For a long time, when a new thunderstorm came through, I'd sit at the bedroom window the way Dane had sat there so many times before me. Watching the lightning skate across the gray-black sky over the mountains. Waiting. Half hoping, as Mom used to do, that he might show up again and it would be as if he'd never been away.

Dane always looked out for me. That's what I remember most about him. He was my brother, my mentor. Always there when I needed him. For twelve years he was there, letting me draw energy from him until he felt I was strong enough to survive without him. Then he was gone.

I guess that's the only thing that matters now: Dane's gone.

Christ, I still miss him.

Haunted World

Robert R. McCammon

 Well, I knew it was the end of the world for sure when I walked into my den and found William Shakespeare sittin' in my BarcaLounger.

At least I think it was him. Anyways, it was one of them fellas wore starched collars and a velvet suit and said a lot of "thees" and "thous" like they used to say every year at the high school senior play down the road. I called Vera in. I said, "Vera, come in here and take a look at this right quick!" and she came runnin'. Of course, we'd seen ghosts before, just like everybody else in the world had by then, but Will Shakespeare sittin' in your den watchin' *Crosswits* on the TV is a damn peculiar sight.

Every so often he'd speak, as if he were tryin' to answer the *Crosswits* questions. Then he'd rest his head back, and I saw him close his eyes and heard him say, "Woe is me," clear as a church bell. By then Ben Junior had come in, and he pressed in between his momma and me, and we all three watched the ghost tryin' to talk to the man on TV. Ol' Will was the same as the other spirits: He wasn't all there. Oh, you could make him out all right, and even see the color of his hair and skin and suit, but he was kinda smoky too, and you could see the chair right through him. He reached out toward the lamp beside him, but his hand was misty and couldn't touch it. "Woe is me," he said again, and then he looked at us standin' in the doorway. His eyes were sad. They were the eyes of a man who was lost on a long trip and couldn't find the right road again.

Vera said, "Would you like me to change the channel?" She was always mannerly to house guests. Even uninvited ones. Ol' Will started to fade away then, bit by bit. Didn't surprise us none, 'cause we'd seen the others do it too. In another minute just his face was left, floatin' in the air like a pale moon. Then nothin' but his eyes. They blinked a couple of times, then those were gone too. But we all knew ol' Will hadn't vanished for good, and he hadn't gone too far away neither. He was like all the other ones roamin' around the haunted world. Hell of a mess, that's for sure.

Wasn't too long before Ben Junior said, "Dad?" and he motioned me and his momma over to the big picture window in the front room, the one that has such a pretty view over the meadow. It was October, and the world was turnin' deep red and purple. The sky was that greenish-gray it gets just before it happens. Vera said a while back that the sky reminds her of a lizard's skin, and I guess that about hits the nail on the head. Ben Junior pointed, and he said in a quiet voice, "There's another one."

Vera and I looked, and of course we saw it. Have to

be blind as a bat in a Bundt cake not to see one of those things, once they get started.

The tornadoes are always that peculiar lizard-skin color. One of 'em whipped right across Pennsylvania Avenue in Washington, D.C., the other day. I saw it on the five o'clock news. Anyway, there was a tornado whippin' and whirlin' down the hillside into our meadow not two hundred yards away. Things started poppin' and creakin' in our house like the whole place was fixin' to come unjointed. A light bulb blew out and right after that the power went. "Lord," Vera whispered, standin' beside me in the lizard-green light. "Lord have mercy."

You could see 'em in the tornado, goin' around and around and tumblin' over each other from the bottom of the cone to the top of the spout. How many were there it was hard to say. Hundreds, I reckon. Some of 'em were smoky, but others looked just as solid as you and me. The tornado was spittin' 'em out hither and yonder, and they were fallin' to earth like autumn leaves. They drifted into the treetops and onto the grass, and they fell over the fence and onto the road that leads to Concordia. Some of 'em were tattered to pieces, like old rags caught in the blades of a lawn mower, but others stood up and staggered around like Saturday night drunks. The tornado took a turn away from our house and marched up the hillside again toward the south, spittin' out ghosts with every whirl, and then Vera reached out and pulled the curtains shut, and we all stood in the twilight listenin' to the trees moan as the tornado went on.

"Well," I said, because there wasn't much else to say. Deep subject, I know. Cold, too. Vera walked over to the wall switch and flicked it up and down with a vengeance, but the power wasn't goin' to come back on for quite a while. "There goes a hot dinner," she said, and she sounded like she was about to cry. I put my hand on her shoulder, and then she kinda folded up against me and hung on. Ben Junior sneaked a peek through the curtain, but what he saw he didn't care for, because he let the curtain drop back real quick.

Someone—somethin'—called from outside. "Mary?" It was a man's voice, and it was terribly lonely. "Mary? Are you in there?"

I started to go to the door, but Vera held me tight. We both knew I had to go. I pulled away from her, and I went to the door and opened it.

On our front porch stood a frail-lookin' man with dark hair slicked back and parted in the middle. He wore a dark suit—black or brown, I couldn't really tell. His face was pale and kinda yellow, like spoiled milk. He took a step back when he saw me, and he was wearin' old high-top shoes. He was shiverin', and he looked around himself. If he saw all the others staggerin' about in the meadow, nothin' registered on his face but pure puzzlement. Then he looked at me again, and when his mouth opened, his voice was like the chilly wind: You felt it more than heard it. "Mary? Is Mary waiting for me?"

"Mary's not here," I told him.

"Mary?" he asked again. "Is she waiting for me?"

"No," I said. "Not here."

He stopped speakin', but his mouth stayed open. His eyes looked wet, like those of a dog that had just gotten kicked in the ribs. "I don't think you know anybody here," I told him, because he seemed to be waitin' for somethin' else. And then his mouth closed, and he turned away from my door and started walkin' across the meadow in his high-topped shoes. "Mary?" I heard him call. "Mary?" He started fadin' away as he passed a Roman soldier sittin' sprawled in the grass, and he was almost gone when a little boy in knickers ran right through him. The man who was searchin' for Mary faded away like a Polaroid left out in the noonday sun too long, but the Roman soldier stayed where he was, and the little boy ran into the woods. There were maybe forty or fifty others out in the meadow, wanderin' around like strangers at a weird garden party. Or a Halloween party, it bein' October and all. Out on the edge of the meadow there was what looked like somebody from Revolutionary times, a skinny man wearin' a powdered wig and a three-cornered hat. Near him was a cowboy in a yellow duster. Over there on the other side was a black-haired woman in a long blue gown that trailed on the grass, and not far from her stood a man in a suit, lookin' around as if he was waitin' for the next bus. The blue mist of ghosts trailed from the trees like cobwebs and drifted over the meadow in an ankle-deep haze. Ghosts were all in the woods, and you could hear 'em babblin' and callin' in a bedlam of accents and languages. "Dan!" I heard one American-speakin' woman—ghost, I mean—shout from over on the edge of the woods. "Damn it, Dan, where's my robe?" she hollered, as she walked buck naked across the grass. Not walked, actually. Kinda wobbled is more like it. The wind hit her and tattered her to pieces so we didn't have to look at her big old flabby butt anymore. Ben Junior was peekin' out beside me, and I shoved him back inside and shut the door.

Vera and I just stared at each other, there in the

gloom, as the ghosts chattered and hollered outside. We heard an Indian war-whoopin', and somebody screamin' that she'd lost her cat, and somebody else raisin' a ruckus in what sounded like Greek to me. They were all searchin' for their own world, the one they used to be part of. But of course they couldn't get back there. They couldn't find anybody or anythin' that was familiar, because this wasn't their world anymore. It was our world. And that's the hell of it. See?

I remember what Burt Truman said. I remember, because it seemed so right. Burt looked at me, his eyes huge behind those bottle-bottom glasses he wears, and he said, "You know why this is happenin', Ben? Well, I'll tell you my opinion. You take the air and the water nowadays. Both so polluted you can't take a safe breath or a decent sip. And what happened on them beaches last summer, all that garbage and crap washin' up 'cause the ocean can't take no more." He lifted up his glasses and scratched his nose. "Seems to me heaven—or hell—can't take no more either. And all the dead folks are gettin' cast back up on shore. Whatever that place is that kept the dead, it's full to overflowin'. The dead folks are washin' back up into our world, and that's God's truth or I ain't sittin' here in Clyde's barbershop."

"Bullshit," Clyde said as he clipped Burt's side-burns. Clyde has a voice like a steam shovel with stripped gears. "Damn ghosts are comin' through the ozone hole. That's what they said on Dan Rather yesterday."

"God's shut with us," Phil Laney offered. He's a deacon at the Baptist church, and he was gloomin'-and-doomin' long before all this started. "Only way for us to fix this is to get down on our knees and pray like we've never prayed before. I mean, serious prayin'. We've got to get right with God before this thing'll be fixed."

"Hell, this thing's done broke to pieces," Luke McGuire said. Ol' Luke's a big fella, stands about six foot three and wears raggedy overalls, but he's got the best farmland in south Alabama. "Just like a machine," he said as he rolled himself another cigarette. "You bust a cylinder on your tractor, ain't prayin' that gets it fixed. You bend a blade on a tiller, you don't get on your knees and kiss the ground until it's straight again. Hell, no. The world's a machine. Thing's done broke to pieces, and the repair shop's shut down."

This was the sort of conversation that could fill most of a Saturday afternoon and evenin' and still leave you goin' in circles. But I mostly thought of what Burt said, about the dead overflowin' and washin' back up into our world. The tornadoes brought 'em back, of course, but I knew what he meant. Heaven and hell were like busted pipes, and the ghosts were spillin' out.

And right about then, as Luke and Phil were arguin' hammer and tongs, a knight in tarnished armor walked past the window of Clyde Butler's barbershop. Walked right out in the street, he did, and Mrs. Beacham in her green Oldsmobile swerved the wheel and crashed into the front of Sammy Kane's Stag Shop for Men. Clothes dummies flew all over the place, broken arms and legs lyin' on the pavement. That knight just kept on goin', fine as you please, and he took a few more rusty steps before he vanished into the unknown. But he didn't go far. We all knew that. He couldn't go far, see. He was still stuck in the haunted world, like all the other dead folks.

After all that commotion had died down, Luke McGuire picked his teeth with a splintered match and brought up the question: "How come the ghosts are wearin' clothes?"

Not all of 'em were, of course, but most of 'em did. We thought about that for a little while, and then Luke went on in that thick drawl of his that always makes me think of mud simmerin' in the bottom of a ditch. "Clothes," he said. "Ghosts of people are one thing. But are they wearin' ghosts of *clothes?*"

We drifted into talkin' about what ghosts were, and that was a tangled thicket. Then Clyde brought up the next skull knocker. "Thank God they're ghosts, that's all I can say." He brushed hairs off Burt's shoulders. "Not solid, I mean." He glanced around at everybody, to see if we'd gotten the point. We hadn't. "You can drive cars through ghosts. You can put your hand through 'em. They don't need food or water, and they can't touch you neither. Take that fella in armor just walked past here. Think you'd like to feel him slap you upside the head? I looked out my window this mornin' and saw the woods full of damn ghosts, blowin' in the breeze like old newspapers. One of 'em had a long black beard and carried a sword 'bout as big as ol' Luke. Think you'd like to get stabbed a few times with somethin' like that?"

"Wasn't a real sword," Luke observed sagely. "Was a ghost of a sword."

"Yeah, and thank God for that," Clyde steam-shoveled on. "What do you think would happen if everybody who ever died in the whole world came back?"

"We might find out," I said. "Seems like that's happenin' right now." I knew, like we all did, that this thing was happenin' not just in Concordia, Alabama, but in Georgia and North Carolina and New York and Illinois and Wyoming and California and everywhere else under the sun. Ghosts were roamin' the streets of London and Paris, and stompin' through Red Square. Even the Australians were seein' ghosts, so when I say haunted world that's exactly what I mean.

"Thank God, they're ghosts and not real," Clyde said, as he finished up on Burt. "There you go." He handed Burt a mirror. "Slicker'n owl shit."

Luke switched on the barbershop's TV to catch the midday news. There was a report from Washington, D.C. It showed somethin' that looked like Thomas Jefferson, sittin' on the steps of the Capitol and cryin' his eyes out.

It hit me then, as I was standin' in the gloom starin' at Vera and the ghosts were catterwaulin' outside. The power was out. How were we gonna see the TV show tonight? They'd been advertisin' it for a week. Tonight Tom Edison was supposed to be a guest on the Johnny Carson show. I'm talkin' about the Tom Edison who invented the light bulb, the genuine article. Seems Edison—his spirit, I mean—had been talked into appearin' on TV. Tonight was the night. Shirley MacLaine was supposed to be a guest too, but she wasn't even dead yet, so what did she know? Anyway, the power was off!

I went to the phone and called Clyde. "They got the juice back on over here," Clyde said, speakin' from eight miles away. The phone was hissin' with static, but I could hear him good enough. "I just got a call from Phil, too," Clyde told me. "His TV's out. I reckon mine is at home too. You want to watch that show, come on over to the barbershop tonight. Hell, I'll get us some beers and we'll have a time of it."

I said that was a fine idea. Ben Junior was tuggin' at my sleeve, and Vera was starin' out the window again. I hung up the phone and walked over to see what had been roused up this time.

More Roman soldiers were out in the meadow. I guess they were Roman, but I'm not sure. There were about a hundred of 'em, and they had shields and swords. Ghost shields and swords, I mean. And there were about a hundred or so Chinese-lookin' fellas too, half-naked and with long braids in their hair. Well, the Romans and the Chinese had taken to fightin'. Maybe they were tryin' to finish up an old battle, or maybe all they knew was fightin' and that was their job. The Romans were swingin' their ghost swords, and the Chinese were kickin' with their ghost legs, and nothin' but mist was bein' hit. From out of the woods swarmed other ghosts: cowboys, musketeers, guys with bowl-shaped haircuts and long robes, women in lacy dresses, and black Africans with animal-skin shields and spears like in that English movie Ben Junior and me watched one Saturday. All the ghosts swirled around each other like they were part of a big churnin' whirlpool, and I'm tellin' you that the noise they made—hollerin' and screamin' at each other—was somethin' fearsome. No doubt about it: Even when people were dead, they still couldn't get along. Then a few dogs were even runnin' around out among the ghosts—ghost dogs, snappin' at ghost ankles. Maybe there was a horse or two out there, but I'm not sure. Anyway, it looked like Animal Heaven had started overflowin' too. "Lord save us!" Vera said, but Ben Junior said, "Neat!" and I saw he was grinnin'. Boy's got a strange sense of humor. Takes after me, I reckon, because I was kinda fascinated at the sight of all those ghosts tanglin' and whirlin'.

Vera turned away from the window, and that was when she screamed.

I looked. I think Ben Junior let out a strangled squawk. It might've been my voice.

Standin' in front of us, right in our pine-paneled livin' room, was a red-bearded man with a double-bladed battle-ax. That sumbitch stood at least six foot six, taller even than Luke McGuire, and he had on some kind of ragged animal skin and a metal skullcup with bull horns sticking out on either side of it. His face looked like a lump of meat wrapped up in wrinkled leather. He had green eyes under red brows as big as scrub brushes, and he let out a holler that shook the room as he lifted that battle-ax up over his head.

What would you have done? I knew he was a ghost and all, but at a time like that you don't think exactly calm. I shoved Vera out of the way of that battle-ax, and I picked up the first thing that came to hand: a lamp table beside the couch. The lamp flew off of it, and I thrust that little wooden table up like a Vikin' shield, my shoulders tensin' for the shock.

It didn't come. The battle-ax, a misty thing, went right through the table. I swear I saw a glint of metal, though, and old blood on the edge. I could smell that sumbitch, sure enough; he smelled like a dead cow. He took another step forward, crowdin' me, and he flailed back and forth with that battle-ax like he really thought he was gonna hit somethin'. His face was splotched with red. Ever heard the expression, "mad as a ghost"? I just made it up, 'cause he was mad as

hellfire sure enough. He chopped the ax back and
forth a dozen times, and the rage on his face would've
been terrible if he'd been flesh and blood instead of
colored mist. I laughed, and that made him madder
still. The ax kept whippin' back and forth, through the
table. I said, "Fella, why don't you put that toy away
and get the hell out of my house?"

He stopped choppin', his big chest heavin' up and
down. He glared at me for a minute, and I could tell
he hated me. Maybe for bein' alive—I don't know.
Then he gave a growl and started to fade away. His
beard was the last thing to go. It hung in the air for a
few seconds, workin' as if it still had a mouth under
it, and then it went.

"Is it gone? Is it gone? Ben, tell me it's gone!" Vera
had scrunched herself up into a corner, her arms hugging herself and her eyes wide and starey. I didn't like
the looks of them. Ben Junior was kinda dazed. He
stood where the Vikin' had been, feelin' around in the
air.

"It's gone, hon," I said to Vera. "Wasn't ever here,
really. You okay?"

"I've never . . . I've never . . . seen anything . . .
like that." She could hardly get a breath, and I set the
table down and put my arms around her while she
trembled.

"They're not real," I told her. "None of them are.
They're just . . . pictures in the air. They hang there
for a while, and then they go away. But they're not
real. Okay?"

She nodded. "Okay," she said, but she sounded
choked.

"Dad?"

"Just a minute. You want me to go get you an aspirin? You want to lie down awhile?" I kept my arms around Vera, for fear her knees might give way.

"Dad?" Ben Junior's voice was a little higher. "Look at this."

"I'm all right," Vera said. She had a strong constitution. Livin' on a farm for over twenty years makes you that way. "See what Ben Junior wants."

I looked over at the boy. He was standin' there, starin' at the table I'd just set down. "Dad?" he repeated. "I . . . don't think this was here before."

"What wasn't there before?" I walked over beside him, and I saw what he was talkin' about.

On the table's surface was a single diagonal scratch. It wasn't much. The tip of a nail might've done it. Only Ben Junior was right, and I knew that at once. The scratch hadn't been there before. I touched it to make sure it was real, and ran my finger along its length. The lamp's base had green backing on it, to keep it from scratchin' anythin'. I looked at Ben Junior. He was a smart boy, and I knew he knew. And he knew I knew, too.

"Vera?" I tried to sound calm, but I don't think I did. "Let's drive on into town and get some dinner. How does that suit you?"

"Fine." She took my hand and wouldn't let go of it, and I walked with her to the closet to get her sweater. Ben Junior went back through the hallway at a cautious pace, stirrin' the air before him with his hands to make sure nothin' was there, and a minute later he returned with a jacket from his room. I got my wallet and the keys to the pickup, and we went outside into the gray-green twilight. The driveway was full of fightin' ghosts: Chinese, Romans, an Indian or two, and a husky fella wearin' a kilt. I backed the truck right through 'em, and none of 'em seemed to mind.

On the drive to Concordia I turned on the radio, but all the stations were screwed up with the most god-awful static you ever heard. I switched it off real quick, because the noise sounded to me like the whole world was screamin'. Vera touched my arm and pointed off toward the right. Another tornado was movin' across the hills, blowin' red leaves before it and leavin' ghosts in its wake. The sky was green and low, shot through with pearly streaks. Half-formed, misty figures swept past the truck. I turned on the windshield wipers.

We passed Bobby Glover's pasture. There were so many ghosts wanderin' and staggerin' around that field it looked like a spirit convention. Things that looked like pieces of filmy cloth were hangin' in Bobby's barbed-wire fence, and they were growin' arms, legs, and heads. An old woman dressed like a Pilgrim was walkin' in the middle of the road, and she saw us comin' and made a noise like a cat gettin' skinned as the truck went through her. I looked back in the rear-view mirror and saw blue mist floatin' in the air where the Pilgrim lady had been a second before. Somethin' occurred to me real strange just about then: Somewhere in the world my own father and mother were wanderin'. Vera's mother, too; her father was in a rest home in Montgomery. Somewhere all our ancestors were out in the haunted world, and the ancestors of everybody who'd ever drawn a breath. I hadn't seen any ghosts of babies yet. I hoped I wouldn't, but you never knew. Peculiar thoughts whirled through my brain, like those red leaves thrown by the tornado: My father had died six years ago, and my mother had gone on a year later. They could be roamin' the jungles of Brazil or the streets of Dallas for all I knew. I hoped my father didn't come back in Tokyo. He'd fought the Japanese in World War II, and that would be pure hell for him.

About three miles from Concordia, we came upon a station wagon that had gone into a ditch. Both the front doors were open, but nobody was around. I stopped the truck and was gonna get out to take a look, but I heard what sounded like Indian war whoops off in the woods somewhere. I thought about that scratch on the table, and I swallowed hard and drove on.

I took the next curve pretty fast. Anyway, we were on him before we knew it. Vera screamed and her foot plunged to the floorboard, but of course the brake pedal was on my side, and I sure as hell wasn't gonna hit it.

He looked more ape than human, really. He was monstrous, and he wore a tattered lion's skin that still had the lion's head on it. He bellowed and charged the pickup, his fangy teeth showin'. I tried to swerve, but there wasn't much use, and I sure didn't want to go into a ditch. The caveman lifted a club that had sharp rocks embedded in it, and he swung that thing like it weighed a feather.

The club turned to mist an instant before it would've hit the fender. I heard the caveman bellow again—right up next to my head, it seemed like—and I gave the truck all the gas she could handle. We sped on down the road, the engine poppin' and snarlin'. I guess that caveman—ghost of a caveman, I mean—must've thought we were somethin' good to eat. I looked in the rearview mirror, but he was gone.

"It wasn't real, was it?" Vera said in a quiet voice. Her gaze was fixed straight ahead. "It was just a picture that hung in the air, wasn't it?"

"Yeah, that's right," I answered. I thought about the scratched table. My fingers were clenched real hard around the steerin' wheel. That table hadn't been scratched before the Vikin' sumbitch had swung his ax at me. My mind was wanderin' in dangerous country. The Vikin' was a ghost, with the ghost of a battle-ax. Just a picture, hangin' in the air. So how come the table was scratched, as if the slightest edge of metal had grazed it?

I didn't care to think about that anymore. Such thoughts made the hair prickle on the back of your neck.

Concordia was a small town, hardly much to look at, but it had never been prettier. The sun was goin' down fast, into a lizard-skin horizon, and Concordia's street lights were glowin' in the murk. We went straight to the Concordia Café. It was crowded, I guess because a lot of folks had the same idea as us. Bein' with real people was a comfort, though the food was as bad as usual. You can be sure that ghosts were the prime topic of conversation, and every so often somebody would holler for everybody else to look out the windows and you could see spirits on Main Street. The sky flashed and flickered, blue lightnin' jumpin' from horizon to horizon, and we all sat in the Concordia Café and watched the parade of ghosts. Here came a fella dressed up in a tuxedo, his hair gleamin' with pomade, and spats on his shoes, and he was callin' for somebody named Lily in a broken voice, ghost tears runnin' down his cheeks. Then a Nazi soldier ran past, carryin' a ghost rifle. A little girl in a nightgown, her hair red and curly, staggered along the street callin' in a language I couldn't understand. Some of the women wanted to go out and help her, but the men blocked the door. It was a ghost little girl, and the hell if we wanted her in here among the livin'.

A whole bunch of 'em wandered past the café: half-naked Egyptians brown as berries, women in gaudy dance-hall duds, a pair of fellas in those tall caps with fur on 'em, and ghosts in rags. And then the ghost of a boy about twelve, Ben Junior's age, came over and peered in the café's window, and he was joined by the ghost of a woman with long white hair and no teeth. A man in a striped prison suit looked in another window, and peerin' in over his shoulder was the ghost of a tall, skinny fella in clown makeup. In a few minutes more they were all around the café, starin' in through the windows at us, and Lord knows our appetites fled. Fifty or sixty ghosts were out there, lookin' in and maybe longin' to join us. Grace Tarpley, the head waitress, started closin' all the blinds, then Mitch Brenner and Tommy Shawcross got up from their tables and helped her. But as soon as all the blinds were down and the windows sealed up, the ghosts outside took to moanin' and catterwaulin' and that was the end of our dinner. Some folks—live folks, I mean—started cryin' and wailin' too, specially some of the children. Hell, I even saw a couple of men break down and start bawlin'. This wasn't no fun, that's for sure.

Anyway, the noise comin' out of the Concordia Café must've scared the ghosts off, because their voices started gettin' fainter and fainter until finally it was just the live people moanin'. Then Gracie let out a scream that almost lifted the roof, because the old farmer sittin' by himself at a booth in the back, an untouched cup of coffee on the table before him, suddenly stood up and faded away. Nobody had known him, but I guess we all figured he was from the next county. It was gettin' so you couldn't tell the livin' from the dead anymore.

The night moved on. It seemed like nobody wanted to go home to their haunted houses. Jack and Sarah Kelton came by our table for a few minutes and said the power was still out their way and they'd heard the lines were all fouled up. Which didn't sound so good, since the Keltons lived about two miles closer to town than us. The lights flickered off and on a few times in the café, which made everybody scream to high heaven, but Gracie said the men were workin' on the wires down the road and not to worry because there were plenty of flashlights and candles. As Jack talked on about seein' a ghost he swore was Abraham Lincoln strollin' along Highway 211, I looked out the blinds and watched the blue lightnin' cracklin' across the sky. It was a bad night here. Hell, it was a bad night everywhere.

I don't know how many cups of coffee Vera and I had. Ben Junior got stuffed on potato chips, and gettin' his belly full is a true miracle. Anyway, the crowd started thinnin' out, folks decidin' to go home to sleep —if they could sleep, that is. It was almost time for the Johnny Carson show, and I paid the bill and took Vera and Ben Junior to Clyde's barbershop down the street.

The regulars were there, and the cast-iron stove was stoked up warm and ruddy. The TV was on, the show about ten minutes away from startin'. We found chairs and sat down next to Phil and Gloria Laney. Luke McGuire was there with his wife Missy and their two kids, the Trumans were there and so was Sammy and Beth Kane. Clyde had a few sixpacks of Bud ready, but none of us felt like a beer.

The show started, Johnny Carson came out—all serious this time, didn't even crack a funny—and he showed a few old pictures of Thomas Edison. The first guest was a fella who'd written a biography of Edison, then Mickey Rooney came on because he played Young Edison in a movie a long time ago. The next guest was a man who talked about the ghosts appearin' all over the world, and he said ghosts had been seen from the Sahara desert to the South Pole. He was an expert, I guess, but exactly what at I don't know. While the talkin' was goin' on, buildin' up to Edison appearin', I was thinkin' about the scratched table. What had made that mark? The edge of that Vikin's battle-ax? No, that couldn't be! The ghosts were just pictures hangin' in the air. They weren't real. But I thought about that station wagon we'd seen in the ditch on the way to town, and the sound of Indians war-whoopin' in the woods.

I remembered Clyde saying, "What do you think would happen if everybody who ever died in the whole world came back?"

Ghosts of everybody who'd ever died was one thing. But what if . . . I liked to choke thinkin' about this . . . what if everybody who'd ever died in the whole world *did* come back? Maybe as ghosts first, yes, but . . . maybe they weren't always gonna stay ghosts. Maybe death had reversed itself. Maybe some of 'em were already turnin' solid, a little piece at a time. As solid as the sharp edge of an ax blade. As solid as

Indians, who'd pulled somebody out of their station wagon and—

I shook those thoughts out of my head. Ghosts were ghosts. Weren't they?

Shirley MacLaine came on next, carryin' a crystal ball. She said Thomas Edison was a good friend of hers.

And then it was time.

They lowered the lights in the studio, I guess so Edison wouldn't get spooked. Then all the guests started callin' his name and Johnny Carson asked the audience to be real quiet. They guests kept on callin' Thomas Edison's name and askin' him to join them, but the seat next to Johnny's desk stayed empty. It went on awhile, and pretty soon Johnny got that look on his face like when he has a talkin' dog on the show and it won't pip a squeak. I mean, the whole thing was almost ridiculous. "I need a beer," Luke said, and he reached for one.

His hand never got there. Because suddenly we all gasped. There was a shape just beginnin' to take form in that empty chair next to Johnny's desk. Some of the audience started talkin', but Johnny hushed them up. The shape was becomin' the body of a man: a white-haired, sad-faced man, dressed in a wrinkled white suit that looked as if it had been slept in for quite some time. The figure got clearer and clearer, and damned if it wasn't the man who was in those old yellowed photographs.

"Got on clothes," Luke rasped. "How can a ghost wear clothes?"

"Shush!" Phil told him, and he leaned closer to the TV.

Clyde turned up the volume. Thomas Edison his

own self was sittin' in that chair on the Carson show, and even though the lights were dim he blinked as he looked around as if they stung his eyes. He was tremblin'. So was Johnny, and 'most everybody else. Thomas Edison looked like somebody's frail, scared old grandpap.

"Hello, Mr. Edison," Johnny finally said. He sounded like he had a chicken bone caught in his throat. "Can I . . . call you Tom?"

Edison didn't answer. He just shook and gasped, plain terrified. "Stage fright," Burt said. "Happened to me once when I gave a speech to the Civitan Club."

"Tom?" Johnny Carson went on. "Do you know who I am?"

Edison shook his head, his eyes wet and glassy.

"Mr. Edison," Shirley said, "we're all your friends here."

Edison gave a soft moan, and Shirley recoiled from him a little bit. "Tom?" Johnny tried again. "Where did you come from?"

"I . . . don't . . ." Edison started to speak, but his voice was wispy. "I . . . don't . . ." He looked around, gasping for words. "I . . . don't . . . belong here." He squinted at the audience. "I don't . . . like this place."

"We all love you," Shirley told him. "Tell us about your journey, and what you've seen on the other si—"

If ever hell broke loose on earth, it was the next instant.

Somebody in the audience took a picture. You could see the quick pop and glare of the flashbulb, right in Tom Edison's eyeballs. Another flash went off, and a third. Johnny Carson jumped up and shouted, "No pictures! I said no pictures! Somebody get those cameras!" The studio lights came on, real sudden. Tom Edison almost jumped out of his chair. People in the audience were rushin' the stage, and Johnny Carson was yellin' for everybody to stay back, but you could hardly hear him over the noise. More flashbulbs were poppin', and I guess somehow the reporters had gotten into the studio when they weren't supposed to be there. Lights flashed in Tom Edison's face, and all of a sudden he reached out and plucked that crystal ball off Shirley's lap, and he threw it straight into the TV camera that was trained on him. The camera smashed, zigzag lines goin' all over the screen. Another TV camera trained on Edison and caught him as he stood up, screamed at the top of his lungs, and vanished in a whirl of blue mist. "Everybody sit down!" Johnny was shoutin'. People were still tryin' to get closer, and now you could see folks grapplin' with each other like a backwoods wrestlin' match. "Everybody please sit—"

The screen went dark. "Somebody stepped on a cord," Burt said. Static jumped and jittered across the screen, and then a message came on: NETWORK DIFFICULTY. PLEASE STAND BY.

We stood by, but the Carson show didn't come back on. "He picked it up," Luke said quietly. "Did you see that? He picked it up."

"Picked what up?" Clyde asked. "What're you babblin' about?"

"Thomas Edison picked up the crystal ball and flung it," Luke told him, and looked around at the rest of us. "A ghost picked up somethin' solid. How can a ghost pick up somethin' solid?"

Nobody answered. I almost did, but I kept my mouth shut. I didn't want what I was thinkin' to be true. Maybe I should have said somethin', but the time slipped past.

Lightnin' flared and crackled over Concordia. About three seconds later, the barbershop's lights flickered once, twice, and went out. All of Concordia lay in darkness. Vera grasped my hand so hard I thought my knuckles were about to bust.

"Well, that's that," Clyde said. He stood up in the dark, and Luke lit a match. In its pale glow we all looked like ghosts. Clyde turned off the dead TV. "I don't know about everybody else," he said, "but I'm goin' home and get a good night's sleep, ghosts or not."

The group started breakin' up, and Clyde locked the doors. "We ought to go to the Holiday Inn over near Grangeville," I told Vera and Ben Junior as we were walkin' back to the pickup. "Maybe they'll have the power on over there. All right?"

Vera wouldn't let go of my hand. "No," she said. "I can't sleep in a strange bed. Lord knows all I want to do is get in my bed and pull the covers over my head and hope I wake up from this nightmare in the mornin'."

"Holiday Inn might be safer," I said. Instantly I regretted it, because Vera stiffened up. "Safer?" she asked. "Safer? What's that mean?"

If I told her what I was thinkin', that would be all she wrote. You'd have to peel Vera off a wall. Ben Junior was listenin' too, and I knew he knew, but still and all, home was where we belonged. "All right, hon," I said, and put my arm around her. "We'll sleep in our own bed tonight." Vera relaxed, and I was mighty glad I hadn't steered her into dark, deep water.

We started off. The pickup's headlights were a comfort. Maybe we should sleep in the truck tonight, I thought. No, we'd all have cricked backs in the mornin'. Best to get on home and pull the covers over our heads just like Vera wanted to. I found myself thinkin' about the rifle down in the basement. I ought to get that out and loaded. Wouldn't hurt to have it beside the bed if I needed—

"Look out, Ben!" Vera shouted, and I went for the brake, but too late.

The caveman was standin' in the road. He snarled and lifted that club studded with sharp-edged rocks, and as he swung it I could see the muscles ripple in his ape-like shoulders.

I expected the club to turn to mist. I wanted it to. I prayed for it, in that long instant as it came at the fender in a powerful blur. Oh, God, I prayed for it.

The club smashed into the front of our pickup truck with a shock that lifted us all off the seat. Vera screamed and so did Ben Junior, and I think Ben Senior let out a scream too. One of the headlights shattered and went out. I felt and heard somethin' boom and clatter in the engine, behind the crushed radiator. The truck lurched, and steam bellowed out around the crumpled hood. The caveman jumped back as the truck passed him, but I think he was scared just as witless as we were. I looked into the rearview mirror and saw him standin' there in the glare of the red taillights. Lightnin' flared behind him, over dark Concordia. I think he was grinnin'. He swung his club, and he started lumberin' along the road in the direction we were goin'.

The truck was laborin'. "Come on, come on!" I said, and I kept my foot to the gas. Vera's scream had broken; she was a shakin' moan, pressed up against my ribs. "He hit us, Dad!" Ben Junior said. "That sumbitch hit us!"

"Yeah," I told him. Wheezed it, really. "Yeah, I know he did."

The truck kept goin'. Chevy builds 'em strong. But I watched the gauges and I listened to the engine racketin', and I knew the eight miles home was askin' way too much.

Finally, with a groan and a shudder, the engine quit. I let the truck coast as far as she'd go, and I prayed again, this time for a slope to take us home, but I knew the road was flat as a flounder all the way to our front porch. We rolled to a stop, and we sat there.

"We've stopped, Dad," Ben Junior said.

I nodded. One part of me wanted to wring his neck. One part of me wanted to wring my own neck. Vera was sobbin', and I put my arm around her tight. "Don't cry," I said. "We're all right. We're gonna be fine. Don't cry, now." She kept cryin'. Words were cheap.

We sat for a while longer. Out in the night we could hear the freight-train roar of a tornado movin' through the hills. "Dad?" Ben Junior said at last, "I don't think we ought to stay here all night." I hadn't raised a dummy, that was for sure; I was the dumb one, for not insistin' we go to the Holiday Inn.

I hesitated at openin' the door. Vera was clingin' to me, and I'm not sure whose heart was poundin' harder. I was thinkin' about the caveman, with his club that must've weighed seventy or eighty pounds. He was between us and Concordia, and every second we wasted brought him closer. I got out of the truck real quick, pulled Vera out, and Ben Junior scrambled out the other side. Lightnin' crackled overhead, and you could hear tornadoes moanin' in the night.

"We've got to get home," I said, maybe just to steady up my own nerves. Once I had my hands on that rifle and we were shut up in our bedroom with our backs to the wall, we'd be just fine. "Sooner we start, the sooner we'll get there."

"It's dark," Vera whispered, her voice shakin'. "Oh, Lord, it's so dark."

I knew she was talkin' about the road that lay ahead. I knew every curve and bump in it, but tonight it was a road that led through the haunted world. Out in the woods were Indians, Roman soldiers, Nazis, Chinese karate kickers, at least one Vikin' with a battle-ax, and God only knew what else. And behind us, maybe stalkin' somethin' good to eat, was a caveman with an eighty-pound club.

And all of 'em, all the ghosts, maybe gettin' more solid by the hour. What was gonna happen, I wondered, when all the billions and billions of people who'd ever died in the world were back on earth again, hungry and thirsty, some of 'em peaceful folks for sure, but others ready to chop your head off or bust your skull with a club? One rifle suddenly seemed an awful puny thing. I had a thought: If we got killed, we wouldn't stay dead very long, would we?

The tornadoes sounded closer, whirlin' more ghosts into the woods. I said, "Come on," in the calmest voice I could manage, and I pulled Vera along with me. Ben Junior walked close to me on the other side, his hands clenched into fists. We had a long way to go. Maybe a car would come along. Maybe. This wasn't a night fit for travelin'. The road ahead was dark, so very dark. We had no choice but to walk it.

Afterword

Dean R. Koontz

Why do we like ghost stories? Why can't we be satisfied to read about private eyes packing .45s, prowling dark streets, beating up—and getting beaten up by—thugs of all sorts, fending off hot babes with secretly cold intentions, and brooding about the Big Sleep, the Long Goodbye? Why can't we readers be satisfied with the sex, romance, adventure, tragedy, comedy, and other thrills to be found in the *sensible* genres of fiction? What *is* it with us that we want to read about the dead, the undead, the walking dead, the living dead? Are we just plain morbid? Perverse? Twisted? Sick?

As a kid, I read spooky stories in my room, huddled under the covers, using a flashlight to illuminate the pages. I had to read everything that way, not just scary stuff; in my house reading books was looked upon as a waste of time and money, and the habit was regarded as barely more respectable than self-abuse and marginally less destructive than serious heroin addiction. But the worst offense in the literary realm was to be caught reading *that* stuff: stories of the supernatural; in fact, any fiction of the fantastic regardless of genre—science fiction, fantasy, horror. In that era those genres were not as widely popular as they now have become; it was fringe reading; catching your son with that material was akin to finding *Das Kapital* and crazed communist tracts hidden beneath the undershirts in his dresser drawer. Subversive material indeed.

It's not like that anymore. In spite of publishers' fevered determination to put blood-drooling, bug-eyed beasts on too many covers in the genre, some respect has been won. Still, for every two people who believe that pornographic books can cause upstanding citizens to become slavering sex fiends, there is at least one who is convinced that reading ghost and horror stories, regardless of how sedate the tales, will certainly transform readers into either mealy-skinned recluses with odd personal habits or foaming-at-the-mouth, pop-eyed sociopaths with a love of chain saws and an interest in dismemberment.

Yet of the many readers of ghost and horror stories whom I know personally, not one is given to violence, most are more civilized than the average citizen, and those who are mealy-skinned are simply not fortunate enough to live here in sunny California, where everyone has an appealing cancer-brown tan. Certain third-rate sociologists and thoroughly *meshuga* psychologists, sucking around for grant money or bending their "sciences" to political purposes, have conducted badly flawed studies in which they purport to show direct links between fiction of the fantastic and everything from schizophrenia to acne. It doesn't wash. Anyone who's a fan of such fiction and who seeks out other fans of it through amateur magazines and conventions, eventually encounters hundreds, if not thousands, of similar-minded folk and discovers that they are both more articulate than the public at large and dramatically less prone to violence than the sociologists and psychologists who, with their intellectually bankrupt theories, would alter whole societies and cultures (by force, if necessary) and blithely disregard the loss of freedom (and sometimes blood) resulting from their policies.

So if we don't turn to these tales to learn how to deal death and bring down modern civilization, as those critics would have it, what *do* we want—and receive—from the genre?

Entertainment, of course. Nothing can fill long, empty hours as satisfyingly as good storytelling. The written word, woven into enchanting spells by a storyteller, has a unique power to bring a new view of the world and the human condition—the author's view—to us, and make it live in our minds and imaginations.

Television rarely does that. In spite of the promise of its early days, TV has become a dead medium, in part because it's a government-protected and government-controlled monopoly, and in part because of its extremely collaborative nature; it spews out committee-conceived and committee-written trash with too little substance to make the viewer care, too little color and texture to convince, too little emotion to enchant, too little wit and wonder to seize the viewer the way that a good story or book does. Can you imagine *anyone* so brain-damaged by video-display radiation and Twinkies as to be utterly spellbound by an episode of "Dynasty" or "She's the Sheriff" or even the sometimes superior "Magnum" in the way that millions have been spellbound by King, Tolkien, Heinlein, and other dealers in the fantastic? No, when a TV show evokes a glimmer of wonder, it's not the same wonder that we readers know; it's wonder in big lead shoes, dressed in a shabby black suit too small for it, brought alive with electricity conducted through rough bolts in its neck, a shambling Frankenstein of wonder, graceless and half dead, a stitched-together travesty of genuine wonder.

Most theatrical films are also too collaborative to produce entertainment with true wonder and passion. And though six or eight really good movies reach the theaters every year, each film enchants for only two hours or less; then the lights come on, and the screen goes blank, and we're reminded of how *passive* a medium film is. Even the best films feed the imagination predigested images and ideas and do not demand active participation as does the printed word.

A book of ghost stories or a novel of the supernatural, if well done, can provide long evenings of surcease from the travails of this world. It can more deeply involve us—and usually it will have more of value to say about life—than any ten good movies. The art of the storyteller, expressed through the printed word, can touch the mind and the heart, establish a special intimacy between writer and reader, and allow an intensity and depth of communion seldom achieved by any other art form.

Ghost stories—all stories of the supernatural—are especially wonder-invoking, for they deal not merely with the unknown but with the *unknowable*. We are curious about what lies beyond death, and good ghost stories, while not always philosophical or intellectual to any great degree, give the illusion of pulling back that black curtain to provide us with a glimpse of what awaits us on the other side. A ghost—any ghost in any story, regardless of the tale's primary intent— is a symbol of our faith in a hereafter and is therefore a symbol, as well, of our deeply held desire to believe that life is more than a biological accident, that human life has purpose and meaning and a destiny beyond this world. Convince me, for the duration of a story, that ghosts are real, and for that same length of time you also convince me that my own spirit will never die.

That is what we get from reading about the supernatural. Hope. Certainly—perhaps primarily—we receive entertainment value. And we get our imaginations stretched, which is a useful exercise for anyone trying to cope with our world of rapid change, in which a healthy imagination is an essential survival tool. And we are induced to think about the enduring mysteries of life. But we also find hope, however subconsciously, in these tales. Even if the fictional ghost or demon is evil, the story is one of hope, for if evil spirits exist, then surely benign shades are out there, too.

Charles Dickens's *A Christmas Carol* is perhaps the greatest ghost story of all time. It is filled with the clank of ghostly chains, frightening figures whose appearance generates drafts of arctic air, and visions of the grave that are sufficiently dark to bring a cold sweat to the perceptive reader who has not been jaded by the numbingly graphic splatter films of our time. Yet in his tale Dickens is most concerned with conveying a message about charity, compassion, love, and the hope for humankind that is embodied in one miserly old man's ability to transform himself into a better person. *A Christmas Carol* takes the hope that is a buried element of all ghost stories and raises it to the surface of the tale, using it as a major theme.

Are we twisted, perverse, or morbid because we are intrigued by these fantastic stories? No. Our fascination springs from our desire to know ourselves, our world, our ultimate fate and purpose—which is the same motive that compels us to read Dostoyevski or James M. Cain or Faulkner.

What disturbs me is that some people *don't* want to read this kind of fiction. Do they have no curiosity about what lies beyond this life? Are they so rigid and inflexible that they cannot bear to have their imaginations stretched? Are they afraid of finding some unsuspected fragment of spirituality in their modern, rational hearts? Are they so in love with death that they cannot bear to read stories in which death is not final and eternal? Does the specter of hope frighten them? Good heavens, what's *wrong* with these people who don't like stories of the supernatural?

About the Authors

MATCH THE CONTRIBUTORS WITH
THEIR PREVIOUS CREDITS

CONTRIBUTORS

1. Kathryn Ptacek
2. Gary Brandner
3. Charles de Lint
4. Steve Rasnic Tem and Melanie Tem
5. Janet Fox
6. Thomas Tessier
7. James Howard Kunstler
8. Charles L. Grant
9. Thomas F. Monteleone
10. Gordon Linzner
11. Ramsey Campbell
12. P. W. Sinclair
13. Donald R. Burleson
14. William F. Nolan
15. Melissa Mia Hall
16. David B. Silva
17. Robert R. McCammon
18. Dean R. Koontz

CREDITS

—A. *Rapture, The Fates, The Nightwalker,* "Food," *Finishing Touches*

—B. *The Influence, The Hungry Moon,* "Mackintosh Willy," *The Doll Who Ate His Mother,* "The Chimney," *Dark Companions, Ancient Images*

—C. *Night Train, The Magnificent Gallery, Lyrica, Crooked House* (with John DeChancie), *Fantasma*

—D. "Pele," *Excavations,* "Bloodwolf," "The Battering," "Spidertalk," "Dark Shapes on the Road"

—E. "Milk," "Family Dentistry," "Mama's Boy," "The Terminator," "The Cryptogram," *H. P. Lovecraft: A Critical Study*

—F. *Lightning, Watchers, Phantoms, Strangers, The Face of Fear, Whispers*

—G. "Valentine," "Clown Black," "Surrogate," "The Ghoul-Children's Halloween," "The Ghost-Winder," Editor of *Scavenger's Newsletter*

—H. *Things Beyond Midnight, Logan's Run,* Screenplay for *Burnt Offerings,* "Dead Call," "He Kilt It With a Stick," Teleplay for *Trilogy of Terror*

—I. *The Howling, Quintana Roo,* "Julian's Hand," *Cameron's Closet, Floater*

—J. *The Hour of the Oxrun Dead, The Nestling, A Glow of Candles, The Pet,* Editor of the *Shadows* anthology series

—K. *The Troupe, The Oni,* Editor of *Space and Time* magazine

—L. *Moonheart, Mulengro, Yarrow, Jack the Giant-Killer, Svaha*

—M. *Child of Darkness, Come Thirteen,* "Ice Sculptures," Editor of *The Horror Show* magazine

—N. *Kachina, Blood Autumn, In Silence Sealed, Shadoweyes,* Editor of *Women of Darkness*

—O. *The Hunt, Thunder Island, Blood Solstice, Wampanaki Tales*

—P. Humor columnist

—Q. "The Glass Doorknob," "Mariana," "Rapture," "Moon-flower"

—R. *Swan Song, They Thirst, Mystery Walk, Usher's Passing,* "Nightcrawlers"

ANSWERS:

1. N	4. D	7. O	10. K	13. E	16. M
2. I	5. G	8. J	11. B	14. H	17. R
3. L	6. A	9. C	12. P	15. Q	18. F